The Sixth Commandment

"IT WILL SURPRISE AND CHILL YOU!"
—*Chicago Tribune*

Thorndecker—Nobel Prize-winning scientist, hero to the small town of Coburn, who is discussed by his neighbors in worshipful whispers...if he is discussed at all.

Todd—Investigator for a private foundation, who discovers that Thorndecker is secretly breaking every law of God and man...and who is faced with the most horrible decision a man could have to make!

Sanders—Master of suspense and mystery, one of America's most popular novelists, who surpasses even his bestselling THE FIRST DEADLY SIN in this "deep and dazzling" new thriller!

"A BLEND OF THRILLER, MYSTERY, LOVE STORY...A TALE OF SINS, CRIMES...AND A NIGHTMARE LURKING IN THE HEART OF A DREAM!"
—*Literary Guild Magazine*

Lawrence Sanders
The Sixth Commandment

BERKLEY BOOKS, NEW YORK

This Berkley book contains the complete
text of the original hardcover edition.
It has been completely reset in a typeface
designed for easy reading, and was printed
from new film.

THE SIXTH COMMANDMENT

A Berkley Book / published by arrangement with
G. P. Putnam's Sons

PRINTING HISTORY
G. P. Putnam's Sons edition published 1979
Berkley edition / January 1980
Tenth printing / December 1983
Eleventh printing / June 1984
Twelfth printing / September 1984

ISBN: 0-425-08012-9

A BERKLEY BOOK ® TM 757,375
Berkley Books are published by The Berkley Publishing Group,
200 Madison Avenue, New York, New York 10016.
The name "BERKLEY" and the stylized "B" with design
are trademarks belonging to Berkley Publishing Corporation.
PRINTED IN THE UNITED STATES OF AMERICA

The Sixth Commandment

LATE NOVEMBER, and the world was dying. A wild wind hooted faintly outside the windows. Inside, the air had been breathed too many times.

"It's got nothing to do with your age," I said.

"Liar," she said.

I tried to groan. Swung my legs out of bed and lighted a cigarette. Sat there smoking, hunched over. She fumbled with my spine.

"Poor baby," she said.

I wouldn't look at her. I knew what I'd see: a small body so supple it twanged. Short brown hair cut like a boy's. All of her sleek. She had me in thrall. Soft swell to her abdomen. A little brown mole on the inside of her left thigh. Her ass was smooth and tight.

"All I'm saying," I said, "is that I've got to go away on a business trip. A week, two weeks, a month—who knows? I've *got* to; it's my job."

"I've got five weeks' vacation coming," she said. "I could get a leave of absence. I could quit. No problem."

I didn't answer.

Her squid arm slid around my neck. Even when she was coming, her flesh was cool. Did she ever sweat? Her skin was glass. But I could never break her.

"It's impossible," I said. "It wouldn't work."

She kneeled on the bed behind me. Put her arms about my neck. Pressed. Pointy little breasts. Very elegant. Pink bosses. All of her elegant. She worked at it: jogging, yoga, dance. I told her once that she even had muscles in her crap, and she said I was vulgar, and I said that was true.

"I'll be back," I said.

"No you won't," she said, and that was true, too.

I leaned forward to stub my cigarette in the ashtray on the floor. She leaned with me. For a moment I was supporting her naked weight on my back. Her warm breath was in my ear. I straightened slowly, pushing her back.

"At least," she said, "let's end things with a bang."

"You're outrageous," I said.

"Am I not?" she said.

See her in one of her tailored Abercrombie & Fitch suits, and you'd never guess. The Gucci brogues. Benjamin Franklin spectacles. Minimal makeup. Crisp. Aloof. All business. But naked, the woman was a goddamned tiger. Joan Powell. How I hated her. How I loved her. She taught me so much. Well, what the hell, I taught her a few things, too. I must have; why else had she endured my infidelities and shitty moods for three years?

"You'll call?" she said, and when I didn't answer, she said, forlornly, "You'll write?"

It wasn't her pleading that disgusted me so much as my own weakness. I wanted her so much, right then, that moment. After psyching myself for weeks, preparing for this break. If she had made the right gesture just then, the right touch, I'd have caved. But she didn't. Which meant she didn't want to, because she knew what the right gesture was, the right touch. She had invented it.

So I shrugged her off, got up, started to dress. She lay back on the rumpled sheets, watching me with hard eyes.

"The best you'll ever get," she said.

"I agree," I said. "Wholeheartedly."

She said she was forty-four, and I believed her. I said I was thirty-two, and she believed me. We didn't lie to each other about things like that. About facts. We lied about important things. It wasn't so much the difference in our ages that bothered me; it was the thralldom. I was addicted. She had me hooked.

I knotted my tie, looking at her in the mirror. Now she had one arm over her eyes. Her upper torso was supine, then, at the waist, her body curved over onto a hip. One knee drawn up. All of her in a sweet S curve, tapering. She kept a year-round tan. Milkier to mark the straps and little triangles of her string bikini. She liked me to shave her. I liked it, too.

"I'm going now," I said.

"Go," she said.

The Bingham Foundation wasn't the Ford or the Rockefeller, but it wasn't peanuts either. We gave away about ten million a year, mostly for scientific research. This was because the original Silas Bingham had been an ironmonger who had invented a new casting process. And his son, Caleb Bingham, had invented a cash register that kept a running total. *His* son, Jeremiah Bingham, had been a surgeon who invented a whole toolbox of clamps, saws, chisels, files, pliers, mallets, etc., for the repair of the human carcass.

Mrs. Cynthia, widow of Jeremiah, ran the Bingham Foundation. She looked like a little old man. The executive director was Stacy Besant. He looked like a little old woman. My name is Samuel Todd. I was one of several field investigators. The Bingham Foundation does not disburse its funds casually.

I was sitting in Besant's office on Friday morning, watching him twist a benzedrine inhaler up one hairy nostril. Fascinating. He unplugged it, with some difficulty, then sniffed, blinked, sneezed. He slid the inhaler into a vest pocket.

"A cold, sir?" I asked.

"Not yet," he said. "But you never know. You've reviewed the Thorndecker file?"

I flipped a palm back and forth.

"Briefly," I said. "I'll take it with me for closer study."

Actually, I had spent the previous night saying goodby to Joan Powell. I hadn't cracked the file. I didn't know who Thorndecker was. Moral: Ignorance really is bliss.

"What do you think?" Besant asked.

"Hard to say," I said. "The application sounds impressive, but all applications sound impressive."

"Of course, of course," he said.

Out came the inhaler again. Into the other nostril this time. Sniff. Blink. Sneeze.

"He's asking for a million," he said.

"Is he, sir?" I said. "They always double it, knowing we'll cut it in half, at least. It's a game."

"Usually," he said. "But in this case, I'm not so sure. He comes highly recommended. His work, I mean. Won a third of a Nobel at the age of thirty-eight."

"What was that for, sir?"

His eyes glazed over. Hunching across the desk toward me, he looked like a Galapagos tortoise clad in Harris tweed.

"Uh, it's all in the file," he said. "The science people are very high on him. Very high indeed." Pause. "His first wife was my niece."

"Oh?"

"Dead now. Drowned in the surf on the Cape. Terrible tragedy. Lovely girl."

I was silent.

The inhaler appeared again, but he didn't use it. Just fondled it. It looked like an oversize bullet. Something for big game.

"Go along then," he said. "Take as much time as you need. Keep in touch."

He held out his hand, and I moved it up and down. I

thought again of a turtle. His flipper was dry and scaly.

Out in the gloomy corridor I met old Mrs. Cynthia. She was moving slowly along, leaning heavily on a polished cane. It had a silver head shaped like a toucan's bill. Handsome.

"Samuel," she said, "you're going up to see Doctor Thorndecker?"

"Yes, ma'am."

"I knew his father," she said. "Knew him well."

"Did you?"

"A sweet man," she said, and something that might have been pain pinched her eyes. "It was all so—so sad."

I stared at her.

"Does that mean you'd like me to approve the grant, Mrs. Cynthia?" I asked bluntly.

Her eyes cleared. She reached out a veined hand and tapped my cheek. Not quite a slap.

"Sometimes, Samuel," she said, "you carry lovable irascibility a little too far. I know you won't let my friendship with Doctor Thorndecker's father affect your judgment. If I thought that, I would never have mentioned it."

There didn't seem to be anything more to say. I went back to my broom-closet office, slid the Thorndecker file into my battered briefcase, and went home to pack. I planned to go over the research on Sunday night, and get an early start the next morning.

I should have slit my wrists instead.

Over the years the Bingham Foundation had developed a reasonably efficient method of processing grant applications. Unless they were obviously from nut cases ("I am on the verge of inventing perpetual motion!"), requests went to three independent investigative organizations that handled this type of work for private foundations and, occasionally, the federal government.

The firm of Donner & Stern, older even than Pinkertons, was too discreet to call their operatives "private detectives." They preferred "inquiry agents," and they provided personal background material on grant applicants. This included family history, education, professional employment record, personal habits (drinking? drug addiction?), and anything else of an intimate nature Donner & Stern felt would assist the Bingham Foundation in forming an opinion on the applicant's merit.

Lifschultz Associates conducted an inquiry into the applicant's financial status, his credit rating, banking history, investments, tax record, current assets, and so forth. The purpose here was to determine the applicant's honesty and trustworthiness, and to insure, as certainly as possible, that upon receipt of a Bingham Foundation grant, he wouldn't immediately depart for Pago Pago with his nubile secretary.

Finally, Scientific Research Records provided an unbiased analysis of the value, or lack of it, of the applicant's proposals: the reasons for which the subsidy was sought. The SRR report usually included a brief summary of similar work being conducted elsewhere, the chances for success, and a compilation of professional judgments on the applicant's intelligence and expertise by associates, colleagues, and rivals.

These three preliminary investigations eliminated about 90 percent of the hopeful scientists who approached the Bingham Foundation, hat in hand. The remaining applications were then handed over to Bingham's own field investigators.

Our job was to make an assessment of what Stacy Besant liked to call "the intangibles, human relations, and things known only to the applicant's priest, psychiatrist, or mistress."

First of all, we tried to discover if his family life was reasonably happy, if his relations with assistants and employees was troublefree, and if he enjoyed a good reputation in his neighborhood and community. If he was himself employed in a university or research facility, it was necessary to make certain the applicant had the confidence and respect of his superiors.

All this was fairly cut-and-dried, necessitating nothing more than talking informally to a great number of people and assuring them their comments would be off the record. But sometimes the results were surprising.

I remember the case of one renowned scientist, happily married, father of four, who applied for a grant for a research project into the nature and origins of homosexuality. During a final interview, the Bigham field investigator discovered the applicant himself was gay. His request was denied, not on moral grounds but because it was feared his predilection would prejudice his research.

In another case, a criminologist's request for funds was rejected when it was learned that he was an avid hunter and gun collector. It was a damaging revelation only because he had asked for the subsidy to make an in-depth analysis of "The Roots of Violence." Bingham decided to let some other foundation have the honor of financing the gunslinger's research.

"Field investigators" may have been our title, but "snoops" was more accurate. I had been doing it for almost five years, and if I was growing increasingly suspicious and cynical, it was because those were exactly the qualities the job required. It gave me no particular pleasure to uncover a weakness or ancient misstep that might mean the end of a man's dreams. But that was what I was being paid for, and paid well.

At least so I told myself. But occasionally, in moments of drunken enlightenment, I wondered if I enjoyed prying into other men's lives because my own was so empty.

The file on the application of Dr. Thorndecker was a fat one. Before I settled down with it, I put out a bottle of Glenlivet Scotch, pitcher of water, bucket of ice cubes. And two packs of cigarettes. I started something on the hi-fi—I think it was Vivaldi—the volume turned down so low the music was only a murmur. Then I started . . .

THORNDECKER, Telford Gordon, 54, BSCh, MD, MSc, PhD, etc., etc., member of this, fellow of that, Nobel Prize Winner for research in the pathology of mammalian cells. Father of daughter Mary, 27, and son

7

Edward, 17. Presently married to second wife Julie, 23.

I took a swallow of Scotch at that. His second wife was four years younger than his daughter. Interesting, but not too unusual. About as interesting as the ten years difference in the ages of his two children.

I sat staring a few moments at the photograph of Dr. Thorndecker included in the file. It was an 8 x 10 glossy, apparently intended for publication; it had that professional type of pose and lighting. It was a head-and-shoulders shot, eyes looking into the camera lens, mouth smiling faintly, chin raised.

He was a handsome man; no doubt of that. Thick shock of dark, wavy hair; heavy, masculine features; surprisingly sensitive lips. Eyes large and widely spaced. High brow, a jaw that was solid without being massive. Smallish ears set close to the skull. Strong, straight nose, somewhat hard and hawkish.

In the photo, the fine lips were smiling, but the eyes were grave, almost moody. I wondered how his voice would sound. I set great store by the timbre of a man's voice. I guessed Thorndecker's would be a rumbling baritone, with deep resonance.

I read on... about his brilliant teaching career, and even more brilliant research into the pathology of mammalian cells. I am not a trained scientist, but I've read a great deal of chemistry and physics, and learned more on my job at Bingham. I gathered, from the SRR report, that Thorndecker was especially interested in the biology of aging, and particularly the senescence of normal mammalian cells. He had made a significant contribution to a research project that produced a statistical study of the reproduction (doublings) of human embryo cells *in vitro*.

After this pioneer work, Thorndecker, on his own, had followed up with a study of the reproduction of human cells *in vitro* from donors of various ages. His findings suggested that the older the donor, the fewer times the donated cells could be induced to reproduce (double). Thorndecker concluded that mammalian cells had a built-in clock. Aging and death were not so much the result of genetic direction or of disease and decay, but were due to the inherent nature of our cells. A time for living, and a time for dying. And all the improved medical skills, diet, and health care in the world could not affect longevity except within very definite natural parameters.

A jolly thought. I had another drink of Glenlivet on that. Then I turned to the report of Lifschultz Associates on the good doctor's finances. It was revealing...

Prior to the death of his first wife by drowning, Dr. Telford Thorndecker apparently had been a man of moderate means, supporting his family on his professor's salary, fees from speaking engagements, the Nobel Prize award, and royalty income from two college textbooks he had written: "Human Cells" and "The Pathology of Human Cells."

He had been sole beneficiary of his wife's estate, and I blinked my eyes when I saw the amount: almost a million dollars. I made a mental note to ask Stacy Besant the source of this inherited wealth. As the first Mrs. Thorndecker's uncle, he should certainly know. And while I was at it, I might as well ask Mrs. Cynthia what she had meant by her lament: "It was all so—so sad," when she mentioned knowing Thorndecker's father.

Shortly after the will was probated, Dr. Thorndecker resigned all his teaching, research, and advisory positions. He purchased Crittenden Hall, a 90-bed nursing and convalescent home located near the village of Coburn, south of Albany, N.Y. The Crittenden grounds and buildings were extensive, but the nursing home had been operating at a loss for several years prior to Thorndecker's purchase. This may have been due to its isolated location, or perhaps simply to bad management.

In any event, Thorndecker showed an unexpected talent for business administration. Within two years, a refurbishing program was completed, a new, younger staff recruited, and Crittenden Hall was showing a modest profit. All this had been accomplished in spite of reducing occupancy to fifty beds and converting one of the buildings to a research laboratory that operated independently of the nursing facility.

Thorndecker managed this by creating a haven for the alcoholic, mentally disturbed, and terminally ill members of wealthy families. The daily rates were among the highest in the country for similar asylums. The kitchen was supervised by a Swiss cordon bleu chef, the staff was large enough to provide a one-to-one relationship with patients, and a wide variety of social activities was available, including first-run movies, TV sets in every room, dances, costume balls, and live entertainment by visiting theatrical troupes. No basket weaving or finger painting at Crittenden Hall.

As chief executive of this thriving enterprise, Dr. Thorndecker paid himself the relatively modest salary of $50,000 a year. All profits of the nursing facility went to the Crittenden Research Laboratory which was, according to the prospectus distributed to potential donors, "Devoted to a continuing inquiry into the biology of aging, with particular attention to cellular morphology and the role it plays in productive longevity."

The Lifschultz Associates' report concluded by stating that the Crittenden Research Laboratory was supported by the profits of the nursing home, by grants and contributions from outside donors, and by bequests, many of them sizable and some of them willed to the laboratory by former patients of Crittenden Hall.

Dr. Thorndecker, I decided, had a nice thing going. Not illegal certainly. Probably not even immoral or unethical. Just nice.

I flipped the stack of records on the hi-fi, visited the can, mixed a fresh highball, lighted the last cigarette in pack No. 1, and settled down to read the original application submitted to the Bingham Foundation by the Crittenden Research Laboratory.

The petition was succinct and well-organized. It made it clear from the outset that despite similar names, the connection between Crittenden Hall, the nursing home, and the Crittenden Research Laboratory was kept deliberately distant. Each facility had its own building, each its own staff. Lab employees were not encouraged to associate with those of the nursing home; they even lunched in separate chambers. What the application was emphasizing was that no Bingham Foundation funds, if granted, would be used in support of Crittenden Hall, a profit-making institution. All monies would go to Crittenden Research Laboratory, a non-profit organization performing original and valuable investigation into the basic constitution of mammalian cells.

The specific purpose for which a million dollars was requested was a three-year study on the effects of the entire spectrum of electromagnetic radiation on human embryo cells *in vitro*. This would include everything from radio waves and visible light to infrared, X rays, ultraviolet, and gamma rays. In addition, the cells' reaction to ultrasound would be explored, as well as laser and maser emissions.

Preliminary experiments, the application stated, indicated that under prolonged exposure to certain wavelengths of electromagnetic radiation, human cells underwent fundamental alterations of their reproductive capabilities, the nature of which the basic research had not clearly revealed. But, it was suggested, the thorough study for which funds were requested could conceivably lead to a fuller understanding of the cause of senescence in mammalian cells. In effect, what the project was designed to discover was the cellular clock that determined the normal life span of human beings.

It was an ambitious proposal. The money requested would be used to pay the salaries of an enlarged staff and to purchase the expensive equipment and instruments needed. A detailed budget was submitted.

I shuffled the file back to the report of Scientific Research Records. It stated that while a great deal of work in this field had already been done by research facilities around the world, the information available was fragmented; no single study of this nature had ever been made, and no researchers, to the knowledge of SRR, had set out with this particular aim: to uncover exactly what it was in human cells that, within a finite time, made our eyesight dim, muscles weaken, organs deteriorate, and brought about aging and death.

That was the stated objective of Dr. Telford Gordon Thorndecker. I didn't believe it for a minute. Here was this brilliant, imaginative, and innovative scientist requesting funds to replicate the experiments of other men and perhaps identify the primary cause of senescence in mammalian cells. I just couldn't see Thorndecker limiting himself to such a goal. The man was a genius; even his rivals and opponents admitted that. Geniuses don't follow; they lead.

I thought I knew the secret ambition of Dr. Telford Thorndecker. It followed the usual pattern of research in the biological sciences: discover, analyze, manipulate. He could never be content with merely identifying and describing the factor in mammalian cells that caused aging and death. He had a hidden desire to control that factor, to stretch our three-score-and-ten, or whatever, and push back the natural limits of human growth.

I grinned, convinced that I had guessed the real motives of Thorndecker in applying for a Bingham Foundation grant. Which only proves how stupid I can be when I set my mind to it.

I took up Thorndecker's photograph, and stared at it again.

"Hello, Ponce de Leon," I said aloud.

Then I finished the whiskey. My own Fountain of Youth.

The First Day

WHEN THE ALARM chattered at 7:00 A.M. on Monday, I poked an arm out from my warm cocoon of blankets and let my hand fall limply on the shut-off button. When I awoke the second time, I looked blearily at the bedside clock. Almost eleven. So much for my early start.

Thirty-two is hardly a ripe old age, but I had recently noticed it was taking me longer and longer to put it together and get going in the morning. Ten years previously, even five years, I could splurge a rough night on the town, maybe including a bit of rub-the-bacon, get home in the wee hours, catch some fast sleep, bounce out of bed at seven, take a cold shower and quick shave, and go whistling off to face the day's challenges.

That morning I moved slowly, balancing my head carefully atop my neck. I climbed shakily out of my warm bed with a grumbled curse. I stared at myself in the bathroom mirror, shuddering. I took a long, hot shower, but the cobwebs were made of stainless steel. Brushing my teeth didn't eliminate the stale taste of all those cigarettes the night before. I didn't even try to shave; I can't stand the sight of blood.

In the kitchen, I closed my eyes and gulped down a glass of tomato juice. It didn't soothe the bubbling in my stomach from all that whiskey I had consumed while reviewing the Thorndecker file. Two cups of black coffee didn't help much either.

Finally, while I was dressing, I said aloud, "Screw it," went back into the kitchen and mixed an enormous Bloody Mary, with salt, pepper, Tabasco, Worcestershire, and horse radish. I got that down, gasping. In about ten minutes I felt like I might live—but still wasn't certain I wanted to.

I looked out the window. It was gray out there, sky lowery, a hard wind blowing debris and pedestrians along West 71st Street. This was in Manhattan, in case you haven't guessed.

A sickeningly cheerful radio voice reported a storm front moving in from the west, with a dropping barometer and plunging thermometer. Snow flurries or a freezing rain predicted; driving conditions hazardous by late afternoon. It all sounded so *good*.

I pulled on whipcord slacks, black turtleneck sweater, tweed jacket, ankle-high boots. I owned a leather trenchcoat. It was a cheapie, and the last rainstorm had left it stiff as a board. But I struggled into it, pulled on a floppy Irish hat, and carried my packed bags down to my Pontiac Grand Prix.

Someone had written in the dust on the hood: "I am dirty. Please wash me." I scrawled underneath, "Why the hell should I?" I got started a little after twelve o'clock. I wouldn't say my mood was depressed. Just sadly thoughtful. I resolved to stop smoking, stop drinking, stop mistreating my holy body. I resolved to—ahh, what was the use? It was *my* holy body, envelope of my immortal soul, and if I wanted to kick hell out of it, who was there to care?

I stopped somewhere near Newburgh for a lunch of steak and eggs, with a couple of ales. There was a liquor store next to the diner, and I bought a pint of Courvoisier cognac. I didn't open it, but it was a comforting feeling knowing it was there in the glove compartment. My security blanket.

Driving up the Hudson Valley was like going into a tunnel. Greasy fog swirled; a heavy sky pressed down between the hills. There was a spatter of hail against the windshield. It turned to rain, then to sleet. I started the wipers, slowed, and got a local radio station that was warning of worse to come.

There wasn't much traffic. The few cars and trucks were moving steadily but cautiously, lights on in the gloom. No one even thought of trying to pass on that slick highway, at least until the sand spreaders got to work. I drove hunched forward, peering into the blackness. I wasn't thinking about the storm. I wasn't even brooding about Dr. Telford Thorndecker. I was remembering Joan Powell.

I had met her three years ago, and there was a storm then much like this one. I wish I could tell you that we met like that couple in the TV commercial, on a hazy, sunlit terrace. We are sipping wine at separate tables, me red, her white. I raise my glass to her. She smiles faintly. The next thing you know, we're sharing the same table, our wine bottles nestling side by side. Don't like that? How about this one, from an old Irene Dunne-Cary Grant movie. We both run for the same cab, get in opposite sides. Big argument. Then the bent-nosed driver (Allen Jenkins) persuades us to share the cab, and we discover we're both going to the same party. You know how *that* turns out.

It wasn't like that at all. On a blowy, rancorous day, I had a late-afternoon appointment with my dentist, Dr. Hockheimer, in a medical building on West 57th Street. It was only for a checkup and cleaning, but I'm terrified of dentists. The fact that Dr. Hockheimer gave all his patients a lollipop after treatment didn't help much.

Hockheimer shared a suite with two other dentists. The waiting room was crowded. I hung up my wet trenchcoat, put my dripping umbrella in the corner rack. I sat down next to a nice looking woman. Early forties, I guessed. She was holding a two-year-old copy of the *National Geographic* in shaking hands. The magazine was upside down. I knew exactly how she felt.

I sat there for almost five minutes, embarrassed to discover I had a lighted cigarette in each hand. I was tapping one out when a god-awful scream of pain came from one of the dentists' offices.

That was all I needed. I jerked to my feet, grabbed up trenchcoat and umbrella, headed for the door. The nice looking lady beat me out by two steps. At the elevator, we smiled wanly at each other.

"I'm a coward," she said.

"Welcome to the club," I said. "Need a drink?"

"Do I ever!" she said.

We dashed across Sixth Avenue, both of us huddling under my umbrella, buffeted by the driving rain. We ran into a dim hotel bar, laughing and feeling better already. We sat at a front table, about as big as a diaper, and ordered martinis.

"Was that a man or a woman who screamed?" I asked.

"Don't talk about it. Joan Powell," she said, offering a firm hand.

"Samuel Todd," I said, shaking it. "You a patient of Hockheimer's?"

She nodded.

"We won't get our lollipops today."

"These are better," she said, sipping her drink.

She stared out the front window. Cold rain was driving in gusts. There was a flash of lightning, a crack of thunder.

She was a severely dressed, no-nonsense, executive-type lady. Sensible shoes. Tailored suit. High-collared

16

blouse. Those crazy half-glasses. Good complexion. Marvelous complexion. Crisp features. A small, graceful, cool lady.

"You're a literary agent," I said. "An executive assistant to a big-shot lawyer. Editor of a women's magazine. Bank officer."

"No," she said. "A department store buyer. Housewares. You're a newspaper reporter. A computer programmer. An undercover cop. A shoe salesman."

"A shoe salesman?" I said. "Jesus! No, I'm with the Bingham Foundation. Field investigator."

"I knew it," she said, and I laughed.

The storm showed no signs of letting up, but I didn't care. It was pleasant in there with her, just talking, having another round. I never made a pass at her, nor she at me. It was all very civilized.

I figured her about ten years older than I. What I liked most about her was that she was obviously content with her age, made no effort to appear younger by dress, makeup, or manner. As I said, a very cool lady. Self-possessed.

After the second martini, she stared at me and said, "You're not the handsomest man I've ever met."

"Oh, I don't know," I said. "Last year I was runner-up in the Miss King of Prussia contest."

She looked down at her drink, expressionless.

"King of Prussia," I said. "A town in Pennsylvania."

"I know where it is," she said. "It wasn't a bad joke, but I very rarely laugh aloud. I chuckle inwardly."

"How will I know when you're chuckling inwardly?"

"Put your hand on my stomach. It flutters. Listen," she went on before I had a chance to react to that, "I didn't mean to insult you. About not being the handsomest man I've ever met. I don't particularly like handsome men. They're always looking in mirrors and combing their hair. You have a nice, plain, rugged face. Very masculine."

"Thank you."

"And you're polite. I like that."

"Good," I said. "Tell me more."

"Your eyes are good," she said. "Greenish-brown, aren't they?"

"Sort of."

"Was your nose broken?"

"A long time ago," I said. "I didn't think it showed."

"It does," she said. "Do people call you Sam?"

"They do. I don't like it."

"All right," she said equably. "Todd, may we have another drink? I'm going to split the check with you. Are you married?"

"No, Powell," I said. "Are you?"

"Not now. I was. Years ago. It was a mistake. Have you ever been married?"

"No," I said. "I was madly in love with my childhood sweetheart, but she ran off with a lion tamer."

"My childhood sweetheart *was* a lion tamer," she said. "Isn't that odd? You don't suppose...?"

The rain had turned to sleet; the streets and sidewalks were layered with slush. There didn't seem much point in trying to get anywhere. So we had dinner right there in the hotel dining room. The food wasn't the greatest, but it was edible. Barely.

We talked lazily of this and that. She was from Virginia. I was from Ohio. She had come directly to New York after graduation from some girls' school. I had come to New York after a two-year detour in Vietnam.

"Army?" she asked.

"Not infantry," I said hastily. "No frontline action or anything like that. Criminal investigation. And there was plenty to investigate."

"I can imagine," she said. She stared down at her plate. "Tom, my younger brother, was killed over there. Marine Corps. I hate violence. *Hate* it."

I didn't say anything.

We had wine during the meal and vodka stingers afterward. I guess we were both more than a little zonked. We started chivying each other, neither of us laughing or even smiling. Very solemn. I don't know if she was chuckling inwardly—I didn't feel her stomach—but I was. What a nice, nice lady.

"Do you have a pet?" she asked. "Dog? Cat?"

"I have this very affectionate oryx," I said. "Name of Cynthia. I've trained her to sit up and beg. You have a pet?"

"A lemur named Pete," she said. "He can roll over and play dead. He's been doing it for a week now."

"Did you ever smoke any pot?"

"All the time. Takes me hours to scrub it clean with Brillo. You're not gay, are you?"

"Usually I'm morose."

And so on, and so on. I suppose it sounds silly. Maybe it was. But it was a pleasant evening. In today's world, "pleasant" is good enough.

After awhile we settled our bill—she insisted on paying half—and staggered out of there. We stood on the wind-whipped sidewalk for half an hour trying to get a taxi. But when a storm like that hits New York, empty cabs drive down into the subways and disappear.

We were both shivering under the hotel marquee, feet cold and wet. We watched the umpteenth occupied cab splash by. Then Joan Powell turned, looked into my eyes.

"The hell with this, Todd," she said firmly. "Let's get a room here for the night."

I stared at her, wondering again if she was chuckling inwardly.

"We've got no luggage," I pointed out.

"So?" she said. "We're a couple in from the suburbs. We've been to the theatre. Now we can't get home because the trains aren't running. Try it. It'll go like a dream."

It did.

I looked at her admiringly in the elevator. The bellhop, key in hand, was examining the ceiling.

"Call the babysitter the moment we get in the room, dear," I said. "Ask her to stay over with the children. I'm sure she'll oblige."

"Oh, she's obliging," Joan Powell said bitterly. "I'm sure you find that out when you drive her home."

The bellhop had a coughing fit.

The room was like our dinner: endurable, but just. A high-ceilinged, drafty barn of a place. A fake gas fireplace that wasn't burning. But a big radiator in the corner hissed steadily. Crackled enamel fixtures in the old-fashioned bathroom. One huge bed that sloped down to the center.

I gave the bellhop a five, and he was so grateful he didn't wink. He closed the door behind him, and I locked it. I turned to Joan Powell.

"Well, here we are, dear," I said. "Just married."

We could hear the world outside. Lash of hard rain against glass. Wail of wind. Thunder clap. Window panes rattled; the air seemed to flutter. But we were sealed off, protected. Warm and dry. Just the two of us in our secret, tawdry place. I didn't want to be anywhere else.

She undressed like an actress changing costumes. Off came the steel-rimmed spectacles, tailored suit, Gucci brogues, opaque pantyhouse. A bra so small it looked like two miniature half-moons.

"What size?" I asked hoarsely, staring at her elegant breasts.

"T-cup," she said.

She kept making sounds of deep satisfaction, "Mmm, mmm," when I put my lips and teeth to her. She was so complete and full. Not a dimple. All of her taut. Bulging hard. Trig, definitely trig. With strength and energy to challenge. I thought this was the real her. The other was role-playing. She was waiting to be free of the pretend.

What did we do? What did we not do? Our howls muffled the wind; our cries silenced the hissing radiator. She didn't give a damn, and after awhile I didn't either.

I topped her by a head, at least, but that can be interesting, too. I could look down with wonder at this cool, intent woman. She was very serious. It wasn't a your-place-or-mine thing. It had meaning for her. It was significant, I knew. And responded.

Sinuous legs came around my waist. Ankles locked.

She pulled me deeper, fingernails digging. Her eyes were open, but glazed.

"Samuel," she said. "Samuel Todd."

"That's me," I said, and gave it my best shot.

I think it was enough. I hope it was enough. But it was difficult to tell. For a woman who hated violence, she was something.

The best part was when, sated, we lay slackly in each other's arms. Half-asleep. Murmuring and moaning nothing. That was nice, being warm and close, kissing now and then, rubbing. The storm was outside, growling, howling, but we were totally gone. Everything was quiet and smelled good.

Three years later I remembered that first night with Joan Powell. The storm was still howling and growling outside, but now I was alone. Well, that's the way I wanted it. Wasn't it?

My headlights picked up a sign through the snow's swirl: COBURN—1 MILE. I leaned forward to the windshield, peering into the darkness, searching for the turnoff. I found it, came down a long, winding ramp. There was a steel sign that had several holes blown through it, like someone had blasted away with a shotgun at close range. The sign said: WELCOME TO COBURN.

I was in the village before I knew it. An hour previously, I later learned, there had been a power failure; Coburn was completely without electricity; all street lamps and traffic signals were out. I glimpsed a few flickering candles and kerosene lanterns inside stores and houses, but this deserted place was mostly black. I drove slowly, and when I saw a muffled pedestrian lumping along with a flashlight for company, I pulled up alongside him and cranked down the window.

"The Coburn Inn?" I yelled.

He motioned forward, in the direction I was heading. I nodded my thanks, sealed myself in, and started up again. For a few moments I thought I was stuck; my wheels spun. But I rocked the Grand Prix back and forth, and

21

after awhile I got traction again and plowed ahead. I found the Coburn Inn dimly lighted with propane lamps. There were a lot of cars parked every which way in the courtyard: tourists who had decided to postpone their trips, to spend this broken night in the nearest warm, dry haven.

In the lobby it looked like most of the stranded travelers had decided to wait out the storm in the restaurant-bar. The flickering lamps gave enough light so I could see crowded tables and stand-up drinkers keeping two bartenders hustling.

There was a kerosene lantern on the front desk.

"Sorry," the bald clerk grinned cheerfully, "we're full up for tonight. The storm, y'know. But you can sit up in the lobby if you like. Plenty to eat and drink. Make a party of it."

"My name's Samuel Todd," I explained patiently. "My office called for a reservation."

"Sorry," he grinned. "No reservations for tonight. We're taking them first-come, first-served."

"I'm here at Dr. Thorndecker's request," I said desperately. "Dr. Telford Thorndecker of Crittenden Hall. He recommended this place. I'm meeting with him tomorrow."

Something happened to the grin. It remained painted on his face, mouth spread, teeth showing, but all the cheer went out of it. The eyes changed focus. I had the feeling that he wasn't seeing me anymore, that he was looking through me to something else. A thousand-yard stare.

"Samuel Todd," I repeated, to shake him out of his reverie. "Reservation. Friend of Dr. Thorndecker."

He shook his head in a kind of shudder, a brief, whip-like motion. His eyes slid down to the big register on the desk.

"Why didn't you say so?" he said in a low voice. "Samuel Todd, sure. Nice, big corner room. Sign here please. You got luggage?"

"Out in my car."

22

"You'll have to bring it in yourself. Half my people didn't show up tonight."

"I'll manage," I said.

He turned to a small bank of cubbyholes, took an old-fashioned skeleton key from 3-F. The key was attached to a brass medallion. He handed it to me, along with a sealed white envelope that had been in the box.

"Message for you," he said importantly. "See, it's got your name on it, and 'Hold for arrival.'"

"Who left it?"

"That I couldn't say."

"Well, when was it left here?"

"Beats me. It was in the box when I came on duty tonight. You might ask the day man tomorrow."

I nodded, and stuffed the envelope into my trenchcoat pocket. I went out into the storm again, and brought in my two suitcases and the briefcase containing the Thorndecker file. And the pint of brandy from the glove compartment.

The single elevator wasn't working. The bald clerk gestured toward the steep staircase. I went clumping slowly up, pausing on the landings to catch my breath. Kerosene lanterns had been set out in all the corridors. I found Room 3-F, and took one of the lanterns in with me. As far as I could see in the wavery light, it was a big corner room, just as the clerk had promised. Nothing palatial, but it seemed reasonably clean. It would do; I wasn't planning to settle permanently in Coburn.

I was peeling off my wet trenchcoat when I found the note that had been left for me. I took the envelope close to the yellowish lantern light to examine it. "Mr. Samuel Todd. Please hold for arrival." Neatly typed.

I opened the flap. A single sheet of white typing paper. I unfolded that. Two words:

"Thorndecker kills."

The Second Day

THE STORM PASSED over sometime during the night and went whining off to New England. When I awoke Tuesday at 7:30, power had been restored; I was able to use the electric shaver I carry in my travel kit. I noticed I had left about three fingers in the brandy bottle, demonstrating massive strength of character.

In daylight, my room looked old-fashioned, but okay. Lofty ceiling, raddled rug, sprung but comfortable armchairs. A small desk, the top tattooed with cigarette burns. Two dressers. The bed was flinty, but that's the way I like it. Biggest bathroom I had ever seen in a hotel, with a crackled pedestal sink, a yellowed tub on clawed legs, a toilet that flushed by pulling a tarnished brass chain hanging from an overhead tank. A Holiday Inn it wasn't, but there were plenty of towels, and the steam radiators were clanking away busily.

I took a peek outside. Instant depression. The sky was slate. Patches of sooty snow were melting; there wasn't a bright color in sight. No pedestrians. No life anywhere. Two of my five windows faced on what I guessed was Coburn's main street. I made a bet with myself that it was called Broadway. (It wasn't; it was called Main Street.) I saw the usual collection of small town stores and shops: Ideal Bootery, Samson's Drugs, E-zee Super-Mart, Bill's 5-and-10, Knowlton's Ladies and Gents Apparel, the Coburn *Sentinel*, Sandy's Liquors and Fine Wines.

Before sallying forth to take a closer look at this teeming metropolis, I spent a few minutes considering what to do about that anonymous billet-doux: "Thorn-decker kills."

I was born a nosy bastard, and all my life I've been less interested in the how of things than in the why of people. I've had formal training in investigation, but you can't learn snoopery from books, any more than swimming, love making, or how to build the Eiffel Tower out of old Popsicle sticks.

Experience is what an investigator needs most. That, plus a jaundiced view of human nature, plus a willingness to listen to the palaver of old cops and learn by *their* experience.

Also, I have one other attribute of an effective shamus: I can't endure the thought of being scammed and made a fool of. I don't have that much self-respect that I can afford to let it be chipped away by some smart-ass con man. Con woman. Con person.

That dramatic note—"Thorndecker kills."—smelled of con to me.

In the groves of academe there's just as much envy, spite, deceit, connivery, and backbiting as in Hackensack politics. The upper echelons of scientific research are just as snaky a pit. The competition for private and federal funding is ruthless. Research scientists rush to publication, sometimes on the strength of palsied evidence. There's no substitute for being first. Either you're a discoverer, and your name goes into textbooks, or you're a plodding replicator, and the Nobel Committee couldn't care less.

So the chances were good that the author of "Thorndecker kills." was a jealous rival or disgruntled aide who felt he wasn't getting sufficient credit. I had seen it happen before: anonymous letters, slanderous rumors slyly spread, even sabotage and deliberate falsification of test results.

And the accusation—"Thorndecker kills."—wasn't all that shocking. All research biologists kill—everything from paramecia to chimpanzees. That's what the job requires. If the note had said: "Thorndecker murders," my hackles might have twitched a bit more. But all I did was slide the letter into an envelope addressed to Donner & Stern, along with a personal note to Nate Stern requesting a make on the typewriter used. I added the phone number of the Coburn Inn, and asked him to call when he had identified the machine. I doubted the information would have any effect on the Thorndecker inquiry.

That was my second mistake of that miserable day. The first was getting out of bed.

I waited and waited and waited for the rackety elevator, watching the brass dial move like it was lubricated with Elmer's Glue-All. When the open cage finally came wheezing down from the top (sixth) floor, the operator turned out to be a wizened colored gentleman one year younger than God. He was wearing a shiny, black alpaca jacket and a little skullcap something like a yarmulke. He was sitting on a wooden kitchen stool. He stopped the elevator five inches below floor level, creaked open the gate slowly. I stepped down and in.

"Close," I said, "but no cigar. How's life treating you this bright, sparkling morning?"

"It's hard but it's fair," he said, closing the gate and shoving the lever forward. "You checking out?"

"I just checked in."

"I thought you was one of those drummers the storm drove in."

"Not me," I said. "I'm here for a few days. Or maybe a few weeks."

"Glad to hear it," he said. "We can use all the customers we gets. My name's Sam. Sam Livingston."

"Sam's my name, too," I said. "Sam Todd. Glad to meet you, Sam."

"Likewise, Sam," he said.

We shook hands solemnly. About this time we were inching past the second floor.

"We'll get there," he said encouragingly. "I hop bells and hump bags and gets you room service, if you want. Like a jug late at night. A sandwich. I can provide."

"That's good to know," I said. "What hours do you work?"

"All hours," he said. "I live here. I got me a nice little place in the basement."

"Where were you last night when I needed you?"

"Hustling drinks in the saloon, I reckon."

"You busy, Sam?" I asked. "Many guests?"

"You," he said, "and half a dozen permanents. It's not our season."

"When is your season?"

He showed me a keyboard of strong, yellow teeth.

"We ain't got a season," he said.

We both laughed, and I looked down into the lobby as we slowly descended.

The floor was a checkerboard of greasy black and white tiles. There were a few small oriental rugs, so tatty the brown backing showed through. The couches and club chairs had once been sleek leather; now they were crackled, cushions lumped with loose springs. Alongside some of the chairs were round rubber mats with ancient brass cuspidors that had been planted with plastic ferns.

Fat wooden pillars, painted to imitate marble, rose from floor to vaulted ceiling. There was ornate iron grillwork around the elevator shaft and cashier's cage. Tucked in one corner was a glass cigar counter, presided over by a shimmering blonde wearing a tight turtleneck sweater punctuated by two Saturn nose cones.

The elevator bobbed to a stop. The gate squeaked open. I moved out. I had the feeling of stepping into the past, a scene of fifty years ago, caught and frozen. Old men slumped in dusty chairs stared at me over the tops of newspapers. The clerk behind the desk, another baldy, looked up from sorting letters into cubbyholes. The creampuff behind the counter paused in the act of opening a carton of cigarettes and raised her shadowed eyes.

It was not a memory, since I was too young to recall an ancient hotel lobby like that, smelling of disinfectant and a thousand dead cigars. I could only guess I remembered the set from an old movie, and any moment Humphrey Bogart was going to shamble over to the enameled blonde, buy a pack of Fatimas, and lisp, "Keep the change, thweetheart."

I shook my head. The vertigo vanished. I was staring at a shabby hotel lobby in a small town that had seen better days none of the citizens could recall. I went to the front desk . . .

"My name's Samuel Todd."

"Yes, Mr. Todd," the clerk said. "Room 3-F. Everything all right?"

He resembled the night clerk, but all bald men look like relatives.

"Everything's fine," I told him. "There was a letter waiting for me when I checked in last night. Could you tell me who left it?"

He shook his head.

"Can't say. I went back in the office for a few minutes. When I came out, the letter was laying right there on the register. Wasn't it signed?"

"Didn't recognize the name," I lied. "Where can I buy a stamp?"

"Machine over there on the cigar counter. Mailing slot's next to the door. Or you can take it to the post office if you like. That's around the corner on River Street. Go out a lot faster if you mail it from there. We don't get a pickup till three, four this afternoon."

I nodded my thanks, and walked over to the cigar counter. The machine sold me a 15-cent stamp for 20 cents. Nice business.

"Good morning, sir," brass head said throatily. "You're staying with us?"

She was something, a dazzle of wet colors: metallic hair, clouded eyes with lashes like inky centipedes, an enormous blooded mouth, pancaked cheeks. The red sweater was cinched with a studded belt wide enough for a motorcycle ride. Her skirt of purple plaid was so tight that in silhouette she looked like a map of Africa. Knee-high boots of white plastic. Tangerine-colored fingernails somewhere between claws and talons. A walking Picasso.

"Good morning," I said. "Yes, I'm staying with you."

I came down hard on the *you*, and she giggled and took a deep breath. It would have been cruel to ignore that. It would have been impossible to ignore that. I bought a candy bar I didn't want.

"Keep the change, sweetheart," I said.

The seediness was getting to me. All I needed was a toothpick in the corner of my mouth, and an unsmoked cigarette behind my ear.

I started for the doorway under the neon Restaurant-Bar sign.

"My name's Millie," the cigar counter girl called after me.

I waved a hand and kept going. Women like that scare me. I have visions of them cracking my bones and sucking the marrow.

One look at the Restaurant-Bar and I understood how the Coburn Inn survived without a season. There were customers at all twenty tables, and only two empty stools at the long counter. There were even three guys bellying up to the bar in an adjoining room, starting their day with a horn of the ox that gored them.

A few women, but mostly men. All locals, I figured: merchants, insurance salesmen, clerks, some blue-collar types, farmers in rubber boots and wool plaid shirts. They all seemed to know each other: a lot of loud talk, hoots of laughter. This had to be the *in* place in Coburn for a scoff or a tipple. More likely, it was the *only* place.

The menu was encouraging: heavy, country breakfasts with things like pork sausages, grits, scrapple, ham steaks, home fries, and so forth. I glanced around, and it looked like no one in Coburn ever heard of cholesterol. I had a glass of orange juice (which turned out to be freshly squeezed), a western omelette, hash browns, hot Danish, and coffee. When in Rome . . .

As I ate, the room gradually emptied out. It was getting on to 9:00 A.M., time to open all those swell stores I had seen, to start the business day thrumming. I figured that in Coburn, the sale of a second-hand manure spreader qualified as a thrum.

I was starting on my second cup of coffee when I realized someone was standing at my shoulder. I glanced around. A cop in khaki uniform under a canvas ranchers' jacket with a shearling collar. His star was on his lapel, his gun belt was buckled tightly. A long, tight man.

"Mr. Samuel Todd?" he asked. His voice was a flat monotone, hard. A pavement voice.

"That's right," I said. "I'm parked in a towaway zone?"

"No, sir," he said, not smiling. "I'm Constable Ronnie Goodfellow." He didn't offer to shake hands. "Mind if I join you?"

"Pull up a stool," I said. "How about a coffee?"

"No, sir. Thank you."

"No drinking on duty, eh?" I said. Still no smile. I gave up.

He took off his fur trooper's hat, opened the gun belt, took off his jacket. Then he buckled the gun belt about his waist again. He hung up hat and jacket, swung onto the stool alongside me.

While he was going through this slow, thoughtful ballet, I was watching him in the mirror behind the counter. I figured him for Indian blood. He was sword-thin, with dark skin, jetty hair, a nose that could slice cheese. He moved with a relaxed grace, but he didn't fool me. I saw the thin lips, squinny eyes. And his holster was oiled and polished.

I had known men like that before: so much pride they shivered with it. You see it mostly in blacks, Chicanos, and all the other put-downs. But some whites have it, too. Country whites or slum whites or mountain whites. Men so sensitive to a slight that they'll kill if they're insulted, derided, or even accidentally jostled. Temper isn't the reason, or merely conceit. It's a hubris that becomes violent when self-esteem is threatened. The image cannot be scorned. You don't chivy men like that; you cross to the other side of the street.

"Reason I'm here," he said in that stony voice, "is Dr. Telford Thorndecker asked me to stop by. Check to see you got settled in all right. See if there's anything you're wanting."

"That's very nice of you and Dr. Thorndecker," I said. "I appreciate your interest. But I'm settled in just dandy. No problems. And the western omelette was the best I've ever tasted."

"Introduce you to folks in Coburn, if you like," he said. "I know them all."

I blew across my coffee to cool it.

"Thorndecker tell you why I'm here?" I asked casually.

Then I turned to look at him. No expression in those tarry eyes.

"About the grant, you mean?" he said.

"The application for the grant," I said.

"He told me."

"That's surprising," I said. "Usually applicants like to keep it quiet. So if they're turned down, which they usually are, there's no public loss of face."

He looked down at his hands, twisted his thin wedding band slowly.

"Mr. Todd," he said, "Crittenden Hall is big business in Coburn. About a hundred people work out there, including the folks in the research lab. Biggest employer around here. They all live hereabouts, take home good paychecks, buy their needs from local stores. It's important to us—you know?"

"Sure," I said. "I understand."

"And with so many local people working out there, it would be pretty hard for Dr. Thorndecker to keep this grant business a secret. He didn't even try. There was a front-page story in the Coburn *Sentinel* a month ago. Everyone in town knows about it. Everyone's hoping it comes through. A million dollars. That would mean a lot to this town."

"Everyone's cheering for Thorndecker?" I said. "Is that it?"

"Just about everyone," he said carefully. "The best people. We're all hoping you give him a good report, and he gets the money. It would mean a lot to Coburn."

"I don't make the decision," I told him. "I just turn in a recommendation, one way or another. There are a lot of other factors involved. My bosses say Yes or No."

"We understand all that," he said patiently. "We just want to make sure you know how the people around here feel about Dr. Thorndecker and his work."

"The best people," I said.

"That's right," he said earnestly. "We're all for him. Dr. Thorndecker is a great man."

"Did he tell you that?" I said, finishing my coffee.

Those dark eyes turned slowly to mine. It wasn't a kindly look he gave me. No amusement at all.

"No," he said. "He didn't tell me. I'm saying it. Dr. Thorndecker is a great man doing fine work."

"Opinion received and noted," I said. "Now if you'll excuse me, Constable Goodfellow, I've got to go mail a letter."

"The post office is around the corner on River Street."

"I know."

"I'll be happy to show you the way."

"All right," I sighed. "Show me the way."

Goodfellow hadn't been exaggerating when he claimed to know all of Coburn. He exchanged greetings with everyone we met, usually on a first-name basis. We stopped a half-dozen times while I was introduced to Leading Citizens. After the Constable carefully identified me and explained what I was doing in Coburn, I was immediately assured that Dr. Telford Gordon Thorndecker was a prince, a cross between Jesus Christ and Albert Schweitzer—with maybe a little Abner Doubleday thrown in.

We mailed my letter. I had hopes then of ditching my police escort. It wasn't that he was *bad* company; he was no company at all. But I had underestimated him.

"Got a few minutes?" he asked. "Something I want to show you."

"Sure," I said, trying to sound enthusiastic. "I'm not on any schedule."

River Street was exactly that. It intersected Main Street, then ran downhill to the Hudson River. We stood at the top, before the street made its snaky descent to the water. The road was potholed, and bordering it were deserted homes and shops; crumbling warehouses, falling-down sheds, and sodden vacant lots littered with rubbish.

The slate sky still pressed down; God had abolished the sun. The air was shivery, wet, and smelled of ash. There was a greasy mist on the river. A current was running, I guess, but all I could see was floating debris, garbage, and patches of glinting oil. Empty crates, grapefruit rinds, dead fish. I don't think travel agents would push Coburn as "two weeks of fun-filled days and glamorous, romance-laden nights."

Constable Ronnie Goodfellow stood there, hands on hips, smoky eyes brooding from under the fur cap pulled low on his forehead.

"My folks lived here for two hundred years," he said. "This was a sweet river once. All the jumping fish you could catch. Salmon, bass, perch. Everything. The river was alive. Boats moving up and down. I mean there was commerce. Busy. Everyone worked hard and made a living. New York people, they wanted to go to Albany, they took the paddlewheel up. This was before trains and

34

buses and airplanes. I mean the river was *important*. We shipped food down to the city by boat and barge. It all moves by truck now, of course. What there is of it. There were big wharves here. You can still see the stubs of the pilings over there. This town was *something*. It's all gone now. All different. Even the weather. My daddy used to tell me the winters were so hard that the river froze deep, and you could walk across the ice to Harrick. Or skate across. Hell, Harrick doesn't even *exist* anymore. Lots of small farms around here then. Good apples. Good grapes. Small manufacturing, like furniture, silverware, glassware. Did you know there was a special color called Coburn Blue? Something to do with the sand around here. They put it into vases and plates. Known all over the country, it was. Coburn Blue. That must have been something. The population was about five times what it is now. The young people stayed right here. This was their home. But now ... This place ..."

His voice got choky. I began to like him.

"I'll tell you what," I said, "it's not only Coburn. It's New York City. It's the United States of America. It's the world. Everything changes. You, me, and the universe. It's the only thing you can depend on—change."

"Yes," he said, "You're right. And I'm a fool."

"You're not a fool," I told him. "A romantic maybe, but there's no law against that."

"A fool," he insisted, and I didn't argue.

We walked slowly back to Main Street.

"You're married?" I said.

He didn't answer.

"Children?"

"No," he said. "No kids."

"Does your wife like Coburn?" I asked him.

"Hates it," he said in that hollow voice of his. "Can't wait to get out."

"Well ...?"

"No," he said. "We'll stay."

We didn't talk anymore until we were standing outside the Coburn Inn.

"Maybe you met my wife," he said, looking over my head. "Works right here in the hotel. Behind the cigar counter. Name's Millie."

I nodded goodby, and marched into the Inn. I considered calling Dr. Thorndecker, but I figured Constable Goodfellow would let him know I was in town. To tell you the truth, I was miffed at the doctor. Not only had he made his Bingham Foundation grant application a matter of public knowledge—something that just isn't done—but he had sent an emissary to greet me. Ordinarily I wouldn't have objected to that, but this agent carried a .38 Police Special. I had a feeling I was being leaned on. I didn't like it.

At this hour in the morning, getting on to eleven o'clock, there was only one customer in the hotel bar. He was a gaffer wearing a checked hunting cap, stained canvas jacket, and old-fashioned leather boots laced to the knees. We used to call them "hightops" where I came from. You bought a pair at Sears after your feet stopped growing, and they lasted for the rest of your life, with occasional half-soling and a liberal application of saddle soap or goose grease before you put them away in the spring. The codger was hunched over a draft beer. He didn't look up when I came in.

The bartender was another baldy, just like the desk clerks. A lot of bald men in one small town. Maybe it was something in the water. I ordered a vodka gimlet on the rocks. He knew what it was, and mixed a fine one, shaking it the way it should be made, not stirred. Most bartenders follow the recipe on the bottle, and make a gimlet tart enough to pucker your asshole. But this one was mostly vodka, with just a flavoring of the lime juice. Drink gimlets and you'll never get scurvy—right? That's my excuse.

The bartender was wearing a lapel badge that read: "Call me Jimmy."

"Good drink, Jimmy," I said.

"Thank you, sir," he said. "I usually have some fresh lime to put in, but that crowd last night cleaned me out.

Maybe I'll have some more by tomorrow, if you're still here."

"I'll be here," I said.

"Oh?" he said. "Staying in Coburn?"

"For awhile," I said.

The old character swung around on his barstool and almost fell off.

"What the hell for?" he demanded in a cracked, screaky voice. "Why would anyone in his right mind want to stay in this piss-ass town?"

"Now, Mr. Coburn," the bartender soothed.

"Don't you 'Now, Mr. Coburn' me," the ancient grumbled. "I knowed you when you was sloppin' hogs, and here you are still in the same line of work."

I turned to look at him.

"Mr. *Coburn?*" I said. "Original settlers?"

"From the poor side of the family," he said with a harsh laugh. "The others had the money and sense to get out."

"Now, Mr. Coburn," Jimmy said, again, nervously.

I saw the beer glass was almost empty.

"Buy you a drink, Mr. Coburn?" I asked respectfully.

"Why the hell not?" he said, and shoved the glass across the bar. "And this time go easy on the head," he told the bartender. "When I want a glass of froth, I'll tell you."

Jimmy sighed, and drew the brew.

"Mind if I join you, Mr. Coburn?" I asked.

"Come ahead," he said, motioning to the stool next to him.

When I moved over, I noticed he had a long gun case, an old, leather-trimmed canvas bag, propped against the bar on his far side.

"Hunting?" I said, nodding toward the case.

"Was," he said, "but it's too damned wet after that storm. Ain't a damned thing left worth shooting around here anyways. Except a few two-legged creatures I could mention but won't. What you doing in town, sonny?"

There was no point in trying to keep it a secret, not after that tour of the village with Constable Goodfellow.

"I'm here to see Dr. Thorndecker," I said. "Of Crittenden Hall."

He didn't say anything, but something happened to that seamed face. Caterpillar brows came down. Bloodless lips pressed. Seared cheeks fell in. The elbow-chin jutted, and I thought I saw a sudden flare in those washed-blue eyes.

Then he lifted his glass of beer and drained it off, just drank it down in steady gulps, the wrinkled Adam's apple pumping away. He slammed the empty glass back down on the bar.

"Do me again, Jimmy," he gasped.

I nodded at the bartender, and motioned toward my own empty glass. We sat in silence. When our drinks were served, I glanced around. The bar was still empty. There were small tables for two set back in the gloom, and a few high-sided booths that could seat four.

"Why don't we make ourselves comfortable?" I suggested. "Stretch out and take it easy."

"Suits me," he grunted.

He picked up his beer and gun case, and led the way. I noticed his limp, a dragging of the right leg. He seemed active enough, but slow. He picked a booth for four, and slid onto one of the worn benches. I sat opposite him. I held out my hand.

"Samuel Todd," I said.

"Al Coburn," he said. His handshake was dry, and not too firm. "No relation to the Todds around here, are you?"

"Don't think so, sir," I said. "I'm from Ohio."

"Never been there," he said. "Never been out of New York State, to tell the truth. Went down to the City once."

"Like it?" I asked.

"No," he said. He glanced toward the bar where Jimmy was studiously polishing glasses, not looking in our direction. "What the hell you want with Thorndecker?"

I told him what I was doing in Coburn. He nodded.

"Read about it in the paper," he said. It was almost a Bostonian accent: "pay-puh." "Think he'll get the money?"

"Not for me to say," I said, shrugging. "You know him?"

"Oh, I know him," he said bitterly. "He's living on my land."

"*Your* land?"

"Coburn land," he said. "Originally. Was still in the family when my daddy died. He left me the farm and my sister the hill." Something happened to his eyes again: that flare of fury. "I thought I got the best of the deal. It was a working farm, and all she got was uncleared woods and a stretch of swamp."

"And then?" I prompted him.

"She married a dude from Albany. Some kind of a foreigner. His name ended in 'i' or 'o'. I forget."

I looked at him. He hadn't forgotten. Would never forget.

"He talked her into selling her parcels off. To a developer. I mean, she sold the *land*. Land that daddy left her."

I watched him raise his beer to his thin lips with a shaking hand. It means that much to some of the old-timers—land. It's not the money value they cherish. It's a piece of the world.

"Then what happened?" I asked him.

"The developer drained the swamp and cleared out most of the trees. Built houses. Sold the hill to a fellow named Crittenden who built the sick place."

"Crittenden Hall," I said.

"This was in the Twenties," he said. "Before the Great Depression. Before your time, sonny. Land was selling good then. My sister did all right. Then she and her foreigner upped and moved away."

"Where are they now?"

"Who the hell knows?" he rasped. "Or cares?"

"And what happened to your farm?"

"Ahh, hell," he said heavily. "My sons didn't take to farming. They moved away. Florida, California. Then I busted up my leg and couldn't get around so good. The old woman died of the cancer. I got tenants on the land now. I get by. But that Thorndecker, he's living on Coburn land. I ain't saying it's not perfectly legal and aboveboard. I'm just saying it's Coburn land."

I nodded, and signaled Jimmy for another round. But a waitress brought our drinks. There were three customers at the bar now, and from outside, in the restaurant, I could hear the sounds of the crank-up for the luncheon rush.

"You know Dr. Thorndecker, Mr. Coburn?" I asked him. "Personally?"

"I've met him," he said shortly.

"What do you think of him?"

His flaky eyelids rose slowly. He stared at me. But he didn't answer.

"Constable Goodfellow tells me all the best people in town are behind him one hundred percent," I said, pressing him. "That's Goodfellow's phrase: 'the best people'."

"Well, I ain't one of the best people," he said, "and I wouldn't trust that quack to cut my toenails."

He was silent a moment, then said sharply, "Goodfellow? How did you meet the Indian? My great-grandpa shot Indians hereabouts."

"He says Thorndecker sent him around. To see if I was settled in, if there was anything I needed, if I wanted to meet anyone in town."

Al Coburn stared down at what was left in his glass of beer. He was quiet a long time. Then he drained his glass, climbed laboriously to his feet, picked up his gun case. I stayed where I was. He stood alongside the table, looking down at me.

"You watch your step, Sam Todd," he said in that hard, creaking, old man's voice.

"Always do," I said.

He nodded and limped away a few steps. Then he stopped, turned, came back.

"Besides," he said, "I'm guessing it wasn't Thorndecker who sent Constable Goodfellow to see you. Thorndecker may be a fraud, but he ain't stupid."

"If not Thorndecker," I asked him, "then who?"

He stared at me.

"I reckon it was that hot-pants wife of his," he said grimly.

He was silent then, just standing there staring at me. It seemed to me he was trying to decide whether or not to say more. I waited. Finally he made up his mind...

"You know what they're doing out there?" he demanded. "In that laboratory of theirs?"

He pronounced it almost in the British manner: la*bor*atory.

I shrugged. "Biological research," I said. "Something to do with human cells."

"Devil's work!" he burst out, so forcibly I felt the spittle on my face. "It's devil's work!"

I sat up straight.

"What are you talking about?" I said harshly. "What does that mean—devil's work?"

"That's for me to know," he said, "and you to find out. Thank you kindly for the drinks."

He actually tipped that checked hunting cap to me. I watched him drag away.

I finished my drink, paid my tab, stalked out of the bar. That country breakfast had been enough; I didn't feel up to lunch. Went into the hotel lobby. Thumbed through magazines in a rack near the cigar counter. Waited until there were no customers. I wanted to talk to her alone.

"Hello, Millie," I said.

"Hi there!" she said, flapping her lashes like feather dusters. "Enjoying your visit to Coburn, Mr. Todd?"

So she had asked the desk clerk my name. I wondered if she had asked my room number, too.

"Lousy town," I said, watching her.

"You can say that again," she said, eyes dulling. "It died fifty years ago, but no one has enough money to give it a decent burial. Can I help you? Cigarettes? A magazine? *Anything?*"

She gave that "anything" the husky, Marilyn Monroe exhalation, arching her back, pouting. God help Constable Ronnie Goodfellow.

"Just information," I told her hastily. "How do I get to

41

Dr. Thorndecker's place? Crittenden Hall?"

I tried to listen and remember as she told me how to drive east on Main Street, turn north on Oakland Drive, make a turn at Mike's Service Station onto Fort Peabody Drive, etc., etc. But I was looking at her and trying to figure why a hard, young Indian cop had married a used woman about five years older than he, and whose idea of bliss was probably a pound box of chocolate bonbons and the tenth rerun of "I Love Lucy."

When she ran down, I said, foolishly, "I met your husband this morning."

"I meet him every morning," she said. Then she added, "Almost."

She stared at me, suddenly very sober, very serious. Challenging.

I tried to smile. I turned around and walked away. I didn't know if it was good sense or cowardice. I did know I had misjudged this lady. Her idea of bliss wasn't the boob tube and bonbons. Far from it.

I found my car in the parking area, and while it was warming up, I scraped the ice off the windshield. Then I headed out of town.

I remember an instructor down in Ft. Benning telling us:

"You can stare at maps and aerial photos until your eyeballs are coming out your ass. But nothing can take the place of physical reconnaissance. Maps and photos are okay, but seeing the terrain and, if possible, walking over it, is a thousand times better. *Learn the terrain.* Know what the hell you're getting into. If you can walk over it before a firefight, maybe you'll walk out of it after."

So I had decided to go have a look at Dr. Telford Thorndecker's terrain.

By following Millie Goodfellow's directions, with a little surly assistance at Mike's Service Station, I found Crittenden Hall without too much difficulty. The grounds were less than a mile east of the river, the main buildings on the hill that had once belonged to Al Coburn's daddy.

The approach was through an area of small farms:

stubbled land and beaten houses. Some of the barns and outbuildings showed light between warped siding; tarpaper roofing flapped forlornly; sprained doors hung open on rusty hinges. I saw farm machinery parked unprotected, and more than one field unpicked, the produce left to rot. It was cold, wet, desolate. Even more disturbing, there was no one around. I didn't see a pedestrian, pass another car, or glimpse anyone working the land or even taking out the garbage. The whole area seemed deserted. Like a plague had struck, or a neutron bomb dropped. The empty, weathered buildings leaned. Stripped trees cut blackly across the pewter sky. But the people were gone. No life. I ached to hear a dog bark.

The big sign read Crittenden Hall, and below was a small brass plaque: Crittenden Research Laboratory. There was a handsome cast iron fence at least six feet tall, with two ornate gates that opened inward. Inside was a guard hut just large enough for one man to sit comfortably, feet on a gas heater.

I drove slowly past. The ornamental iron fence became chain link, but it entirely enclosed the Thorndecker property. Using single-lane back roads, I was able to make a complete circuit. A lot of heavily wooded land. Some meadows. A brook. A tennis court. A surprisingly large cemetery, well-tended, rather attractive. People were dying to get in there. I finally saw someone: a burly guy in black oilskins with a broken shotgun over one arm. In his other hand was a leash. At the end of the leash, a straining German shepherd.

I came back to the two-lane macadam that ran in front of the main gate. I parked off the verge where I couldn't be seen from the guard hut. I got out, shivering, found my 7x50 field glasses in the messy trunk, got back in the car and lowered the window just enough. I had a reasonably good view of the buildings and grounds. The light was slaty, and the lens kept misting up, but I could see what I wanted to see.

I wasn't looking for anything menacing or suspicious. I just wanted to get a quick first impression. Did the buildings look in good repair? Were the grounds reasonably well-groomed? Was there an air of prosperity and good management—or was the place a dump, run-down and awaiting foreclosure?

Dr. Thorndecker's place got high marks. Not a broken window that I could see. Sashes and wooden trim smartly painted. Lawn trimmed, and dead leaves gathered. Trees obviously cared for, brick walks swept clean. Bushes and garden had been prepared for the coming winter. Storm windows were up.

All this spelled care and efficiency. It looked like a prosperous, functioning set-up with strong management that paid attention to maintenance and appearance even in this lousy weather at this time of year.

The main building, the largest building, was also, obviously, the oldest. Probably the original nursing home, Crittenden Hall. It was a three-story brick structure sited on the crest of the hill. The two-story wings were built on a slightly lower level. All outside walls were covered with ivy, still green. Roofs were tarnished copper. Windows were fitted with ornamental iron grilles, not unusual in buildings designed for the ill, infirm, aged, and/or loony.

About halfway down the hill was a newer building. Also red brick, but no ivy. And the roof was slated. The windows were also guarded, but with no-nonsense vertical iron bars. This building, which I assumed to be the Crittenden Research Laboratory, was not as gracefully designed as Crittenden Hall; it was merely a two-story box, with mean windows and a half-hearted attempt at an attractive Georgian portico and main entrance. Between nursing home and laboratory was an outdoor walk and stairway, a roofed port set on iron pillars, without walls.

There were several smaller outbuildings which could have been kitchens, labs, storehouses, supply sheds, whatever; I couldn't even guess. But everything seemed precise, trim, clean and well-preserved.

Then why did I get such a feeling of desolation?

It might have been that joyless day, the earth still sodden, the sky pressing down. It might have been that disconsolate light. Not light at all, really, but just moist steel. Or maybe it was Coburn and my mood.

All I know is that when I put down the binoculars, I had seen nothing that could possibly count against Dr. Telford Gordon Thorndecker and his grant application to the Bingham Foundation. Yet I felt something I struggled to analyze and name.

I stared at those winter-stark buildings on the worn hill, striving to grasp what it was I felt. It came to me on the trip back to Coburn. It wasn't fear. Exactly. It was dread.

After that little jaunt to the hinterland, Coburn seemed positively sparkling. I counted at least four pedestrians on Main Street. And look! There was a dog lifting his leg at a hydrant. Marvelous!

I parked and locked the car. What I wanted right then was—oh, I could think of a lot of things I wanted: vodka gimlet. Straight cognac. Coffee and Danish. Club sandwich and ale. Hot pastrami and Celery Tonic. Joan Powell. On rye. So I walked across Main Street to the office of the Coburn *Sentinel*.

It was a storefront with a chipped gold legend on the plate glass window: "Biggest little weekly in the State!" Just inside the door was a stained wooden counter where you could subscribe or buy a want-ad or complain your name was spelled wrong in that front-page story they did on the anniversary party at the Gulek Fat Processing Plant.

Behind the counter were a few exhausted desks, typewriters, swivel chairs. There was a small private office enclosed by frosted glass partitions. And in the rear was the printing area. Everything was ancient. Hand-set type, flatbed press. I guessed they did business cards, stationery, and fliers to pay the rent.

The place was not exactly a humming beehive of activity. There was a superannuated lady behind the counter. She was sitting on a high stool, clipping ads from old *Sentinels* with long shears. She had a bun of iron-gray hair with two pencils stuck into it. And she wore a cameo brooch at the ruffled neck of her shirtwaist blouse. She had just stepped off a *Saturday Evening Post* cover by Norman Rockwell.

Behind her, sitting at one of the weary desks, was a lissome wench. All of 18, I figured. The cheerleader type: so blond, so buxom, so healthy, so glowing that I immediately straightened my shoulders and sucked in my gut. Vanity, thy name is man. Miss Dimples was pecking away at an old Underwood standard, the tip of a pink tongue poked from one corner of her mouth. I'd have traded my Grand Prix for one—Enough. That way lies madness.

Farther to the rear, standing in front of fonts in the press section, a stringy character was setting type with all the blinding speed of a sloth on Librium. He was wearing an ink-smeared apron and one of those square caps printers fold out of newsprint. He was also wearing glasses with lenses like the bottoms of Coke bottles. I wondered about the *Sentinel*'s typos per running inch . . .

That whole damned place belonged in the Smithsonian, with a neat label: "American newspaper office, circa 1930." Actually, all of Coburn belonged in the same Institution, with a similar label. Time had stopped in Coburn. I had stepped into a warp, and any minute someone was going to turn on an Atwater Kent radio, and I'd hear Gene Austin singing "My Blue Heaven."

"May I help you?" the old lady said, looking up from her clipping.

"Is the editor in, please?" I asked. "I'd like to see him."

"Her," she said. "Our editor is female. Agatha Binder."

"Pardon me," I said humbly. "Might I see Miss, Mrs., or Ms. Binder?"

"About what?" she said suspiciously. "You selling something? Or got a complaint?"

I figured the Coburn *Sentinel* got a lot of complaints.

"No, no complaints," I said. I gave her my most winning smile, with no effect whatsoever. "My name is

Samuel Todd. I'm with the Bingham Foundation. I'd like to talk to your editor about Dr. Telford Thorndecker."

"Oh," she said, "*that*. Wait right here."

She slid off the stool and went trotting back into the gloomy shop. She went into the closed office. She was out in a minute, beckoning me with an imperious forefinger. I pushed through the swinging gate. On the way back, I passed the desk of the nubile cheerleader. She was still pecking away at the Underwood, tongue still poked from her mouth.

"I love you," I whispered, and she looked up in alarm.

The woman sprawled behind the littered desk in the jumbled office was about my age, and fifty pounds heavier. She was wearing ink-stained painter's overalls over a red checkerboard shirt that looked like it was made from an Italian restaurant tablecloth. Her feet were parked on the desk, in unbuckled combat boots of World War II. There was a cardboard container of black coffee on the floor alongside her, and she was working on the biggest submarine sandwich I've ever seen. Meatballs.

Everything about her was massive: head, nose, jaw, shoulders, bosom, hips, thighs. The hands that held the sub looked like picnic hams, and her wrists were as thick as my ankles. But no ogre she. It all went together, and was even pleasing in a monumental way. If they had a foothill left over from Mt. Rushmore, they could have used it for her: rugged, craggy. Even the eyes were granite, with little sparkling lights of mica.

"Miss Binder," I said.

"Todd," she said, "sit down."

I sat.

Her voice was like her body: heavy, with an almost masculine rumble. She never stopped munching away at that damned hoagie while we talked, and never stopped swilling coffee. But it didn't slow her down, and the meatballs didn't affect her diction. Much.

"Thorndecker getting his dough?" she demanded.

"That's not for me to say," I told her. How many times would I have to repeat that in Coburn? "I'm just here to do some poking. You know Thorndecker? Personally?"

"Sure, I know him. I know everyone in Coburn. He's a conceited, opinionated, sanctimonious, pompous ass. He's also the greatest brain I've ever met. So smart it scares you. He's a genius; no doubt about that."

"Ever hear any gossip about that nursing home of his? Patients mistreated? Lousy food? Things like that?"

"You kidding?" she said. "Listen, buster, I should live like Thorndecker's patients. Caviar for breakfast. First-run movies. He's got the best wine cellar in the county. And why not? They're paying for it. Listen, Todd, there are lots and lots of people in this country with lots and lots of money. The sick ones and the old ones go to Crittenden Hall to die in style—and that's what they get. I know most of the locals working up there—the aides, cooks, waitresses, and so forth. They all say the same thing: the place is a palace. If you've got to go, that's the way to do it. And when they conk off, as most of them eventually do, he even buries them, or has them cremated. At an added cost, of course."

"Yeah," I said, "I noticed the cemetery. Nice place."

"Oh?" she said. "You've visited Crittenden Hall?"

"Just a quick look," I said vaguely. "What about the research lab?"

"What about it?"

"Know anything about what they're doing up there?"

She kept masticating a meatball, but her expression changed. I mean the focus of her eyes changed, to what I call a "thousand-yard stare." Meaning she was looking at me, through me, and beyond. The same look I had seen in the eyes of the night clerk at the Coburn Inn when I had checked in and mentioned Thorndecker's name.

I had interrogated enough suspects in criminal cases in the army to know what that stare meant. It didn't necessarily mean they were lying or guilty. It usually meant they were making a decision on what and how much to reveal, and what and how much to hide. It was a signal of deep thought, calculating their own interests and culpability.

48

"No," she said finally, "I don't know what they're doing in the lab. Something to do with human cells and longevity. But all that scientific bullshit is beyond me."

She selected that moment to lean over and pick up her coffee cup. So I couldn't see her face, and maybe guess that she was lying?

"You know Thorndecker's family?" I asked her. "Wife? Daughter? The son? Can you tell me anything about them?"

"The wife's less than half his age," she said. "A real beauty. She's his second wife, you know. Julie comes into town occasionally. She dresses fancy. Buys her clothes on Fifth Avenue. Not your typical Coburn housewife."

"Thinks she's superior?"

"I didn't say that," she said swiftly. "She's just not a mixer, that's all."

"She and the doctor happy?"

Again she leaned away from me. This time to set the coffee container back on the floor.

"As far as I know," she said in that deep, rumbling voice. "You really dig, don't you?"

I ignored the question.

"What about the daughter?" I asked. "Does she mix in Coburn's social life?"

"What social life?" she jeered. "Two beers at the Coburn Inn? No, I don't see much of Mary either. It's not that the Thorndeckers are standoffish, you understand, but they keep pretty much to themselves. Why the hell shouldn't they? What the fuck is there to do in this shithole?"

She peered at me, hoping I had been shocked by her language. But I had heard those words before.

"And the son?" I asked. "Edward?"

"No secret about him," she said. "He's been bounced from a couple of prep schools. Lousy grades, I understand. Now he's living at home with a private tutor to get him ready for Yale or Harvard or wherever. I met him a few times. Nice kid. Very handsome. Like his pa. But shy, I thought. Doesn't say much."

"But generally, you'd say the Thorndeckers are a close, loving American family?"

She looked at me suspiciously, wondering if I was putting her on. I was, of course, but she'd never see it in my expression.

"Well... sure," she said. "I suppose they've got their problems like everyone else, but there's never been any gossip or scandal, if that's what you mean."

"Julie Thorndecker," I said, "the wife... she's a good friend of Constable Ronnie Goodfellow?"

The combat boots came off the desk onto the floor with a crash. Agatha Binder jerked toward me. Her mouth was open wide enough so I could see a chunk of half-chewed meatball.

"Where the hell did you hear that?" she demanded.

"Around," I shrugged.

"Shit," she said, "that's just vicious gossip."

"You just said there's never been any gossip about the Thorndeckers."

She sat back, finished chewing and swallowing.

"You're a smartass, aren't you, Todd?"

I didn't answer.

She pushed the remnants of her sandwich aside. She leaned across the desk to me, ham-hands clasped. Her manner was very earnest, very sincere. Apparently she was staring directly into my eyes. But it's difficult to look steadily into someone else's eyes, even when you're telling the truth. The trick is to stare at the bridge of the nose, between the eyes. The effect is the same. I figured that's what she was doing.

"Look, buster," she said in a basso profundo rumble, "you're going to hear a lot of nasty remarks about the Thorndeckers. They're not the richest people hereabouts, but they ain't hurting. Anytime there's money, you'll hear mean, jealous gossip. Take it for what it's worth."

"All right," I said agreeably, "I will. Now how about Thorndecker's staff? I mean the top people. Know any of them?"

"I know Stella Beecham. She's an RN, supervisor of nurses and aides in Crittenden Hall. She practically runs the place. A good friend of mine. And I've met Dr. Draper. He's Thorndecker's Chief of Staff or Executive Assistant or whatever, in the research lab. I've met some of the others, but their names didn't register."

"Competent people?"

"Beecham certainly is. She's a jewel. Draper is the studious, scientific type. I've got nothing in common with him, but he's supposed to be a whiz. I guess the others in the lab are just as smart. Listen, I told you Thorndecker is a genius. He's a good administrator, too. He wouldn't hire dingbats. And the staff in the nursing home, mostly locals, do their jobs. They work hard."

"So Thorndecker's got no labor problems?"

"No way! Jobs are scarce around here, and he pays top dollar. Sick leave, pensions, paid vacation . . . the works. I'd like to work there myself."

"The hell you would," I said.

"Yeah," she said, grinning weakly. "The hell I would."

"You know Al Coburn?"

"That old fart?" she burst out. "He's been crazy as a loon since his wife died. Don't listen to anything *he* says."

"Well, I've got to listen to *someone*," I said. "Preferably someone who knows Thorndecker. Where does he bank?"

"Locally?" she said. "That would have to be the First Farmers & Merchants. The only bank in town. Around the corner on River Street. Next to the post office. The man to see is Arthur Merchant. He's president. That really is his name—Merchant. But the 'Merchants' in the bank's name has nothing to do with his. That means the bank was—"

"I get it, I get it," I assured her. "Just a fiendish coincidence. Life is full of them. Church? Is Thorndecker a church-goer?"

"He and his wife are registered Episcopalians, but they don't work at it."

"You're a walking encyclopedia of Coburn lore," I said admiringly. "You said, 'He and his wife.' What about the daughter? And the son?"

"I don't know what the hell Eddie is. A Boy Scout, I suspect."

"And the daughter? Mary?"

"Well..." she said cautiously. "Uh..."

"Uh?" I said. "What does 'Uh' mean?"

She punched gently at the tip of her nose with a knuckle.

"What the hell has that got to do with whether or not Dr. Thorndecker gets a grant from the Bingham Foundation?"

"Probably not a thing," I admitted. "But I'm a nosy bastard."

"You sure as hell are," she grumbled. "Well, if you must know, I heard Mary Thorndecker goes to a little church about five miles south of here. It's fundamentalist. Evangelical. You know—being born again, and all that crap. They wave their arms and shout, 'Yes, Lord!'"

"And speak in tongues," I said.

She looked at me curiously.

"You're not so dumb, are you?" she said.

"Dumb," I said, "but not so." I paused a moment, pondering. "Well, I can't think of anything else to ask. I want to thank you for your kind cooperation. You've been a big help."

"I have?" she said, surprised. "That's nice. I hope I've helped Thorndecker get his bread. He deserves it, and it would be a great help to this town."

"So I've heard," I said. "Listen, if I come up with any more questions, can I come around again?"

"Often as you like," she said, rising. I stood up too, and saw she was almost as tall as I am. A *big* woman. "Go see Art Merchant at the bank. He'll tell you anything you want to know. By the way, he's also mayor of Coburn."

"Fantastic," I said.

We were standing there, shaking hands and smiling

idiotically at each other, when there was a timid knock on the door.

"Come in," Agatha Binder roared, dropping my hand.

The door opened hesitantly. There was my very own Miss Dimples. She looked even better standing up. Miniskirt. Yummy knees. Black plastic boots. A buttery angora sweater. I remembered an old army expression: "All you need with a dame like that is a spoon and a straw." She was holding a sheaf of yellow copy paper.

"Yes, Sue Ann?" the *Sentinel* editor said.

"I've finished the Kenner funeral story, Miss Binder," the girl faltered.

"Very good, Sue Ann. Just leave it. I'll get to it this afternoon."

The cheerleader dropped the copy on the desk and exited hastily, closing the door behind her. She hadn't glanced at me, but Agatha Binder was staring at me shrewdly.

"Like that?" she asked softly.

"It's okay," I said, flipping a palm back and forth. "Not sensational, but okay."

"Hands off, kiddo," she said in a harder voice, eyes glittering. "It's mine."

I was glad to hear it. I felt better immediately. The sensation of Coburn being in a time warp disappeared. I was back in the 1970s, and I walked out of there with my spirit leaping like a demented hart.

When I strolled into the lobby of the Coburn Inn, the baldy behind the desk signaled frantically.

"Where have you been?" he said in an aggrieved tone.

"Sorry I didn't check in," I said. "Next time I'll bring a note from home."

But he wasn't listening.

"Dr. Thorndecker has called you *three* times," he said. "He wants you to call him back as soon as possible. Here's the number."

Upstairs in my room, I peeled off the trenchcoat, kicked off the boots. I lay back on the hard bed. The telephone was on the rickety bedside table. Calls went through the hotel switchboard. I gave the number and waited.

"Crittenden Hall."

"Dr. Thorndecker, please. Samuel Todd calling."

"Just a moment, please."

Click, click, click.

"Crittenden Research Laboratory."

"Dr. Thorndecker, please. Samuel Todd calling."

"Just a monent, please."

Click, click, click.

"Lab."

"Dr. Thorndecker, please. Samuel Todd calling."

No clicks this time; just, "Hang on."

"Mr. Todd?"

"Yes, Dr. Thorndecker?"

"No. I'm sorry, Mr. Todd, but Dr. Thorndecker can't come to the phone at the moment. I'm Dr. Kenneth Draper, Dr. Thorndecker's assistant. How are you, sir?"

It was a postnasal-drip kind of voice: stuffed, whiny, without resonance.

"If I felt any better I'd be unconscious, thank you. I have a message to call Dr. Thorndecker."

"I know, sir. He's been trying to reach you all afternoon, but at the moment he's involved in a critical experiment."

I was trying to take my socks off with my toes.

"So am I," I said.

"Pardon, sir?"

"Childish humor. Forget it."

"Dr. Thorndecker asks if you can join the family for dinner tonight. Here at Crittenden Hall. Cocktails at six, dinner at seven."

"Be delighted," I said. "Thank you."

"Do you know how to get here, Mr. Todd? You drive east on Main Street, then—"

"I'll find it," I said hastily. "See you tonight. Thank you, Dr. Draper."

I hung up, and took off my socks the conventional

way. I lay back on the bed, figuring to grab a nap for an hour or so, then get up and shower, shave, dress. But sleep wouldn't come. My mind was churning.

You've probably heard the following exchange on a TV detective drama, or read it in a detective novel:

Police Sergeant: "That guy is guilty as hell."

Police Officer: "Why do you say that?"

Police Sergeant: "Gut instinct."

Sometimes the sergeant says, "Gut feeling" or "A hunch." But the implication is that he's had an intuitive feeling, almost a subconscious inspiration, that has revealed the truth.

I asked an old precinct dick about this, and he said: "Bullshit."

Then he said: "Look, I don't deny that you get a gut feeling or a hunch about some cases, but it doesn't just appear out of nowhere. You get a hunch, and if you sit down and analyze it, you discover that what it is, is a logical deduction based on things you know, things you've heard, things you've seen. I mean that 'gut feeling' they're always talking about is really based on hard evidence. Instinct has got nothing to do with it."

I didn't have a gut feeling or a hunch about this Thorndecker investigation. What I had was more like a vague unease. So I started to analyze it, trying to discover what hard evidence had triggered it, and why it was spoiling my nap. My list went like this:

1. When a poor wife is killed accidentally, people cluck twice and say, "What a shame." When a rich wife is killed accidentally, people cluck once, say, "What a shame," and raise an eyebrow. Thorndecker's first wife left him a mil and turned his life around.

2. Thorndecker had released the story of his application for a Bingham Foundation grant to the local press. It wasn't unethical, but it was certainly unusual. I didn't buy Constable Goodfellow's story that it was impossible to keep a secret like that in a small town. Thorndecker could have prepared the application himself, or with the help of a single discreet aide, and no one in Coburn would have

known a thing about it. So he had a motive for giving the story to the Coburn *Sentinel.* To rally the town on his side, knowing there'd be a field investigation?

3. Someone dispatched an armed cop to welcome me to Coburn. That was a dumb thing to do. Why not greet me in person or send an assistant? I didn't understand Goodfellow's role at all.

4. Al Coburn might have been an "old fart" to Agatha Binder, but I thought he was a crusty old geezer with all his marbles. So why had he said, "You watch your step, Sam Todd?" Watch my step for *what?* And what the hell was that "devil's work" he claimed they were doing in the research lab?

5. Agatha Binder had called Thorndecker a "pompous ass" and put on a great show of being a tough, cynical newspaper editor. But she had been careful not to say a thing that might endanger the Bingham grant. Her answers to my questions were a beautiful example of manipulation, except when she blew her cool at my mention of the Julie Thorndecker-Ronnie Goodfellow connection. What the hell was going on *there?*

6. And while I was what-the-helling, just what the hell were Crittenden Hall (a nursing home) and the research laboratory doing with an armed guard and an attack dog patrolling the grounds? To make sure no one escaped from the cemetery?

7. That anonymous note: "Thorndecker kills."

Those were most of the reasons I could list for my "gut instinct" that all was not kosher with Dr. Thorndecker's application. There were a few other little odds and ends. Like Mrs. Cynthia's comment in the corridor of the Bingham Foundation: "I knew his father... it was all so sad... A sweet man." And the fact that the Crittenden Research Laboratory was supported, in part, by bequests from deceased patients of Crittenden Hall.

I agree that any or all of these questions might have had a completely innocent explanation. But they nagged, and kept me from sleeping. Finally, I got up, dug my case notebook from my suitcase, and jotted them all down, more or less in the form you just read.

They were even more disturbing when I saw them in writing. Something about this whole business reeketh in the nostrils of a righteous man (me), and I didn't have a clue to what it was. So I solved the whole problem in my usual decisive, determined manner.

I shaved, showered, dressed, went down to the bar, and had two vodka gimlets.

I started out for Crittenden Hall about five-thirty. At that time of year it was already dark, and once I got beyond the misty, haloed street lights of Coburn, the blackness closed in. I was falling down a pit, and my low beams couldn't show the end of it. Naked tree trunks whipped by, a stone embankment, culvert, a plank bridge. But I kept falling, leaning forward over the steering wheel and bracing for the moment when I hit bottom.

I never did, of course. Instead of the bottom of the pit, I found Crittenden Hall, and pulled up to those ornate gates. The guard came ambling out of his hut and put a flashlight on me. I shouted my name, he swung the gates open, I drove in. The iron clanged shut behind me.

I followed the graveled roadway. It curved slowly through lawn that was black on this moonless night. The road ended in a generous parking area in front of Crittenden Hall. As I was getting out of the car, I saw portico lights come on. The door opened, someone stepped out.

I paused a moment. I was in front of the center portion of the main building, the old building. The two wings stretched away in the darkness. At close range, the Hall was larger than I expected: a high three stories, mullioned windows, cornices of carved stone. The style was vaguely Georgian, with faint touches—like narrow embrasures—of a castle built to withstand Saracen archers.

A lady came forward as I trudged up to the porch. She was holding out a white hand, almost covered by the ruffled lace cuff of her gown.

"Welcome to Crittenden, Mr. Todd," she said, smiling stiffly. "I'm Mary Thorndecker."

While I was shaking the daughter's cold hand and

murmuring something I forget, I was taking her in. She was Alice in Wonderland's maiden aunt in a daisied gown designed by Tenniel. I mean it billowed to her ankles, all ribbons and bows. The high, ruffled collar matched the lace cuffs. The waist was loosely crumpled with a wide velvet ribbon belt. If Mary Thorndecker had breasts, hips, ass, they were effectively concealed.

Inside the Hall, an attendant came forward to take my hat and coat. He was wearing a short, white medical jacket and black trousers. He might have been a butler, but he was built like a linebacker. When he turned away from me, I caught the bulge in his hip pocket. This bucko was carrying a sap. All right, I'll go along with that in an establishment where some of the guests were not too tightly wrapped.

"Now this is the main floor," Mary Thorndecker was babbling away, "and in the rear are the dining room, kitchen, social rooms, and so forth. The library, card room, and indoor recreational area. All used by our guests. Their private suites, the medical rooms, the doctors' offices and nurses' lounges, and so forth, are in the wings. We're going up to the second floor. That's where we live. Our private home. Living room, dining room, our own kitchen, daddy's study, sitting room . . . all that."

"And the third floor?" I inquired politely.

"Bedrooms," she said, frowning, as if someone had uttered a dirty word.

It was a handsome staircase, curving gracefully, with a gleaming carved oak balustrade. The walls were covered with ivory linen. I expected portraits of ancestors in heavy gilt frames. At least a likeness of the original Mr. Crittenden. But instead, the wall alongside the stairway was hung with paintings of flowers in thin black frames. All kinds of flowers: peonies, roses, poppies, geraniums, lilies . . . everything.

The paintings blazed with fervor. I paused to examine an oil of lilac branches in a clear vase.

"The paintings are beautiful," I said, and I meant it.

Mary Thorndecker was a few steps ahead of me, higher than me. She stopped suddenly, whirled to look down.

"Do you think so?" she said breathlessly. "Do you *really* think so? They're mine. I mean I painted them. You *do* like them?"

"Magnificent," I assured her. "Bursting with life."

Her long, saturnine face came alive. Cheeks flushed. Thin lips curved in a warm smile. The dark eyes caught fire behind steel-rimmed granny glasses.

"Thank you," she said tremulously. "Oh, thank you. Some people . . ."

She left that unfinished, and we continued our climb in silence. On the second floor landing, a man stumbled forward, hand outstretched. His expression was wary and hunted.

"Yes, Mary," he said automatically. Then: "Samuel Todd? I'm Kenneth Draper, Dr. Thorndecker's assistant. This is a . . ."

He left that sentence unfinished, too. I wondered if that was the conversational style in Crittenden Hall: half-sentences, unfinished thoughts, implied opinions.

Agatha Binder had said Draper was a "studious, scientific type . . . supposed to be a whiz." He might have been. He was also a nervous, jerky type . . . supposed to be a nut. He shook hands and wouldn't let go; he giggled inanely when I said, "Happy to meet you," and he succeeded in walking up my heels when he ushered me into the living room of the Thorndeckers' private suite.

I got a quick impression of a high vaulted room richly furnished, lots of brocades and porcelains, a huge marble-framed fireplace with a blaze crackling. And I was ankle-deep in a buttery rug. That's all I had a chance to catch before Draper was nudging me forward to the two people seated on a tobacco-brown suede couch facing the fireplace.

Edward Thorndecker lunged to his feet to be introduced. He was 17, and looked 12, a young Botticelli prince. He was all blue eyes and crisp black curls, with a complexion so enameled I could not believe he had ever shaved. The hand he proffered was soft as a girl's, and about as strong. There was something in his voice that was not quite a lisp. He did not say, "Pleathed to meet you, Mithter Todd," it was not that obvious, but he did have trouble with his sibilants. It made no difference. He could have been a mute, and still stagger you with his physical beauty.

His stepmother was beautiful, too, but in a different way. Edward had the beauty of youth; nothing in his smooth, flawless face marked experience or the passage of years. Julie Thorndecker had stronger features, and part of her attraction was due to artifice. If Mary Thorndecker found inspiration for her art in flowers, Julie found it in herself.

I remember well that first meeting. Initially, all I could see were the satin evening pajamas, the color of fresh mushrooms. Full trousers and a tunic cinched with a mocha sash. The neckline plunged, and there was something in that glittery, slithery costume that convinced me she was naked beneath, and if I listened intently I might hear the whispery slide of soft satin on softer flesh. She was wearing high-heeled evening sandals, thin ribbons of silver leather. Her bare toes were long, the nails painted a crimson as dark as old blood. There was a slave bracelet of fine gold links around one slender ankle.

I was ushered to an armchair so deep I felt swallowed. Mary Thorndecker and Dr. Draper found chairs—close to each other, I noted—and there was a spate of fast, almost feverish small talk. Most of it consisted of questions directed at me. Yes, I had driven up from New York. Yes, Coburn seemed a quiet, attractive village. No, I had no idea how long I'd stay—a few days perhaps. My accommodations at the Inn were certainly not luxurious, but they were adequate. Yes, the food was exceptionally good. No, I had not yet met Art Merchant. Yes, it had certainly been a terrible storm, with all the lights off and power lost. I said:

"But I suppose you have emergency generators, don't you, Dr. Draper?"

"What?" he said, startled at being addressed. "Oh, yes, of course we do."

"Naturally," I nodded. "I imagine you have valuable cultures in the lab under very precise temperature control."

"We certainly do," he said enthusiastically. "Why, if we lost refrigeration even for—"

"Oh, Kenneth, please," Julie Thorndecker said lazily. "No shop talk tonight. Just a social evening. Wouldn't you prefer that, Mr. Todd?"

I remember bobbing my head violently in assent, but I was too stunned by her voice to make any sensible reply.

It was a husky voice, throaty, almost tremulous, with a kind of crack as if it was changing. It was a different voice, a stirring voice, an adorable voice. It made me want to hear her murmur and whisper. Just the thought of it rattled my vertebrae.

Before I had a chance to make a fool of myself by asking her to read aloud from the Coburn telephone directory, I was saved by the entrance of the gorilla who had taken my hat and coat. He was pushing a wheeled cart laden with ice bucket, bottles, mixes, glasses.

"Daddy will be along in a few minutes," Mary Thorndecker told us all. "He said to start without him."

That was fine with me; I needed something. Preferably two somethings. I was conscious of currents in that room: loves, animosities, personal conflicts that I could only guess from glances, tones of voice, turned shoulders, and sudden changes of expression I could not fathom.

Julie and Edward Thorndecker each took a glass of white wine. Mary had a cola drink. Dr. Draper asked for a straight bourbon, which brought a look of sad reproof from Mary. Not seeing any lime juice on the cart, I opted for a vodka martini and watched the attendant mix it. He slugged me—a double, at least—and I wondered if those were his instructions.

While the drinks were being served, I had a chance to make a closer inspection of the room from the depths of my feather bed. My first impression was reinforced: it was a glorious chamber. The overstuffed furniture was covered with brown leather, beige linen, chocolate velvet. Straight chairs and tables were blond French provincial, and looked to me to be antiques of museum quality. There was a cocktail table of brass and smoked glass, the draperies were batik, and the unframed paintings on the walls were abstracts in brilliant primary colors.

In the hands of a decorator of glitchy taste, this eclecticism would have been a disaster. But it all came together; it pleased the eye and was comfortable to a sinful degree. Part of the appeal, I decided, was due to the noble proportions of the room itself, with its high ceiling and the perfect ratio between length and width. There are some rooms that would satisfy even if they were empty, and this was one of them.

I said something to this effect, and Julie and Edward exchanged congratulatory smiles. If it was their taste reflected here, their gratification was warranted. But I saw Mary Thorndecker's lips tighten slightly—just a prim pressing together—and I began to glimpse the outlines of the family feuds.

We were on our second round—the talk louder now, the laughs more frequent—when the hall door banged open, and Dr. Telford Gordon Thorndecker swept into the room. There's no other phrase for it: he swept in, the President arriving at the Oval Office. Dr. Kenneth Draper jerked to his feet. Edward stood up slowly. I struggled out of my down cocoon, and even Mary Thorndecker rose to greet her father. Only Julie remained seated.

"Hello, hello, hello, all," he said briskly, and I was happy to note I had been correct: it was a rumbling baritone, with deep resonance. "Sorry I'm late. A minor crisis. Very minor! Darling..." He swooped to kiss his young wife's cheek. "And you must be Samuel Todd of the Bingham Foundation. Welcome to Crittenden. This *is* a pleasure. Forgive me for not greeting you personally, but I see you've been well taken care of. Excellent! Excellent! How are you, Mr. Todd? A small scotch for me, John. Well, here we are! This *is* nice."

I've seen newsreels of President Franklin Roosevelt, and this big man had the same grinning vitality, the energy, and raw exuberance of Roosevelt. I've met politicians, generals, and business executives, and I don't impress easily. But Thorndecker overwhelmed me. When he spoke to you, he gave the impression of speaking only to *you*, and not talking just to hear the sound of his own voice. When he asked a question, he made you feel he was genuinely interested in your opinion, he was hanging on your every word, and if he disagreed, he still respected your intelligence and sincerity.

The photograph I had seen of him was a good likeness; he was a handsome man. But the black-and-white glossy hadn't prepared me for the physical presence. All I could think of was that he was smarter, better looking, and stronger than I was. But I didn't resent it. That was his peculiar gift: your admiration was never soured with envy. How could you envy or be jealous of an elemental force?

He took command immediately. We were to finish our drinks at once, and file into the dining room. This is how we'd be seated, this is what we'd eat, these were the wines we'd find superb, and so forth. And all this without the touch of the Obersturmführer. He commanded with humor, a self-deprecating wit, and a cheerful willingness to bend to anyone's whims, no matter how eccentric he found them.

If the table in the rather gloomy dining room had been set to make an impression on me, it did. Pewter serving plates, four crystal wine glasses and goblets at each setting, a baroque silver service, fresh flowers, slender white tapers in a cast iron candelabrum.

I sat on Thorndecker's right. Next to me was Dr. Draper. Julie was at the foot of the table. On her right was Edward, and across from me was Mary, on Thorndecker's left. Cozy.

The moment we were seated, two waitresses with starched white aprons over staid black dresses appeared and began serving. We had smoked salmon with chopped onion and capers; a lobster bisque; an enormous Beef Wellington carved at the table; a potato dish that seemed to be mixed tiny balls of white and sweet potatoes, boiled and then sautéed in seasoned butter; fresh green beans; buttered baby carrots; endive salad with hearts of palm; raspberry sherbet; espresso or regular coffee.

I've had better meals, but never in a private home. If the beans were overcooked and the crust of the Wellington a bit soggy, it could be forgiven or forgotten for the sake of the wines Thorndecker uncorked and the efficiency of the service. Every time my wine glass got down to the panic level, one of the waitresses or the gorilla-butler was at my elbow to refill it. Hot rolls and sweet butter were passed incessantly. It seemed to me that I had only to wish another spoonful of those succulent potatoes, when presto! they appeared on my plate.

"Do your patients eat as well?" I asked Thorndecker.

"Better," he assured me, smiling. "We have one old lady who regularly imports truffles from the south of France. Two years ago we had an old gentleman who brought along his private chef. That man—the chef, I mean—was a genius. A genius! I tried to hire him, but he refused to cook for more than four at a time."

"What happened to him?" I asked. "Not the chef, the old gentleman."

"Deceased," Thorndecker said easily. "Are you enjoying the dinner?"

"Very much so," I said.

"Really?" he said, looking into my eyes. "I thought the beans overcooked and the Wellington crust a bit soggy. Delighted to hear I was wrong."

The conversation was dominated by Dr. Thorndecker. Maybe "directed" is a better word, because he spoke very little himself. But he questioned his children and wife about their activities during the day, made several wry comments on their reports, asked them about their plans for the following day. I had a sense of custom being honored, a nightly interrogation. If Thorndecker had planned to present a portrait of domestic felicity, he succeeded admirably.

Between courses, and during Thorndecker's quizzing, I had an opportunity to observe the ménage more closely. I picked up some interesting impressions to store away, for mulling later.

Edward Thorndecker had been reasonably alert and cheerful prior to his father's appearance; after, he became subdued, somewhat sullen.

Julie wore her hair cut quite short. It was fine, silvered, brushed close to her skull. It appeared to be an extension of her satin pajamas, as if she was wearing a helmet of the same material.

Dr. Kenneth Draper drank too much wine too rapidly, looking up frequently to Mary Thorndecker to see if she was noticing.

Thorndecker himself had a remarkably tanned face. At that time of year, it was either pancake makeup or regular use of a suntan lamp. When I caught him in profile, it suddenly occurred to me he might have had a face-lifting.

The servants were efficient, but unsmiling. Conversations between servants and family were kept to a minimum. Instructions for serving were given by Mary Thorndecker. I had the oddest notion that she was mistress of the house. In fact, on appearance alone, she could have been Thorndecker's wife, and Julie and Edward their children.

Thorndecker's pleasantness had its limits; his elbow was joggled by one of the waitresses, and I caught the flash of anger in his eyes. I didn't hear what he muttered to her.

After his fourth glass of wine, Dr. Draper stared at Mary Thorndecker with what I can only describe as hopeless passion. I was convinced the poor mutt was smitten by her charms. What they were escaped me.

I wondered if Julie and Edward Thorndecker were holding hands under the tablecloth, improbable as that seemed.

Dr. Thorndecker was wearing a cologne or after-shave lotion that I found fruity and slightly sickening.

Mary Thorndecker, with her thin, censorious lips, seemed disapproving of this flagrant display of rich food and strong drink. She ate sparingly, drank nothing but mineral water. Very admirable, even if it was imported water.

Julie was a gamine, with an inexhaustible supply of expressions: pouts, smiles, moues, frowns, grins, leers. In repose, her face was a beautifully tinted mask, triangular, with high cheekbones and stung lips. Occasionally she bit the full lower lip with her sharp upper teeth, a stimulating sight.

Never once during the meal did Mary address Julie directly, or vice versa. In fact, they both seemed to avoid looking at each other.

That was about all I was able to observe and remember. It was enough.

I was on my second cup of espresso, replete and wondering how I might cadge a brandy, when the butler-gorilla entered hurriedly. He went directly to Dr. Kenneth Draper, leaned down, whispered in his ear. I saw this happen. I saw Draper's Bordeaux-flushed cheeks go suddenly white. He looked to Dr. Thorndecker. If a signal passed between them, I didn't catch it. But Draper rose immediately, weaving slightly. He excused himself, thanking the Thorndeckers for the "'nificent dinner," addressing himself to Mary. Then he was gone, and no one commented on it.

"A brandy, Mr. Todd?" Telford Thorndecker sang out. "Cognac? Armagnac? I have a calvados I think you'll like. Let's all move back to the living room and give them a chance to clean up in here and get home at a reasonable hour. All right, everyone . . . up and out!"

We straggled back into the living room: Julie, Edward, Thorndecker, me. Mary stayed behind, for housewifely chores I suppose. Maybe to make sure that no one swagged a slice of that soggy Beef Wellington.

The calvados was good. Not great, but good. Julie

took a thimbleful of green Chartreuse. Edward got a stick in the eye.

"Don't you have homework to do, young man?" Thorndecker demanded sternly.

"Yes, father," the youth said. A crabbed voice, surly manner.

But he said his goodnights politely enough, kissing his stepmother and father, on their cheeks, offering me his limp hand again. We watched him leave.

"Good-looking boy," I offered.

"Yes," Thorndecker said shortly. "Now take a look at this, Mr. Todd. I think you'll be interested."

We left Julie curved felinely in a corner of the suede couch, running a tongue tip around the rim of her liqueur glass. Thorndecker showed me a small collection of eighteenth-century miniatures, portaits painted on thin slices of ivory. I admired those, and Sevres porcelains, a beautifully crafted antique microscope in gleaming brass, a set of silver-mounted flintlock duelling pistols, an ornate Italian mantel clock that showed the time of day, date, phases of the moon, constellations, tides and, for all I know, when to take the meatloaf out of the oven.

Thorndecker's attitude toward these treasures was curious. He knew the provenance of everything he owned. He was proud of them. But I don't think he really *liked* them. They were valuable possessions, and fulfilled some desire he had to surround himself with beautiful things of value. He could have collected Duesenbergs or rare Phoenician coins. It would be all the same to him.

"It's a magnificent room," I told him.

"Yes," he said, nodding, looking about, "yes, it is. A few pieces I inherited. But Julie selected most of them. She decorated this room. She and Edward. It's what I've wanted all my life. A room like this."

I said nothing.

We strolled back to his wife. She rose as we approached, finishing her Chartreuse, set the empty glass on the serving cart. Then she did an incredible thing.

She lifted her slender arms high above her head and

stretched wide, yawning. I looked at her with amazement. She was a small, perfectly formed woman: a cameo body. She stood there, weight on one leg, hip-sprung, her feet apart. Her head was back, throat taut, mouth yawned open, lips wet and glistening.

Thorndecker and I stood there, frozen, staring at that strained torso, hard nipples poking the shining stuff. Then she relaxed, smiling at me.

"Please forgive me," she said in that throaty voice. "The wine...I think I'll run along to bed."

We exchanged pleasantries. I briefly held the sinewy hand she offered.

"Don't be long, darling," she said to her husband, drawing fingertips down his cheek.

"I—I—I won't," he stammered, completely undone.

We watched her sway from the room. The gleaming satin rippled.

"Another calvados?" Thorndecker said hoarsely.

"Another drink, thank you," I said. "But I see you have cognac there. I'd prefer that, if I may, sir."

"Of course, of course," he muttered.

"Then I'll be on my way," I promised him. "I'm sure you have a full day tomorrow."

"Not at all," he said dully, and poured us drinks.

We sat on the suede couch, staring into dying embers.

"I suppose you'll want to see the place?" he said.

"I would, yes," I acknowledged. "The nursing home and the lab."

"Tomorrow morning? And stay for lunch?"

"Oh no," I said. "Not after that dinner! I'll skip lunch tomorrow. Would—oh, say about one o'clock be convenient? I have things to do in the morning."

"One o'clock would be fine," he said. "I may not be able to show you around myself, but I'll tell Draper to be available. He'll show you everything. I'll make that very clear. Anything and everything you want to see."

"Thank you, sir," I said.

We were turned half-sideways to converse. Now his heavy eyes rose to lock with mine.

"You don't have to call me 'sir'," he said.

"All right," I said equably.

"If you have any questions, Draper will answer them. If he can't, I will."

"Fine."

Pause, while we both sipped our drinks daintily.

"Of course," he said, "you may have some personal questions for me."

I considered a moment.

"No," I said, "I don't think so."

He seemed surprised at that. And maybe a little disappointed.

"I mean about my personal life," he explained. "I know how these grant investigations work. You want to know all about me."

"We know a great deal about you now, Dr. Thorndecker," I said, as gently as I could.

He sighed, and seemed to shrivel, hunching down on the couch. He looked every one of his 54 years. Suddenly I realized what it was: this man was physically tired. He was bone-weary. All the youthful vigor had leaked out of him. He had put in a strenuous, stressful day, and he wanted nothing more at this point than to crawl into bed next to his warm, young wife, melt down beneath the covers, and sleep. To tell you the truth, I felt much the same myself.

"I suppose," he said, ruminating in a low voice, "I suppose you find it odd that a man my age would have a wife young enough to be my daughter. Younger than my daughter."

"Not odd," I said. "Understandable. Maybe fifty, or even thirty or twenty years ago, it would have been considered odd. But not today. New forms of relationships. The old prejudices out the window. It's a whole new ballgame."

But he wasn't listening to my cracker-barrel philosophy.

"She means so much to me," he said wonderingly. "So much. You have no idea how she has made—"

His confessions disturbed me and embarrassed me. I drained my drink and stood up.

"Dr. Thorndecker," I said formally, "I want to thank

69

you and your wife and your family for your gracious hospitality. A very pleasant evening, and I hope we—"

But at that precise instant the hall door was flung open. Dr. Kenneth Draper stood rooted. He was wearing a stained white lab coat. He had jerked his tie loose and opened his collar. His eyes were blinking furiously, and I wondered if he was about to cry.

"Dr. Thorndecker," he said desperately, "please, can you come? At once? It's Petersen."

Thorndecker finished his drink slowly, set the glass slowly aside. Now he looked older than his 54 years. He looked defeated.

"Do you mind?" he asked me. "A patient with problems. I'm afraid he won't last the night. We'll do what we can."

"Of course," I said. "You go ahead. I can find my way out. Thank you again, doctor."

We shook hands. He smiled stiffly, moved brokenly to the door. He and Draper disappeared. I was alone. So, what the hell, I poured myself another small brandy and slugged it down. I took a final look around that splendid room and then wandered out onto the second floor landing. In truth, I was feeling no pain.

I had taken one step down the stairway when I heard the sound of running feet behind me. I turned. Mary Thorndecker came dashing up.

"Take this," she said breathlessly. "Don't look at it now. Read it later."

She thrust a folded paper into my hand, whirled, darted away, the long calico gown snapping about her ankles. I wondered if she was heading for a brisk run through the heather, shouting, "Heathcliff! Heathcliff!"

I stuffed the folded paper into my side pocket. I walked down that long, long stairway as erect and dignified as I could make it. The butler-gorilla was waiting below with my coat and hat.

"Nighty-night," I said.

"Yeah," he said.

I drove slowly, very, very slowly, around the graveled

road to the gates. They opened magically for me. I turned onto the paved road, went a few hundred yards, then pulled off onto the verge. I switched off engine and lights. It was raw as hell, and I huddled down inside my leather trenchcoat and wished I had a small jug of brandy to keep me alive. But all I could do was wait. So I waited. Don't ask me what I was waiting for; I didn't know. Maybe I figured it was best not to drive on unfamiliar roads in my condition. Maybe I was just sleepy. I don't know what my motives were; I'm just telling you what happened.

The cold woke me up. I snapped out of my daze, shivering. I glanced at the luminous dial of my watch; it was almost 2:00 A.M. I had left Crittenden Hall before midnight. Now I was sober, with a headache that threatened to break down the battlements of my skull. I lighted a cigarette and tried to remember if I had misbehaved during the evening, insulted anyone, done anything to besmirch the Bingham Foundation escutcheon. I couldn't think of a thing. Other than developing an enormous lech for Julie Thorndecker—which no one could possibly be aware of, except, perhaps, Julie Thorndecker—I had conducted myself in exemplary fashion as far as I could recall.

I was leaning forward to snub out my cigarette when I saw the lights. One, two, three of them, bobbing in line from the rear of Crittenden Hall, heading out into the pitchy grounds.

I slid from the car, leaving the door open. I went loping along outside the chain-link fence, trying to keep the lights in view. They moved up and down in a regular rhythm: marching men carrying flashlights or battery lanterns.

The fence curved around. I ran faster to catch up, happy that whoever had planned the security of Crittenden had cleared the land immediately outside the fence. No bushes, no trees. I was running on half-frozen stubble, the ground resisting, then squishing beneath my feet.

I came up to them, raised a hand to shield my mouth so

they might not spot the white vapor of my breath. Another light came on, a more powerful lantern. I moved along with them, hanging back a little, the fence between us, and the bare trees on the Crittenden grounds.

Four men, at least. Then, in the lantern's beam, I saw more. Six men, heavily muffled against the cold. Three of them were hauling a wheeled cart. And on the cart, a black burden, a bulk, a box, a coffin.

When they stopped, I stopped. Crouched down. Lay down on the frost-silvered grass. The beams of flashlights and lanterns concentrated. I could see an open grave. A mound of loose earth at one side. I had not seen that during my afternoon reconnaissance.

The load was taken off the cart. A plain box. I could hear the grunts of the lifting men from where I lay. The coffin was slid into the open hole. One end first, and then it was dropped and allowed to thump to the bottom. Shovels had been brought. Two men attacked the mound of loose dirt, working slowly but steadily. The first few shovelfuls rattled on the coffin lid. Then, as the grave filled, they worked in silence. All I could see were the steady beams of light, the lifting, swinging, dumping shovels. Then the flash of empty shovel blades.

The grave was filled, the loose earth smacked down and rounded. Squares of sod were placed over the raw dirt. Then the procession, still silent, turned back to Crittenden Hall. I watched them go, knowing a chill without, a chill within. The lights bobbed slowly away. They went out, one by one.

I lay there as long as I could endure it, teeth making like castanets, feet and hands lumpy and dull. Then I made a run for my car, hobbling along as fast as I could, trying to flex my fingers, afraid to feel my nose in case it had dropped off.

I got the heater going, held my hands in front of the vents, and in a few minutes reckoned I'd live to play the violin again. I drove away from there at a modest speed, hoping the gate guard and roving night sentinel (if there was one) wouldn't spot my lights.

I told myself that both Thorndecker and Draper were licensed MD's, and could sign a death certificate. I told myself that one of the shrouded figures with flashlight or lantern could have been a licensed mortician. I told myself all sorts of nonsense. The cadaver was infected with a deadly plague and had to be put underground immediately. Or, all burials were made at this hour so as not to disturb the other withering guests of Crittenden Hall. Or, the dead man or woman was without funds, without family, without friends, and this surreptitious entombment was a discreet way of putting a pauper to rest.

I didn't believe a word of it. Of any of it. That slow procession of shadowed figures and bobbing lights scared the hell out of me. I had a wild notion of giving Dr. Telford Gordon ·Thorndecker an A-plus rating and, as quickly as possible, getting my ass back to the familiar violence of New York City. A dreadful place with one saving grace: the dead were buried during daylight hours.

The lobby of the Coburn Inn did nothing to lift my spirits or inspire confidence in a better tomorrow. It was almost three in the morning; only a night light on the desk shed a ghastly, orange-tinted glow. The place was totally empty. I guessed the night clerk was snoozing in the back office, and Sam Livingston was corking off in his basement hideaway.

I looked around at the slimy tiled floor, the shabby rugs, the tattered couches and armchairs. Even the plastic ferns in the old brass spittoons seemed wilted. And over all, the smell of must and ash, the stink of age and decay. The Coburn Inn: Reasonable Rates and Instant Senescence.

I didn't have the heart to wake Sam Livingston to run me up, so I trudged the stairway, still bone-chilled, muscle-sore, brain-dulled. I got to room 3-F all right, seeing not a soul in the shadowed corridors. But there was enough illumination to see that the door of my room was open a few inches. I had left it locked.

Adrenaline flowed; I moved cautiously. The room was dark. I kicked the door open wider, reached around, flicked the light switch. Someone had paid me a visit. My suitcases and briefcase had been upended, contents dumped on the floor. The few things I had stowed away in closet and bureaus had been pulled out and trashed. Even my toilet articles had been pawed over. The mattress on that hard bed had been lifted and tipped. Chairs were lying on their sides, the bottom coverings slit, and the few miserable prints on the walls had been taken off their hooks and the paper backing ripped away.

I made a quick check. As far as I could see, nothing was missing. Even my case notebook was intact. My wallet of credit cards was untouched. So why the toss? I gave up trying to figure it, or anything else that had happened that black night. All I wanted was sleep.

I restored the bed to reasonable order, but left all the rest of the stuff exactly where it was, on the floor. I started undressing then, so weary that I was tempted to flop down with my boots on. It was when I was taking off my jacket that I found, in the side pocket, the folded paper that Mary Thorndecker had slipped me just before I left Crittenden Hall.

I unfolded it gingerly, like it might be a letter bomb. But it was only a badly printed religious tract, one of those things handed out on street corners by itinerant preachers. This one was headed: WHERE WILL YOU SPEND ETERNITY?

Not, I hoped, at the Coburn Inn.

The Third Day

CONSTABLE RONNIE GOODFELLOW stood with arms akimbo, surveying the wreckage of my hotel room.

"Shit," he said.

"My sentiments exactly," I said. "But look, it's no big deal. Nothing was stolen. The only reason I wanted you to know was if it fits a pattern of hotel room break-ins. You've had them before?"

Sleek head turned slowly, dark eyes observed me thoughtfully. Finally...

"You a cop?" he said.

"No, but I've had some training. Army CID."

"Well, there's no pattern. Some petty pilferage in the kitchen maybe, but there hasn't been a break-in here since I've been on the force. Why should there be? What is there to steal in this bag of bones? The regulars who live here are all on Social Security. Most of the time they haven't got two nickels to rub together."

He took slow steps into the room, looking about.

"The bed tossed?" he asked.

"That's right. I put it straight so I could get some sleep last night."

He nodded, still looking around with squinty eyes. Suddenly he swooped, picked up one of those vomit-tinted prints that had hung on the tenement-green wall. He inspected the torn paper backing.

"Looking for something special," he said. "Something small and flat that could be slid between the backing and the picture. Like a photo, a sheet of paper, a document, a letter. Something like that."

I looked at him with new respect. He was no stupe.

"Got any idea what it could be?" he asked casually.

"Not a clue," I said, just as off-handedly. "I haven't got a thing like that worth hiding."

He nodded again, and there was nothing in that smooth, saturnine face to show if he believed me or not.

"Well..." he said, "maybe I'll go down and have a few words with Sam Livingston."

"You don't think—" I began.

"Of course not," he said sharply. "Sam's as honest as the day is long. But maybe he saw someone prowling around late at night. He's up all hours. You say you got in late?"

I hadn't said. I hoped he didn't catch the brief pause before I answered.

"A little after midnight," I lied. "I had dinner with the Thorndeckers."

"Oh?" he said. "Have a good time?"

"Sure did. Great food. Good company." Then I added, somewhat maliciously: "Mrs. Thorndecker is a beauty."

"Yes," he said, almost absently, "a very attractive woman. Well, I'll see what I can do about this, Mr. Todd. Sorry it had to happen to a visitor to our town."

"Happens everywhere," I shrugged. "No real harm done."

I closed and locked the door behind him. He hadn't

inspected that lock, but I had. No sign of forced entry. That was one for me. But he had seen that the object of the search had been something small and flat, something that could be concealed in a picture frame. That was one for him.

I knew what it was, of course. My visitor had been trying to recover that anonymous note. The one that read: "Thorndecker kills."

With only a half-dozen regulars and me staying at the Coburn Inn, the management didn't think it necessary to employ a chambermaid. Old Sam Livingston did the chores: changing linen, emptying wastebaskets, throwing out "dead soldiers," vacuuming when the dust got ankle-deep.

I was still trying to set my room to rights when he knocked. I let him in.

"I'll straighten up here," he told me. "You go get your morning coffee."

"Thanks, Sam," I said gratefully.

I handed him a five-dollar bill. He stared at it.

"Abraham Lincoln," he said. "Fine-looking man. Good beard." He held the bill out to me. "Take it back, Mr. Todd. I'd clean up anyways. You don't have to do that."

"I know I don't *have* to do it," I said. "All I *have* to do is pay taxes and die. I *want* to do it."

"That's different," he said, pocketing the bill. "I thank you kindly."

I took another look at him: an independent old cuss in his black alpaca jacket and skullcap. He had a scrubby head of grayish curls and a face as gnarled as a hardwood burl. All of him looked like dark hardwood: chiseled, carved, sanded, oiled, and then worked for so many years that the polish on face and hands had a deep glow that could only come from hard use.

"Live in Coburn all your life?" I asked him.

"Most of it," he said.

"Seventy-five years?" I guessed.

"Eighty-three," he said.

"I'll never make it," I said.

"Sure you will," he said, "you lay off the sauce and the women."

"In that case," I said, "I don't want to make it. Sam, I want to come down to your place sometime, maybe have a little visit with you."

"Anytime," he said. "I ain't going anywhere. The French toast is nice this morning."

I can take a hint. I left him to his cleaning and went down for breakfast. But I skipped the French toast. Juice, unbuttered toast, black coffee. Very virtuous. On my way out, I looked in at the bar but Al Coburn wasn't there. Just Jimmy the bartender reading the *Sentinel*. I waved at him and went out to the lobby. I stopped for cigarettes. I really did need cigarettes. Honest.

"Good morning, Millie," I said.

"Oh, Mr. Todd," she said excitedly, "I heard about your trouble. I'm so sorry."

I stared at her glassily, trying to figure which trouble she meant.

She was wearing the same makeup, probably marketed under the trade name "Picasso's Clown." But the costume was different. This morning it was a voluminous shift, a kind of muumuu, in an orange foliage print. It had a high, drawstring neckline, long sleeves, tight cuffs. The yards and yards of sleazy synthetic fell to her ankles. Hamlet's uncle could have hidden behind that arras.

Strange, but it was sexier than the tight sweater and skirt she had worn the day before. The cloth, gathered at the neck, jutted out over her glorious appendages, then fell straight down in folds, billows, pleats. She was completely covered, concealed. It was inflammatory.

"Your trouble," she repeated. "You know—the robbery."

"Burglary," I said automatically. "But the door didn't seem to be jimmied."

"That's what Ronnie said. He thinks whoever did it had a key."

So the Indian had caught it after all. That pesky

redskin kept surprising me. I resolved never to underestimate him again.

Millie Goodfellow crooked a long, slender forefinger, beckoning me closer. Since the glass cigar counter was between us, I had to bend forward in a ridiculous posture. I found myself focusing on the nail of that summoning finger. Dark brown polish.

"A passkey," she whispered. "I told Ronnie it was probably a passkey. There's a million of them floating around. Everyone has one." Suddenly she giggled. "I even have one myself. Isn't that awful?"

I was in cloud-cuckoo land.

"*You* have a hotel passkey, Millie?" I asked. "Whatever for?"

"It gets me in the little girls' room," she said primly. Then she was back in her Cleopatra role. "And a lot of other places, too!"

I think I managed a half-ass grin before I stumbled away. My initial reaction had been correct: this lady was scary.

Wednesday morning in Coburn, N. Y. . . .

At least the sun was shining. Maybe not exactly shining, but it was there. You could see it, dull and tarnished, glowing dimly behind a cloud cover. It put a leaden light on everything: illumination but no shadows. People moved sluggishly, the air was cold without being invigorating, and I kept hoping I'd hear someone laugh aloud. No one did.

Around to River Street and the First Farmers & Merchants Bank. It had the flashiest storefront in Coburn, with panels of gray marble between gleaming plateglass windows, and lots of vinyl tile and mirrors inside. The foreclosure business must be good.

There were two tellers' windows and a small bullpen with three desks occupied by New Accounts, Personal Loans, and Mortgages. There was one guard who could have been Constable Ronnie Goodfellow fifty years older and fifty pounds heavier. I went to him. His side-holstered revolver had a greenish tinge, as if moss was growing on it.

I gave my name and explained that I'd like to see the president, Mr. Arthur Merchant, although I didn't have an appointment. He nodded gravely and disappeared for about five minutes, during which time two members of the Junior Mafia could have waltzed in and cleaned out the place.

But finally he returned and ushered me to a back office, enclosed, walled with a good grade of polished plywood. A toothy lady relieved me of hat and trenchcoat, which she hung on a rack. She handled my garments with her fingertips; I couldn't blame her. Finally, finally, I was led into the inner sanctum, and Arthur Merchant, bank president and Coburn mayor, rose to greet me. He shook my hand enthusiastically with a fevered palm and insisted I sit in a leather club chair alongside his desk. When we were standing, I was six inches taller than he. When we sat down, he in his swivel chair, he was six inches taller. That chair must have had 12-inch casters.

He was a surprisingly young man for a bank president and mayor. He was also short, plump, florid, and sweatier than the room temperature could account for. Young as he was, the big skull was showing the scants; strands of thin, black hair were brushed sideways to hide the divot. The face bulged. You've seen faces that bulge, haven't you? They seem to protrude. As if an amateur sculptor started out with an ostrich egg as a head form, and then added squares and strips of modeling clay: forehead, nose, cheeks, mouth, chin. I mean everything seems to hang out there, and all that clay just might dry and drop off. Leaving the blank ostrich egg.

We exchanged the usual pleasantries: the weather, my reaction to Coburn, my accommodations at the Inn, places of interest I should see while in the vicinity: the place where a British spy was hanged in 1777; Lovers' Leap on the Hudson River, scene of nineteen authenticated suicides; and the very spot where, only last summer, a bear had come out of the woods and badly mauled, and allegedly attempted to rape, a 68-year-old lady gathering wild strawberries.

I said it all sounded pretty exciting to me, but as Mr. Merchant was undoubtedly aware, I was not in Coburn to sightsee or visit tourist attractions; I had come to garner information about Dr. Telford Gordon Thorndecker. That's when I learned that Arthur Merchant was a compulsive fusser.

The pudgy hands went stealing out to straighten desk blotter, pencils, calendar pad. He tightened his tie, smoothed the hair at his temples, examined his fingernails. He crossed and recrossed his knees, tugged down the points of his vest, brushed nonexistent lint from his sleeve. He leaped to his feet, strode across the room, closed a bookcase door that had been open about a quarter-inch. Then he came back to his desk, sat down, and began rearranging blotter, pencils, and pad, aligning their edges with quick, nervous twitches of those pinkish squid hands.

And all during this *a cappella* ballet he was explaining to me what a splendid fellow Thorndecker was. Salt of the earth. Everything the Boy Scout oath demanded. Absolutely straight-up in his financial dealings. A loyal contributor to local charities. And what a boon to Coburn! Not only as the biggest employer in the village, but as a citizen, bringing to Coburn renown as the home of one of the world's greatest scientists.

"One of the *greatest*, Mr. Todd," Art Merchant concluded, somewhat winded, as well he should have been after that ten-minute monologue.

"Very impressive," I said, as coldly as I could. "You know what he's doing at Crittenden?"

It was a small sneak punch, but Merchant reacted like I had slammed a knee into his groin.

"What? Why...ah..." he stammered. Then: "The nursing home," he burst out. "Surely you know about that. Beds for fifty patients. A program of social—"

"I know about Crittenden Hall," I interrupted. "I want to know about the Crittenden Research Laboratory. What's going on in the lab?"

"Well, ah, you know," he said desperately, limp hands

flailing. "Scientific stuff. Don't ask me to understand; I'm just a small-town banker. But valuable things—I'm sure of that. The man's a genius! Everyone says so. And still young. Relatively. He's going to do great work. No doubt about that. You'll see."

He maundered on and on, turning now to what an excellent business manager Thorndecker was, what a fine executive, and how rare it was to find that acumen in a doctor, a professor, a man of science. But I wasn't listening.

I was beginning to feel slight twinges of paranoia. I am not ordinarily a subscriber to the conspiracy theory of history. For instance, I do not believe an evil cabal engineered the deaths of the Kennedys and Martin Luther King, the disappearance of Jimmy Hoffa, or even the lousy weather we've been having.

I believe in the Single Nut theory of history, holding that one goofy individual can change the course of human affairs by a well-placed bomb or a well-aimed rifle shot. I don't believe in conspiracies because they require the concerted efforts of two or more people. In other words, a committee. And I've never known a committee that achieved anything but endless bickering and the piling up of Minutes of the Last Meeting that serve no useful purpose except being recycled for the production of Mother's Day cards.

Still, as I said, I was beginning to feel twinges. I thought Agatha Binder had lied to me. I thought Art Merchant was lying to me. These two, along with the Thorndeckers, Dr. Draper, and maybe Ronnie Goodfellow and a few other of the best people of Coburn, all knew something I didn't know, and wasn't being told. I didn't like that. I told you, I don't like being conned.

I realized Arthur Merchant had stopped talking and was staring at me, expecting some kind of response.

"Well," I said, rising to my feet, "that's certainly an enthusiastic endorsement, Mr. Merchant. I'd say Dr. Thorndecker is fortunate in having you and the other citizens of Coburn as friends and neighbors."

I must have said the right thing, because the fear went out of his eyes, and some color came back into those clayey cheeks.

"And we are fortunate," he sang out, "in having Dr. Thorndecker as a friend and neighbor. You bet your life! Mr. Todd, you stop by again if you have any more questions, any questions at all, concerning Dr. Thorndecker's financial affairs. He's instructed me to throw his books open to you, as it were. Anything you want to know. Anything at all."

"I've seen the report of Lifschultz Associates," I said, moving toward the door. "It appears Dr. Thorndecker is in a very healthy financial position."

"Healthy?" Art Merchant cried, and did everything but leap into the air and click his heels together. "I should say so! The man is a fantastic money manager. Fan-tas-tic! In addition to being one of the world's greatest scientists, of course."

"Of course," I said. "By the way, Mr. Merchant, I understand you're the mayor of Coburn?"

"Oh . . ." he said, shrugging and spreading his plump hands deprecatingly, "I guess I got the job because no one else wanted it. It's unpaid, you know. About what it's worth."

"The reason I mention it," I said, "is that I haven't seen any public buildings around town. No courthouse, no city hall, no jail."

"Well, we have what we call the Civic Building, put up by the WPA back in 1936. We've got our fire department in there—it's just one old pumper and a hose cart—the police station, a two-cell jail, and our city hall, which is really just one big office. We have a JP in town, but if we get a serious charge or trial, we move it over to the courthouse at the county seat."

"The Civic Building?" I said. "I'd like to see that. How do I find it?"

"Just go out Main Street to Oakland Drive. It's one block south, right next to the boarded-up A&P; you can't miss it. Not much to look at, to tell you the truth. There's been some talk of replacing it with a modern building, but the way things are..."

He let that sentence trail off, the way so many Coburnites did. It gave their talk an effect of helpless futility. Hell, what's the point of finishing a sentence when the world's coming to an end?

I thanked him for his kind cooperation and shook that popover with fingers. I claimed hat and trenchcoat, and got out of there. No customers in the bank, and the people at the desks marked New Accounts, Personal Loans, and Mortgages didn't seem to have much to do. I began to appreciate how much a big, active account like Thorndecker's meant to First Farmers & Merchants, and to Mayor Art Merchant.

Having time to kill before my visit to Crittenden at 1:00 P.M., I spent an hour wandering about Coburn. If I had walked at a faster clip, I could have seen the entire village in thirty minutes. I made a complete tour of the business section—about four blocks—featuring boarded-up stores and Going Out of Business sales. Then I meandered through residential districts, and located the Civic Building. I kept walking until vacant lots became more numerous and finally merged with farms and wooded tracts.

When I had seen all there was to see, I retraced my steps, heading back to the Coburn Inn. I had my ungloved hands shoved into my trenchcoat pockets, and I hunched my shoulders against a whetted wind blowing from the river. I was thinking about what I had just seen, about Coburn.

The town was dying—but what of that? A lot of villages, towns, and cities have died since the world began. People move away, buildings crumble, and the grass or the forest or the jungle or the desert moves back in. As I told Constable Goodfellow, history is change. You can't stop it; all you can do is try to keep from getting run over by it.

It wasn't the decay of Coburn that depressed me so

much as the layout of the residential neighborhoods. I saw three-story Victorian mansions right next to leaky shacks with a scratchy yard and tin garage. Judging by homes, Coburn's well-to-do didn't congregate in a special, exclusive neighborhood; they lived cheek-by-jowl with their underprivileged brethren.

You might find that egalitarian and admirable. I found it unbelievable. There isn't a village, town, or city on earth where the rich don't huddle in their own enclave, forcing the poor into theirs. I suppose this has a certain social value: it gives the poor a *place* to aspire to. What's the point of striving for what the sociologists call upward mobility if you have to stay in the ghetto?

The problem was solved when I spotted a sign in a ground-floor window of one of those big Victorian mansions. It read: "Rooms to let. Day, week, month." Then I understood. *All* of the Incorporated Village of Coburn was on the wrong side of the tracks. As I trudged back to the Inn, the sky darkening, the smell of snow in the air, I thought this place could have been the capital city of Gloom.

I went into the bar and asked the spavined waiter for a club sandwich and a bottle of beer. While I waited, I looked idly around. It was getting on to noon; the lunch crowd was beginning to straggle in. Then I became aware of something else about Coburn, something I had observed but that hadn't really registered until now.

There were no young people in town. I had seen a few schoolkids on the streets, but no one in the, oh, say 18-to-25 age bracket. There was Miss Dimples in the *Sentinel* office, but except for her, Coburn seemed devoid of young people. Even the gas jockeys at Mike's Service Station looked like they were pulling down Spanish-American War pensions.

The reason was obvious, of course. If you were an eager, curious, reasonably brainy 20-year-old with worlds to conquer, would you stay in Coburn? Not me. I'd shake the place. And that's what Coburn's young people had done. For Albany, New York, Miami, Los Angeles. Or maybe Paris, Rome, Amsterdam, Karachi. *Any* place was better than home.

On my way out, I stopped at the bar for a quick vodka gimlet. I know it was a poor choice on top of my luncheon beer. But after the realization, "*Any* place was better than home," I needed it.

Once again I drove to Crittenden through that blasted landscape, and was admitted by the gate guard. He was pressing a transistor radio against his skull. There was a look of ineffable joy on his face, as if he had just heard his number pulled in the Irish Sweeps. I don't think he even saw me, but he let me in; I followed the graveled road to the front of Crittenden Hall.

Dr. Kenneth Draper came out to greet me. I took a closer look at him. You know the grave, white-coated, eye-glassed guy in the TV commercials who looks earnestly at the camera and says, "Have you ever suffered from irregularity?" That was Draper. As a matter of fact, he looked like he was suffering himself: forehead washboarded, deep lines from nose to corners of mouth, bleached complexion, and a furtive, over-the-shoulder glance, wondering when the knout would fall.

"Well!" Draper said brightly. "Now what we've planned is the grand tour. The nursing home first. Look around. Anything you want to see. Meet the head staff. Then to the lab. Ditto there. Take a look at our setup, what we're doing. Meet some of our people. Then Dr. Thorndecker would like to speak with you when we're finished. How does that sound?"

"Sounds fine," I assured him. The poor simp looked so apprehensive that I think if I had said, "Sounds lousy," he would have burst into tears.

We turned to the left, and Draper hauled a ring of keys from his pocket.

"The wings are practically identical," he explained. "We didn't want to waste your time by dragging you through both, so we'll take a look at the west wing. We keep the door locked for security. Some of our patients are mentals, and we try to keep access doors locked for their protection."

"And yours?" I asked.

"What?" he said. "Oh yes, I suppose that's true, although the few violent cases we have are kept pretty, uh, content."

There was a wide, tiled, institutional corridor with doors on both sides.

"Main floor": Dr. Draper recited, "Doctors' and nurses' offices and lounges. Records and admitting room. X ray and therapy. Clinic and dispensary. Everything here is duplicated in the east wing."

"Expensive setup, isn't it?" I said. "For fifty patients?"

"They can afford it," he said tonelessly. "Now I'm going to introduce you to Nurse Stella Beecham. She's an RN, head nurse in Crittenden Hall. She'll show you through the nursing home, then bring you over to the lab. I'll leave you in her hands, and then take you through the Crittenden Research Laboratory myself."

"Sounds fine," I said again, trying to get some enthusiasm into my voice.

Stella Beecham looked like a white stump: squat, straight up and down. She was wearing a short-sleeved nurse's uniform, and I caught the biceps and muscles in her forearms and thick wrists. But nurses are usually strong; they have to be to turn a two-hundred-pound patient in his bed, or lift a deadweight from stretcher to wheelchair.

Beecham wasn't the prettiest angel of mercy I've ever seen. She had gross, thrusting, almost masculine features. No makeup. Her complexion was rough, ruddy, with the beginnings of burst capillaries in nose and cheeks. To me, that signals a heavy drinker. She had a faint mustache. On the left side of her chin, just below the corner of her pale mouth, was a silvery wen with two short, black hairs sticking out. It looked for all the world like a transistor, and I consciously avoided staring at it when I talked to her.

Dr. Kenneth Draper cut out, and Nurse Beecham took

me in tow, spouting staccato statistics. It went like this, in her hard, drillmaster's voice:

"Fifty beds. Today's occupancy rate: forty-nine. We have a waiting list of thirty-eight to get in. Seven addicts at present: five alcoholics, two hard drugs. Six mentals. Prognosis: negative. All the others are terminals. Cancer, MS, emphysema, myasthenia gravis, cardiacs, and so forth. Their doctors have given up. About all we can do is try to keep them pain-free. A hundred and fifty meals prepared each day in the main kitchen, not counting those for staff, maintenance personnel, and security guards. Plus special meals. Some of our guests like afternoon tea or a late-night snack. We have a chef on duty around-the-clock. These are the nurses' offices and lounges. The doctors' are across the hall."

"You have MD's in residence?" I asked—not that I was so interested, but just to let her know I was listening.

"Two assigned to each wing. Plus, of course, Dr. Thorndecker and Dr. Draper. They're both MD's. Two RN's around-the-clock in each wing. Plus a pharmaceutical nurse for each wing. Three shifts of aides and orderlies. Our total staff provides a better than one-to-one ratio with our guests. Here's the X-ray room. We have a resident radiologist. Therapy in here. Our resident therapist deals mostly with the addiction cases, particularly the alcoholics. Spiritual therapy, if desired, is provided by the Reverend Peter Koukla of the First Episcopal Church. We also have an Albany rabbi on call, when needed. Examination room here, dispensary here. Combined barber and beauty shop. This is handled by a concession. Dietician's office here. We send out all our laundry and drycleaning. I think that about completes the main floor of this wing."

"What's in the basement?" I asked, in the friendliest tone possible.

"Storage," she said. "Want to see it?"

"No," I said, "that won't be necessary."

It was a short, brusque exchange—brusque on her

part. She had the palest blue eyes I've ever seen, almost as colorless as water, and showing about as much. All they did was glitter; I could read nothing there. So why did I have the feeling that my mention of the cellar had flicked a nerve? Just a tensing, almost a bristling of her powerful body.

"Now we'll go upstairs," she said. "The vacant suite is in this wing, so I'll be able to show it to you."

We had passed a few aides, a few orderlies. But I hadn't seen anyone who looked like a patient.

"Where is everyone?" I asked. "The place seems deserted."

She gave me a reasonable explanation:

"It's lunchtime. The dining room is in the rear of the main entrance hall. Most of our guests are there now, except for those who dine in their rooms. The aides and doctors usually eat in the dining room also. Dr. Thorndecker feels it helps maintain rapport with our patients."

"I hope I haven't interrupted *your* luncheon," I said.

"Not at all," she said. "I'm on a diet. I skip lunch."

That sounded like a friendly, personal comment—a welcome relief from the officialese she had been spouting—so I followed up on it.

"I met an acquaintance of yours," I said. "Agatha Binder. I had a talk with her yesterday."

"Did you?" she said. "Now you'll notice that we have no elevators. But during Dr. Thorndecker's refurbishing program, the stairways at the ends of the corridors were made much narrower, and ramps were installed. So we're able to move wheeled stretchers and wheelchairs up to the top floors without too much trouble. Actually, there's very little traffic. Non-ambulatory guests are encouraged to remain in their suites. What do you think of Crittenden Hall so far?"

The question came so abruptly that it confused me.

"Well...uh," I said. "I'll tell you," I said. "I'm impressed," I said, "by how neat and immaculate and sparkling everything is. I almost suspect you prepared for my visit—like sailors getting ready for a white-glove inspection on a U. S. Navy ship."

I said it in a bantering tone, keeping it light, but she had no humor whatsoever—except, possibly, bad.

"Oh no," she said, "it's like this all the time. Dr. Thorndecker insists on absolutely hygienic conditions. Our cleaning staff has been specially trained. We've gotten highest ratings in the New York State inspections, and I mean to keep it that way."

It was a grim declaration. But she was a grim woman. And, as I followed her up the narrow staircase to the second floor, I reflected that even her legs were grim: heavy, thick, with clumped muscles under the white cotton stockings. I wouldn't, I thought, care to be given a needle by Nurse Stella Beecham. She was liable to pin me to the goddamned bed.

"I won't show you any of the occupied suites," she said. "Dr. Thorndecker felt it might disturb our guests unnecessarily."

"Of course."

"But he wanted you to see the one vacant suite. We have a guest arriving for it tomorrow morning."

"Was it occupied by a man—or maybe it was a woman—named Petersen?" I asked.

I don't know why I said that. My tongue was ahead of my brain. I just said it idly. Nurse Beecham's reaction was astonishing. She was standing on the second-floor landing, three steps above me. When I said, "Petersen," she whirled, then went suddenly rigid, her lumpy features set in an ugly expression that was half fear, half cunning, and all fury.

"Why did you say that?" she demanded, the "say" hissed so that it came out "ssssay."

"I don't know," I told her honestly, staring up at her transistor-wen. "But I was at the Thorndeckers for dinner last night, and late in the evening Dr. Thorndecker was called away by Dr. Draper. I got the impression it involved some crisis in the condition of a patient named

Petersen. Dr. Thorndecker said he was afraid Petersen wouldn't last the night."

The gorgon's face relaxed, wax flowing. She took a deep breath. She had an awesome bosom.

"He didn't," she said. "He passed. The empty suite is just down the corridor here. Follow me, please."

She unlocked the door, and stood aside. I walked in ahead of her. It was a suite all right: sitting room, bedroom, bathroom. There was even a little kitchenette, with a waist-high refrigerator. But no stove. The windows faced the sere fields of Crittenden.

The rooms were clean and cheerfully decorated: chintz drapes and slipcovers. Bright, innocuous paintings on the warm beige walls. A new, oval-shaped rag rug. Windows were washed, floor polished, upholstery spotless, small desk set neatly with blotter, stationery, ballpoint pen, Bible. The bed had been freshly made. Spotless white towels hung in the bathroom. The closet door was open. It was empty of clothes, but wooden hangers were precisely arranged along the rod.

Nurse Beecham stood patiently at the hallway door while I prowled around. A quiet, impersonal suite of rooms. Nothing of Petersen showed, nor of any of the others who had gone before. No cigarette butts, worn slippers, rumpled pillows. No initials carved in the desk top. There was a faint scent of disinfectant in the air.

I stood at the window, staring down at the withered fields. It was a comfortable place to die, I supposed. Warm. Lighted. And he had been well cared for. Pain-free. Still, the place had all the ambience of a motel suite in Scranton, Pa. It had that hard, machine look, everything clean enough, but aseptic and chilling.

I turned back to Stella Beecham.

"What did he die of?" I asked. "Petersen?"

"Pelvic cancer," she said. "Inoperable. He didn't respond to chemotherapy. Shall we go now?"

I followed her in silence down the stairway to the main floor. We stopped three times while she introduced me to staff: one of the resident MD's, the radiologist, and another RN. We all smiled and said things. I don't remember their names.

Nurse Beecham paused outside the back door of the west wing.

"It's a few steps to the lab," she said. "Would you like your coat?"

"No, I'll leave it here," I said. "Thank you for showing me around. It must be very boring for you."

"I don't mind," she said gruffly.

We walked out to that roofed port that led down the hill to the Crittenden Research Laboratory. It was a miserably rude day, the sun completely hidden now, air biting, wind slicing. But I didn't see Beecham hurry her deliberate tread or hug her bare arms. She just trundled steadily along, a boulder rolling downhill.

The side door of the lab was locked. Nurse Beecham had the key on an enormous ring she hauled from her side pocket. When we were inside, she double-locked the door.

"Wait here, please," she said, and went thumping down a wide, waxed linoleum corridor. I waited, looking around. Nothing of interest to see, unless closed doors excite you. In a few minutes, Dr. Kenneth Draper came bustling down the hall, rubbing his palms together and trying hard to look relaxed and genial.

"Well!" he said again. "Here we are! See everything you wanted in the Hall?"

"I think so," I said. "It appears to be a very efficient operation."

"Oh, it is, it is," he assured me. "Quality care. If you'd care to test the patients' food, just drop in unexpectedly, for any meal. I think you'll be pleasantly surprised."

"I'm sure I would be," I said. "But that won't be necessary, Dr. Draper. By the way, Nurse Beecham strikes me as being a very valuable member of your staff. How long has she been with you?"

"From the start," he said. "When Dr. Thorndecker took over. He brought her in. I understand she was the first Mrs. Thorndecker's nurse during a long illness prior to her—her accident. I don't know what we'd do without

Beecham. Perhaps not the most personable, outgoing woman in the world, but she certainly does a job running the Hall. Keeps problems to a minimum so Dr. Thorndecker and I can devote more time to the lab."

"Where your real interests lie?" I suggested.

"Well...uh, yes," he said hesitantly, as if afraid of saying too much. "The nursing home is our first responsibility, of course, but we are doing some exciting things here, and I suppose it's natural..."

Another Coburnite who couldn't finish his sentences. I wondered how these people expressed love for one another. Did they just say, "I love..." and let it go at that?

"Now this is our main floor," Dr. Draper was saying. "Here you'll find our offices, records room, reference library, a small lounge, a locker and dressing room, showers, and a room we've equipped with cots for researchers who might want to sleep here after a long day's work or during a prolonged project. Do you want to see any of these rooms?"

"I'd like to glance at the reference library, if I may," I said. "Just for a moment."

"Of course, of course. Along here, please."

This place was certainly livelier than the nursing home. As we walked along the corridor, I heard voices from behind closed doors, hoots of laughter, and once a shouted argument in which I could distinguish one screamed statement: "You're full of shit!"

We stopped several times for Dr. Draper to introduce me to staff members hustling by. They all seemed to know who I was, and shook my hand with what appeared to be genuine enthusiasm. There were almost as many women as men, and all of them seemed young and—well, I think "keen" would describe them best. I said something about this to Draper.

"Oh, they're top-notch," he said proudly. "The best. Dr. Thorndecker recruited them from all over: Harvard, Duke, Berkeley, Johns Hopkins, Chicago, MIT. We have two Japanese, one Swede, and a kid from Mali you wouldn't believe, he's so smart. We pay them half of what they could be making with any of the big drug companies."

"Then why...?" I said. I was beginning to suffer from the Coburn Syndrome.

"Thorndecker!" Dr. Draper cried. "It's Thorndecker. The opportunity of working with him. Learning from him. They're very highly motivated."

"Or he's charmed them," I said, smiling.

Suddenly he was sober.

"Yes," he said in a low voice. "That, too. Here's our library. Small, but sufficient."

We stepped inside. A room about twenty by forty feet, lined with bookcases. Several small oak tables with a single chair at each, and one long conference table with twelve captain's chairs. A Xerox machine. The shelves were jammed with books on end and periodicals lying flat. It wasn't too orderly: the ashtrays filled, wastebaskets overflowing, books and magazines lined up raggedly. But after a visit to the late Mr. Petersen's abode, it was a pleasure to see human mess.

"Looks like it's used," I commented, wandering around.

"All the time," he told me. "Sometimes the researchers will get caught up in something, read all night, and then flop into one of those cots I told you about. Very irregular hours. No one punches a time clock. But if they do their jobs, they can work any hours they please. A very relaxed atmosphere. Dr. Thorndecker feels it pays off in productivity."

Meanwhile I was inspecting the titles of the books and periodicals on the shelves. If I had hoped they'd give me a clue to what was going on at the Crittenden Research Laboratory, I was disappointed. They appeared to me to be standard scientific reference texts, with heavy emphasis on human biology and the morphology of mammalian cells. A thick stack of recent oncological papers. One shelf of US Government publications dealing with demography, census, and public health statistics. I didn't see a single volume I'd care to curl up with on a cold winter night.

"Very nice," I said, turning to Draper. "Where do we go now—the labs?"

"Fine," he said. "They're on the second floor. On each side of the corridor is a large general lab used by the researchers. And then a smaller private lab used by the supervising staffers."

"How many supervisors do you have?"

"Well..." he said, blushing, "actually just Dr. Thorndecker and me. But when the grant—*if* the grant comes through, we hope to expand. We have the space and facilities to do it. Well, you'll see. Let's go up."

Unlike nursing homes and hospitals, research laboratories don't necessarily have to be sterile, efficient, and as cozy as a subway station. True, I've been in labs that look like operating rooms: all shiny white tile and equipment right out of *The Bride of Frankenstein*. I've also been in research labs not much larger than a walk-in closet and equipped with not much more than a stained sink and a Bunsen burner.

When it comes to scientific research, there's no guarantee. A million dollars sunk into a palace of a lab with all the latest and most exotic stainless steel doodads can result in the earth-shaking discovery that when soft cheese is exposed to the open air, mold results. And from that little closet lab with roaches fornicating in unwashed flasks can come a discovery that remakes the world.

The second-floor working quarters of the Crittenden Research Laboratory fell about halfway between palace and closet. The space was ample enough; the entire floor was divided in two by a wide corridor, and on each side was a huge laboratory. Each had, at its end, a small, private laboratory enclosed by frosted glass panels. These two small supervisors' labs had private entrances from the corridor, and also etched glass doors leading into the main labs. All these doors, I noted, could be locked.

The main laboratories were lighted with overhead

fluorescent fixtures, plus high-intensity lamps mounted near microscopes. Workbenches ran around the walls, with additional work tables in the center areas. Plenty of sinks, garbage disposal units, lab stools, metal and glass welding torches and tanks—from which I guessed they had occasional need to fabricate their own equipment.

But it was the profusion of big, complex, obviously store-bought hardware that bewildered me.

"I can recognize an oscilloscope when I see one," I told Draper. "And that thing's a gas diffusion analyzer, and that's a scanning electron microscope. But what's all this other stuff?"

"Oh... various things," he said vaguely. "The big control board is for an automated cell culture, blood and tissue analyzer. Very complete readings, in less time than it would take to do it by hand. Incidentally, in addition to our own work, we do all the tests needed by the nursing home. That includes blood, urine, sputum, stools, biopsies—whatever. We have pathologists on staff."

There had been half a dozen researchers working in the first lab we visited, and I saw about the same number when we walked into the lab across the hall. A few of them looked up when we entered, but most didn't give us a glance.

The second lab had workbenches along three walls. The fourth, a long one, was lined with stainless steel refrigerators and climate-controlled cabinets. Through the front glass panels I could see racks and racks of flasks and tubes of all sizes and shapes.

"Cell cultures?" I asked Dr. Draper.

"Mostly," he nodded. "And some specimens. Organ and tumor slices. Things of that sort. We have some very old, very valuable cultures here. A few originals. We're continually getting requests from all over the world."

"You give the stuff away?"

"Sometimes, but we prefer to trade," he said, laughing shortly. "'Here's what we've got; what have *you* got?' Research laboratories do a lot of horse-trading like that."

"You have bacteria?" I asked.

"Some."

"Viruses?"

"Some."

"Lethal?"

"Oh yes," he nodded. "Including a few rare ones from Africa. They're in those cabinets with the padlocks. Only Dr. Thorndecker and I have the key."

"What are they all doing?" I said, motioning toward the researchers bent over their workbenches. "What's your current project?"

"Well, ah," he said, "I'd prefer you direct that question to Dr. Thorndecker. He specifically said he wished to brief you personally on our current activities. After we've finished up here."

"Good enough," I said. Just seeing the Crittenden Research Laboratory in action revealed nothing. If they were brewing up a bubonic plague and told me they were making chicken noodle Cup-a-Soup, I wouldn't have known the difference.

"The only thing left to see is the basement," Draper said.

"What's down there?"

"Mostly our experimental animals. A dissection room. Mainly for animals," he added hastily. "We don't do any human PM's unless it's requested by relatives of the deceased."

"Why would they request it?"

"For various reasons. Usually to determine the exact cause of death. We had a case last year in which a widow authorized an autopsy of her deceased husband, a mental who had been at Crittenden Hall for two years. She was afraid of a genetic brain disorder that might be inherited by their son."

"Did you find it?"

"Yes," he said. "And there have been some postmortems authorized by the subjects themselves, prior to their death. These were people who wished to donate organs: kidneys, corneas, hearts, and so forth. But these cases have been few, considering the advanced age of most of the patients in the nursing home. Their organs are rarely, ah, desirable."

And on that cheery note, we descended the stairway to the basement of the Crittenden Research Laboratory. Dr. Kenneth Draper paused with his hand on the knob of a heavy, padded steel door. He turned to me.

He seemed suddenly overcome by embarrassment. Spots of color appeared high on his cheeks. His forehead was pearled with sweat. Wet teeth appeared in a hokey grin.

"We have mostly mice, dogs, cats, chimps, and guinea pigs," he said.

"Yes?" I said encouragingly. "And...?"

"Well," he said, tittering nervously, "you are not, by any chance, an anti-vivisectionist, are you, Mr. Todd?"

"Rather them than me," I said, and looked at him. But he had turned away; I couldn't see his face.

When we stepped inside, I heard immediately the reason for that outside door being padded. The big basement room was an audiophile's nightmare: chirps, squeals, barks, hisses, honks, roars, howls. I looked around, dazed.

"You'll get used to it," Draper shouted in my ear.

"Never," I shouted back.

We made a quick tour of the cages. I didn't mind the smell so much as that cacophony. I really am a sentimental slob, and I kept thinking the imprisoned beasts were making all that racket because they were suffering and wanted out. Not a very objective reaction, I admit; most of them looked sleek and well-fed. It's just that I hate to see an animal in a cage. I hate zoos. I see myself behind those bars, with a neat label: "Samuel Todd, Homus Americanus, habitat New York City. A rare species that feeds on vodka gimlets and celery stalks stuffed with anchovy paste."

There were a few aproned attendants around who grinned at us. One of them was wearing a set of heavy earphones. Maybe he was just blocking out that noise, or maybe he was listening to Mahler's Fifth.

After inspecting the spitting cats, howling dogs, barking chimps, and squealing mice, it was a relief to get into a smaller room closed off by another of those padded steel doors.

This one was also lined with cages. But the occupants were those animals being used in current experiments and were reasonably quiet. Some of them lay on their sides, in what appeared to be a comatose state. Some were bandaged. Some had sensors taped to heads and bodies, the wires leading out to a battery of recording machines.

And some of them—one young chimpanzee in particular—were covered with tumors. Great, monstrous growths. Blossoms of wild flesh. Red and blue and yellow. A flowering of raw tissue. The smell in there was something.

The young chimp was almost hidden by the deadly blooms. The eruptions covered his head, body, limbs. He lay on his back, spreadeagled, breathing shallowly. I could see his black, glittering eyes staring at the cage above him.

"Carcinosarcoma," Dr. Draper said. "He's lasted longer than any other in this particular series of tests."

"You infected him?" I asked, knowing the answer.

"Yes," Draper said. "To test the efficacy of a drug we had high hopes for."

"Your hopes aren't so high now?"

"No," he said, shrinking.

I felt like a shit.

"Forgive me, doctor," I said. "I know in my mind this kind of thing has to be done. I know it's valuable. I'd just prefer not to see it."

"I understand," he said. "Actually, we all try to be objective. I mean all of us—attendants, researchers. But sometimes we don't succeed. We give them names. Al, Tony, Happy Boy, Sue. When they die, or have to be destroyed, we feel it, I assure you."

"I believe you," I said.

I took a quick look at the dissecting room. Just two stainless steel tables, sinks, pots and pans for excised organs. Choppers. Slicers. Shredders. Something like a kitchen in a gourmet restaurant.

We walked back through the animal room. I was happy to get out of there. The stairway up to the main floor was blessedly quiet.

"Thank you, Dr. Draper," I said. "I'm sure you're a busy man, and you'll probably have to work late to catch up. But I appreciate your showing me around."

"My pleasure," he said.

Of course I didn't believe him.

"And now," I said, "I understand a meeting with Dr. Thorndecker is planned?"

"Correct," he said, obviously pleased that everything had gone so well, and one of his wild, young researchers hadn't dropped a diseased guinea pig's spleen down my neck. "I'll call Crittenden Hall from here. Then I'll unlock the back door, and if you'll just go back the way you came, someone will be at the Hall to let you in."

"Thanks again," I said, shaking his damp hand.

I figured him for a good second-level man: plenty of brains, but without the energy, ambition, and obsessive drive to make it to the top level. His attitude toward Thorndecker seemed ambivalent; I couldn't figure it. But he seemed enthusiastic enough about his work and the Crittenden Research Laboratory.

He made his phone call and was unlocking the back door when suddenly, on impulse, I asked him, "Are you married, Dr. Draper?"

His reaction reminded me of that analyzing computer I had just seen. Lights flashing, bubbles bubbling, bleeps bleeping; I could almost *see* him computing, wondering how his answer might affect a grant from the Bingham Foundation to the Crittenden Research Laboratory. Finally . . .

"Why no," he said. "I'm not."

"I'm not either," I said, hoping it might make him feel better. He might even get to like me, and start calling me Sam, or Happy Boy, like one of his experimental animals in that room of the doomed I had just seen.

Turned out into the cold, I trudged determinedly up the steps, back to Crittenden Hall. But then I realized how pleasant it was to be alone, even for a moment or two. It seemed to me I had been accompanied almost every minute I had been on the grounds. And it was possible I had been under observation for the few seconds I had been alone when Nurse Beecham went to fetch Dr. Draper.

I shook my head. Those paranoiac twinges again. But, looking around at the ruined day, the decayed fields of Crittenden, I figured they came with the territory.

A little, snub-nosed nurse's aide had the back door of Crittenden Hall open for me when I arrived. She escorted me down the corridor and delivered me to the white-jacketed goon in the entrance hall. He told me Dr. Thorndecker was awaiting me in his second-floor study, and waved me up the wide staircase. I went about halfway up, raised my eyes, and saw an aproned maid waiting for me on the second-floor landing. I glanced down to see the goon still watching me from the main floor entrance hall.

Then I was certain; it wasn't paranoia at all. They were keeping me in sight. Every minute. They didn't want me wandering around by myself. Who knew what closed door I might open?

Dr. Thorndecker's study was a rumpled warehouse of a room. It looked like an attic for furniture that wasn't good enough for the other rooms in Crittenden Hall, but was too good to give to the Salvation Army. No two chairs, styles, or colors matched. The desk was a scarred and battered rolltop. The lamps had silk shades with beaded fringe. The couch was one big, lumpy stain, and books and periodicals were stacked higgledy-piggledy on the floor. Some of the stacks had collapsed; there were puddles of magazines, scientific papers, spiral-bound notebooks. I had to step over them to get in.

Thorndecker made no apology for this mess, for which I admired him. He got me seated in a cretonne-covered armchair that had stuffing coming out one arm. I wriggled around cautiously until I could sit comfortably without being goosed by a loose spring. The doctor slumped in a swivel chair swung around from his desk.

"Your wife decorate this room?" I asked politely.

He laughed. "To tell you the truth, I like it just the way it is. It's my own private place. A hideaway. No one ever comes in here except the cleaning woman."

"Once every five years?" I suggested. "Whether it needs it or not?"

He laughed again. He seemed to enjoy my chivying. He had whipped off his glasses the moment I entered, but not before I had noted they made him look older. Not older than his 54 years, but just as old. He certainly looked younger without them.

The tanned complexion helped. Perfect teeth that I guessed were capped, not store-bought. Thick billows of dark hair; not a smidgen of gray. No jowls. No sagging of neck flesh. The skin was ruddy and tight, eyes clear and alert. He moved lithely, with an energetic bounce. If he had told me he was 40 years old, I might have thought he was shaving five years. But 54? Imfuckingpossible.

The clothes helped. Beige doeskin slacks, sports jacket of yummy tweed, open-collar shirt with a paisley ascot. Glittering, tasseled moccasins on his small feet. A very spiffy gentleman. When he spoke in that rich, fruity baritone, I could understand how he could woo whiz-kids away from drug cartels at half the salary. He had charm, and even the realization that it was contrived was no defense against it.

Suddenly I had a suspicion that not only the charm, but the man himself might be contrived. The artfully youthful look of bronzed skin, California whites, and hair unblemished by a speck of gray. That appearance might have been a perfectly natural bounty but was, more likely, the result of sunlamp, expensive dental work, facials, and hair dye. And those too-young clothes. I didn't expect Dr. Telford Gordon Thorndecker to dress like a mortician, but I didn't expect him to dress like a juvenile lead either.

Supposing my suspicions correct, what could possibly be his motive? The first one that occurred to me—the *only* one that occurred to me—was that this Nobel winner, this gifted scientist, this *genius* was trying to keep himself attractive and exciting to his young wife. The pampered body was for her. The elegant duds were for her. Even this mess of a room was to prove to her that disorder didn't faze him, that he was capable of whim and youthful nuttiness. He might be an amusing character, an original personality. But he was not a fuddy-duddy; *he was not*.

Irrational? No, just human. I don't mean my own suspicions; I mean Thorndecker's conduct. I had seen how swiftly his vigorous exuberance collapsed the night before when his wife was not present. I began to feel sorry for the man, and like him more.

He looked at me narrowly.

"The animals shake you up?" he asked.

"How did you know that?" I said.

"They usually do. But it must be done."

"I know."

"I have some brandy here. Join me?"

I nodded. He poured us small drinks from a bottle he took from a file drawer in his desk. He used plastic throwaway cups, and again made no apology or excuse. He took one of my cigarettes, and we lighted up.

"I'd be interested in hearing your reactions, Mr. Todd," he said. "On or off the record."

"Oh, on," I said. "I won't try to mislead you. I thought the nursing home a very efficient operation. Of course, it only has a peripheral bearing on your application, but it's nice to know you run a clean, classy institution. Good food, good care, pleasant surroundings, sufficient staff, planned social activities and all that stuff."

"Yes," he said, not changing expression, "all that stuff."

"From what I've read of our preliminary investigation reports, Crittenden Hall makes a modest profit. Which goes to the Crittenden Research Laboratory. Correct?"

He gestured toward the stacks of papers on his desk.

"Correct," he said. "And that's what I've been doing this afternoon, and why I couldn't show you around personally; I've been shuffling papers: bills, checks, requisitions, budgets, vouchers, salaries, and so forth. We have an accountant, of course; he comes in once a month. But I do the day-to-day management. It's my own fault; I could delegate the responsibility to Draper or Beecham— or hire a smart bookkeeper to do it. But I prefer doing it myself. I want to know where every penny comes from and where it goes. And you know, Mr. Todd, I hate it. Hate every minute of it. This paper shuffling, I mean. I'd much rather be in the lab with Dr. Draper and the others. Hard at work. The kind of work I enjoy."

It sounded swell: gifted scientist not interested in the vulgar details of making money, but only in pure research. For the benefit of mankind. What a cynical bastard I am! I said:

"That's a natural lead-in to my next question, Dr. Thorndecker. What kind of work? Everyone I saw in the lab seemed gung-ho and busy as hell. What's going on? What are you doing in the lab? I mean right now. Not if you get the grant, but what's going on *now?*"

He leaned back in his swivel chair, clasped his hands behind his head. He stared at plaster peeling off the high ceiling. His face suddenly contorted in a quick grimace, a tic that lasted no more than a second.

"Know anything about science?" he said. "Human biology in particular? Cells?"

"Some," I said. "Not much. I read your application and the report by our research specialists. But I'm not a trained scientist."

"An informed layman?"

"I guess you could say that."

"Anything in the application or report you didn't understand?"

"I caught the gist of it. I gather you're interested in why people get old."

His ceiling-aimed stare came slowly down. He looked directly into my eyes.

"Exactly," he said. "That's it in a nutshell. Why do people get old? Why does the skin lose its elasticity at the age of thirty-five? Why, at a later age, do muscles grow slack and eyesight dim? Why does hearing fail? Why should a man's cock shrink and his ass sink, or maybe shrivel up until there's nothing there but a crack on a spotted board? Why do a woman's breasts sag and wrinkle? Why does her pubic hair become sparse and scraggly? Why does a man go bald, a woman get puckered thighs? Why do lines appear? What happens to muscle tone and skin color? Did you know that some people actually shrink? They do, Mr. Todd, they *shrink*. Not only in body weight, but in their bone structure. Not to mention teeth falling out, a hawking of phlegm, an odor of the flesh like ash or loam, a tightening of the bowels."

"Jesus," I gasped, "I can hardly wait. Could I have a little more brandy, please?"

He laughed, and filled up my plastic cup. And his own, I noted. Once again I noted that sudden, brief twitching of his features. Almost a spasm of pain.

"I'm not telling you anything you didn't know," he said. "You just don't want to think about it. No one does. Mortality. A hard concept to grasp. Maybe even impossible. But the interesting thing about senescence, Mr. Todd, is that science was hardly aware of it as a biological phenomenon until the last—oh, let's say fifty years. Back in the Middle Ages, if you lived to the ripe old age of thirty or forty, you were doing well. Oh sure, there were a few oldsters of fifty or sixty, but most humans died in childbirth or soon after. If they survived a few years, disease, accidents, pestilence, or wars took them off before they really achieved maturity. Now, quite suddenly, with the marvelous advances in medical science, public health, hygiene, improved diet, and so forth, we have more and more people living into their sixties, seventies, eighties, nineties, and no one thinks it remarkable. It isn't. What is remarkable is that, in spite of medical care, diet, exercise, and sanitary toilets, very few humans make it to a hundred. Why is that, Mr. Todd?"

"Have no idea."

"Sure you do," he said gently. "They don't necessarily

sicken. They don't get typhoid, the plague, smallpox, or TB. They just decay. They degenerate. The body not only stops growing, it simply stops. It's not a sudden thing; in a healthy human it takes place over a period of thirty or forty years. But we can see it happening, all those awful things I mentioned to you, and there's no way we can stop it. The human body declines. Heart, liver, stomach, bowels, brain, circulation, nervous system: all subject to degenerative disorders. The body begins to waste away. And if you study actuarial tables, you'll see there's a very definite mathematical progression. The likelihood of dying doubles every seven years after the age of thirty. How does that grab you? But it's only been in the past fifty years that science has started asking Why? Why should the human body decay? Why should hair fall out and skin become shrunken and crepey? We've extended longevity, yes. Meaning most people live longer than they did in the Middle Ages. But now we find ourselves up against a barrier, a wall. Why don't people live to be a hundred, two hundred, three hundred? We can't figure it out. No matter how good our diet, how efficient our sewers, how pure our air, there seems to be something in the human body, in our species, Mr. Todd, that decrees: Thus far, but no farther. We just can't seem to get beyond that one-hundred-year limit. Oh, maybe a few go a couple of years over, but generally a hundred years seems to be the limit for *Homo sapiens*. Why? Who or what set that limit? Is it something in *us?* Something in our physical makeup? Something that decrees the time for dying? What is it? What the hell *is* it? And that, Mr. Todd, is what those gung-ho, busy-as-hell young researchers you just saw in the Crittenden Research Laboratory are trying to find."

I must admit, he had me. He spoke with such earnestness, such fervor, leaning toward me with hands clasped, that I couldn't take my eyes from him, couldn't stop listening because I was afraid that in the next sentence he might reveal the miracle of creation, and if I wasn't paying attention, I might miss it.

When he paused, I sat back, took a deep breath, and drank half my brandy.

I stared at him over the rim of my plastic cup. This time the contraction that wrenched his features was more violent than the two I had previously noted. This one not only twisted his face but wracked his body: he stiffened for an instant, then shuddered as his limbs relaxed. I don't think he was aware that it was evident. When it passed, his expression was unchanged, and he made no reference to it.

"Wow," I said. "Heady stuff, even for an informed layman. And I don't mean the brandy. Are you saying that the Biblical three-score-and-ten don't necessarily have to be that? But could be more?"

He looked at me strangely.

"You're very quick," he said. "That's exactly what I'm saying. It doesn't *have* to be three-score-and-ten. Not if we can find what determines that span. If we can isolate it, we can manipulate it. Then it could become five-score-and-ten, or ten-score-and-ten. Or more. Whatever we want."

I was staggered. Almost literally. If that spring-sprung armchair hadn't clasped me close, I might have trembled. After reading his application, I had suspected Thorndecker wanted Bingham Foundation to finance a search for the Fountain of Youth. Everything I had seen of him up to that moment reinforced that suspicion. Older man-youthful wife. Cosseted body and the threads of a swinger. Contrived enthusiasm and the energy of a spark. It all made a kind of very human sense.

But now, if I understood him, he wasn't talking about the Fountain of Youth, of keeping smooth-skinned and romping all the days of our lives; he was talking about immortality—or something pretty close to it. I couldn't believe it.

"Dr. Thorndecker," I said, "let me get this straight ... Are you saying there is a factor in human biology, in our bodies, that causes aging? And that once this agent—

let's call it the X Factor—can be discovered and isolated, then the chances are that it can be manipulated, modified, changed—whatever—so that the natural span of a man's years could be increased without limit?"

He put his feet up on his desk. He sipped his brandy. Then he nodded.

"That's exactly what I'm saying."

I leaned back, lighted another cigarette, crossed my legs. I couldn't look at him. I was afraid that if I did, and he said, "Now jump out of the window," out I'd go.

Because I can't tell you how convincing the man was. It wasn't only the manner: the passionate voice, the deep, unblinking gaze. But it was the impression of personal confession he gave, as if he were revealing the secret closest to his heart, a secret he had never revealed to anyone but me, because he knew I would understand and be sympathetic. It was as moving as a murmured, "I love you," and could no more be withstood.

"All right," I said finally, "supposing—just supposing—I go along with your theory that there is something in human biology, in the human body, that determines our lifespan—it is just a theory, isn't it?"

"Of course. With some hard statistical evidence to back it up."

"Assuming I agree with you that we all have something inside us that dictates when the cock shrinks and the ass sinks, what is it? What is the X Factor?"

"You read my application, and my professional record?"

"Yes."

"Then you must know that I believe the X Factor—as you call it—is to be found in the cell. The human cell."

"Germ cells? Sex cells?"

"No, we're working with body cells. Heart, skin, lung."

"Why cells at all? Couldn't the X Factor, the aging factor, be a genetic property?"

He gave me a glassy smile.

"You *are* an informed layman," he said. "Yes, I admit many good men working in this field believe senescence has a genetic origin. That the lifespan of our speices, of all species, is determined by a genetic clock."

"It makes sense," I argued. "If my parents and grandparents live into their eighties and nineties, chances are pretty good that, barring a fatal accident or illness, I'll live into my eighties or nineties, too. At least, the insurance companies are betting on it."

"You may," he acknowledged. "And the geneticists make a great point of that. Perhaps the X Factor exists in DNA, and determines the lifespan of every human born. And perhaps the X Factor in DNA could be isolated. Then what?"

I shook my head. "You've lost me. You speak of manipulating the X Factor in human cells, if and when it can be isolated. So . . . ? Why couldn't it be manipulated if found in the genetic code? I understand gene splicing is all the rage these days."

"Oh, it's the rage," he said, not laughing. "But recombination with *what?* If you isolated the senescence gene, what would you combine it with—the tortoise gene? They grow to a hundred and fifty, you know. As my son Edward might say, 'Big deal!' What I'm trying to say, Mr. Todd, is that, in this case, gene splicing does not offer anything but the possibility of extending the human lifespan by fifty years. I happen to believe that my cellular theory offers more than that. Much more. You ask if it's a theory, I reply that it is. You ask if I have any proof that the cellular approach to senescence is viable, I reply that there is much proof that the X Factor exists in human cells, but it has not been isolated. As of this date. You ask if I have anything to go on, other than my own conviction, that the X Factor can be isolated and manipulated, and I must reply in all honesty: no, nothing but my own conviction."

I took a deep breath.

"All right, Dr. Thorndecker," I said, "I appreciate your honesty. But why in hell didn't you spell all this out in your application? Why did you base it all on that crap about exposing human embryo cells to electromagnetic radiation?"

"First of all, that was accurate. We intend to do exactly that, in our effort to isolate the X Factor. Second of all, if I had stated in the application that my ultimate aim was to make humans immortal, would the Bingham Foundation even have bothered to process the application, or would it have been immediately consigned to deep six?"

"You know the answer to that," I said. "If you had stated your true reason for requesting the subsidy, I wouldn't be here now."

"Of course not," he said.

I looked at him in wonderment.

"So why are you telling me now?" I asked him. "Aren't you afraid I'll roll up my tent and go home?"

"It's a possibility," he acknowledged. "You could tell your superiors I misled the Bingham Foundation. I didn't, of course. But I admit I was not as totally forthright as I might have been. Still, my application is entirely truthful. It is not dishonest."

"You draw a fine line," I told him. I stared at that handsome, brooding face a long time. "And you're confessing," I said, still marveling. "Are you that sure of me?"

"I'm not sure of you at all," he said, somewhat testily. "But I think you're a shrewd man. I'm paying you the compliment of not trying to deceive you. You can report this conversation to your superiors or not, as you please. The decision is yours."

"You don't care?"

"Mr. Todd, I care a great, goddamned deal. That grant is important to me. It's essential I get it. And it's vital, as I'm sure you're aware, to all of Coburn. But as I say, the decision is yours."

I drained my plastic cup, struggled out of that creaking armchair.

"You're certain," I said, "that the X Factor, the aging factor, will be found in human body cells and not in the genetic code?"

He grinned at me. "I'm certain. No one else is."

"Dr. Thorndecker, you stated there is hard statistical evidence to back up your belief in the existence of the X Factor in human body cells."

"That's correct; there is."

"Could I take a look at it?"

"Of course," he said promptly. "It consists not only of my work, but the work of others in this field. I'll have it collected and prepared for you. It will be ready in a day or so."

"Fine," I said. "Let's let it go until then. You've given me enough to think about for one day."

He walked me out onto the second-floor landing, chatting amiably, hand on my shoulder. He held me fast, went on and on about this and that, and I wondered— why the stall? Then I saw his eyes flickering to the lobby below. Sure enough, when the white-jacketed goon-doorman appeared, Thorndecker released my shoulder, shook my hand, told me how much he had enjoyed our palaver—his word: "palaver"—and gave me a smile of super-charm. I was becoming impervious to it. You can endure just so much charm in a given period. After that, it's like being force-fed a pound of chocolate macaroons.

I ambled slowly down that sweeping staircase. I was handed my coat and hat. I was ushered out the front door of Crittenden Hall.

I stood on the graveled driveway a moment, belting my trenchcoat, turning up the collar. Something odd was happening to that day: it was going ghostly on me. There was a cold mist in the air. At the same time, a whitish fog was rolling down.

Everything was silvered, swathed in the finest chain mail imaginable. It was a metallic mesh, wrapped around the physical world. I could see my car looming, but dimly, dimly, all glitter and glint. Beyond, even dimmer, the bare trunks of trees appeared, disappeared, appeared again, wavery in the hazy light. I could feel the wet on my face, and see it on my black leather coat.

I heard a weird chonking sound, and turned toward it.

Then it became clopping. I heard the whinny of a horse, and out of the shivery mist, coming at a fast trot, rode Julie Thorndecker, sitting astride a big bay gelding. She pulled up alongside me. I stepped back hastily as the horse 'took a few skittering steps on the gravel, his eyes stretched. Then she quieted him, stroking his neck, whispering to him. I moved closer.

They had obviously been on a gallop. Steam came drifting from the beast's flanks and haunches; its breath was one long plume of white. It still seemed excited from the run: pawed the driveway, moved about restlessly, tossed its head. But Mrs. Thorndecker continued her ministering, solid in the English saddle. That was one hell of a horse. From my point of view, it seemed enormous, with a neck that was all glistening muscle, and a mouthful of teeth as big as piano keys.

Julie was wearing brown boots, whipcord jodhpurs, a creamy flannel shirt, suede jacket, gloves. There was a red silk scraf about her throat: the only splash of color in that somber scene. Her head was not covered, and the mist had matted down her fine hair so that it clung to her skull.

Before I could say, "Hi," or "Hello," or "Does he bite?" she had slipped from the saddle and landed lightly on her feet alongside me. She flipped the reins over the horse's head, then wrapped them around her hand.

"You always ride in the rain?" I asked her.

"It isn't raining," she said. "Just dampish. When the ground freezes, and the snow comes, I don't ride at all. Today was super."

"Glad to hear it."

"I have to cool him off," she said. "Take a little walk?"

"Sure," I said. "You walk between me and the horse."

"Are you afraid of horses?"

"Lady," I said, "I'm afraid of cocker spaniels."

So off we went, strolling slowly, that great beast following us like an equine chaperon.

"Have a nice visit?" she asked.

I hadn't forgotten that husky voice, that throaty, almost tremulous voice. It still seemed to promise everything a man might desire, and more. I began to warm under my trenchcoat.

"I like your hat," she said suddenly.

"Thanks," I said, flipping the limp brim at her. "It was made in Ireland, so I suppose it loves weather like this. Might even begin to grow. How long do we walk before that monster cools off?"

"A few minutes," she said. "Bored with me already?"

"No," I said. "Never," I vowed.

She laughed, a deep, shirred chuckle.

"Aren't you sweet," she said.

"I am," I acknowledged.

It seemed to me we were walking down a narrow road of packed earth. On both sides, indistinct in the fog, were the black trunks of winter-stripped trees, with spidery branches almost meeting overhead. It was like walking into a tunnel of smoke: everything gray and swirling. Even the light seemed to pulse: patches of pearl, patches of sweat.

"Did you have a good visit?" she asked again.

"Very good."

"And did you like what you saw?"

"Oh yes."

"Glad to hear it. You had a talk with my husband?"

"I did. A long talk. A long, interesting talk."

"Good," she said. "Perhaps he'll forgive me."

I turned to look at her. "Oh? For what?"

"For sending Ronnie Goodfellow to see you. I did that, you know. From the best motives in the world."

"I'm sure they were," I said.

"You aren't angry, are you?"

She stopped, I stopped, the horse stopped. She put a hand on my arm. She came a half-step closer, looked up at me.

"It won't hurt Telford, will it?" she breathed. "My sending Ronnie to see if you were settled in? It won't hurt our chances of getting the grant?"

That young face was as damp as mine. I remember seeing tiny silver beads of moisture on her long, black lashes. Her cheeks were still flushed from the gallop, and those ripe lips seemed perpetually parted, waiting. Everything about her seemed complaisant and yearning. Except the eyes. The eyes were wet stones.

Why, I wondered, with hard eyes like that, should she seem so peculiarly vulnerable to me? It was her crackly voice, I decided, and the little boy's hair-do, and the warmth of her hand on my arm, and the loose, free way she moved. The giving way.

"Of course not," I said. "You didn't do anything so awful. As a matter of fact, I liked Goodfellow. No harm done."

"Thank you," she said faintly. "You've made me feel a lot better." She came another half-step closer. "It's so important, you see. To Telford. To me. To all of us."

If, at that moment, she had looked into my eyes, batted her lashes, and murmured, "I'll do anything to get my husband that grant—*anything*," I think I would have burst out laughing. But she wasn't that obvious. There was just the warm hand on my arm, the two half-steps toward me, the implied intimacy in that furry scene of smoke, lustrous mist, shadowy trees, and a steaming horse making snorting noises behind us and beginning to paw impatiently at the earth.

We turned back, slowly. We walked a few minutes in silence. She hauled on the reins with both hands until the gelding's head was practically over her shoulder. She reached up to stroke that velvety nose.

"You darling," she said. "Darling."

I didn't know if she meant the horse or me. But then, at that moment, I suspected I might be happy.

We were about halfway back to the Hall when faintly, from far off, I heard the cry, "Julie! Julie!" Dimmed by distance, muffled by fog, that wailed cry stopped us dead in our tracks. It seemed to come from everywhere, almost howled, distorted: "Joo-lee! Joo-lee!" We looked around in the tunnel, trying to determine the direction. "Joo-lee! Joo-lee!" Louder now.

Then, first a drifting shade, then a dark presence, and

then a figure wavering in the putty light, came running Edward Thorndecker. He pounded up to us, stood accusingly, hands on waist, chest heaving.

"Where *were* you?" he demanded of his stepmother. "You didn't come back from your ride and, my God, I was so worried! I thought you might have been thrown. Hurt. Killed! Julie, you've got to—"

"Edward," she interrupted sweetly, putting a hand on his arm (the same goddamned hand that had been on *my* arm!), "say hello to Mr. Todd."

"Hello, Mr. Todd," he said, not bothering to look at me. "Julie, you have no idea how frantic I was. My God, I was ready to call the cops."

"Were you, dear?" she said with that throaty chuckle. "You *must* have been upset if you were ready to call the cops."

I guessed it was an inside joke, because they both started laughing, he hesitantly at first, then without restraint. I didn't catch the enormous humor of it all, but it gave me a chance to take a closer look at him.

He was wearing a prep school uniform: dark blue blazer, gray flannel slacks, black shoes, black knitted tie. No coat, no hat. He was a beautiful, beautiful boy, clear cheeks flushed from running, red lips open, blue eyes clear and sparkling. And those crisp black curls, glittering with the wet.

"Julie," he said, "I've got to talk to you. Do you know what father—"

She leaned forward and pressed a gloved forefinger softly to his lips, silencing him. If she had done that to me, I'd have—ahh, the hell with it.

"Shh, Edward," she said, smiling with her mouth but not with her eyes. "We have a guest, and I'm sure Mr. Todd is not interested at all in a minor family disagreement. Mr. Todd, will you excuse us, please?"

Both looked at me, he for the first time. Since neither showed any indication of moving, I gathered I was being given the bum's rush.

"Of course," I said. I removed my sodden tweed hat

and held it aloft. "Mrs. Thorndecker," I said. "Edward," I said.

I replaced the lid, turned, and plodded away from them. I trudged back to my car, resolved that I absolutely would not turn around to look back at them. I did about twenty steps before I turned around to look back at them.

I could see them glimmering through that scrim of fine chain mail. They were framed in the billowing fog between the rows of black trees and veiny, arching branches. Their figures wavered. I wiped a hand across my eyes, hoping to get a clearer look. But it was not clear. It was all smoke and shadow. Still, it seemed to me they were in each other's arms. Close. Close.

Somewhere, on the way back to Coburn, I pulled off the road. I left the motor running, the heater on. I lowered the window a bit so I wouldn't take the long, long sleep. I lighted a cigarette, and I pondered. I'm good at that. Not concluding, just pondering. In this case, my reflections were a mishmash: objective judgments of things I had observed that afternoon interspersed with subjective memories of parted lips, silvered hair plastered flat, husky laughs, and a loose, yielding way of moving.

Conclusions? You'll never guess. The only hard fact I came up with was that Al Coburn was a wise old owl. He had guessed Julie Thorndecker had sicced Constable Goodfellow onto me, and he had been right. Decision: cultivate Al Coburn and see what other insights the old fart might reveal.

As for the rest: all was confusion. But if you can't endure that, you shouldn't be in the snooping business. Sooner or later (if you're lucky), actions, relationships, and motives get sorted out and begin to make sense. It might not be rational sense, but I was dealing with human beings—and who says people have to be logical? Not me. And I speak from self-knowledge.

But there was one thing I could nail down, and had to. So I finished my cigarette, flicked the butt into what was now a freezing rain, and completed my drive into Coburn. It was about four-thirty, and I hoped I'd get there before the place closed for the day.

I made it—but not by much. Art Merchant had been right: the Coburn Civic Building was definitely not a tourist attraction. It was a two-story structure of crumbling red brick, designed along the general lines of an egg crate. The fire department occupied the ground level in front, the police department the ground level in back. The second floor was the City Hall: one big, hollow room. A bronze plaque on the outside wall stated: "This building erected by the Works Progress Administration, 1936; Franklin D. Roosevelt, President." Some loyal Democrat should have destroyed that.

I tramped up a wooden stairway, steps dusty and sagging. The wall was broken by tall, narrow windows affording a splendid view of the boarded-up A&P. At the top of the stairs were frosted glass doors bearing the legend: "oburn ity all." The lettering was in black paint, which had lasted. I figured the capital letters had been in gilt which had flaked off years ago and had never been replaced.

In all that cavernous room there was one middle-aged lady spraying her blue hair with a long aerosol can that could have been "Sparkle-Clear" or "Roach-Ded," for all I knew. She looked at me disapprovingly.

"We're closed," she yelled at me from across the room.

I made a big business of looking at my watch.

"Nah," I called, smiling winsomely, "you wouldn't do that to me—would you? You've got to finish spraying your lovely hair, and then the nails to touch up, and a few phone calls to your girlfriends, and it's only fifteen minutes to five, and I swear what I want won't take more than two minutes. Three maybe. Five at the most. Look at me—a poor traveler from out of town, come to your fair city seeking help in my hour of need. Can you turn me away? In your heart of hearts, can you really reject me?"

I don't apologize for this shit.

"Real estate?" she guessed. "The plats are over on the left, and if you—"

"No, no," I said. "Something much sadder. An uncle of mine passed away in Coburn only last night. Poor man. I need copies of the death certificate. You know—for insurance, bank accounts, the IRS and so forth. I need about ten copies."

"Sorry," she sang out. We were shouting at each other across at least fifty feet of empty office. "Death certificates go to the county seat. The Health Department. They have fire-proof files."

"Oh," I said, deflated. "Well, thanks, anyway."

"Of course, we keep photocopies of Coburn deaths," she said. "They're in the Deceased file on your right, between Bankruptcies and Defaults."

"May I take a quick look, ma'm?" I asked politely. "Just to make sure there is a certificate filed on my uncle?"

"Help yourself," she called. "I have to make a phone call. Then I'm locking up, so don't be long."

"Won't take a minute," I promised.

She got busy on the phone. I got busy on the Deceased file. The photocopy of Petersen's certificate was easy to find; it was in front, the most recent Coburn death. Chester K. Petersen, 72, resident of Crittenden Hall. The certificate was signed by Dr. Kenneth Draper.

But that wasn't what I was looking for. My eyes raced to find Cause of Death. There it was:

Congestive heart failure.

I glanced at the blue-haired lady. She was still giggling on the phone. I fumbled through the file as quickly as I could. I managed to go back through the previous two years. There had been twenty-three death certificates filed that listed Crittenden Hall as place of residence. The certificates were signed by Dr. Kenneth Draper and several other doctors. I guessed they were the resident MD's in Crittenden Hall.

Item: Two years ago, there had been six certificates filed, signed by four different MD's, including Draper. There had been a variety of causes of death.

Item: During the past year, there had been eighteen certificates filed, including Petersen's. Of these, fourteen had been signed by Draper, the others by residents.

Item: Of the fourteen death certificates in the past year signed by Dr. Kenneth Draper, eleven listed congestive heart failure as cause of death. The other three noted acute alcoholism, emphysema, and leukemia.

Nowhere, on any of the death certificates, did the name Dr. Telford Gordon Thorndecker appear.

"Finished?" the blue-haired lady called.

"Yes, thank you."

"Find what you wanted?" she yelled.

I smiled, waved, and got out of there. Did I find what I wanted? What did I want?

Driving back to the Coburn Inn, I recalled the exact conversation:

Me: "What did he die of? Petersen?"

Nurse Stella Beecham: "Pelvic cancer. Inoperable. He didn't respond to chemotherapy."

Someone was lying. Beecham or Draper, who had signed the certificate stating congestive heart failure was the cause of death.

And all those other puzzling statistics...

I needed a drink.

So, apparently, did half of Coburn. The bar at the Inn was two-deep with stand-up drinkers, and all of the booths were occupied. I took a small table, and grabbed the harried waiter long enough to order a vodka gimlet and a bag of potato chips with a bowl of taco-flavored cheese dip. My brain was whirling—why not my stomach?

I was working on drink and dip, using both hands, when I heard a breathless...

"Hi! Buy a thirsty girl a drink?"

I lurched to my feet.

"Hello, Millie," I said, gagging on a chip. "Sure, sit down. What'll you have?"

"My usual," she said. "Chivas Regal and 7-Up."

I don't think she saw me wince. I shouted the order at the passing waiter, then looked around nervously; I don't enjoy being seen in public with a cop's wife. It's not a matter of morality; it's a matter of survival. But fortunately, there was an old John Wayne movie on the bar's seven-foot TV screen, and most of the patrons were staring at that.

"Don't worry," Millie laughed. "Ronnie's working a

twelve-hour shift tonight: four to four."

I looked at her with respect, and began to revise my opinion. I pushed the dip toward her, and she dug in.

"Besides," she said, spraying me with little bits of potato chip, "he doesn't give a damn who I drink with."

"Besides," I added, "he'd be happy to know you're helping make my stay in Coburn a pleasant one. He wants me to be happy."

"Yeah," she said, brightening, "that's right. Am I really helping?"

"You bet your sweet patootie," I said. "Love that tent you're wearing."

She looked down at the flowered muumuu.

"Really?" she said doubtfully. "This old thing? It doesn't show much."

"That's what makes it so exciting," I told her. "It leaves everything to the imagination."

She leaned forward and whispered:

"Know what I've got on underneath?"

I knew the answer to that one, but I couldn't spoil her big yock.

"What?" I asked.

"Just perfume!" she shouted, leaned back and laughed like a maniac.

Her drink arrived, and she took a big gulp, still spluttering with mirth. It gave me a chance to take a closer look at her.

The face was older than the body. There were lines at the corners of eyes and mouth. Beneath the heavy makeup, the skin was beginning to look pouchy and tired. And there was something in her expression perilously close to defeat. But the neck was strong and smooth, firm breasts poked, the backs of her hands were unblemished. Nothing defeated about that body.

"Where do you and Ronnie live, Millie?" I asked idly.

"Way to hell and gone," she said sullenly. "Out on Fort Peabody Drive."

I thought a moment.

"Near Crittenden Hall?"

"Yeah," she said sourly, "right *near* it. Their fence runs

along the back line of our property."

"What have you got—a house, farm, mobile home?"

"A dump," she said. "We got a dump. Could I have another one of these?"

I ordered another round of drinks.

"Tell me, Millie," I said, "where do the good citizens of Coburn go when they want to cut loose? Don't tell me they all come in here and watch television?"

"Oh, there's a few places," she said, coming alive. "Roadhouses. Out on the Albany post road. Nothing fancy, but they have jukes and dancing. Sometimes Red Dog Betty's has a trio on Saturday night."

"Red Dog Betty's?"

"Yeah. There's a big poodle in red neon outside the place. It's kind of a rough joint. A lot of truckers stop there. But loads of fun."

She looked at me hopefully, but I wasn't having any. I wasn't drunk enough for Red Dog Betty's and loads of fun.

"Tell me about the places you go to in New York," she said.

I didn't tell her about the places I go to; she'd have been bored silly. But I told her what I thought she wanted to hear, describing fancy restaurants, swinging bars, discos, outdoor cafes, beaches, pick-up joints and make-out joints.

Her face became younger and wistful. She asked eager questions. She wanted to know how the women dressed, how they acted, what it cost to live in New York, could she get an apartment, could she get a job.

"Could I have fun there?" she asked.

I felt like weeping.

"Sure, you could," I said. "Maybe not every minute. It can be the loneliest place in the world. But yes, you could have fun."

She thought about that a moment. Then the defeat came back in her eyes.

"Nah," she said mournfully. "I'd end up peddling my tail on the street."

It was another revelation. No dumbbell she. I had

underestimated her. The clown makeup and the tart's costume she was wearing the first time I saw her had misled me. Maybe she wasn't intelligent, but she was shrewd enough to know who she was and what she was.

She knew that in Coburn she was *somebody*. Men came to the Inn lobby to buy their cigars and cigarettes and magazines and newspapers, just to wisecrack with her, to get a look at the finest lungs west of the Hudson River, to flirt, to dream. The femme fatale of Coburn, N.Y. As much a tourist attraction as Lovers' Leap and the place where the British spy was hanged. And in New York City, she'd end up hawking her ass on Eighth Avenue, competing with 15-year-old hookers from Minneapolis, and she knew it.

She knew it in her mind, but knowing couldn't entirely kill the dream, end the fantasy. The wild, crazy, raucous, violent city drew her, beckoned, lured, seduced. Loads of fun down there. *Loads* of fun.

The bar was emptying, the patrons going off grumbling to farms, homes, wherever. There were several empty booths.

"Have dinner with me, Millie," I said impulsively. "You'd be doing me a favor. I get tired of eating alone, and I'd—"

"Sure," she said promptly. "We'll eat right here. Okay? I hear the meat loaf is very good tonight."

It was good, as a matter of fact. I think it was a mixture of beef, pork, and lamb, very juicy and nicely seasoned. With it, they served thick slices of potato that had been baked, then browned and crusted in a skillet. Creamed spinach. We both had warm apple pie a la mode for dessert. I figured if this Thorndecker investigation went on much longer, I was going to need a new wardrobe, three sizes larger.

We had a bottle of New York State red with the meal, and brandy stingers with our coffee. Millie Goodfellow sat there, chin propped on her hand, a benign smile on her face, and I admit I was feeling the way she looked: slack, satisfied, and grinny. The memory of those eleven congestive heart failures in the past year at Crittenden Hall slid briefly into my mind, and slid right out again.

"You were talking about going to New York," I said. "Just you? Or you and your husband?"

"What do you think?" she said scornfully. "He'll never leave this turd-kicking town. He *likes* it here, for God's sake."

"Well..." I said, "it's his home. I understand his family have lived her for years and years."

"That's not the reason," she said darkly. "The reason he won't get out."

"Oh?" I said. "What is the reason?"

She put her two forefingers together and her two thumbs together, and made an elongated spade-shaped opening. She looked down at it, then up at me.

"Know what I mean?" she said.

"Yes," I said, "I think I know what you mean."

We were sitting across from each other in a highbacked booth. The checkered tablecloth hung almost to the floor. Millie Goodfellow squirmed around a bit, and before I knew it, she had a stockinged foot in my groin, tapping gently.

"Hi there!" she said brightly.

"Uh...hi," I said, sliding a hand below the tablecloth to grip her ankle. It wasn't passion on my part; it was fear. One sharp kick would have me singing soprano.

"Sex is keeping him in Coburn?" I asked.

She winked at me.

"You said it, I didn't," she said.

"Let me guess," I said. "Julie Thorndecker."

She winked again.

"You catch on fast," she said. "She's got him hypnotized. He's in heat for her all the time. Walks around with his tongue hanging out. And other things a lady can't mention. He can't think straight. He runs errands for her. If she told him to, he'd jump in the river. He's gone nuts. He's out there all the time. I think they're making it in the back seat of his cruiser. Hell, maybe they're making it in our place while I'm working. She'd get a charge out of that: screwing my husband in my bed."

"Are you sure, Millie?"

"Sure, I'm sure," she said roughly. "But you think I give a damn? I don't give a damn. Because you know what the funny thing is?"

"What's the funny thing?"

"He thinks he's the only one, but he's only one of many, son. She's laying everything in pants. Maybe even that bull dyke Agatha Binder. Maybe even that sissy stepson of hers, that kid Edward. I wouldn't be a bit surprised. I'm telling you, Constable Ronald H. Goodfellow is in for a rude awakening one of these days. Oh yes. And I couldn't care less. But you know what burns my ass?"

"A flame about this high?" I asked, holding my palm at table level.

She was drunk enough to think that funny.

"What burns me," she said, still giggling, "is that I've got the reputation for being the fast one. Always playing around—you know? Cheating on my husband with every drummer and trucker who comes to town. That's what people think. And she's the re-*feened* Mrs. Lah-de-dah, wife of the big scientist, the first lady of Coburn. And she's just a randy bitch. She out-fucks me three to one. But I get the reputation. Is that fair? You know what I'm going to do? I'm going to hire a private detective and get pictures of them together. You know—naked as jaybirds and banging away. Then I'm going to sue Ronnie for divorce and smear her name and the pictures all over the place."

"No, Millie," I said, "you're not going to do that."

"No," she said dully, "I won't. I can't. Because Ronnie knows about me. Names, dates, places. He's got it all in that little goddamned notebook of his. He knows about me, and I know about him. Hey!" she said brightly. "What happened to our happy little party?" Her stockinged toes beat a rapid tattoo on my cringing testicles. "Let's you and me go up to your room. You show me the New York way, and I'll show you the Coburn way."

"What's the Coburn way?"

"Standing up in a hammock."

"Hell," I said laughing, "I don't even know the New York way. Unless it's impotence. I'm going to beg off, Millie. I appreciate your kind offer, but I'm somewhat weary and I'm somewhat drunk, and I wouldn't want to disappoint you. Another time. When I'm in tip-top condition."

The toes dug deeper.

"Promise?" she breathed.

"Promise," I nodded.

I paid the tab, we collected hats and coats, and I walked her out to her Ford Pinto in the parking lot. She was feeling no pain, but she was talking lucidly and wasn't staggering or anything. I believed her when she said she could get home all right.

"As a matter of fact," she said, "I'm practically stone cold sober. I might even stop by Red Dog Betty's and see if there's any action tonight."

"Don't do that, Millie," I urged. "Go home, go to bed, and dream of me. I'll go upstairs, go to bed, and dream of you. We'll have a marvelous dream together."

"Okay," she said, "that's what we'll do. You're so sweet, I could eat you up. Come in and sit with me a minute while the car warms up."

She pulled me into the car with her, started the engine, turned on the heater. I fumbled for a cigarette, but before I knew what was happening, she was all over me like a wet sheet. Her mouth was slammed against mine, a frantic tongue was exploring my fillings.

I knew it wasn't my manly charm. It wasn't even her physical wanting. It was misery and loneliness and hurt. It was despair. And the only way she could exorcise that was to cleave to a warm bod, any bod. I just happened to be the nearest.

She pulled her mouth away.

"Hold me," she gasped. "Please. Just hold me."

I held her, and hoped it was comfort. She took my hand and thrust it under her coat, under that long, voluminous skirt. She had been truthful: all she had on beneath the shift was perfume. She pressed my palm against a long, cool thigh. She just held it there and closed her eyes.

"Sweet," she whispered. "So sweet. Isn't it sweet?"

"Yes," I said. "Millie, I've—"

"I know," she said, releasing my hand and smiling bravely, "you've got to go. Okay. You'll be in town awhile?"

"Another few days at least," I said.

"We'll get together?" she asked anxiously.

"Sure we will."

"Listen, all that stuff I said about Julie Thorndecker— I shouldn't have said all that. It's all bullshit. None of it's true. I'm just jealous, that's all. She's so beautiful."

"And young," I said, like an idiot.

"Yes," she said in a low voice. "She's young."

I kissed her cheek and got out of there. I watched her drive away. When she turned onto Main Street, I waved, but I don't think she saw me. I hoped she wasn't going to Red Dog Betty's. I hoped nothing bad would happen to her. I hoped she'd be happy. I hoped I'd wake in the morning without a hangover. I hoped I'd go to Heaven when I died.

I knew none of these things was going to happen.

I went back into the bar. I had two straight brandies, figuring they'd settle the old tum-tum, and I'd be able to sleep without pills. Something was nagging at me. A memory was nagging, and I couldn't recall, couldn't define, couldn't pin it down. It had nothing to do with the Thorndecker investigation. It was a memory revived by something that had happened in the past hour, something that had happened with Millie Goodfellow.

It was more than an hour before I grabbed it. I was up in my room, hunched over on the bed, two boots and one sock off, when it came to me. I sat there, stunned, a wilted sock dangling in my fingers. The memory stunned me. Not the memory itself, but the fact that when it happened, I was convinced it would turn my life around, and I'd never forget it. Now it took me an hour to dredge it out of the past. So much for the woes of yesteryear.

What happened was this...

About two years previously—Joan Powell and I enjoying a sharp, hard, bright, and loving relationship—I was assigned a field investigation in Gary, Indiana: not *quite* the gardenspot of America.

An assistant professor in a second-rate engineering school had submitted an application for a modest grant. His specialty was solar energy, and he had been doing independent research on methods to increase the efficiency of solar cells. They're squares of gallium arsenide that convert sunlight directly to electricity. Even the types used in the space program were horribly expensive and not all that efficient.

The professor had developed, he said, a method of electronic amplification that boosted the energy output above that of fossil fuels at half the cost. Not only did I not know what the hell his diagrams and equations meant, but Scientific Research Records, who analyzed his proposals, more or less admitted they were stumped: "The claims made herein represent a totally new and unique approach to this particular problem, and there is nothing in current research to substantiate or refute the applicant's proposals." In other words: "We just don't know."

Lifschultz Associates reported the professor was small potatoes, financially speaking. He had a mortgage, a car loan, two kids in college, and a few bucks in the bank. Small insurance, small investments, small everything. Mr. Everyman.

Donner & Stern didn't have much to add of a personal nature. The professor had been married to the same woman for twenty-six years, had those two kids, drove a five-year-old car, didn't drink, gamble, or carouse, was something of an enigma to neighbors and colleagues. He was polite, quiet, withdrawn, didn't seem to have any close friends, and apparently his only vice was playing viola in a local amateur string quartet.

I went out to Gary to see him, and it was pretty awful. He had fixed up a basement lab in his home, but it looked like a tinkerer's workshop to me. He didn't talk much, and his dumpy wife was even quieter. I remember they served me a glass of cranberry juice, and put out a plate of Milky Ways cut into little cubes.

I thought he was a loser—the whole family were losers—and I guess some of this crept into my report. Anyway, his application was denied, and he got one of our courteous goodby letters.

A few days later he tried to swallow a shotgun and blew his brains all over his basement workshop.

I don't know why it hit me so hard. The professor wasn't rejected just on the basis of my report; the special investigators had been as unenthusiastic as I was. But I couldn't get rid of the notion that his suicide was my fault; I had done him in. If I had been a little kinder, more sympathetic, more understanding, maybe he'd have gotten his ridiculously small grant, and maybe his cockamamie invention would have proved out. Maybe the guy was another Edison. We'll never know, will we?

The night after I heard of his death, I had dinner with Joan Powell. We ate at a restaurant on West 55th Street that specialized in North Italian cooking. Usually I thought the food was great. That night the pasta tasted like excelsior. Powell knew my moods better than her own, and asked me what was wrong. I told her about the suicidal professor in Gary, Indiana.

"And don't tell me it wasn't my fault," I warned her. "Don't tell me that logically I have no business blaming myself. I don't want to listen to any logic."

"I wasn't going to serve you any," she said quietly.

"It goes beyond logic," I said. "It's irrational, I know. I just feel like shit, that's all."

"*Must* you use words like that?"

"You do," I reminded her.

"Not at the dinner table," she said loftily. "There is a time and place for everything."

I poked at my food, and she stared at me.

"Todd, you're really hurting, aren't you?"

"He was such a sad schlumpf," I groaned. "A little guy. And plain. His wife was plain, too. I mean they had nothing: no wit, no personality, and they weren't even physically attractive. Do you think that affected my judgment?"

"Probably," she said.

"You're a big help."

"Do you want advice or sympathy?"

"Neither," I said. "But five minutes of silence would be nice."

"Fuck you," she said.

"*Must* you use words like that?"

"I told you, there's a time and place for everything."

"Powell, what am I going to *do?*"

"Do? You can't do anything, can you? It's done, isn't it?"

"How long am I going to feel this lousy? The rest of my life?"

"Nooo," she said wisely, "I don't think so. A week. A month maybe. It'll pass."

"The hell you say," I growled. "Let's go."

"Go? Where?"

"Anywhere. I've got to get out of here."

"All right," she said equably. "You owe me half a veal cutlet Parmesan."

"Put it on my bill," I said.

"You're running up a big tab, buster," she said. "I'm not sure you're good for it."

If I had been in a better mood, I would have enjoyed that night: late September, with balm in the air over a little nip that warned of what was coming. I don't know how long we drove—an hour maybe. No, it was longer than that. We went up to the George Washington Bridge, turned around, and drove back down to the Battery. Not what you'd call a restful, bucolic drive. But working the traffic helped keep my mind off my misery. I don't think Joan Powell and I exchanged a dozen words during that trip. But she was there beside me, silent. It helped.

After we watched a Staten Island ferry pull in and pull out—about as exciting as watching grass grow—I drove back up the east side to Powell's home. She lived in one of those enormous high-rise luxury apartment houses that have an institutional look: hospitals, office buildings, or just a forty-story file cabinet.

There were two below-ground parking levels. Powell didn't own a car—didn't drive, as a matter of fact—but after I started seeing her, dating her, spending time in her apartment, including weekends, I persuaded her to rent a parking space. It cost fifty a month, and I paid it gladly. A lot easier than trying to find parking space on the street in that neighborhood. Plus the fact that my hubcaps were relatively secure.

Our parking space was down on the second level. A little like parking in the Lincoln Tunnel. It was a scary place: pools of harsh light and puddles of black darkness. Silent cars, heavy and gleaming. Concrete pillars and oil stains. I parked, switched off the motor. We lighted cigarettes, and were very alone.

I went through it all again. The schlumpfy professor, his crazy scheme, his mousy wife. The glass of cranberry juice and cubes of cut-up Milky Ways. The amateurish home laboratory, and how I couldn't understand what the hell he was mumbling about when he showed me his equations, demonstrated his equipment, and made an electric fan run on the power of a 100-watt lightbulb shining on a chip of white, glassy stuff.

Joan Powell let me gabble. She sat apart, hugging herself against the basement chill. A cigarette burned down in her lips. Her sleek head was tilted to keep the smoke from her eyes. She didn't say a word while I spun out my litany of woe and declaimed my guilt.

I ended my soliloquy and waited for a reaction. Nothing.

"Well?" I demanded.

"You know what I think you need right now?" she said.

"What?"

"A good fuck."

"Oh my," I said. "Listen to the lady."

We put out our cigarettes, turned to stare at each other. Powell was looking at me steadily, and there was something in her fine features I had never seen before: strength and knowing and calm acceptance. Maybe we're all created equal, in the sight of God and under the law, but there is quality in people. I mean human character runs the gamut from slug to saint. I realized, maybe for the first time, that this was one superior human.

And because I was feeling so deeply it embarrassed me, I had to say something brittle and smart-alecky. But I never did get it out. I choked on the words, and just came apart. I don't apologize for it; it had been coming on since I heard of the professor's messy death. But I wasn't mourning just for him; I was crying for all the sad, little schlumpfs in the world. For all of us. The losers.

Powell was holding me in her arms then, and I was gasping and moaning and trying to tell her all those things.

"Shh," she kept saying. "Shh. Shh."

I remembered she stroked my hair, kissed my fingers, touched my lips. She held me until I stopped shivering, pulling my head down to her warm breast. She rocked a little, back and forth, like a mother holding an infant. She smelled good to me, warm and fragrant, and I nuzzled my nose down into her neckline and kissed the soft skin.

It all went so slowly. After awhile it went in silence. I had the feeling, and I think she did too, that we were alone on earth. We were locked in a car, in an underground garage, the weight of an enormous building above, the whole earth below. We were in a coffin in a cavern in a mine. I had never known such sweet solitude, closed around like that.

And I had never known such intimacy, such closeness, not even naked on a sweated sheet. Without speaking, we opened to each other. I could feel it, feel the flow between us. My anguish was diluted by her strength; I suppose she took some of my hurt into her. Sharing eased the pain. When I kissed her, it was almost like kissing myself. A strange experience, but there it was. She was me, and I was her. It was peace. That's the only way I can describe it: it was total peace.

Well...that happened two years previously. I was convinced that night was going to remake my life, that I would suddenly become saintly and good, full of kindness and understanding. I didn't change, of course. The next day I was my normal shitty self, and a week later I had forgotten all about the dead professor, and a week after that I had forgotten all about an hour of total peace in an underground garage with Joan Powell when we had done nothing but hold each other and share. If I remembered it at all, it was to wonder why we hadn't screwed.

Now, two years later, sitting in a lonely room in Coburn, N.Y., the memory of that night came back. I knew what had triggered it: those few moments alone in the car with Millie Goodfellow. I had felt the stirring of the same emotion, the feeling of closed-in intimacy, of being the only survivors in the world, everything blocked out but the two of us, comforting, consoling.

I had been deceiving myself to think I was the only comforter, the lone consoler. She had given warm assurance to me as well, and when I waved goodbye, the lights of her car fading into the black night, I was sorry to see her go. Because then I was really alone. And I was afraid.

I knew what it was. It all came back to Thorndecker. I could hear the name itself, boomed out by the Voice of Doom, with deep organ chords in the background: "Thooorn-deck-er. Thoorn-deck-er." It was like the tolling of a mournful bell. And even when I was in bed, covers pulled up, anxious for sleep to come, in my fear I heard that slow dirge and saw a dark funeral procession moving across frozen ground.

The Fourth Day

I WOKE SUDDENLY, tasting my tongue, smelling my breath. I stared at the crackled ceiling and wondered how long I had been buried in Coburn, N.Y.

I had been through that mid-case syndrome before. In any investigation, the disparate facts and observations pile up, a jumble, and you'd like nothing better than to walk away whistling, tossing a live grenade over your shoulder as you go. Then you close the door carefully and—*boom!*—all gone.

I think, in my case, the discouragement comes from a hopeless romanticism. I want people to be nice. Everyone should be sweet-tempered, polite, considerate, and brush their teeth twice a day. There should be no stale breaths and furry tongues in the world. I like happy endings.

I stared morosely at my sallow face in the mirror of the bathroom medicine cabinet, and I knew the Thorndecker investigation wasn't going to have a happy ending. It saddened me, because I didn't dislike any of the people involved. Some, like Stella Beecham and banker Art Merchant, left me indifferent. But most of the others I liked, or recognized as fallible human beings caught up in fates they could not captain.

Except Dr. Telford Gordon Thorndecker. I couldn't see him as a willy-nilly victim. The man was master of his soul; that much was obvious. But his motives were wrapped around. At that dinner party—his youthful vigor and raw exuberance. A part he was playing? And then, in his study, another role: the serious, intent man of science, with a politician's use of charm and a secret delight in the manipulation of others. Which man was Thorndecker? Or was there another, another, another? A whole deck of Thorndeckers: Jack, Queen, King, and finally...the Joker?

I showered, shaved, dressed, and had a terrible desire to telephone Joan Powell, that complete woman. Not even to talk. Just to hear her say, "Hello?" Then I'd hang up. I didn't call, of course, I just mention it here to illustrate my state of mind. I wasn't *quite* out of the tree, but I was swinging.

Sam Livingston took me down in the ramshackle elevator. We exchanged mumbles. We both seemed to be in the same surly mood. If I had given him a bright, "Good morning, Sam!" he'd have kicked me in the jewels, and if he had sung out, "Nice, sunny morning," I'd have delivered a sharp karate chop behind his left ear. So we both just mumbled. It was that kind of a morning.

I saw Millie Goodfellow behind the cigar counter, and was pleased to know she was still alive. She was in one of her biddy's costumes again: a ruffled blouse cut down to the pipik, wide black leather belt, short denim skirt with rawhide lacing down the front, like a man's fly. She was also wearing dark, dark sunglasses.

I bought another pack of cigarettes I didn't need.

"Incognito this morning, Millie?" I inquired casually.

She lifted those dark cheaters, and I saw the mouse: a beauty. She had tried to cover it with pancake makeup, but the colors came through: glistening black, purple, yellow. The whole eye was puffed and bulging.

"Nice," I said. "Did you collect that at Red Dog Betty's?"

"No," she said, replacing the glasses, "this one was home-grown. I told him what I thought about him and his fancy lady."

I really didn't want to hear it. I didn't know if she was lying. I didn't know what the truth was. And on that feckless morning, I didn't care.

"See you around," I said, and started away.

A hand shot out, grabbed my arm.

"Remember what you promised last night?" she whispered.

That was last night, in another mood, another world, and before I knew her husband got physical.

"What?" I said. "Oh. Sure."

I stared at blank glass, not seeing her eyes.

"I remember," I said with a sleazy grin, more determined than ever to get my ass back to civilization as soon as possible.

I had another of those big, bulky country breakfasts. This one involved pancakes and pork sausages. I don't know what it did for my cholesterol count, but at least it took my mind off such topics as hanging, cyanide, and a long walk off a short pier. When I returned to the city, I decided, I'd diet, join a health club, exercise regularly, manufacture a hard stomach, and put the roses back in my cheeks. Is there no end to self-delusion?

On the way out, I detoured through the bar. Jimmy was behind the taps. I nodded at him. I didn't see anyone else, until I heard a rasped, "Todd. You there." I turned, and there was old Al Coburn sitting alone in a booth. He had a beer in front of him. I walked over.

"May I join you, Mr. Coburn?" I asked.

"No law against it," he said—as gracious an invitation as I've ever had.

I slid in opposite, called to Jimmy, pointed at Coburn's beer, and held up two fingers.

While we waited for our drinks to come, I said to him,

"What's it like outside? Is the sun shining?"

"Somewhere," he said.

That seemed to take care of that. I stared at him. Have you ever seen bald land after a bad drought? Say the banks of a drained reservoir, or a parched river bed? That's the way Al Coburn's face looked. All cracks and lines, cut up like a knife had been drawn deep, the flesh without juice, squares and diamonds of dry skin.

But there was nothing juiceless about those washed-blue eyes. Looking into those was like staring into the Caribbean off one of the Bahamian cays. You stared and stared, seeing deep, deep. Moving things there, shifting shadows, sudden shapes, and then the clean, cool bottom. A few shells. Hard coral.

Maybe it was those pork sausages bubbling in my gut, but I felt uneasy. I felt there was more to Al Coburn than I had reckoned. I had misread Millie Goodfellow; there was more to her than the frustrated wife, the Emma Bovary of Coburn, N.Y. There was more to Al Coburn. If that was true, then it might be true of Agatha Binder, Art Merchant, Constable Goodfellow, Stella Beecham, Dr. Kenneth Draper—for the whole lot of them.

Maybe I was making an awful mistake. I was seeing them all (except Dr. Thorndecker) as two-dimensional cutouts. Types. Cardboard characters. But the longer I stayed around, the deeper I dug, the more they sprouted a third dimension. I was beginning to glimpse hidden motives and secret passions. It was like picking up Horatio Alger and finding William Faulkner. In *Coburn, N.Y.!?* A boggling thought, that in this brackish backwater there were characters who, if they didn't qualify for a Greek tragedy, were at least a few steps above, or deeper, than a TV sitcom.

We sipped our beers and looked vaguely at each other.

"How you coming?" Al Coburn asked in his scrawly voice.

"Coming?" I said. "On what?"

He looked at me with disgust.

"Don't play smarty with me, sonny," he said. "This

Thorndecker thing. That's what I mean."

"Oh," I said. "That. Well, I'm making progress. Talking to people. Learning things."

He grunted, finished his old beer, started on the new.

"He's doing all right, ain't he," he said. "On Coburn land. Got a nice business going."

"It appears to be prosperous," I said cautiously. "Yes. I looked it over."

"That's what you think," he said darkly.

"What's that supposed to mean, Mr. Coburn?"

"The death of a man?" he said. "The world's heart don't skip a beat."

I shook my head, bewildered. I grabbed at a straw, and came up with nothing.

"Are you talking about Petersen?" I asked.

"Who?"

"Chester K. Petersen."

"Never heard of him."

"All right," I sighed. "You've lost me completely."

We drank awhile in silence. He glowered at his glass of beer, almost snarling at it. What a cantankerous old geezer he was. I watched him, damned if I'd give him another opening. If he had something to say, let him say it. Finally:

"Was he another?" he said.

"Petersen? I don't know. Another *what?*"

"Heart attack?"

"He died of congestive heart failure."

"Who says?"

"The death certificate says."

He smiled at me. I hope I never see another smile like it. It was all store teeth and blanched lips. A skeleton could smile with more warmth than that.

"The death certificate says," he repeated. "You believe *that?*"

This isn't original with me; I remember reading somewhere that the worst American insult, absolutely the *worst*, is to say, "Do you believe everything you read in the papers?" Al Coburn's last question had the same effect. I immediately went on the defensive.

"Well, uh, of course not," I stammered. "Not necessarily."

"Tell you a story," he said. More of a statement than a question.

I nodded, waved for two more beers, and settled back. I had nothing to lose but my sanity.

"Feller I knew name of Scoggins," he started. "Ernie Scoggins. We was friends from way back. Grew up together, Ernie and me. His folks had a sawmill on the river, but that went. They had an ice house, too. That was before refrigerators, you know, and them with all that sawdust to pack it in. Cut it on Loon Lake in the winter, and cover it over with burlap and sawdust in the ice house. Ernie and me used to sneak in there in the summer and suck on slivers of ice. I guess we was two crazy kids."

I could feel my eyeballs beginning to harden, and knew I was getting a glassy stare. I wanted to yelp, "Get on with it, for God's sake!" But Al Coburn wasn't the kind of man you could hurry. He'd just shutter on me, and I'd never learn what he had on his mind. So I let him yabber.

"Bad luck," Coburn said. "Ernie sure had bad luck. His son got killed in Korea, and his two daughters just up and moved on. His wife died the same year my Martha went, and that brought us closer together, Ernie and me. Something in common—you know? Anyway, the sawmill went, and the ice house, of course. Ernie tried this and that, but nothing come out good for him. He took a lick at farming, and lost his crop in a hailstorm. Tried a hardware store, and that went bust. Put some money in a Florida land swindle, and lost that."

"Bad luck," I said sympathetically, repeating what he had said. But now he disagreed.

"Mebbe," he said. "But Ernie wasn't all that smart. I knew it, and I think sometimes he knew it. He just didn't have much above the eyebrows, Ernie didn't. Throwing his money around. But I'll tell you this: he was the best friend a man could have. Shirt off his back. Always cheerful. Could he tell a joke? Land! And a good word for everyone. Wasn't a soul in Coburn who didn't like Ernie Scoggins. Ask anyone; they'll tell you. Old Ernie Scoggins..."

He fell silent then, staring at his empty beer glass, ruminating. I took it for a hint, and signaled Jimmy for two more.

"What happened to him?" I asked Al Coburn. "Old Ernie Scoggins—is he still around?"

He didn't answer until Jimmy brought over our beers, collected the empty glasses, and went back behind the bar again.

"No, he ain't around," Coburn said in a low voice. "Not for almost a month now."

"Dead?"

He glanced at Jimmy, then leaned across the table to me.

"No one knows," he whispered. "Mebbe dead, mebbe not. He just disappeared."

"Disappeared?" I said incredulously. "You mean one fine day he just turned up missing?"

"That's right."

"Didn't anyone try to find him? His family?"

"Ernie didn't have no family," Coburn said, "rightly speaking. No one even knows where his two daughters are, if *they're* still alive. No brothers or sisters. I reckon you could say I was Ernie Scoggins' family. So after he didn't show up for a few days, I asked around. No one knew a thing."

"Did you report his disappearance to the police?"

Coburn snorted disdainfully, then took a long swallow of beer.

"To that Indian," he nodded. "Ronnie Goodfellow. The two of us went out to Ernie's place. He was living in a beat-up trailer out on Cypress Road. Goodfellow tried the door, it was open, and we went in. Everything looked all right. I mean the place wasn't broken up or anything like that. But most of Ernie's clothes was gone, including his Sunday-go-to-meeting suit, and a battered old suitcase I knew he owned. Goodfellow said it looked to him like Ernie just took off of his own free will. Just packed up and left."

"Sounds like it," I said. "Did he have any debts in town?"

"Oh hell, Ernie *always* had debts. All his life."

"Well then? He just flew the coop. Got fed up and decided to try his luck somewhere else."

Al Coburn looked at me with a twisted face. I couldn't read it. Contempt there for me, and something else: indecision, and something else. Fear maybe.

"I'll tell you," he said. "The debts wasn't all that big. And for about two years before he disappeared, Ernie Scoggins had been working for Thorndecker out in Crittenden Hall."

"Oh," I said.

"It wasn't much of a job," Coburn said. "'Maintenance personnel' was what they called it. Raking leaves, cutting down dead branches, taking care of the wife's bay gelding. Like that. But Ernie said it wasn't too hard, he was outside most of the time, you know, and the pay was good. I don't figure he ever paid a penny to Social Security in his life, and he needed that job. I can't see him just walking away from it. He wasn't any spring chicken, you know. My age."

I moved my beer glass around, making interlocking rings on the tabletop.

"What do you think happened?" I asked him. "Why did he leave?"

His answer was so faint I had to lean forward to hear his scratchy voice.

"I don't think Ernie Scoggins did leave," he said. "First of all, if he was taking off, he'd have stopped by to say so-long to me. I *know* that. Second of all, Ernie was in World War One, with the Marines. And he still had his helmet. You know, one of those pie-shaped hats with a brim. The old hunk of rusty tin was the one thing Ernie treasured. It was valuable to him. He never would have moved on without taking it with him. But when Goodfellow and I went into his place, the helmet was still there, setting on his little TV set."

"But his clothes were gone?"

"Most of them."

"And a suitcase?"

"Yes."

"And the door was open?"

He nodded.

I sat back, propped myself against the wall, put my feet up on the booth bench, sitting sideways to Coburn. I watched Jimmy polishing glasses behind the bar.

"I don't know," I said slowly. "I'll have to go along with Goodfellow. Ernie Scoggins packed some clothes and walked away. And left the door open because he wasn't coming back. He didn't take the helmet because there was no room for it in the valise. What's he going to do—wear it?"

He stared at me.

"Don't be a wisenheimer," he said.

I took a deep breath, blew it out, brought my feet down with a thump, and faced him.

"All right," I said, "you've obviously got more. What is it?"

"His car. It was still parked outside his trailer."

"So he took a bus, a train, a plane."

"He didn't," Al Coburn said. "I checked."

"*You* checked? Didn't Constable Goodfellow check?"

"Not so's you know it."

"Scoggins could have walked, or hitched a ride."

"With his car there? Gas in the tank? You believe that?"

"No," I said unhappily. "All right, let's have it: what happened to Ernie Scoggins?"

When he didn't answer, I said:

"Look, Mr. Coburn, I've listened patiently to this sad story. You apparently think it's important enough for me to know about it. So I guess it's got something to do with Thorndecker. So why are you holding back? Is that all there is to the whole thing? An old boyhood pal of yours disappeared? What's the *point?*"

"Finish your beer," he said, finishing his.

I finished my beer. He jerked a thumb, got up, hobbled toward the exit. I paid Jimmy, then hurried after Coburn.

He stumped his way through the lobby, out to the parking lot. We got in the cab of his dented Chevy pickup. I had time to note that it was a phlegmy day again, the sun hidden, an iron sky pressing down. And rawly cold.

"I think he's dead," Al Coburn said. "Ernie Scoggins. Dead and buried somewheres around here. I think they took some of his clothes and his suitcase to make it look like he just took off."

"They?" I cried. "Who's *they?"*

He wouldn't answer that.

"Besides..." he said. "Besides..."

I held my breath. I had a feeling we had finally come to it. Coburn was gripping the steering wheel with bleached knuckles, leaning forward, staring unseeingly through the splattered windshield.

"Besides," he said, "about six months or so before he disappeared, Ernie gives me something to hold for him. A letter, in an envelope. If anything happens to me, he says, you open this and read it. Otherwise you just leave it sealed. He knew he could trust me, you see."

The old man had gotten to me. It was damned cold in that pickup cab, but I could feel sweat trickling down my spine, a pressure under the sternum.

"All right, all right," I said tersely. "So something happened to him, and you opened it—right?"

He nodded.

"You read it?"

He nodded.

"Well, goddammit!" I exploded. "What the hell *was* it?"

He hunched forward a little further, still staring out that stupid windshield. I saw him in profile, saw what an ancient man he was: wattled and mottled, the jowls hanging slack, face cut and pitted deep. He looked terribly frail and vulnerable then. A strong wind might blow him away, a push crack a hip, a blow puddle the white, fragile skull showing through wisps of hair fine as corn silk.

"I haven't made up my mind," he said heavily. "Haven't decided."

"Is it a police matter?" I asked. "Should the cops know?"

"I can't," he said dully.

"Then show it to me, Mr. Coburn. Or tell me what it's all about. Maybe I can help. I think you need help."

"I've got notes at the bank," he said suddenly.

"What?" I said, bewildered by this new tack. "What are you talking about?"

"Notes," he said. "Loans with Art Merchant. He's given me one extension. I need another."

I caught on.

"And you think if you talk about what's in Ernie Scoggins' letter, you won't get your extension?"

"They'll crucify me."

"*They?*" I shouted again. "*They?* Who in God's name is *they?*"

"All of them," he said.

"Thorndecker?" I demanded.

But I couldn't get any more information out of him. All he'd say was that he had some thinking to do. The stubborn old coot! I slammed out of the cab and went back into the Inn, furious with him and furious with myself for listening to him. He didn't even thank me for the beers.

As usual, the lobby looked like the showroom of an undertaking parlor. The only thing lacking was a selection of caskets, lids open and waiting. I went over to the desk where one of the baldies was slowly turning the pages of *Hustler*, making "Tch, tch" sounds with tongue and teeth.

"I hate to interrupt your studies," I said, taking out my peevishness on him, "but I'd like to visit your local Episcopal Church. You got one?"

"Sure do," he said proudly. "First Episcopal Church of Coburn. My church. Nice place. The Reverend Peter Koukla. A marvelous preacher."

"How do I find it?"

"Easy as pie," he said happily. "East on Main Street to Cypress. Make a left, and there you are. You an Episcopalian?"

"Today I am," I said. "Thanks for the directions."

I started away.

"Mr. Todd," he said.

I turned back. He was looking somewhere over my head.

"Can I give you some advice, Mr. Todd?" he said in a low voice, in a rush.

"Sure. Everyone else does."

"I seed you with Al Coburn. You being a stranger in town and all, I got to tell you: Al Coburn is a nut. Always has been, always will be. I wouldn't pay no attention to anything he says, if I was you."

"Thank you," I said.

"A nut," he repeated. "He just shoots off his mouth. Everyone in town knows it. Senile, I guess. You know how they get."

"Sure," I said. "Thanks for the tip."

"Craperoo," he called after me. "He just talks craperoo."

I drove slowly east on Main Street, watching the rusted street signs for Cypress Road. Old Ernie Scoggins had lived on Cypress Road, I recalled. And the First Episcopal Church of Coburn was on Cypress Road. A coincidence that meant precisely nothing.

I was certain that sometime during the year, on favored days, blessed weeks, the sun shone on Coburn, N.Y. But I couldn't testify to it personally. It was now Thursday, and as far as I knew, there was a permanent shroud over the village. It seemed to have its own cloud cover. Sometimes, around the horizon, I could see a thin strip of blue sky and the sun shining on someone else. But an inverted bowl hung over Coburn. When it wasn't drizzling, it was misting, raining, snowing, sleeting. Or, as it was that day, just growly and frowning. It was only early December. What it might be like in January and February, I hated to think.

But the Episcopal Church was cheerful enough. Not a new building, but the weathered brick was warm and solid, wood trim white and freshly painted. A sign on the lawn gave the times for Sunday services, Sunday school, luncheon of the women's club, trustees' meeting, young folks' hootenanny, and so forth. Also, the subject of next Sunday's sermon: LOVE IS THE ANSWER. I wondered what the question was.

The wide front door was unlocked, and I walked into a big, pleasant nave. The most prosperous public setting I had seen in Coburn. Polished floor. Glistening pews. Well-designed altar and choir stall. Handsome organ. Everything clean and shipshape. A well-tended House of God, smelling faintly of Lemon Pledge.

I don't care how cynical you are, a church—any church—has a chastening effect. You find yourself speaking in whispers, walking on tiptoe, and trying very hard not to fart. Anyway, that's what church-going does to me. Religion is a language I don't understand, but I'm prepared to accept the fact that people communicate in it. Like Sanskrit.

I had the whole place to myself. If I knew how to fence new hymnals, I could have made a fine haul. I stepped gently up the center aisle, then heard the sound of hammering coming from somewhere. Bang, bang, bang. Pause. Bang, bang, bang. I followed the sound, through a side door, down a wide flight of iron steps. Bang, bang, bang. Louder now. There was a recreation room in the basement. Two Ping-Pong tables, and a sign on the wall: TRUST IN JESUS. Rather than a good backhand.

I walked down a cement corridor, and the banging stopped. He must have heard me coming because when I entered a small storage-workshop area, a man was facing the door with a hammer in his hand, raised.

"Beg your pardon," I said, "but I'm looking for the Reverend Peter Koukla."

"That's me," he smiled with relief, putting aside his weapon. "How may I be of service?"

"Samuel Todd," I said. "I'm here in—"

"Mr. Todd!" he cried enthusiastically, rushing forward to pump my hand. "Of course, of course! The Thorndecker grant! I heard you were in town. A pleasure. This *is* a pleasure!"

I don't know what I expected. A moth-eaten Moses, I

suppose. But this Man of God was about my own age, or maybe a few years younger. He was shorter than me, and skinny as a fencer, nervy as an actor. Black hair covered his ears. Very long. Prince Valiant. A precisely trimmed black mustache and Vandyke beard. A white T-shirt that had IT'S FUN TO BE A CHRISTIAN printed on the front. Tailored, hand-stitched jeans that must have set him back a C-note, and Gucci loafers. But he wasn't wearing earrings; I'll say that for him.

We chatted of this and that for openers. Or rather, he chatted, and I listened, grinned, and nodded like one of those crazy dogs in the rear window of a car with Georgia license plates. The Reverend Peter Koukla was sure a talker.

He mentioned Dr. Thorndecker, Agatha Binder, and Art Merchant—all in one sentence. He commented on the weather, and assured me such muck was unusual, unique; usually Coburn, N.Y. enjoyed a blazing tropical sun cooled by the trade winds. He showed me what he had been hammering on: a miniature stable that was to become part of a crèche for the church's Christmas celebration.

"Ping-Pong is all very well," he informed me gravely, "but the traditions cannot be slighted. No indeed! The golden generation is heartened by this remembrance of the rituals of their youth, and the youngsters are introduced to the most sacred rites of their church."

Beautiful. I noted he had not repeated himself, using the words celebration, traditions, rituals, and rites. Guys who deliver a sermon every Sunday can do that: the Bible on their right hand, Roget's Thesaurus on their left.

"Do you have many youngsters in your congregation, Father?" I asked, a trifle nastily. "Pardon me, I'm not up on correct usage. Do I call you Father, Pastor, Padre, Reverend—or what?"

"Oh, call me anything you like," he laughed merrily. "But don't call me late for supper!"

He looked at me, suddenly stern, and didn't relax until I laughed dutifully.

"No," he said, "frankly, we don't have too many youngsters. Simply because Coburn is not a young community. Not too many young married couples. Ergo, not too many children. That is not to say the problems of our senior citizens are not of equal importance. Oh, I *am* enjoying this talk, and the opportunity to exchange opinions."

I wasn't aware that I had voiced any opinions, but I was willing to go along with him. He dusted off a shop stool, and made me sit down. He took a little leap and ended up sitting on his workbench, his legs dangling. I was bemused to note that he was wearing no socks inside those Gucci loafers. Very *in*. In Antibes and Southampton. A little uncomfortable, I guessed, in Coburn, N.Y., in early December.

"It's a challenge," he was saying. "The average age of our population increases every year. More and more of those over sixty-five. Can we ignore them? Discard them? Cut them off from the mainstream of American thought and culture? I say no! What do you think?"

"Very interesting," I said. "Your ideas. Refreshing."

"Refreshing," he repeated. "I like that. No, please, don't light a cigarette. We voted last year to ban the smoking of cigarettes, cigars, and pipes on church grounds. Sorry."

"My fault," I said, putting the pack back in my pocket. "It'll do me good to go without."

"Of course it will," he caroled, throwing back his head and shouting at Heaven. "Of course, of course!"

I don't know . . . maybe he was just high on God. If he had been a theatrical agent, I would have suspected cocaine, and if he had been an advertising copywriter, I would have suspected grass. But this guy was high on ideas. Loony ideas, possibly, but they were enough to keep him floating.

At the moment, the Reverend Peter Koukla was expounding on how the steady increase in the median age of the American population would affect national political attitudes. I was getting woozy with his machine-gun delivery: spouted words accompanied by a fine spray of saliva.

"Very interesting," I broke in. "A challenging concept. But I really came to talk to you about Dr. Thorndecker."

"Of course, of course!" he yelped, and changed gears in mid-course without a pause.

What followed were the same panegyrics I had heard from Ronnie Goodfellow, Agatha Binder, Art Merchant: that is, Dr. Telford Gordon Thorndecker was a prince of princes, one of God's noblemen. They were spreading it on thickly. Didn't the man have any warts? Koukla obviously didn't think so; he told me the doctor was a "great friend" of the church, lent his name and time to special activities, and made frequent and sizable contributions.

"I only mention this," the Reverend added, "to give credit where credit is due. The man is much too modest to tell you himself. I really don't know what we'd do without him."

"Attends services regularly, does he?"

"Frequently," Koukla said—which, I reflected, is a little different from "regularly."

"His wife and son, also?"

"They are members, yes."

"But not his daughter?"

"Ah...no. She has her own religious preferences, I understand. Somewhat more fundamental than our teachings."

"Is Draper one of your members? Dr. Kenneth Draper?"

"He was," Koukla said shortly. "I have not seen him at services recently. But we do get many staff members from the Hall and the research laboratory."

All his answers were bright, swift, delivered with every appearance of openness and honesty. It was hard to fault this perky little man. I went at him from another direction...

"Nurse Beecham told me that occasionally you are

called to Crittenden Hall to provide spiritual comfort for some of the patients?"

"When they request it, yes. I had a discussion with Dr. Thorndecker about the possibility of providing a regular Sunday afternoon service, after my duties here are completed. But so many of the guests are bedridden, it probably wouldn't be a satisfactory arrangement. I do conduct a service in the Hall on Christmas and Easter, however."

"Reverend, I was surprised to learn that Crittenden has its own cemetery. When a patient dies, isn't the body usually claimed by his family? I mean, isn't he returned to his home for burial?"

"Usually," he said, "but not always. Sometimes the family of the deceased prefer burial on the Crittenden grounds. It's very convenient. Sometimes the deceased request it in their wills."

"Do you ever, ah, officiate at these burials?"

"Of course, of course! Several times. Sometimes the final service is held here at the church, and the casket returned to Crittenden for interment."

I nodded, wondering how far I might go without having my interest reported back to Dr. Thorndecker. The hell with it, I decided. Let Koukla report it. It just might stir things up. So I asked my question:

"Didn't attend the burial of a man named Petersen, did you? Chester K. Petersen?"

"Petersen?" he said. "No, I don't think so. When did he pass?"

"Two nights ago."

"Oh, no," he said, "definitely not. My last funeral service for a Crittenden guest was about a month ago. But if the deceased was of another faith—Catholic, perhaps, or Jewish—naturally I wouldn't be..."

His sentence trailed off, in the approved Coburn manner. He had started his last speech with a confident rush, then slowed, slowed, until his final words were a doubtful drawl. I could almost see him begin to wonder if he wasn't talking too much, revealing something (in all innocence) that the church's "great friend" wouldn't want revealed.

I rose quickly to my feet, before he got the notion of asking what the death of Chester K. Petersen had to do with the Thorndecker grant.

"Thank you very much, sir," I said briskly, holding out my hand. "You've been very cooperative, and I appreciate it."

He hopped spryly off the workbench, and clasped my proffered hand in both of his.

"Of course, of course!" he said. "Happy to oblige. If you're still in town on Sunday morning, it would give me great pleasure to welcome you to our Sabbath services. I believe and preach the religion of joy. I think you'll find it invigorating."

"I might do just that," I nodded. "Well, I'm sure you're anxious to get back to your carpentry. Don't bother showing me out; I can find my way. Thanks again for your trouble."

"No trouble, no trouble!" he shouted, and waved a farewell.

I walked noisily down the cement corridor, then tramped heavily up the iron steps. At the top, I opened and slammed shut the side door leading to the church nave. But I remained inside, on the stairway landing, standing, listening, wondering if the hammering would commence again. It didn't. But I figured it wouldn't. I had seen the telephone in the Reverend Peter Koukla's workshop.

I went slowly down those iron steps again, moving as quietly as I could. I didn't have to go far along the cement corridor before I heard him speaking:

"This is Reverend Koukla," he was saying. "Could I talk to Dr. Thorndecker, please?"

I slipped silently away, and went out the side entrance into the church nave, easing the door shut behind me. I didn't have to listen to the rest of Koukla's conversation. I knew what he was going to say.

Walked out to my car, lighted a cigarette, took three fast, greedy drags. Nasty habit, smoking. So is drinking. So is burying dead men at two in the morning.

I felt I was running one of those Victorian garden mazes, my movements all false starts and retracings. The box hedges walled me around, higher than my head, and all I could do was wander, trying to find the center where I might be rewarded with a candy apple, or the hand of a princess and half the kingdom. I told you I was a closet romantic.

I was floundering and thinking crazy; I knew it. All I had was a hatful of suspicions, and there wasn't one of them I couldn't demolish with a reasonable, acceptable, *legal* explanation. I tried to convince myself that my mistrust was all smoke, and the smart thing for me to do was to stamp Thorndecker's application A-OK, and say, "Goom-by" to Coburn, N.Y.

So why did I sit in my car shivering, and not only from the cold? The hand holding the cigarette trembled. I had never felt so hollow in my life. It was a presentiment of being in over my head, up against something I couldn't handle, wrestling with a force I couldn't define and was powerless to stop.

I started the car and drove along Cypress Road, away from the business section. I left the heater off and cranked the window down a few inches, hoping the cutting air might blow through my skull and take the jimjams along with it. I drove slowly until the houses became fewer and fewer. Then I was in a section of scrabby wooded plots and open fields that looked like they had been shaved a week ago.

I drove past a sign that read: NEW FRONTIER TRAILER COURT, and kept on going. Then I braked hard, backed up, and read the smaller print: "Trailer parking by day, week, or month. All conveniences. Reasonable rates." In Coburn, N.Y., they still called it a "trailer court." The rest of the country called them "mobile home communities."

But it was on Cypress Road, and Al Coburn had said his old buddy, Ernie Scoggins, had lived in a trailer on

Cypress Road. So I followed the bent tin arrow nailed to a pine stump, and rattled and jounced down a rutted dirt road to a clearing where maybe twenty trailers, camper vans, and mobile homes were drawn up in a rough circle. Maybe they were expecting an attack by Mohawks on the New Frontier.

I parked, got out of the car, looked around. God, it was sad. There wasn't a soul to be seen, and under that mean sky the place looked crumbling and abandoned. Maybe the Mohawks really had come through, scalped all the men, carried off the women and kids. Fantasy time. There were overflowing garbage cans, and lights on in some of the vans. People lived there; no doubt about it. Although "lived" might be an exaggeration. It looked like the kind of place where, if all the TV sets konked out simultaneously, they'd go for each other's throats. Nothing else to do.

I wandered around and finally found a mobile home that had a MANAGER sign spiked into the hard-scrabble front yard. There was another sign over the door with two painted dice showing seven, and the legend: PAIR-O-DICE. Those dice should have shown crap.

The steps were rough planks laid across piled bricks; they swayed when I stepped cautiously up. I knocked on the door. From inside I could hear the sound of gunfire, horses' hooves, wild screams. If it wasn't a TV western, I was going to skedaddle the hell out of there.

I knocked again. The guy who answered the door looked familiar. I had never met him, but I knew him. You'd have known him, too. Soiled undershirt showing a sagging beer belly. Dirty chinos. Unlaced work shoes over gray wool socks. A fat head with a cigar sprouting from the middle. An open can of a local brew in his hand. He wasn't happy about being dragged away from the boob tube. It was filling the room behind him with flickering, blue-tinted light, and the gunfire sounded like thunder.

"Yeah?" he said, glowering at me.

"Who is it, Morty?" a woman shrieked from inside the room.

152

"You shut your mouth," he screamed, not bothering to turn his head, so for a moment I thought he was yelling at me.

"I understand there's a trailer out here for sale," I began my scam, "and I was—"

"What?" he roared. "Iola, will you turn that god-damned thing down? I can't hear what the man is saying."

We waited. The gunfire was reduced to a grumble.

"Now," he said, "you want a place to park? We got all modern conveniences. You can hitch up to—"

"No, no," I said hastily. "I understand there's a trailer out here for sale."

His piggy eyes got smaller, if possible, and he removed the sodden cigar from his mouth with an audible *plop!*

"Who told you that?" Morty demanded.

"Fellow I met in the bar at the Coburn Inn. Name of Al Coburn. He says a friend of his, name of Ernie Scoggins, lived out here. That right?"

"Well . . . yeah," he said mistrustfully. "He did."

"I understand this Scoggins took off, and his rig's up for sale."

He rubbed his chin with the back of his beer-can hand. I could hear the rasp of the stubble.

"I don't know about that," he said. "I ain't even sure he owned the thing. He's got debts all over town. He took off owing me a month's rent. I'm holding the rig and his car until I get mine."

"Maybe we can work something out," I said. "The bank's holding the title. Al Merchant's willing to work a deal if I decide to buy. All I want to do is take a look at the thing."

"Well . . ."He couldn't decide. "What the hell you want Scoggins' pisspot for? It ain't worth a damn."

"Just for summer," I said hurriedly. "You know— holidays and weekends in the good weather. I figure it would be cheaper than buying a cottage."

"Oh, hell," he said heavily, "it'd be cheaper than buying an outhouse. Well . . . it's your money. It's that gray job over there. The one with the beat-up VW parked alongside. Take a look if you want to; the door ain't locked."

"Thank you very much," I said, turned carefully on those rickety steps, started down.

"Hey, listen," he called after me, "if you decide to buy, I got to get that month's rent he owes me."

"Off the top," I promised him, and he seemed satisfied. He went back in, slammed the door, and in a few seconds I heard the thunder of gunfire again.

I took a look at the VW first. Either Scoggins had been a lousy driver, or he had bought it fourth-hand after it had endured a series of horrendous accidents. You could see the geography of its history: dents, scars, scrapes, nicks, cuts, patches of several-colored paints, rust spots, places where bare metal showed through. All the hubcaps were missing. The front trunk lid was wired shut to the bumper with a twisted coat hanger.

I looked through one of the dirty windows. Nothing to see but torn upholstery, rags on the floor, some greasy road maps, and a heap of empty Copenhagen snuff tins. I would have liked to unbend that coat hanger and take a look in the trunk, but I was afraid Morty might be watching me from one of his windows.

Scoggins' trailer was exactly that: a trailer, not a mobile home. It was an old, *old* model, a box on wheels, narrow enough and light enough to be towed by a passenger car on turnpikes, highways, or secondary roads. It was a plywood job, with one side door and two windows that were broken and covered with tacked shirt cardboards.

It had been propped up on cement blocks; the wheels were missing. A tank of propane was still connected, and a wire led to an electrical outlet in a pipe that poked above the ground at every parking space. There was a hose hookup to another underground pipe, for water.

There were no stairs; it was a long step up from ground to doorway. The door was not only unlocked, it was ajar an inch or so. I pushed it open, stepped up and in. A cold, damp, musty odor: unwashed linen and mouldering furniture. There was a wall switch (bare, no plate), and when I flicked it, what I got was a single 60-watt bulb hanging limply from the center of the room.

And it was really one room. There was a small alcove with waist-high refrigerator, small sink, a grill over propane gas ring, plywood cupboard. No toilet or shower. I hoped the New Frontier offered public facilities. The bed folded up against the wall. Mercifully, it was up. Judging by the rest of the interior, I really didn't want to see that bed. One upholstered armchair, torn and molting. A twelve-inch, portable TV set on a rusted tubular stand. A varnished maple table with two straight-back kitchen chairs. An open closet with a few scraps of clothing hanging from wall hooks. A scarred dresser with drawer knobs missing.

That was about all. The World War I helmet was still where Al Coburn had said it was, atop the TV set. There were some unwashed dishes in the sink, clotted and crusted. Brownish water dripped from the tap. The plywood floor squeaked underfoot. The only decoration was last year's calendar from Mike's Service Station, showing a stumpy blonde in a pink bikini. She was standing on a beach, one knee coyly bent, with palm trees in the background. She had an unbelievable mouthful of teeth, and was holding a beachball over her head.

"A little chilly in here, honey?" I asked her.

Compared to that place, my room at the Coburn Inn was the Taj Mahal. I looked around, trying to imagine what it was like for old Ernie Scoggins—wife dead, son dead, daughters moved away—to do a hard day's work at Crittenden Hall, and then to lump home to this burrow in his falling-apart VW. Take off his shoes, fry a hamburger, open a beer. Collapse into the sprung armchair in front of the little black-and-white screen. Drink his beer, munch his hamburger, and watch people sing and dance and laugh.

I tried to imagine all that, but it didn't work. It was like trying to imagine what war was like if you had never been there.

I went through the Grand Rapids dresser but found nothing of interest. A pair of torn longjohns, some gray, unpressed handkerchiefs, a blue workshirt, wool socks that needed toes, junk. I figured Constable Goodfellow or Al Coburn had taken the old man's papers away, if there were any. I found nothing.

I poked around in the cabinet over the sink. All I found were a few cockroaches who stared at me, annoyed at being interrupted. One interesting thing: there was an eight-ounce jar of instant coffee, practically new, with no more than one or two teaspoonsful taken out. The jar still bore the supermarket pricetag: $5.45. Odd that a poor old man would take off for parts unknown and leave that treasure behind.

I didn't unlatch the bed, let it down, and paw through it. I just couldn't.

So that was that, I figured. Nothing plus nothing equals nothing. I stood in the doorway, my finger on the light switch, taking a final look around. My God, that must have been a cold place to live. There was a small electric heater set into one wall, and I suppose he used the propane stove for added warmth, but still...The chill came right up through that bare, sagging plywood floor and stiffened my toes inside my boots.

Maybe the trailer had been carpeted when it was new. But now the only piece of rug was under the old man's armchair. It was about a three-foot square, with ravelled edges. It looked like a remnant someone had thrown out, a piece left over after a cheap wall-to-wall carpeting job had been completed.

I stared at it, wondering why I was staring. Just a ragged piece of rug in a shit-brown color. It was under the armchair and stuck out in front where his feet would rest when he gummed his hamburger and watched TV. Keep his tootsies relatively warm while he stared at young, handsome people winning Cadillacs and trips to Bermuda on the game shows.

It made sense; that's why the rug was there. So far so good. But why wasn't the rug scarred and scuffed and stained in front of the armchair, where his feet rested and he dribbled food while guffawing at the funny, funny Master of Ceremonies? It wasn't scarred or scuffed or stained. It looked new.

I took my finger off the light switch. I went back to the armchair, got down on my knees, peered underneath. The portion of the rug *under* the chair was scarred and scuffed and stained.

"Shit," I said aloud.

I stood, lifted the armchair, set it aside. He could have turned the rug, I acknowledged. Shortly before he departed, he noticed the rug under his feet was getting worn and spotted. So he just turned it around. Then the worn part would be under the chair, and he'd have a nice, new, thick pile under his feet in front of the chair.

Except... Except...

There were special stains on the portion of the rug that had been under the armchair. I got down on my knees again, put my nose right down to them. They didn't look like food stains to me. They were reddish-brown, crusted. There were several heavy blobs with crowns of smaller stains radiating around them. Like the heavy blobs had fallen from a distance and splashed.

I smelled the stains. It wasn't a scientific test, I admit, but it was good enough for me. I knew what those stains were. They weren't Aunt Millie's Spaghetti Sauce.

I replaced the armchair in its original position, switched off the light, got out of there. I didn't look toward the manager's mobile home. I slid into the Grand Prix, jazzed it, spun away.

They didn't have much time: that's what I was thinking as I drove back to the Coburn Inn. They were in a hurry, frantic, afraid of being seen by Manager Morty or some other denizen of the New Frontier Trailer Court. So they

did what they had come to do. And then they got him out
of there—what was left of him—with some clothes
thrown hastily into his old suitcase, trying to make it look
like he had scampered of his own free will. And because
the blood was ripe and thick and glistening in front of the
armchair, they had turned the rug around so the stains
would be hidden under the chair.

Time! Time! They were working so fast, so anxiously.
Maybe even desperately. They just wanted him snuffed
and out of there. What about his car? Maybe it was one
killer, and he couldn't handle the VW and the car he came
in. Maybe it was two killers, and one couldn't drive. Fuck
the car. And fuck the helmet; they didn't know it was his
most prized possession. And they didn't have time to
search the place and find that almost-full jar of coffee.
They didn't have time, they didn't plan it well, they
weren't thinking. Amateurs.

I went at it over and over again. The final thought as I
pulled into the parking lot of the Coburn Inn: they
couldn't have known that he had written a letter, or they
would have tossed the place to find it. And Al Coburn had
said, "...the place wasn't broken up, or anything like
that."

I felt so goddamned smug with my brilliant ratiocina-
tion. My depression was gone. I walked into the lobby
humming a merry tune. I should have been droning a
dirge. I was so wrong, so *wrong!*

But at the moment I was in an euphoric mood,
bouncing and admiring the way the overhead fluorescent
lights gleamed off the nude pate of the guy behind the
desk. *Another* baldy!

"Oh, Mr. Todd," he called in a lilting, chirpy voice, and
held up one manicured finger.

In my new humor, I was willing to accommodate; I
walked over for my message.

"The Reverend Koukla has called you *twice,*" he
breathed, in hushed and humble tones. "Such a *fine* man.
Could you call him at once, *please?*"

"I'm going in for lunch," I said. "I'll call him as soon as I'm finished."

"Please, *please*," he said. "It sounded so *urgent*. You can talk to him right here on the desk phone. I'll put it through for you."

"Okay," I said, shrugging, "if it's so important."

"I'm not supposed to let people use the desk phone for personal calls," he whispered. "But it's the *Reverend Koukla!*"

"Have you caught his walking-on-the-water act?" I asked him. "A smash."

But he was already inside the office, where the switchboard was located, and I don't think he heard me.

Koukla came on immediately.

"Mr. Todd," he said briskly, "I owe you an apology."

"Oh?"

"Yes indeedy!" he said, then went on with a rush: "I'm afraid I was not as hospitable as I should have been to a visitor to Coburn, a stranger in our midst. As a matter of fact, I'm having some people in this evening for good talk and a buffet supper. No occasion; very informal. Just a friendly get-together. The Thorndeckers will be here, and Art Merchant, Agatha Binder, others you've met, and people who would like to meet *you*. Could you possibly join us? About sixish? For refreshments and talk and then a cold supper later? It should be fun."

That had to be the most quickly arranged buffet supper in the annals of Coburn's social life. I figured Dr. Thorndecker had put the Reverend up to it, and sometime during the evening I'd get a casual explanation of what happened to Chester K. Petersen.

"Sounds good to me," I said. "Thank you for the invitation. I'll be there."

"Good, good, good," he gurgled, making it sound like, "Googoogoo." "I'm in the Victorian monstrosity just west of the church. You can't miss it; the porch light will be on."

"See you at six," I said, and hung up.

I went into the bar a little subdued, a little thoughtful. It seemed to me Thorndecker was over-reacting. If there was nothing fishy about Petersen's death and burial, he didn't have to do a thing until I inquired, and then he could set me straight. If it was a juggle, then he had to go on the con, preferably in an atmosphere of good cheer, of bonhomie. That's the way I figured he figured it, and I resented it. They were taking me for an idiot.

The bar was full, and the restaurant was crowded: all seats taken. I gave up, came back to the lobby, and asked Sam Livingston if he could get me a club sandwich and a bottle of Heineken, and bring it up to my room. He said it might take half an hour, and I said no problem. He went immediately to the kitchen, and I tramped up the stairs to Room 3-F.

Skinned off damp hat, damp trenchcoat, damp boots. Lighted another cigarette. Stood in my stockinged feet at the window, staring down at Main Street but not seeing it. Thinking. I wish I could tell you my thoughts came in a neat, logical order. They didn't; I was all over the place. Something like this:

1. Maybe they tried to take Scoggins's car, but it was locked.

2. Why didn't they roll up the blood-stained rug and take it with them? I could brainstorm a lot of reasons for that. Maybe Al Coburn and other friends had seen that cheap scrap of carpet many times, and would wonder at its absence. Maybe it was just easier and faster to turn the carpet front to back. They figured no one would notice, and no one did. Not investigating officer Constable Ronnie Goodfellow, not best friend Al Coburn.

3. Why was I using the mysterious pronoun "they," when I had become so furious when Al Coburn used it?

4. Those debts of Al Coburn at the bank ... Was he afraid of Art Merchant? Or was it Thorndecker, working through Merchant?

5. How could Nurse Beecham tell me Petersen died of cancer when the death certificate, signed by Dr. Draper,

listed congestive heart failure as cause of death? Was one of them innocent, and one of them lying? Or were they both in on it, and just got their signals crossed?

6. What color were Julie Thorndecker's eyes?

At this point Sam Livingston knocked and came in with my club sandwich and Heineken. I signed, slipped Livingston a buck, and locked the door behind him. I went back to my station at the window, chomping ravenously at a quarter-wedge of sandwich and swilling the beer. The rambling went on...

7. If Al Coburn was right, and Ernie Scoggins was "buried somewheres around here," where would be the logical place to put him under? Easy answer: in the Crittenden cemetery. Who'd go digging there?

8. Something's going on in that lab that's not quite kosher, and Scoggins tumbled to it.

9. Just what in hell was in that letter Scoggins left with Al Coburn? It couldn't be a vague accusation; it had to be hard evidence of some kind if it had that effect on Coburn. A photograph? Something lifted from the Crittenden Research Laboratory? A photocopy of someone else's letter? A microfilm? What?

10. Was Julie Thorndecker really making it with her stepson?

11. How was I going to get out of my promise to Millie Goodfellow?

12. Who killed Cock Robin?

I had finished the beer and sandwich, and was licking mayonnaise off my fingers, when the phone rang. I wiped my hands on the back of an armchair slipcover and picked up the handset.

"Todd," I said.

"Nate Stern," the voice said.

"Nate. Good to hear from you. How're the wife, kids, grandchildren?"

"Fine," he said. "You?"

Nate Stern, a man of few words, was boss of Donner & Stern. Lou Donner had been shot dead by a bank officer who had been dipping in the till. Lou made the mistake of trying to get back some of the loot before turning the guy over to the blues.

"I'm surviving, Nate," I said.

"Switchboard?" he asked.

"Yes," I said, beginning to talk just like him.

"That sample . . ."

"Yes?"

"Olympia Standard, about five years old."

"Thanks."

"Any help?"

"Not much. Be talking."

"Sure."

We both rang off.

In case you forgot, we were talking about that anonymous note: "Thorndecker kills." I had tried to get a look at the typewriters out at Crittenden. I hadn't seen any in the nursing home. The two I saw in the research lab were both IBM electrics. So? So nothing.

There was a telephone call of my own I had to make. I admitted that maybe I had been putting it off because I was afraid it might cause pain to the people I had to talk to. But I couldn't postpone it any longer. It couldn't go through the hotel switchboard, where the desk baldy might be listening in, nodding, and busily taking notes.

So I pulled on damp boots, damp trenchcoat, damp hat again. I crossed Main Street to Samson's Drugs, and crowded myself into an old wooden phone booth. I made a person-to-person call, collect, to Mr. Stacy Besant at the Bingham Foundation in New York City. I knew he'd be in; he never went out to lunch. He always brought a peanut butter sandwich from home in a Mark Cross attaché case.

"Samuel," he said, "how are matters progressing?"

"Slowly," I said, "but surely."

Something in my voice must have alerted him.

"Problems?" he asked.

Problems! The man asked if I had problems! I was *selling* problems.

"Some," I said, "yes, sir."

I heard a long, sniffing wheeze, and figured he had jammed that inhaler up his nose again.

"Anything we can do at this end?"

"Yes, Mr. Besant," I said. "I have a few questions. You said the first Mrs. Thorndecker was your niece. Was she older than Thorndecker?"

There was a silence a moment. Then, quietly:

"Does that have a bearing on your investigation?"

"Yes, sir, it does."

"I see. Well, the first Mrs. Thorndecker, Betty, was approximately ten years older than her husband."

It was my turn to say, "I see." I thought a moment, then asked Besant: "Thorndecker inherited a great deal. Could you tell me the source of the first Mrs. Thorndecker's wealth?"

"Old money," he said. "Pharmaceuticals. That's how Thorndecker met Betty. He was running a research project for her company."

"That takes care of that. Could you tell me a little more about the circumstances of her death?"

Again I heard the sniffing wheeze.

"Well..." he said finally, "Betty had a drinking problem, and—"

"Pardon the interruption, sir," I said, "but did she have the problem before she married Thorndecker, or did it develop afterward."

Silence.

"Sir," I said. "Are you there?"

"I'm here," he said in a low voice. "I had never considered that aspect before, and I am attempting to search my memory."

"Take your time, Mr. Besant," I said cheerily.

"Do not be insolent, Samuel," he said sharply. "I am not as senile as you sometimes seem to think. I would say that prior to her marriage, Betty was an active social drinker. Her marriage appears to me now to have exacerbated her problem."

"She became an alcoholic?"

The old man sighed. "Yes. She did."

"And exactly how did she die?"

"It was summer. The family went to the Cape. She had the habit, Betty did, when she was, ah, in her cups, so to speak, to take midnight swims. Or in the early hours of the morning."

"Cold sea at the Cape. Even during the day."

"Oh yes," the old man mourned. "Everyone warned her. Husband, daughter, son—everyone. But they couldn't lock her up, could they? When possible, someone went with her. No matter what the hour. But she would sneak away, go off by herself."

"Asking for it?"

"What?"

"Was she courting death, sir? Seeking it? Did she want to die?"

Silence again. Then a heavy sigh.

"Samuel," he said, "you are a very *old* young man. The thought had never occurred to me. But perhaps you're right, perhaps she was courting death. In any event, it came. One morning she wasn't there when the household awoke. Her body was found in the surf."

"Uh," I said, "any signs of—you know?"

"Just minor bruises and scrapes. Things to be expected in such a death. No unusual wounds, no abnormalities. Salt water in the lungs."

"Was she a good swimmer?"

"An excellent swimmer. When sober."

"How about Thorndecker?" I asked. "A good swimmer?"

"Samuel, Samuel," he groaned. "I have no idea. *Must* you be so suspicious?"

"Yes, sir," I said, "I must. Any evidence of his having something on the side? You know—mistress? Girlfriend? Anything like that?"

He cleared his throat.

"No," he said.

"You're sure?"

"As a matter of fact," he said, and I could almost see that tortoise head ducking defensively, "I made a few discreet inquiries of my own."

"Oh-ho," I said. "And he was pure?"

"Absolutely."

"Where was he the night his wife died? Home in bed?"

"No," he said. "At a medical conference in Boston. He had departed that evening. His presence in Boston that night was verified."

"Oh," I said, deflated. "I guess he *was* pure. Unless..."

"Unless what, Samuel?"

"Nothing, sir. You're right; I *am* very suspicious. I was just imagining a way he could have jiggered it."

The old man shocked me.

"I know," he said. "A drug in her bottle. He had easy access to drugs."

I sucked in my breath.

"You're right again, sir," I said. "I do tend to underestimate you, and I apologize for it. Were the contents of her bottle analyzed?"

"Oh yes," he said. "Everything was done properly; I saw to that. The contents were just gin; no foreign substances. But, of course, by the time the body was found, the authorities called, and the investigation started, Thorndecker had been summoned back to the Cape from Boston."

"What you're saying is that he could have switched bottles, or replaced the contents?"

"There is that remote possibility, yes."

"Do you think he did?"

The silence lasted a long time. It was finally ended by another deep sniff, then another: a two-nostril job.

"I would not care to venture an opinion," Mr. Stacy Besant said gravely.

"All right," I said. "It's a moot point anyway. Barring a confession, we'll never know, will we?"

"No," he said, "we never will."

"One final question, sir. I'm puzzled by the dates and

ages involved. Particularly the ten-year difference between Mary and Edward, Thorndecker's two children. A little unusual, isn't it?"

"A simple explanation," he said. "Betty was a widow when Thorndecker married her. Mary is her daughter by her first husband. Edward is the son of Betty and Telford Thorndecker. So Mary and Edward are really half-brother and half-sister."

"Thank you, sir," I said. "That explains a great deal."

"Does it?" he said surprised.

"Mr. Besant," I said, "I wonder if you'd be kind enough to switch me to Mrs. Cynthia, if she's available."

"Of course," he said. "At once. Hang on."

I'll say this for the old boy: he wouldn't dream of asking why I wanted to talk to the boss-lady of the Bingham Foundation. If she wanted him to know about her conversation with me, she'd tell him.

He had my call switched, and in a few seconds I was talking to Mrs. Cynthia. We exchanged news about the states of our health (good), and the weather (miserable), and then I said:

"Ma'am, just before I came up here, I met you in the corridor, and you mentioned you had known Dr. Thorndecker's father."

"Yes," she said, "so I did."

"You also said he was a sweet man—those are your words, ma'am—and then you added, 'It was all so sad.' What did you mean by that?"

"Samuel," she said, "I wish I had your memory."

"Mrs. Cynthia," I said, "I wish I had your brains and beauty."

She laughed.

"You scamp," she said. "If I was only fifty years younger..."

"If I was only fifty years older," I said.

"You will be, soon enough. Yes, I knew Dr. Thorndecker's father. Gerald Thorndecker. Gerry. I knew him quite well."

She didn't add to that, and I didn't pry any deeper. The

statement just lay there, given and accepted.

"And what was so sad, Mrs. Cynthia?"

"The manner of his death," she said. "Gerald Thorndecker was killed in a hunting accident. Shocking."

"A hunting accident?" I repeated. "Where was this?"

"In Maine. Up near the border."

"How old was his son at the time?"

"Telford? Thirteen perhaps. Fourteen. Around there."

"Thank you," I said, ready to say goodby.

"He was with him when it happened."

It took me a second to comprehend that sentence.

"The son?" I asked. "Telford Thorndecker? He was there when his father was killed in a hunting accident?"

"That is correct," she said crisply.

"Do you recall the details, Mrs. Cynthia?"

"Of course I recall the details," she said sharply. "I'm not likely to forget them. They had flushed a buck, and—"

"They?" I said. "Gerald Thorndecker and his son?"

"Samuel," she said, sighing, "either you let me tell this story in my own, old woman's way, or I shall ring off this instant."

"Sorry, ma'am," I said humbly. "I promise not to interrupt again."

"The hunting party consisted of Gerald Thorndecker, his young son Telford, and four friends and neighbors. Six in all. They flushed a buck, spread out on a line, and pressed forward. Later, at the coroner's inquest, it was stated that Gerald Thorndecker walked faster than the rest of them. Trotting, moving out ahead of them. I believe it. He was that kind of man. Eager. In any event, the others were behind him. They heard a crashing in the brush, saw what they thought was the buck doubling back, and they fired. They killed Gerald. Now you may ask your questions."

"Thank you," I said, without irony. "How many of the hunters fired at Gerald?"

"Three, I believe."

"Including the son, Telford?"

"Yes."

"Were ballistics tests made?"

"Yes. He had been hit twice."

"Including a bullet from his son's rifle?"

"Yes. And another."

I should have known. You think that in any investigation, criminal or otherwise, you get the facts, put them together, and the whole thing opens up like one of those crazy Chinese lumps you drop in water and a gorgeous blossom unfolds? Not so. Because you rarely deal with facts. You deal with half-facts, or quarter-, eighth-, or sixteenth-facts. Little bitty things that you can't prove or disprove. Nothing is ever sure or complete.

"All right," I said to Mrs. Cynthia, "Gerald Thorndecker was killed by two bullets, one fired by his son. What about the mother?"

"Her name was Grace. She died of breast cancer when Telford was just a child. I think he was three. Or four. His father raised him."

"Money?"

"Not much," she said regretfully. "Gerald was foolish that way. He squandered. He had a standard of living and was determined to maintain it. He inherited a good income, but it goes fast when nothing new is coming in."

"What did he do? Did he have a job or profession?"

"Gerald Thorndecker," she said severely, "was a poet."

"A poet? Oh my God. I can understand why the money went. Was he published?"

"Privately. By himself." Then she added softly, "I still have his books."

"Was he any good?" I asked.

"No," she said. "His genius was for living."

"Telford was an only child."

"How did you know?"

"He *looks* like an only child. He *acts* like an only child. Mrs. Cynthia, just let me recap a moment to see if I've got this straight. Dr. Thorndecker is an only child. His mother dies when he's three or four. He's brought up by his father, a failed poet rapidly squandering his inheritance. The father is killed accidently when the boy is thirteen."

"Or fourteen," she said.

"Or fourteen," I agreed. "Around there. Now, what happened to the boy? Who took him in?"

"An aunt. His father's sister."

"She put him through medical school?"

"Oh no," Mrs. Cynthia said. "She was poor as a church mouse. Telford never would have made it without his father's insurance. That's all he had. The insurance saw him through medical school and his post-graduate work."

"Wow," I said.

"Wow?" she said.

"He wanted to be a doctor all along?" I asked.

"Oh yes. For as long as I can remember. Since he was just a little boy."

"Mrs. Cynthia, I thank you," I said. "Sorry to take up so much of your time."

"That's quite all right, Samuel," she said. "I hope what I've told you may be of some help in your inquiry. If you see Dr. Thorndecker, please give him my love. He may remember me."

"How could he forget you?" I said gallantly.

She made a humphing sound, but I knew she was pleased. She really was a grand old dame, and I loved her and didn't want to hurt her. Which is why I didn't make a snide comment about the extraordinary coincidence of two violent deaths in the life of Dr. Telford Thorndecker, both of which he might possibly have caused, and from both of which he had profited handsomely. But maybe it wasn't an extraordinary coincidence; maybe it was just a plain coincidence, and I was seeing contrivance where only accident existed.

I walked slowly back to the Inn. One good thing about Coburn: you didn't have to look about fearfully for traffic when you crossed the street.

Stacy Besant and Mrs. Cynthia had given me a lot to think about. Now I knew much more; my plate was full. A full plate, hell; my platter was overflowing. The investigation was slowly becoming two: the history, character, personality, and ambitions of Dr. Telford Gordon Thorndecker; and the strange events that had taken place in and around Crittenden during the past month. That the two would eventually come together, merge, and make some kind of goofy sense, I had no doubt. But meanwhile I didn't know what the hell to do next.

What I did was to go back across Main Street to Sandy's Liquors and Fine Wines. I bought a fifth of a twelve-year-old Scotch. It came all gussied up in a flashy box. Carrying that in a brown paper sack, I returned to the Coburn Inn. I looked around for Sam Livingston, but he was nowhere to be seen. The lobby was enjoying its early afternoon siesta. Even Millie Goodfellow was somnolent, filing slowly at her talons behind the cigar counter.

I walked down the stairway into the basement, pushed through a fire door, and wandered along a cement corridor lined with steam and water pipes. I found a door with a neat sign that read: SAMUEL LIVINGSTON. PLEASE KNOCK BEFORE ENTERING. I knocked, but I didn't enter; I waited.

He came to the door wearing his usual shiny, black alpaca jacket and little skullcap. He also had on half-glasses and was carrying a closed paperback novel, a forefinger marking his place. I took the bottle of Scotch from the sack and thrust it at him.

"Greeks bearing gifts," I said. "Beware."

His basalt face warmed in a slow smile.

"For me?" he said. "Now I take that kindly of you. Come in, get comfy, and we'll sample a taste of this fine sippin' whiskey."

He had a snug little place down there. One low-ceilinged room with kitchenette, and a small bathroom. Everything neat as a pin. A sleeping sofa, two overstuffed armchairs, a table with ice cream parlor chairs. A chest of drawers. No TV set, but a big bookcase of paperbacks. I took a quick look. Barbara Cartland. Frank Yerby. Daphne du Maurier. Elsie Lee. Like that. Romantic novels. Gothics. Edwardians. Regencies. Women with long, glittering, low-cut gowns. Men with mustaches, wearing open, ruffled shirts and carrying swords. Castles in dark mountains with one light burning in a high window. Well...what the hell; I read H. Rider Haggard.

He had me sit in one of the soft armchairs, and he brought us each a small glass of the Scotch.

"We don't want to hurt this with water," he said.

"Straight is fine," I agreed.

He lowered himself slowly into the other armchair, lifted his glass to me, then took a small sip. His eyes closed.

"Yes," he breathed. "Oh my yes." He opened his eyes, passed the glass back and forth under his nose, inhaling with pleasure. "How you finding Coburn, Sam? Slow and quiet enough for you?"

"You'd think so," I said, "judging from the surface. But I'm getting the feeling that underneath, things might be faster and noisier."

"Could be," he said noncommittally. "I hear you been doing some digging?"

"Just talking to people," I said. "I figured you might be able to help me."

"How might I do that?"

"Well, you've lived here a long time, haven't you?"

"Thirty years," he said. "And I figure to live out the rest of it right here. So you, being a smart man, won't expect me to bad-mouth any of the people I got to live with."

"Of course not," I said. "It's just that I've picked up some conflicting opinions, and I thought you could straighten me out."

He stared at me over the rim of his glass. It was a dried apple of a face: lines and creases and a crinkly network of wrinkles. Black and gleaming. The teeth were big and yellow. His ears stuck out like flags, and his eyes had seen everything.

"Tell you what," he said. "Supposin' you asks your questions. If I want to answer, I will. If I don't, I won't. If I don't know, I'll tell you so."

"Fair enough," I said. "My first question is about Al Coburn. You know him?"

"Sure, I know him. Everyone in town knows Al Coburn. His people *started* this place."

"You think he's a nut?"

He showed me that keyboard of teeth.

"Mr. Coburn?" he said. "A nut? Nah. Sly as a fox, that man. Good brain on him."

"Okay," I said. "That was my take, too. Art Merchant?"

"The banker man? He's just a banker. What do you expect?"

"You think that newspaper, the *Sentinel*, is making money?"

He took a sip of his drink, then looked at me reflectively.

"Just," he said.

"You think they've got loans from the bank?"

"Now how would I know a thing like that?"

"Sam," I said, "I got the feeling that there's not much going on in Coburn that you don't know about."

"Agatha Binder could have some notes at the bank," he acknowledged. "Most business folks in Coburn do."

"You know the Thorndeckers?"

"I've seen them," he said cautiously.

"To speak to?"

"Only Miz Mary. We're friends."

"Constable Goodfellow? You know him?"

"Oh sure."

I threw my curve.

"Anything between him and Dr. Thorndecker's wife?"

The curtain came down.

"I wouldn't know," he said.

"Ever hear any gossip about what's going on at the Crittenden Research Laboratory?"

"I never believe in gossip."

"But you listen to it?"

"Some."

"Ever hear about a man named Petersen? Chester K. Petersen?"

"Petersen? Can't say that I have."

"Scoggins? Ernie Scoggins?"

"Oh my yes, I knew Ernie Scoggins. He sat right where you're sitting many's a time. Stop by here to chew the fat. Bring me a jug sometimes. Sometimes he was broke, and I'd make him a little something to eat. Nice, cheerful man. Always joking."

"They say he just took off," I said.

"So they say," he nodded.

"Do you think he did?" I asked him.

He thought a long moment. Finally...

"I don't know what happened to Ernie Scoggins," he said.

"What do you *think* happened?"

"I just don't know."

"When was the last time you saw him?"

"Couple of days before he disappeared."

"He came here?"

"That's right."

"When? What time of day?"

"In the evening. When he got off work."

"Anything unusual about him?"

"Like what?"

"What was his mood? Was he in a good mood?"

"Yeah, he was in a good mood. Said he was going to get some money pretty soon, and him and me would go up to Albany and have a steak dinner and see the sights."

"Did you tell Constable Goodfellow this?"

"No."

"Why not?"

"He didn't ask."

"Did Scoggins tell you how much money he'd be getting?"

"No."

"But could you guess from what he said how much it'd be? A lot of money?"

"Anything over a five-dollar bill would be a lot of money to Ernie Scoggins."

"Did he tell you where the money would be coming from?"

"No, and I didn't ask."

"Could you make a guess where it was coming from?"

"I just don't know."

I went along like that, with his "I don't know's" getting more frequent. I couldn't blame him. As he said, he had to survive in Coburn; I was going home one blessed day. I knew he wouldn't reveal the town's secrets—until thumbscrews come back in fashion.

I ran out of questions, and accepted another small Scotch. Then we just sat there sipping, talking of this and that. I discovered he had a deadpan sense of humor so subtle, so hidden, that you could easily miss it if you weren't watching for it. For instance:

"Are you a church-going man?" I asked him.

"I certainly am," he said. "Every Saturday—that's my afternoon off here—I sweep and dust the Episcopalian Church."

Said with no smile, no lifted eyebrow, no irony, no bitterness. Apparently just an ingenuous statement of fact. Ingenuous, my ass! This gaffer was *deep*. He was laughing, or weeping, far down inside himself. If you caught it, fine. If it went over your head, that was also fine. He didn't give a damn.

But he could say profound things, too.

"What do you think of Millie Goodfellow?" I inquired.

He said: "She's lonely with too many men."

I asked him if he was the only black in town. He said no, there were two families, a total of nine men, women, and children. The men farmed, the women worked as domestics, the kids went to a good school.

"They doin' all right," Sam Livingston said. "I don't mess with them much."

"Why is that?"

"I don't mess with *anyone* much."

"No family of your own, Sam?"

"No," he said. "They all gone."

Whether that meant they were dead or had deserted Coburn, I didn't know, and didn't ask.

"Sam," I said, "you say you and Mary Thorndecker are

friends. How is that? I mean, does she visit you here? What opportunity do you have to talk to her?"

"Oh..." he said vaguely. "Here and there."

I stared at him, remembering what Agatha Binder had said about Mary Thorndecker going to an evangelist church about five miles south of Coburn. A fundamentalist church. The Reverend Peter Koukla had said something similar.

"Your church?" I asked Livingston. "You and Mary Thorndecker go to the same church? A born-again place about five miles south of here?"

The glaze came down over his ocherous eyes again.

"Sam," he said, "you do get around."

"I'd like to visit that church," I said. "How do I get there?"

"Like you said: five miles south. Take the river route, then make a left. You'll see the signs."

"You drive there?"

"No," he said, "I don't drive. Miz Mary, she stops by for me."

"When are services?" I asked. "Sunday?"

"Sunday, and every other night in the week. Every night at eight."

"I think I'll go," I said. "Good minister?"

"Puts on a good show," he said, grinning. "A joy to hear."

The Scotch was making me drowsy. I thanked him for his hospitality, and stood up to leave. He thanked me for the whiskey, and offered to take me up in the elevator. It came down into the basement, alongside his little apartment, and he could hear the bell from inside his room. I told him I'd walk up, the exercise would do me good.

I started down the cement corridor. He was still standing at his open door. A small, wizened figure, a frail antique. I had walked perhaps five steps when he called my name. I stopped, turned around. He didn't say anything more.

"What is it, Sam?" I asked him.

175

"It's worse than you think," he said, moved inside his room, and closed the door.

I stood there, surrounded by cement and iron, trying to decipher: "It's worse than you think." What did he mean by that? Coburn? The Thorndecker investigation? Or maybe life itself?

I just didn't know.

Not then I didn't.

I trudged slowly up the stairway to Room 3-F. I was pondering the sad fate of Ernie Scoggins. Thought he was coming into some money, did he? The hopeful slob. As Al Coburn had said, he just didn't have much above the eyebrows. After what Sam Livingston had told me, this was the scenario I put together:

Scoggins had seen something or heard something. Or both. Probably on his job at Crittenden Hall. If Constable Ronnie and Julie Thorndecker really did have the hots for each other, maybe Scoggins walked in on them while they were rubbing the bacon. Somewhere. In the woods. In the stall of that big bay gelding. In the back seat of Goodfellow's cruiser. Anywhere.

So Scoggins, having watched plenty of *Kojak, Baretta,* and *Police Woman,* thinks he knows just how to profit from this unexpected opportunity, the poor sod. He tries a little cut-rate blackmail (which in Coburn, N.Y., would be on the order of $9.95). If they don't pay up, Scoggins threatens to report their hanky-panky to Dr. Thorndecker. Who knows—maybe he's got some hard evidence: a tape recording, photograph, love letter—something like that.

But the lovers, realizing like all blackmail victims that the first demand is just a down payment, decided that Ernie Scoggins had to be scrubbed. I figured Goodfellow did it himself, driving his cruiser; he had the balls for it. And the Constable working alone would explain why Scoggins's car hadn't been taken away, and why Goodfellow had said nothing about the blood-stained rug when he "investigated" Scoggins's disappearance. It

would also explain what was in that letter left with Al
Coburn: the hard evidence of Julie and Ronnie putting
horns on the head of the august Dr. Telford Gordon
Thorndecker—photograph, love letter, tape recording,
whatever.

That scenario sounded good to me. I could buy it.

And tomorrow, I reflected sourly, I would solve the
riddle of Chester K. Petersen's death and burial, on
Saturday I would discover what was meant by that note:
"Thorndecker kills," and on Sunday I would rest.

Ordinarily I keep a case notebook during an
investigation, filling it with observations, bits of dialogue,
suggestions for further inquiries. The notebook is a big
help when it comes time to write my final report.

But after the tossing of my room at the Coburn Inn, I
hadn't put anything on paper. I kept it all in my pointy
little head. It was a mess up there. Nothing seemed neat.

I couldn't get a handle on what the hell was going on.
Or even know positively that anything *was* going on.

I sprawled on the hard bed, boots off, hands clasped
behind my head. I tried to find a thread, an element, a
theme that might pull it all together. I had been
flummoxed like this on other investigations, and had
devised a trick that sometimes worked for me.

What I did was try my damnedest to stop *thinking*
about the case. I mean, try to ignore who did what, who
said what, and the things I had seen, done, guessed. Just
wash the whole shmear out of my consciousness and leave
myself open to emotions, sensations, instincts. It was an
attempt to get down to a very primitive level. Reasoning
was out; *feeling* was in.

When I tried to determine what I felt about the
Thorndecker inquiry, what my subjective reactions were,
I came up with an odd one: I suddenly realized how much
this case was dominated by the conflicts of youth and age,
the problems of senescence, the puzzles of natural and
perverse death.

Start with the Thorndecker application. That was for a

grant to investigate and, hopefully, isolate and manipulate the X Factor in mammalian cells that causes aging and the end of life.

Add a nursing home with a high death rate: normal for institutions that provided care of the terminally ill.

Add a middle-aged doctor married to a very young wife who, possibly, was finding her jollies elsewhere with, amongst others, a macho Indian cop and, maybe, a stepson younger than she.

Add a bedraggled covey of old, old men: Scoggins, Petersen, Al Coburn. Even Sam Livingston.

Add a staff of very young, whiz-kid researchers who might be long on talent and short on ethics.

Add a village that was a necropolis of fractured dreams. A village that seemed to be stumbling toward oblivion, that was not merely old but obsolete, showing its toothless mouth and sounding its creaks.

All these were notes in a player piano roll: holes punched in thin paper. And the discordant melody I heard was all about age, the enigma of age. I could understand Thorndecker's passion to solve it. Compared to what he hoped to do, a walk on the moon was a stroll to the corner drugstore. I mean the man wanted it *all*.

One other factor crept into my merry-go-round brain... Maybe *I* was obsessed with youth and age, their mysteries and collisions. I had rejected Joan Powell for what I imagined was a good and logical reason: the difference in our years. But was that really a rational reaction, or had I demonstrated an inherited response I was not even aware of? Something in my cells, or genes, that forced me to discard that good woman? Something to do with the preservation of my species?

I didn't, I decided, understand *anything*. All I knew was that right then, I wanted her, needed her. Loved her? Who said that?

I spent the late afternoon that way: stewing. It had been a yo-yo day: I was up, I was down, I was up, I was down. When it came time to shower and dress, preparing for the Reverend Peter Koukla's "friendly get-together," I had resolved to put in a token appearance, split as quickly as I reasonably could, and return to the sanctuary of Room 3-F with a jug of comfort provided by Sandy's Liquors and Fine Wines.

So much for high hopes and good intentions...

Koukla had been right; his place was easy to find. Not only was the porch light on, but the front door was open and there were guests standing outside, drinks in hand, even though it was a sharp night. Cars were parked in Koukla's driveway, and on both sides of the street. I took my place at the tail end of the line, about a block away, left coat and hat in my locked car, walked back to the party.

If he had organized that bash on short notice, the Reverend had done one hell of a job. I reckoned there were forty or fifty people milling about, drinking up a storm. But after I plunged into the throng, shaking hands and grinning like an idiot, I saw that most of the guests were researchers from the lab and off-duty staff from Crittenden Hall. In other words, Thorndecker had called out the troops.

Most of them were in civvies, but a few were wearing white trousers and short white jackets, as if they had just rushed over from nursing home or laboratory. I didn't see Mary Thorndecker, but the rest of the clan was there. And Agatha Binder, Art Merchant, Dr. Kenneth Draper, and Ronnie Goodfellow, self-conscious in his uniform. There were others whose names I had forgotten but whose faces were vaguely familiar: the "best people" Goodfellow had introduced on my first morning in Coburn.

There was a punch bowl, and white wine was available. No hard booze. But the kids out on the porch were puffing away like mad, and even inside the house the smell of grass was sweet and thick. Include me out. I had tried pot twice, with Joan Powell, and each time, at the crucial moment, I fell asleep. I'd rather have a hangover.

It was all genial enough, everyone talking, laughing, mixing. No one leaned on me, and Koukla didn't try to introduce me to everyone; just left me free to roam. I met some of the kid researchers and listened to their patter.

The fact that I couldn't understand their sentences didn't bother me so much as the fact that I couldn't understand their *words*. I had a hazy notion of what "endocrinology" meant, but when they moved down the dictionary to "endocytosis," they lost me.

"Do you understand what they're talking about?" I asked Julie Thorndecker.

"Not me," she said, rewarding me with a throaty chuckle. "I leave all that to my husband. I prefer words of one syllable."

"Me, too," I said. "Four-letter words." Then, when she froze, I added, "Like 'love' and 'kiss'." I laughed heartily, signifying it was all a big yock, and after awhile her lips smiled.

"Enjoying your stay in Coburn, Mr. Todd?" she asked me.

"Not really. Quiet place. Lonely place."

"My, my," she said mockingly. She put a hand on my arm again. She seemed to have a need to touch. "We'll have to do something about that."

She was wearing a pantsuit of black velvet. Stud earrings of small diamonds. The gold-link ankle bracelet. She looked smashing. But she could have made a grease monkey's coveralls look chic.

In that crush, in the jabber of voices around us, it would have been possible to say the most outrageous things—make an assignation: "You do this to me, and I'll do that to you."—and no one would have heard. But actually we talked inconsequentialities: her horse, my car, her home, my job. All innocent enough.

Except that as we said nothing memorable, we were jammed up against each other by the mob. I could feel her heat. She made no effort to pull away. And while we yakked, our eyes were locked—and it was like being goosed with an icicle: painful, shivery, pleasurable, frightening, mind-blowing. The look in her eyes wasn't flirty or seductive; it was elemental, primeval. It was raw sex, stripped of subterfuge. No game-player she. My scenario sounded better to me; I could understand how a man could kill for such a woman.

"There you are!" Dr. Thorndecker said, slipping an arm about his wife's shoulders. "Entertaining our guest, are you? Splendid! Suppose we get a cup of that excellent punch?"

We worked our way over to the punch bowl. In the process, Julie Thorndecker moved away. If a signal had passed between the doctor and her, I hadn't caught it.

"A lot of your people here tonight," I mentioned, sampling a plastic cup of the punch and setting it carefully aside.

Later, thinking about it, I had only admiration for the way he used that offhand comment to lead into exactly what *he* wanted to say. I think if I had offered, "The price of soybeans in China is going up," he could have done the same thing. The man was masterful.

"Oh yes," he said, looking around, suddenly serious. "We should plan more social activities like this. These people work very hard; they not only deserve a break, they *need* it. It's not the happiest place to work. I refer to the nursing home, of course, not the lab."

"I can imagine," I murmured, pouring myself a paper cup of the white wine. That was a *little* better.

"Can you?" he said. "I'm not sure anyone not intimately associated with such an institution can even guess the emotional stress involved. We try to remain objective, to refrain from becoming personally involved. But it's impossible. We *do* become involved, intimately involved. Even with those we know have only a week, a month, a year to live. Some of them are such marvelous human beings."

"Of course," I said. "Maybe, when they accept their fate, know their days are numbered, maybe then they become superior human beings. More understanding. Kinder."

"You think so?" he asked. His dark eyes came down from the ceiling to focus on me. "Maybe. Although I'm not certain any of us is capable of believing in our own mortality. One effect I have noted, though: the closer to death our patients grow, the more exaggerated their eccentricities become. That's odd, isn't it? A man who might have sung aloud occasionally, just sung for his own amusement with no one else present, begins to sing constantly as death approaches. A vain woman becomes vainer, spending all her waking hours making-up and doing her hair. Whatever weakness or whim they might have, intensifies as death approaches."

"Yes," I agreed, "that *is* odd."

"For instance..." he said, almost dreamily.

No, not dreamily. But he was away from me, disconnected from his surroundings, off someplace I couldn't reach. It was not just that he was lying; I knew he was. But, while lying, he had retreated deep within himself, to a secret dream. I was seeing another facet of this many-sided man. Now there was almost a stillness in him, a certainty. His stare turned inward, and he seemed to be listening to his own falsehoods, with approval. He was so *sure*, so sure that what he was doing was right, that the splendid end justified any sordid means.

"He came to us a few years ago," he said, speaking in a steady voice, but so low that I had to bend close to hear him in that hubbub. Finally, he was almost whispering in my ear. "A man named Petersen. Chester K. Petersen. Pelvic cancer. Terminal. Inoperable. I talked to his personal physician. Petersen had always been a solitary. Almost a recluse. A wealthy man, unmarried, who had let his family ties dwindle. And as his illness worsened, his craving for solitude intensified. Meals were left outside his door. He refused to submit to medical examinations. He seemed anxious to end all human contact. It was as I told you: in the last stages, the eccentricity becomes a dreadful obsession. We've seen it—all of us who serve in this field—happen again and again."

I knew it was a fairy tale, beautifully spun, but I had to hear it out. The man had me locked. I could not resist his certitude.

But in spite of my fascination with what he was saying, I have to tell you this: I was observing him. What I mean is that I was two people. I was a witness, spellbound by his resonant voice and intriguing story. I don't deny it. But at the same time I was an investigator, searching. What I was looking for was evidence of what I had seen in our previous meetings: the weariness that concluded the first, those racking spasms of pain I had noted during our second interview.

On that night, at that moment, I saw no indication of either: no weariness, no pain.

What I did see were preternaturally bright eyes, that secretive expression, and movements, gestures, that were slowed and glazed. It hit me: this man was drugged. Somehow. On something. He was so drawled out, so spaced and deliberate. He was functioning; no doubt about that. And functioning efficiently. But he was gone. That's the only way I can express it: he was gone. Off somewhere. Maybe he was dulling the weariness, the pain. I just didn't know.

"What became of him?" I asked. "This Petersen?"

"He left a will," Thorndecker said, smiling faintly. "Quite legal. Drawn by a local attorney. Signed and witnessed. In the event of his death, he desired to be buried late at night, or in the early morning hours. Between midnight and dawn. The wording of the will was quite specific. He was to be buried in the Crittenden cemetery. No religious service, no mourners, no funeral. With as little fuss as possible. He just didn't want the world to note his passing."

"Weird," I said.

"Wasn't it?" he nodded.

"And you respected his wishes?"

"Of course."

"He died of cancer?"

"Well..." Thorndecker said, pulling gently at the lobe of one ear, "the immediate cause of death was congestive heart failure. But, of course, it was the cancer that brought it on."

He looked at me narrowly, tilting his head to one side. He had me, and I knew it. Try to fight that diagnosis and that death certificate in a court of law, and see how far you'd get.

He must have glimpsed confusion and surrender in my eyes, for he suddenly slapped me on the shoulder.

"Good Heavens!" he cried. "Enough of this morbidity! Let's enjoy this evening. Now I'll leave you to your own devices, and let you meet and talk with some of these fine young people. I'm happy you could attend the Reverend Koukla's party, Mr. Todd."

I put a hand on his arm to stop him.

"Before you go," I said, "I must tell you. Mrs. Cynthia Bingham asked me to give you her regards. Her love."

The change in him was startling. He froze. His face congealed. Suddenly he was looking back, remembering. He was alone in that crowded room.

"Cynthia Bingham," he repeated. I couldn't hear him, but I saw his lips move.

His features became so suddenly tragic that I thought he might burst out weeping.

"Can we ever escape the past, Mr. Todd?" he asked me.

I mean he really *asked* me. It wasn't a rhetorical question. He was confounded, and wanted an answer.

"No, sir," I told him. "I don't think we can."

He nodded sadly.

He disappeared into the crowd. What a great performance that had been. A bravura! The man had missed his calling; he should have been an actor, playing only Hamlet. Or Lear. He left me stunned, shaken, and almost convinced.

"Mr. Todd," Dr. Kenneth Draper said, with his nervous smile, "enjoying the party?"

"Beginning to," I said, pouring myself another cup of white wine. "I haven't seen Mary Thorndecker this evening. Is she around?"

"Ah, regretfully no," he said, wiping a palm across a forehead that as far as I could see was completely dry. "I understand she had a previous engagement."

"Lovely young woman," I said. "And talented. I liked her paintings."

He came alive.

"Oh yes!" he said. "She does beautiful things. Beautiful! And she's such a help to us."

"A help?"

"In Crittenden Hall. She visits our guests, talks to them for hours, brings them flowers. Things of that sort. She's very people-oriented."

"People-oriented'," I repeated, nodding solemnly. "Well, I guess that's better than being horse-oriented."

He didn't pick up on that at all, so I let it slide.

"By the way," he said, looking about, searching for someone, "Dr. Thorndecker asked us to prepare a report for you. A precis of the research that's been done to date on aging and its relationship to human cells."

"Yes, he said he'd get something together for me."

"Well, we've completed it. Mostly photocopies of papers and some original things we've been doing in the lab. Are you familiar with the term *in vitro?*"

"Means 'In glass,' doesn't it?"

"Specifically, yes. Generally, it means under laboratory conditions. That is, in test tubes, dishes, flasks— whatever. In an artificial environment. As opposed to *in vivo*, which means in the body, in living tissue."

"I understand."

"Most of the papers you'll receive report on experiments with mammalian cells *in vitro.*"

"But you have experimented on living tissue, haven't you?" I said. "I saw your animals."

Also, at that moment, I saw the sudden sweat on his forehead.

"Of course," he said. "Rats, guinea pigs, chimps, dogs. It's all there. My assistant has the package for you. Linda Cunningham. She's around here somewhere."

He looked about wildly.

"I'll bump into her," I soothed him. "And if we don't get together, you can always drop the package off at the Coburn Inn."

"I suppose so," he said doubtfully, "but Dr. Thorndecker was most explicit about getting it to you tonight."

185

I nodded, and wandered away. Geniuses might be great guys: fun to read about, fun to know. But I'm not sure I'd care to work for one.

"*So* glad you could make it, Mr. Todd," the Reverend Peter Koukla said, clasping my hand in both of his. "You have a drink? Good. It's a *nice* white wine, isn't it?"

"Very nice."

"Excuse me, please. I must see to the chow."

I hadn't heard food called "chow" since Boy Scout camp. Unless, I reflected idly, Koukla was referring to his dog—the kind with a black tongue.

I worked my way across the room to where Agatha Binder and Nurse Stella Beecham were standing stolidly, close together, backs against the wall. They looked like a bas relief in mahogany.

"Ladies," I greeted them.

"Watch your language, buster," Agatha Binder said, grinning. "So you made it, did you? Well, what would a party be without a guest of honor?"

"Is that what I am?" I asked, smiling with all my boyish charm at Nurse Beecham.

If looks could kill, I'd have been bundling with Chester K. Petersen.

"Mr. Todd!" Art Merchant caroled, twitching. "Nice to see you again. How is your investigation progressing?"

"Leaps and bounds," I said, turning to him. "Tell me something, Mr. Merchant . . . Do you ever lend money on trailers?"

"Trailers?"

"Mobile homes."

"Oh," he said. "Well . . . it depends."

"Thank you," I said.

I moved away. I'm tall enough to see over heads. I saw Dr. Telford Thorndecker crowding his wife into a corner. He was all over her, not caring. His hands were on her shoulders, arms, stroking her hip, touching her hair. Once he put a finger to her lips. Once he leaned down to kiss her ear. Another role: Dr. Telford Thorndecker, sex fiend.

"They seem very happy," I said to Constable Ronnie

Goodfellow, who was watching the same scene. "Not drinking? Oh...on duty, are you?"

"Yes," he said, staring at the Thorndeckers. "Just stopped in to say hello."

"Something I've been meaning to ask you," I said. "You're not the only cop in town, are you?"

He turned those black eyes to look at me. Finally...

"Of course not," he said. "We've got the county sheriff's deputies and the state troopers."

"No," I said, "I mean here in Coburn. Are you the only constable?"

"No, sir," he said. "Four constables. I work mostly nights."

"Who's top man?"

"Chief Constable? That's Anson Merchant."

"Merchant?" I said. "Related to Art Merchant, the banker?"

"Yes," Ronnie Goodfellow said shortly, turning his eyes back to the Thorndeckers loving it up in the corner. "The chief is the mayor's brother."

"Are you Mr. Todd?" she asked breathlessly.

A plump, little butterball. A Kewpie doll. She was holding out a sealed manila envelope.

"And you must be Linda Cunningham," I said. "Dr. Draper's assistant."

"Right on!" she cried, slapping the envelope into my hand. "And here's your report. Now you tell Kenneth you got it, y'hear? He was so *nervous!*"

"I'll tell him," I promised. "But what if I have questions about it? Who do I contact?"

"Me," she said, giggling. "My name, address, and phone number are on the report."

"Super," I said, getting high on her breath. "You may be hearing from me."

"Super," she said, still giggling.

I folded the heavy envelope lengthwise and jammed it into my jacket pocket. I was prepared to talk nonsense to her a little longer, just to hear her giggle, but a long drink of water in a lab coat dragged her away. I looked around the crowded room. Most of the guests were straggling into the dining room where I could see a table laid with cold meats, potato salad, dishes of this and that. I saw Thorndecker talking to the Reverend Koukla. I turned back to Constable Goodfellow, but he was gone.

"Hello, Mr. Todd," Edward Thorndecker said in his half-lisp. "Going to get something to eat?"

"Soon," I said. "How are you, Edward?"

"Okay, sir," he said politely. "I wanted to get Julie a plate. Have you seen her?"

"Not recently." I said.

"She's around here somewhere," he said fretfully, his beautiful eyes anxious. "I saw her, and then she just disappeared."

"You'll find her," I said.

He moved away without replying. I watched the mob at the buffet, and decided I wasn't all that hungry. I wandered out onto the porch to smoke a cigarette. The tobacco kind. But a flock of chattering guests came after me, juggling filled paper plates and plastic cups of coffee. I didn't want noisy company; I wanted quiet, solitude, and the chance to sort things out.

I stepped down from the porch. Cigarette in my lips, hands jammed into pockets, shoulders hunched against the cold, I sauntered slowly down the deserted street.

What happened next was a scene from an Italian movie: as wildly improbable.

There were street lights on both corners: orange globes with dim and flickering halos. But mid-block, sidewalks and street were shadowed, black as sin and not half as inviting. I was moving toward my parked Grand Prix. Across the street I could see, dimly, the official cruiser of Constable Ronnie Goodfellow. In 1976, it had been painted in a gaudy Bicentennial design. Now the bold stars were faded, the brave stripes mud-encrusted and indistinct.

It seemed to me, as I glanced at the cruiser, that slender white arms were beckoning me from the back seat. I spat out my cigarette, ground it out quickly. I slipped farther back into the gloom, behind a tree. I waited until my eyes became accustomed to the dark. I peered cautiously around. I saw...

Not slender white arms, but bare feet, ankles, calves. The window frame cut off the legs at mid-thigh. A woman's legs, waving in the air as languidly as a butterfly's wings. A slave bracelet glinted about one ankle. I watched without shame. I could make out a man's shirted back bent between those stroking legs. The image, in that somber light, had the eerie and stirring quality of a remembered dream.

I glanced back toward Koukla's house. I saw the lights, the guests on the porch. I heard faintly the tinkle of talk and laughter. But the two in the car were oblivious to everything but their own need. The broad back rose and fell, faster and faster. The slender white legs stretched and flexed in response.

I caught something in peripheral vision: the brief flare of a lighted match. I turned slowly...

I was not the only silent stalker, the only bemused witness. Halfway between me and the lighted Koukla home, Dr. Telford Gordon Thorndecker stood back from the sidewalk, observing the scene in the cruiser, quiet and contemplative while his wife was being done. There was no mistaking his massive frame, his leonine head. He smoked his cigarette with care and deliberation. Nothing in his manner or posture showed anger or defeat. Resignation, possibly.

Then I moved, as silently and stealthily as I could. I slid down the row of trees to my car. I unlocked the door, pulled it quietly shut behind me. I started the engine, but didn't turn on the lights. I backed up to the corner, so I wouldn't have to pass that busy official cruiser of the Coburn constabulary.

On my way back to the Inn, I did not reflect on Thorndecker's hurt or on the lovers' scorn. All I could think was that if they had dared it, in such a place, at such a time, then they knew he was aware. And his knowledge had no significance for them. They just didn't care.

And if he knew, and they didn't care, then why was Ernie Scoggins snuffed? My beautiful scenario evaporated.

It was not until I had parked in the lot of the Coburn Inn, and was stumbling across Main Street to Sandy's Liquors and Fine Wines, that the squalidness of the scene I had just witnessed bludgeoned me. I saw again that calm, silent husband watching his wife getting it off with a man half his age. I saw again the frantically pounding back, the jerking, naked legs.

Did he love her that much? Did they both love her that much?

I wanted to weep. For their misery and doomed hopes. For the splintered dreams of all of us.

I had no desire for food, wasn't sure I ever wanted to eat again. But I did want to numb my dread. I drank warm vodka from a bathroom glass caked with Pepsodent around the rim.

I sat in one of the gimpy armchairs, pulled a spindle lamp close. I began going through the report Linda Cunningham had delivered. I think I mentioned that I've had no formal education or training in science, so most of the research papers meant little to me. But I could grasp, hazily, the conclusions.

They weren't very startling, because I had read much the same in the preliminary investigation of Dr. Thorndecker's work by Scientific Research Records for the Bingham Foundation. It had been found that normal human body cells reproduced (doubled) a finite number of times *in vitro*. There seemed to be a significant correlation between the number of doublings and the age of the donor.

When normal human embryo cells were nurtured and reproduced *in vitro*, about fifty doublings could be expected. As donor age increased, the number of doublings decreased. The normal cultured cells did not die, exactly, but after each doubling became less differentiated and simpler, until they bore little resemblance to the original normal cells.

All this argued forcibly, as Dr. Thorndecker had said,

for a "cellular clock," an X Factor that determined how long a normal human cell remained viable. When I read the reports on reproduction *in vitro* of normal mammalian cells other than human, the same apparently held true. So, obviously, each species had a built-in lifespan that was reflected in the lifespan of each body cell of which it was composed. When the cells completed their allotted number of doublings and died, the organism died.

"I'll drink to that," I said aloud, and took another hefty belt of Pepsodent-flavored vodka.

One thing bothered me here. It concerned a paper on original research done by the Crittenden lab on the morphology of normal chimpanzee body cells. The conclusions were consistent with the research on normal body cells of other species.

But there was nothing in the report concerning the testing of an experimental cancer drug on chimps. Yet I had seen that young, comatose specimen in the basement of the Crittenden Research Laboratory. He had been a mass of putrescent, cancerous tumors, and Dr. Draper had stated that the animal had been deliberately infected, then treated, and the experimental drug had failed.

There was nothing of this in the report I received. But after thinking about it awhile, I could understand why it might not be mentioned. The lab was undoubtedly engaged in several research projects. One of them might be the development of drugs efficacious against sarcomas and carcinomas. But information on this project was not included in the report prepared for me simply because it was extraneous. It had nothing to do with Dr. Thorndecker's application for funds to investigate the cause of aging. It had nothing to do with my inquiry.

That made sense, I told myself.

Finally, the report tossed aside, vodka in the bottle getting down to the panic level, I closed my eyes, stretched out my legs, and tried to determine exactly what it was in that report that was nagging at me. There was a question I wanted answered, and for the life of me I couldn't determine what it was.

Sighing, I picked up the report and skimmed it through

again. It told me nothing more, but the feeling persisted that I was missing something. It was something that wasn't stated in the report, but was implied.

I gave up. I capped the vodka bottle. I went into the bathroom. I peed. I washed hands and face in cold water. I combed my hair. I slapped cologne on my jaw. I decided to go down to the bar. Maybe Millie Goodfellow was lounging about, and I could buy her a drink. After all, it was only what any other normal, red-blooded American boy would—

I stopped. "Normal, red-blooded American boy." The key word was "normal." I rushed back to the living room. I grabbed up the research report from the floor. I flipped through it wildly.

It was as I remembered. *Now* I remembered. It was all about *normal* body cells, *normal* mammalian cells, *normal* human embryo cells, *normal* chimpanzee cells. In every instance, in every report on reproduction, doubling, aging, the qualifying adjective "normal" had been used to describe the cells *in vitro*.

I took a deep breath. I didn't know what the hell it meant, but I thought it had to mean something. I found the phone number of Linda Cunningham.

"Hi!" she said, and giggled. "Whoever you are."

"Samuel Todd," I said. "How're you doing?"

"Super!" she said, and I believed her. I could hear punk rock blaring in the background—it sounded like the Sex Pistols—and there was a lot of loud talk, yells, groans, screams of laughter. I figured she had invited a few friends to her home, for something a little stronger than fruit punch and white wine.

"Sorry to interrupt your party," I said, "but this will just take a minute. Linda? Linda, are you there?"

"Super!" she said.

"Linda, in that report—you know what report I'm talking about, don't you?"

"Report?" she said. "Oh sure. Report. Who is this?"

"Samuel Todd," I repeated patiently. "I'm the guy you gave the report to earlier tonight at the Reverend Koukla's party."

"Oh wow!" she cried. "Harry, don't you *ever* do that again! That *hurt*."

"Linda," I said desperately, "this is Sam Todd."

"Super!" she said.

There was a louder blast of music, then the sound of scuffling. A male voice came on the phone.

"Are you an obscene phone caller?" he asked drunkenly. "I can breathe heavier than you."

More scuffling sounds. Crash of dropped phone. I heard Linda say, "Now stop it. You're just *awful*."

"Linda!" I yelled. "Linda? Are you there?"

She came back on the line.

"Who is this?" she said. "Who—whom are you calling?"

"This is Samuel Todd. I am calling Linda Cunningham, that's whom."

"Mr. Todd?" she cried. "Really? Super! Come on right over. We have a marvelous party all our—"

"No, no," I said hastily. "Thanks very much, but I can't come over. Linda, I have a question about the report. You said I could contact you if I had a question about the report."

"Report? What report?"

"Linda," I said as calmly as I could, "tonight at Koukla's party you gave me a report. Dr. Draper prepared it on orders of Dr. Thorndecker."

"Oh," she said, suddenly sober. "*That* report. Well, yes, sure, I remember. This is Mr. Todd?"

"Right," I said gratefully. "Just one little question about the report, and then I'll let you get back to your party."

"Super party," she said, giggling.

"Sounds like it," I said, hearing glass smashing in the background. "Sounds like a jim-dandy party. I wish I could join you, I really do. Linda, in that report you keep talking about normal cells. Normal embryo cells, and normal mammalian cells, and so forth. All the statistics have to do with normal cells—right?"

"Right," she said, and it came out "Ri." She giggled. "All normal cells. Normal body cells."

"Now my question is this:" I said. "Do all those statistics hold true for *ab*normal cells, too? Do abnormal cells decay or die after a limited number of reproductions?"

"Abnormal cells?" she said, beginning to slur. "What kind of abnormal cells?"

"Well, say cancer cells."

"Oh no," she said. "No no no no. Cancer cells go on forever. *In vitro*, that is. They never die. Harry, I *told* you not to *do* that again. It's really very embarrassing."

"Cancer cells never die?" I repeated dully.

"Didn't you know?" she said, giggling. "Cancer cells are immortal. Oh wow, Harry, do *that* again. That's super!"

I hung up softly.

I didn't go down to the bar that night. I didn't finish the quart of vodka either, though I put a hell of a dent in it. But the more I drank, the more sober I became. Finally I undressed and got into bed. I didn't know when sleep would come. Maybe in about ten years.

Didn't you know? Cancer cells are immortal.

I had a vision of a pinhead of pulsing jelly. Becoming something about as large as a dried pea. Discolored and wrinkled. Growing. Swelling. Expanding. The tiny wrinkles becoming folds and valleys. The discolorations becoming blobs of corruption. Larger and larger. A tumor as big as the Ritz. Taking over. Something monstrous. Blooming in wild colors. Runny tissue. The stink of old gardenias. Spreading, oozing, engulfing. And never dying. Never, never, never. But conquering, filling a slimed universe.

Immortal.

The Fifth Day

I DON'T KNOW what your life is like, but sometimes, in mine, I just don't want to get out of bed. It's not a big thing, like I've suddenly come to the conclusion that life is a scam. It's a lot of little things: Con Edison just sent me a monthly bill for $3,472.69.; a new shirt was missing when my laundry was returned; a crazy woman on the bus asked me why my nose was so long; a check from a friend, in repayment of a loan, promptly bounced. *Little* things. Maybe you could cope with them one at a time. But suddenly they pile up, and you don't want to get out of bed; it just isn't worth it.

That's how I felt on Friday morning. I looked toward the light coming through the window. It was the color of snot; I knew the sun wasn't shining. I wasn't hung over. I mean my head didn't ache, my stomach didn't bubble. But I felt disoriented. And I had all these problems. It seemed easier to stay exactly where I was, under warm blankets, and forget about "taking arms against a sea of troubles." Hamlet's soliloquy. Hamlet should have spent a week in Coburn, N. Y. He'd have found a use for that bare bodkin.

But why the hassle? There was no reason, I told myself, why I *should* get out of bed. What for? No one I wanted to see. No one I wanted to talk to. Events were moving smoothly along without my intervention. Corpses were getting shoveled into the ground at two in the morning, old geezers were disappearing, young wives were cuckolding their husbands in the back seats of police cars, cancer cells were reproducing like mad. God's in His Heaven; all's right with the world. What could I do?

It went on like that until about ten in the morning. Then I got out of bed. I wish I could tell you it was from stern resolve, a conviction that I owed myself, my employers, and the human race one more effort to tidy up the Thorndecker mess. It wasn't that at all. I got out of bed because I had to pee.

This led to the reflection that maybe the memorable acts of great men were impelled by similarly basic drives. Maybe Einstein came up with $E=MC^2$ while suffering from insomnia. Maybe Keats dashed off "Ode on a Grecian Urn" while he was constipated. Maybe Carnot jotted down the second law of thermodynamics while enduring an attack of dyspepsia and awaiting the arrival of Mother Tums. It was all possible.

I record this nonsense to illustrate my state of mind on that Friday morning. I may not have been hung over, but I wasn't certain I was completely sober.

Breakfast helped bring me back to reality. A calorie omelette, with a side order of cholesterol. Delicious. Three cups of black coffee.

"Another?" the foot-sore waitress asked when I ordered the third.

"Another," I nodded. "And a warm Danish. Buttered."

"It's your stomach," she said.

But it wasn't. It belonged to someone else, thank God. And my brain was also up for grabs.

I came down to earth during that final black coffee. Then I knew who I was, where I was, and what I was doing. Or trying to do. Caffeine restored my anxieties; I was my usual paranoiac self. Stunned by what I had seen and heard the previous evening. Wanting to put the jigsaw together, and looking frantically for those easy corner pieces.

I signed my breakfast tab, then wandered through the bar on my way to nowhere.

"Hey you, Todd," Al Coburn called in his raspy voice. "Over here."

He was seated alone in one of the high-backed booths. I slid in opposite, and before I looked at him, I glanced around. Jimmy was behind the bar, as usual. Two guys in plaid lumberjackets were drinking beer and arguing about something. I turned back to Al Coburn. He was drinking whiskey, neat, with a beer wash.

I jerked my chin at the booze.

"Taking your flu shot?" I asked.

"They killed my dog last night," he said hoarsely. "Poisoned her."

"Who's 'they?' Who poisoned your dog?"

"I come out this morning, and there she was. Stiff. Tongue hanging out."

"You call a vet?"

"What the hell for?" he said angrily. "Any fool could see she was dead."

"How old a dog?"

"Thirteen," he said.

"Maybe she died of natural causes," I said. "Thirteen's a good age for a dog. What makes you think she was poisoned?"

He tried to get the full shot glass up to his lips, but his hand was trembling too much. Finally, he bent over it and slurped. When he straightened up, whiskey dripped from his chin. He hadn't shaved for a few days; I watched drops run down through white stubble.

"Two nights ago," he said, "someone fired off a rifle, through my windows."

"Joy-riding kids," I said.

"That hound," he said, choking. "The best."

This time he got the shot glass to his mouth, and drained it. I went over to the bar and bought him another, and a beer for me. I carried the drinks back to the booth.

Grief must have mellowed him; this time he thanked me.

"You tell Goodfellow about this?" I asked him.

He shook his head. His rough, liver-spotted hands were still trembling; he gripped the edge of the table to steady himself.

"You tell any cop about it?"

"What's the use?" he said despairingly. "They're all in on it."

"In on what?"

He wouldn't answer, and we were back on the merry-go-round: vague hints, intimation, accusations—and no answers.

"Mr. Coburn," I said, "why would anyone want to poison your dog?"

He leaned across the table. Those washed-blue eyes were dulled and rheumy.

"That's simple, ain't it? A warning to me to keep my trap shut. A sign of what might happen to me."

"Why you?" I asked him. "Because you were Ernie Scoggins's best friend?"

"Maybe just that," he said. "Or maybe they looked for that letter, couldn't find it, and figured Ernie give it to me. Listen, maybe they *hurt* him, and he *told* them he give me the goddamned letter. Ernie, he wouldn't do anything to cause me harm, but maybe he told them I had the letter, hoping it would keep them from killing him. But it didn't. Now they're after me."

"What are you going to do?"

He sat back, folded his twitchy hands in his lap, stared down at them.

"I don't know," he muttered. "Killed my dog. Shot out my windows. I don't know what to do."

"Mr. Coburn," I said, as patiently as I could, "if you feel your life's threatened because of the Scoggins letter, why don't you do this: put the letter in a safe deposit box at the bank. Then tell it around town how Scoggins gave you that letter, and it's in a safe place, and it will only be opened in the event of your death. That's a good insurance policy."

"No," he said, "I don't trust the bank. That Art Merchant. How do I know them boxes are safe?"

"They can't open the box without your key."

He laughed scornfully. "That's what *they* say."

I didn't try to argue. He was so spooked, so irrational, that compared to him, my paranoia seemed like a mild whim.

"All right," I said, "then show me the letter. Let me read it. Tell everyone in town I've seen it. They're not going to kill both of us."

"What makes you think so?" he said.

I didn't even have sense enough to be frightened. All I could think of was that I was drinking beer with a psychotic old man who kept talking about how "they" poisoned his dog, shot holes in his windows, and wanted to kill him. And I was going right along with him as if what he was saying was real, logical, believable.

"The hell with it," I said suddenly.

"What?" he said.

"Mr. Coburn, I've had it. I've enjoyed our little chats. Interesting and instructive. But I've gone as far as I can go. Either you tell me more, or I'm cutting loose. I can't go stumbling along in the dark like this."

"Yeah," he said unexpectedly, "I can see that."

He took his upper denture from his mouth, wiped it carefully on a cocktail napkin, slipped it back in. A jolly sight to see.

"Tell you what," he said. Then he stopped.

"What?" I asked. "Tell me what?"

He went through the same act with the lower plate. His

way of gaining time, I suppose. I would have preferred finger-drumming or a trip to the loo.

"Maybe I can get this whole thing stopped," he said. "If I can, then there's no need to worry."

"And if you can't?"

He looked up sharply. Bleached lips pressed tighter. That elbow chin jutted. Resolve seemed to be returning.

"You figuring on being here tomorrow?" he asked.

"Sure. I guess so. Another day at least."

"I'll see you. Here at the Inn."

"I may not be in."

"I'll leave a message."

"All right. Are you sure you don't want to tell me now what this is all about?"

"Maybe tomorrow," he said evasively. "I'll know by tomorrow."

I wanted to nail it down. "And if you don't get the whole thing stopped, like you said, then you'll show me Ernie Scoggins's letter?"

"You'll see it," he said grimly.

Later, when it was all over, I realized I should have leaned on him harder. I should have leaned on all of them harder, bulldozing my way to the truth. But hindsight is always 20-20 vision. And at the time, I was afraid that if I came on too strong, they'd all clam, and I'd have nothing.

Besides, I doubt if what I did or did not do had much effect on what happened. Events had already been set in motion before I arrived in Coburn and visited Crittenden Hall. Perhaps my presence acted as a catalyst, and the Thorndecker affair rushed to its climax faster simply because I was there. But the final outcome was always inevitable.

Al Coburn went stumping off, and I went thoughtfully out into the hotel lobby. Millie Goodfellow beckoned me over to the cigar counter. She was wearing a tight T-shirt with a road sign printed on the front: SLIPPERY WHEN WET.

"How do you like it?" she said, arching her back. "Cute?"

"Cute as all get out," I said, nodding.

The dark glasses were still in place, the black eye effectively concealed.

"I know something you don't," she said, making it sound like a 6-year-old girl taunting her 8-year-old brother.

"Millie," I said, sighing, "*everyone* knows something I don't know."

"What will you give me if I tell you?" she asked.

"What do you want—a five-pound box of money?"

"I could use it," she giggled. "But I want you to keep your promise, that's all."

"I would have done that anyway," I lied. "What do you know that I don't know?"

She glanced casually about. The lobby was in its usual state of somnolence. A few of the permanent residents were reading Albany newspapers in the sagging armchairs. The baldy behind the desk was busy with scraps of paper and an old adding machine.

Millie Goodfellow beckoned me closer. I leaned across the counter, which put my face close to that damned road sign. I felt like an idiot, and undoubtedly looked like one.

"You remember when someone broke into your room?" she said in a low voice, still watching the lobby.

"Of course I remember."

"You won't tell anyone will you?"

"Tell anyone what?"

"Tell anyone that I told you."

It would have been laughable if it wasn't so goddamned maddening.

"Told me *what*?" I said angrily.

"My husband," she whispered. "I think it was Ronnie who did it."

I stared at her, blinking. If she was right, that Indian cop had done a hell of an acting job when he came up to "investigate" the break-in.

"Why do you think that, Millie?"

"He took my keys that night. He thinks I didn't notice, but I did. I told you I've got a passkey. And the next morning my keys were back."

"Why didn't you tell me this before?"

She lifted the black glasses. The mouse under her eye was a rainbow.

"I didn't have *this* before," she said. "You won't tell him I told you, will you? I mean about the keys?"

"Of course I won't tell him," I said. "Or anyone else. Thank you, Millie."

"Remember your promise," she called after me.

The elevator door bore a hand-printed sign: NOT WORKING. That would do for me, too, I thought glumly, walking up the stairs. Oh, I was working—but nothing was getting done. Bits and pieces—that's what I was collecting: bits and pieces. I wondered, if Constable Goodfellow *had* been my midnight caller, how he had learned of that anonymous note and why he was so anxious to recover it. Every time I got the answer to one question, it led to at least two more. The whole damn thing kept growing, spreading. Of course I made the comparison to cancerous cells *in vitro*. No end to it.

When I got to my room, the door was open, and I discovered why the elevator was out of operation: Sam Livingston was in 3-F, sweeping up, making the bed, setting out a clean drinking glass and fresh towels.

"Morning, Sam," I said grumpily.

"Morning, Sam," he said. He held up the quart vodka bottle. Maybe two drinks were left. "You have friends in?" he asked.

"No, I did that myself."

"My, my. Someone must have been thirsty."

"Someone must have been disgusted. Have a belt, if you like."

"A little early in the morning for me," he said, "but I thank you kindly. What you disgusted about?"

He kept moving around the room, emptying ashtrays, rearranging the dust.

"You want a complete list?" I asked him. "The weather, for starters. With this lousy town running a close second."

"Nothing you can do about the weather," he said. "God sends it; you take it."

"That doesn't mean I can't bitch about it."

"As for this town, I don't reckon it's much worse than any other place. Trouble is, it's so small, you see it clearer."

"I'm not tracking, Sam."

"Well, like in New York City. Now, you got a lot of rich, powerful people running that town—right?"

"Well...sure."

"And maybe some of them, you don't even know their names. Like bankers maybe, newspaper editors, preachers, union people, big property owners, businessmen. They really run the town, don't they? I mean, they got the muscle."

"I suppose so."

"I know so. And you don't even know who they are, because that city is so big, and they like to keep their names out of the papers and their faces off the TV. They want to be invisible. They can do that in a great big city. But in Coburn, now, we're small. Everyone knows everyone else. No one can keep invisible. But otherwise it's the same."

"You mean a small group of movers and shakers who run things?"

"Pretty much," he said. "Also, this town's in such a bad money way—no jobs around, the young folks moving out, property values dropping—that these here people they got to stick together. They can't go fighting amongst theirselves."

I stared at him, saw that old, black face deliberately expressionless. It was a mask that had been crumpled up, then partly smoothed out. But the wrinkles were still there, the scars and wounds of age.

"Sam," I said softly to him, "I think you're trying to tell me something."

"Nah," he said, "I'm just blabbing to pass the time whilst I tidy up in here. Now you get a lot of people in a lifeboat, and they all got to keep rowing and bailing, bailing and rowing. If they don't want the whole damn boat to go down."

I thought about that pearl of wisdom for a moment or two.

"Sam, are you hinting that there's a conspiracy? Amongst the movers and shakers of Coburn? About this Thorndecker grant?"

"Conspiracy?" he said.

"What does that mean—a bunch of folks get together and make a plan? Nah. They don't have to do that. They all know what they got to do to keep that lifeboat floating."

"Rowing and bailing," I said.

"Now you got it," he said. "These people, they don't want to get wet, floating around out there in the ocean, boat gone, not a prayer. So they go along, no matter what they hear or what they guess. They *gotta* go along. They got no choice, do they?"

"Self-preservation," I said.

"Sure," he said cheerfully. "That's why you finding it so tough to get people to talk to you. No one wants to kick holes in the boat."

"Are things really that bad in Coburn?" I asked.

"They ain't good," he said shortly.

"Well, let me ask you this: would the 'best people' of Coburn, the ones who run the town, would they go along with something illegal, something criminal or evil, just to keep the boat floating?"

"You said it yourself," he said. "Self-preservation. Mighty powerful. Can make a man do things he wouldn't do if he don't have to. Just to hang onto what he's got, you understand."

"Yes, I do understand," I said slowly. "Thank you, Sam. You've given me something else to think about."

"Aw hell," he said, gathering up broom, mop, pail and rags, "I'd have thought you'd have figured that out for yourself."

"I was getting to it," I said. "I think. But you spelled it out for me."

He turned suddenly, looked at me with something like alarm in his face.

"What did I say?" he demanded. "I didn't say nothing."

I turned my eyes away. It was embarrassing to see that fear.

"You didn't say anything, Sam," I assured him. "You didn't tell me word one."

He grunted, satisfied.

"I got a message for you," he said. "From Miz Thorndecker."

"Mary?"

"No," he said, "the married one."

I couldn't tell if his "Miz" meant "Miss" or "Mrs."

"Mrs. Julie Thorndecker?" I asked.

"That's the one," he said. "She wants to meet with you."

"She does? When did she tell you this?"

"She got the word to me," he said vaguely.

"Where does she want to meet?"

"There's a place out on the Albany post road. It's—"

"Don't tell me," I said. "A roadhouse. Red Dog Betty's."

"You know it?" he said, surprised. "Yeah, that's the place. It's got a big parking lot. That's where she'll meet you. She don't want to go inside."

"When?"

"Noon today," he said. "She drives one of these sporty little foreign cars."

"She would," I said. "All right, I'll meet her. Thanks again, Sam."

He told me how to get to Red Dog Betty's. I gave him five dollars, which he accepted gratefully and with dignity.

I had more than an hour to kill before my meeting with Julie Thorndecker. There was only one thing I wanted to do: I got into the Grand Prix and drove out to Crittenden. I didn't have anything planned; I just wanted to look at the place again. It drew me.

It was another lost day: someone had destroyed the sun and thrown a gauzy sheet across the world. The sky came right down—you wanted to duck your head—and the light seemed to be coming through a wire strainer, and a rusty one at that. Damp wood smell, and the river, and frosted fields. The melancholy of that place seeped into my bones. The marrow shriveled, and if someone had tapped my tibia, I'd have gone *ting!* Like a crystal goblet.

Nearing Crittenden, I passed a Village of Coburn cruiser going the other way. The constable driving wasn't Ronnie Goodfellow, but he raised a hand in greeting as we passed, and I waved back. I was happy to see another officer. I was getting the idea that the Indian worked a twenty-four-hour shift.

I drove slowly around the Crittenden grounds. The buildings looked silent and deserted. I had the fantasy that if I broke in, I'd hear a radio playing, see hot food on the tables, smell hamburgers sizzling on the grill—and not a soul to be found. A new *Marie Celeste* mystery. All the signs of life, but no life.

I saw a blue MGB parked on the gravel before the main entrance of Crittenden Hall, and figured it was Julie's "sporty little foreign car" that Sam Livingston had mentioned. But I didn't see her, or anyone else.

I drove around the fenced estate. Fields and woods dark and empty under the flat sky. No guard with shotgun and attack dog. Just a vacant landscape. I came up to the cemetery, still rolling gently, and then I saw someone. A black figure moving quietly among the tombstones, not quite sauntering.

There was no mistaking that massive, almost monumental bulk: Dr. Telford Gordon Thorndecker surveying his domain, a shadow across the land. He was overcoated, hatless; heavy brown hair fluffed in gusts of wind. He walked with hands clasped behind him, in the European fashion. His head was slightly bowed, as if he was reading the tombstones as he passed.

Something in that wavery air, that tainted light, magnified his size, so that I imagined I was seeing a giant stalking the earth. He tramped the world as if he owned it, as indeed he did—at least that patch of it.

He was doing nothing suspicious. He was doing nothing at all. Apparently just out for a morning stroll. But his posture—bowed head, slumped shoulders, hands clasped in back—spoke of deep, deep thoughts, heavy pondering, dense reflection. A ruminative figure.

Even at a distance, seeing him as a silhouette cut from black paper and pasted against a frosty scene, the man dominated. I thought of how we all revolved around him, whirling our crazy, uncertain courses. But he was the eye of the storm, the sure calm, and everyone looked to him for answers.

I had a wild desire to walk alongside him through that home of the dead and ask him all the questions that were troubling me:

Did you shoot your father deliberately, Dr. Thorndecker?

Did you contrive your first wife's death?

Why did you marry such a young second wife, and how are you able to endure her infidelities?

Why are you obsessed with the problems of aging, and do you really hope to unlock the secret of immortality?

He might, I dreamed, tell me the whole story: father, wife, love, dream—everything. In grave, measured tones, that resonant baritone booming, he would tell me the complete story, leaving nothing out, and the tale would be so wondrous that all I'd be able to say would be, "And then what happened?"

And nothing in his story would be vile or ugly. I wanted it all to be the chronicle of a hero, moving from triumph to triumph. I wanted him to succeed, I really did, and hoped all my doubts and suspicions were due to envy, because I could never be the man he was, never be as handsome, know as much, or have the ability to win a woman as beautiful as Julie.

I had spent only a few hours in the man's company, but I had come under his spell. I admit it. Because he was endless. I could not get to his limits, couldn't even glimpse them. The first colossus I had ever met, and it was a chastening experience.

I didn't want to stop the car to watch him, and after awhile he and the graveyard were hidden behind a copse of bare, black trees stuck in the hard ground like grease pencils. I completed the circuit of Crittenden. As I headed for the Albany post road, the Coburn constabulary cruiser passed me again.

This time the officer didn't wave.

The place wasn't hard to find. There was a big red neon poodle out in front, and underneath was the legend: RED DOG BETTY'S. Even at noontime the sign was flashing on and off, and there were three semitrailers and a score of private cars parked in the wide blacktop lot. I made a complete circle, and then selected a deserted spot as far from the roadhouse as I could get. I parked where I had a good view of arrivals and departures. I switched off, opened the window a bit, lighted a cigarette.

It was larger than I had imagined: a three-story clapboard building with a shingled mansard roof and dormer windows on the top floor. I couldn't figure what they needed all that space for, unless they were running games upstairs or providing hot-pillow bedrooms for lonely truckers and traveling salesmen. But maybe those upper floors were something as innocent as the owner's living quarters.

There were neon beer signs in the ground floor windows, and I could hear a juke box blaring from where I sat. As I watched, another semi pulled into the lot, and two more private cars. That place must have been a gold mine. Over the entrance was a painted sign: STEAKS, CHOPS, BAR-B-QUE. I wondered how good the food was. The presence of truckers was no indication; most of those guys will eat slop as long as the beer is cold and the coffee hot.

I sat there for two cigarettes before the blue MGB turned off the road and came nosing slowly around. I rolled down the window, stuck out my arm, and waved. She pulled up alongside, and looked at me without expression.

"Your place or mine?" she called.

Funny lady.

"Why don't you join me?" I said. "More room in here."

She came sliding out of her car, feet first. Her skirt rode up, and I caught a quick flash of bare legs. If she wanted to catch my attention, she succeeded. She took the bucket seat next to me, and slammed the door. I lighted her cigarette. Her hands weren't shaking, but her movements were brittle, almost jerky.

"Mrs. Thorndecker," I said, "nice to see you again."

"Julie," she said mechanically.

"Julie," I said, "nice to see you again."

She tried a small laugh, but it didn't work.

She was wearing a white corduroy suit. Underneath was a white turtleneck sweater, a heavy Irish fisherman's sweater. Her fine, silvered hair was brushed tight to the scalp. No jewelry. Very little makeup. Maybe something around the eyes to make them look big and luminous. But the lips were pale, the face ivory.

She was one beautiful woman. All of her features were crisp and defined. That heavy suit and bulky sweater made her look fragile. But there was nothing vulnerable in the eyes. They were knowing and, looking at her, all I could see was a gold slave bracelet glittering on a naked ankle high in the back seat of a cop's car.

"Been here before?" she said absently.

"No, never," I said. "Looks like an okay place. How's the food?"

She flipped a palm back and forth.

"So-so," she said. "The simple stuff is good. Steaks, stews—things like that. When they try fancy, it's lousy."

I wasn't really hearing her words. I was hearing that marvelous, husky voice. I had to stop that, I decided. I had to listen to this lady's words, and not get carried away by her laughing growls, murmurs, throaty chuckles.

I didn't give her any help. I didn't say, "Well?" Or, "You wanted to see me?" Or, "You have something to say?" I just waited.

"I like Coburn," she said suddenly. "I know you don't, but I do."

"It's your home," I observed.

"That's part of it," she agreed. "I never had much of a home until I married. Also, I think part of it is that in Coburn I'm a big frog in a little pond. I don't think I could live in, say, Boston or New York. Or even Albany. I know. I've tried. I was lost."

"Where are you from, Julie? Originally?"

"A little town in Iowa. You never heard of it."

"Try me."

"Eagle Grove."

"You're right," I said. "I never heard of it. You don't speak like a midwesterner."

"I've been away a long time," she said. "A long, *long* time. I wanted to be a dancer. Ballet."

"Oh?" I said. "Were you any good?"

"Good enough," she said. "But I didn't have the discipline. Talent's never enough."

"How did you meet your husband?"

"At a party," she said. "He saved my life."

She said that very simply, a statement of absolute fact. So, of course, I had to joke about it because I was embarrassed.

"Choking on a fishbone, were you?" I said lightly.

"No, nothing like that. It was the last party I was going to go to. I had been to too many parties. I was going to have a good time, then go back to my fleabag and eat a bottle of pills."

I couldn't believe it. She was young, young, young. And beautiful. I just couldn't make the connection between suicide and this woman with the cameo face and limpid body who sat beside me, filling the car with her very personal fragrance, a scent of warm breath and fresh skin.

All I could think of to say was: "Where was it? This party?"

"Cambridge. Then Telford came over to me. He had been staring at me all evening. He took me aside and told me who he was, how old he was, what he did, how much money he had, how his wife had died a few months before. He told me everything. Then he asked me to marry him."

"Just like that?"

"Just like that," she said, nodding. "And I said yes—

just like that. The shortest courtship on record."

"You think he knew?" I asked her. "What you intended to do?"

"Oh yes," she said in a low voice. "I didn't tell him, but he knew. I didn't tell him a thing about myself, but he knew. And asked me to marry him."

"And you've never regretted it?"

"Never," she said firmly. "Never for a minute. Do you have any idea of what kind of man he is?"

"I've been told he's a genius."

"Not his work," she said impatiently. "I mean *him*?"

"Very intelligent," I said cautiously. "Very charming."

"He's a great man," she said definitely. "A *great* man. But I have a problem."

Sure you do, I thought cynically; you fuck Indian cops: that's your problem.

"His daughter," she went on, leaning forward to peer out the fogged windshield. "Mary. She's really his stepdaughter. His first wife was a widow when she married Telford."

I didn't tell her this was old news to me. I lighted cigarettes for us again. She was slowly calming, her movements and gestures becoming easier, more fluid as she talked. I wanted to keep her talking. I was conscious of that suggestive voice, but I was listening to her words now.

"Mary is older than me," she said. "Four years older. She loves her stepfather very much."

She suddenly turned sideways on the seat. She drew up her legs so those bare knees were staring at me. They were round, smooth, hairless as breasts.

"*Very* much," she repeated, staring into my eyes. "Mary loves her stepfather *very* much. So she resents me. She hates me."

I made a sound. I waved a hand.

"Surely it's not that bad," I said.

"It's that bad," she said solemnly. "And also—I don't know whether you know this or not—Mary is a very, uh, disturbed woman. She's into this religious thing. Goes to some outhouse church. Shouts. Reads the Bible. Born again. The whole bit."

"Maybe she's sincere," I said.

She put a soft hand on my arm, leaned closer.

"Of *course* she's sincere," she whispered. "Believes every word of that shit. That's one of the reasons she hates me. Because I took her mother's place. She thinks I'm committing adultery with her father."

I was bewildered.

"But Thorndecker isn't her father," I said.

"*I* know that. *You* know that. But Mary is so mixed up, she thinks of Telford as her father. She thinks I stole her father from her and her dead mother. It's very complex."

"The understatement of the year."

"Sex," Julie Thorndecker said. "Sex has got a lot to do with it. Mary is so in love with Telford, she can't think straight. She thinks we—she and I—are competing for the love of the same man. That's why she hates me."

"What about Dr. Draper? Where does he fit into all this?"

"He'd marry Mary tomorrow if she'd have him. She never will. She wants Telford. But Draper keeps tagging after her like a puppy, hoping she'll suddenly see the light. I feel sorry for him."

"And for Mary?"

"Well . . . yes. I feel sorry for Mary, too. She's so mixed up. But also, I'm scared of her."

"Scared?" I said. "I can't picture you being frightened of anything or anyone."

"I thank you, kind sir," she said, tilting her head, giving me a big smile, tightening her grip on my arm.

She shouldn't have said that. It was a false note. She was not the flirty, girlish type of woman who says, "I thank you, kind sir." I began to get the idea that I was witnessing a performance, and when she finished, the audience would rise, applauding, and roses would be tossed.

"Why are you frightened of Mary?" I asked her.

She shrugged. "She's so—so unbalanced. Who knows what she might do? Or say? Oh, don't get me wrong. I'm not frightened of what she might say about me. That's of no importance. But I'm afraid for my husband. I'm afraid crazy Mary might endanger his career, his plans. That's really why I asked you to meet me here today, to have this talk."

"You're afraid Mary might—well, let's say slander her stepfather?"

If she had said, "Yes," then I was going to say, "But why should Mary endanger Thorndecker's career and his plans if she loves him as much as you say?"

But Julie didn't fall into that trap.

"Oh, she'd never do or say anything against Telford. Not directly. She loves him too much for that. But she might slander *me*. Say things. Spread stories. Because she hates me so much. Not realizing how it might reflect on Telford, how it might affect the grand dreams he has."

I leaned forward to stub out my cigarette. The movement had the added advantages of removing my arm from Julie's distracting grasp and tearing my eyes away from those shiny knees.

"What you're saying," I said slowly, "is that you hope whatever Mary might say about you will not affect Dr. Thorndecker's application for a Bingham Foundation grant. Isn't that it?"

"Yes," she said, "that's it. I just wanted you to know what a disturbed woman she is. Whatever she might say has absolutely nothing to do with my husband's application or his work."

Then we sat without speaking. I became more conscious of her scent. I'm sensitive to odors, and it seemed to me she was exuding a tantalizing perfume that was light, fragrant, with an after-scent, the way some wines have an after-taste. Julie's after-scent was deep, rich, musky. Very stirring. I thought of rumpled sheets, howls, and wet teeth.

I came back to this world to see the Coburn constabulary cruiser move slowly by. It drove up behind us, passed, made the turn behind the roadhouse, and disappeared. The officer driving, the same one I had twice met near Crittenden, didn't turn his head as he drove by. I don't know if he saw us sitting together or not. It didn't seem important. But we both watched him as he went by.

"I love my husband," Julie Thorndecker said thoughtfully.

I was silent. I hadn't even asked her.

"Still..." she said.

I said nothing.

"You're not giving me much encouragement," she said.

"When did you ever need encouragement?" I asked her.

"Never," she said. "You're right. Could I have a cigarette, please?"

We lighted up again. I ran the window down to get rid of the smoke.

"Too cold for you?" I said.

"Yes," she said, "too cold. But not the weather. Leave the window down. The trouble is..."

Another Coburnite. The unfinished sentence.

"What's the trouble?" I said.

She turned her head slowly to stare at me. I could read nothing in her eyes. Just eyes.

"I'd like to fuck you," she said steadily. "I really would. The trouble is, you'd think I was flopping so you'd give Telford a good report."

I don't care how much experience you've had, what a hot-shot cocksman you are. You're still going to feel fear when a woman says, "Yes."

"That's exactly what I'd think," I said. "What I'm thinking."

"Too bad," she said. "It's not like that at all. If you picked me up in a bar...?"

"Or met you at a party? A different can of worms."

"A lovely figure of speech. Thank you."

"You know what I mean," I said. "In another place, another time."

She looked at me shrewdly.

"You're sure you're not making excuses?" she said.

"I'm not sure," I said. "I'm not sure of anything. I'm especially not sure of a woman who makes an offer like that right after she's told me she loves her husband."

She looked at me in astonishment.

"What has one got to do with the other?" she asked.

She wasn't dissembling. She meant it.

There's so much about living I don't understand.

"Mrs. Thorndecker," I said. "Julie. I'm not making any value judgment. I'm just saying it's impossible. For me."

"All right," she said equably. "I can live with it. What about Millie Goodfellow?"

"What about her?"

"She's married. Is your fine sense of propriety working there?"

"Not much point to this conversation," I said. "Is there?"

"You're something of a prig, aren't you?" she said.

"Yes," I said. "Something. I'll just have to live with it."

She opened her door, then turned back.

"About Mary," she said. "She *is* disturbed. Please remember what I told you."

"I'll remember," I said.

She gave me a brief smile. Very brief. I watched her drive away. I took a deep breath and blew it out slowly. I felt like a fool. But I've felt like that before, and will again.

I put up the window. I scooched far down on the seat. I tilted my lumpy tweed hat over my closed eyes. I wasn't dreaming of my lost chance with Julie Thorndecker; I was remembering a somewhat similar incident with Joan Powell. It had started similarly; it had ended differently.

We had spent a whole Saturday together, doing everything required of an unmarried couple on the loose in Manhattan: wandering about Bloomingdale's for an hour, lunch at Maxwell's Plum, a long walk over to the Central Park Zoo to say hello to Patty Cake, then a French movie in which the actors spent most of their time climbing sand dunes, dinner at an Italian place in the Village, and back to Powell's apartment.

It should have been a great day. The sun was shining. Garbage had been collected; the city looked neat and clean. I think Joan enjoyed the day. She acted like she did. She said she did. But sometime during the afternoon, it began going sour for me. It wasn't the movie or the restaurants. It wasn't Joan. It was just a mood, a foul mood, without reason. I couldn't account for it; I just knew I had it.

Powell assumed we'd end our busy day in bed. A reasonable assumption based on past experience. When we got back to her place, she went into the bathroom for a quick shower. She came out bareass naked, rubbing her damp hair with a big pink towel.

Joan Powell is something to see naked. She really fits together. Nothing extra, nothing superfluous. She's just there, complete. She's a small woman, but so perfectly proportioned that she could be tarnishing in the garden of the Museum of Modern Art.

I was sitting on the edge of her Scarpa sofa, leaning over, hands clasped between my knees.

"How about mixing us something?" she suggested.

"No," I said. "Thanks. I think I better take off."

She looked at me.

"Sick?" she said.

"No," I said, "just lousy. I don't know what it is. Instant depression. I think I better be alone. I don't want to bore you."

"That's what I want you to do," she said. "Bore me."

"When you get out of those Gucci loafers," I said, "you can be incredibly vulgar."

"Can't I though?" she said cheerfully. "Take off your clothes."

"Oh God," I groaned, "haven't you understood a thing I've said? I just don't *feel* like it."

She tossed the towel aside. She moved naked about the room. Lighted her own cigarette. Mixed her own Cutty and soda.

"You don't feel like it," she repeated. "So what?"

"So what?" I said, outraged. "I've just said I don't feel

like fun and games tonight. What are you going to do—rape me? For God's sake, it's got nothing to do with you. I just don't feel like a toss, so I'm taking off."

"Go ahead," she said. "Take off. But don't come back."

This was during a time when the last thing in the world I wanted was to lose her. We were just in the process of working out a sweet, easy, take-it-as-it-comes relationship, and I thought I could be completely honest with her.

"I can't believe you," I said. "One night—*one* night; the first time—I don't want to rub the bacon, and you're ready to call it quits."

She looked at me narrowly.

"It's been more than one time for me, kiddo," she said.

Then she may have seen in my face what that did to my ego, because she came over to sit beside me and slid a cool arm around my neck.

"Look, Todd," she said, "there have been times when I've climbed between the sheets with you when I didn't feel like it. Because you wanted to. Because I love you. And doing something you wanted to do, and I didn't want to, was a sacrifice that proved that love. More important, it turned out to be the best sex we've ever had—for me. Because I was proving my love. And in addition to the physical thing, I was feeling so warm and tender and giving. Try it; you'll like it."

She was right. It was the best sex we ever had—for me. I told you she taught me a lot.

But I didn't think it would work that way with Julie Thorndecker. There was no love between us; I wasn't ready to make a willing sacrifice so she could be happy. And something else kept me away from her. Maybe she was right; I was a prig. Maybe I was just a hopeless romantic. It had to do with Thorndecker. Screwing his wife would be like throwing mud at a statue.

Just to complicate matters further, there was an additional factor involved in my rejection of Julie Thorndecker.

As you've probably gathered by now, I'm a fantasist. I could get twenty years in the pokey for what I dream in one day. For instance, I've had a lot of sexual daydreams about Joan Powell. Some I told her about; some I didn't. I even had some recent fantasies about Millie Goodfellow.

But I found myself totally incapable of fantasizing about Julie Thorndecker. God knows I tried. But the dreams just slid away and dissolved. It wasn't all due to the fact that she was married to a man I admired. It was that she was so beautiful, the body so young and tender, that I couldn't dream about her.

Fantasies, to be pleasurable, must have *some* relation to reality. Even daydreams must be *possible* to be stirring. You can't, for instance, successfully fantasize about hitting the sheets with Cleopatra because a part of your brain keeps telling you that she was smooched by an asp centuries ago, and any fantasy involving her would be a waste of time.

I could fantasize about Joan Powell and Millie Goodfellow because those daydreams were possible. But when I attempted a sexual fancy involving Julie Thorndecker... nothing. I told myself it was because of her husband and her superbeauty.

But there was another reason. Powell and Goodfellow were living, breathing, warm, eager women. Julie Thorndecker was not. She was, I thought, a dead lady.

After all that heavy thinking, I decided that if I didn't get a drink immediately I might shuffle off to Buffalo from a hyperactive cerebellum. So I got out of the car, locked up, stomped over to Red Dog Betty's.

Inside, the place looked like it had originally been a private home: a dozen connecting rooms. The doors had been removed, but the hinge butt plates were still there, painted over. The wall between what I guessed were the original living room and parlor had been knocked down to make a long barroom. The other rooms, smaller, were used for dining. It was an attractive arrangement: a lot of intimate nooks; you didn't feel like you were eating in a barn, and the jukebox in the barroom was muffled to an endurable decibel level.

The barroom itself wasn't fake English pub, or fake

fishermen's shanty, or fake anything. The decorations
didn't look planned; just accumulated. A few Tiffany
lamps shed a pleasantly mellow glow. The long, scarred
mahogany bar was set with stools upholstered in black
vinyl. There were a few battered oak tables with captain's
chairs. A wall of booths had table candles stuck in empty
whiskey bottles covered with wax drippings.

The light was dim, the air redolent of stale beer. There
was no chrome or plastic. A snug place, with no cutesy
signs. In fact, the only sign I saw bore the stern
admonition: BE GOOD OR BE GONE. There was a big array of
liquor bottles behind the bar—much larger than the
selection at the Coburn Inn—and I was happy to see they
kept their "garbage" on the bar, in plain view.

"Garbage" is what bartenders call their little containers
of cherries, olives, onions, lemon peel, lime wedges, and
orange slices. Keeping these garnishes atop the bar is a
tip-off to a quality joint; you know you're getting fresh
fixings in your drinks. When the "garbage" is kept below
the bar, out of sight, that olive in your martini was
probably the property of a previous martini drinker who
either forgot to eat it, ignored it, or tasted it and spit it
back into his empty glass. A schlock bar can keep one
olive going a week that way.

I hung up my coat and hat on a brass tree, gratified to
note the absence of a hatcheck attendant. I swung onto
one of the barstools and looked around. Sitting near me
were three guys who looked like traveling salesmen. They
were working on double martinis and exchanging
business cards. Down the other end were two truckers in
windbreakers, wearing caps decorated with all kinds of
metal badges. They had boilermakers on the bar in front
of them, and were already shaking dice in a cup to see
who'd pay for the next round.

There were no other customers in the barroom; all the
action was in the dining areas. They were crowded, and
there was a crew of young, fresh-faced waitresses serving
drinks, taking orders, lugging in trays of food from the
kitchen in the rear.

There was one black bartender doing nothing but working the service section of the bar, preparing drinks for the diners as the waitresses rushed up with their orders. The other bartender, the one who waited on me, was a heavy woman of 50-55, around there. She was comfortably upholstered, wearing a black silk dress two sizes too tight for her. She had a ring on every finger—and she hadn't found those in Crackerjack boxes. Her face was at once doughy and tough. A lot of good beef and bourbon had gone into that complexion.

She flashed diamond earrings, and a doubled strand of pearls. A brooch of what looked to me like rubies in the shape of a rose bloomed on her awesome bosom. Her black wig went up two feet into the air, and was pierced with long, jeweled pins. As the ad says: if you got it, flaunt it.

Like a lot of heavy people, she was light on her feet, and worked with a skillful economy of movement that was a joy to watch. When I ordered Cutty and soda, she slid a napkin in front of me, poured an honest shotglass to the brim, uncapped a nip of soda, placed a clean twelve-ounce glass on the napkin, and half-filled it with ice from a little scoop. All this in one continuous, flowing motion. If I owned a bar, I'd like to have her working for me.

"Mix?" she asked, looking at me.

"Please," I said.

She dumped the Scotch into the tall glass without spilling a drop, added an inch of soda, then waited until I took a sip.

"Okay?" she asked. Her voice was a growl, low and burred.

"Just what the doctor ordered," I said.

"What doctor is that?" she said. "I'd like to send him a few of my customers. You passing through?"

"Staying a few days in Coburn," I told her.

"We all got troubles," she said philosophically, then went down the bar to the truckers to pour them another round. A chubby little waitress came up to the bar to whisper something to her. She walked back to the three salesmen. "Your table's ready, boys," she rasped. "The waitress will bring your drinks."

"Thanks, Betty," one of them said.

I waited until they disappeared into one of the dining rooms. The diamond-studded barmaid began washing and rinsing glasses near me.

"Your name's Betty?" I asked.

"That's right."

"*The* Betty? You own the place?"

"Me and the bank," she growled. She dried her hand carefully and stuck it over the bar. I shook a fistful of silver, gold, and assorted stones. And not, I bet, a hunk of glass in the lot. "Betty Hanrahan," she said. "You?"

"Samuel Todd."

"A pleasure. I don't want to hustle you, Mr. Todd, take your time, but I just wanted you to know that if you're alone and thinking of eating, we can serve you right here at the bar."

"Thanks," I said. "I might do that. But maybe I'll have another first."

"Sure," she said, and refilled the shotglass with one swift, precise motion. She also gave me a fresh highball glass and fresh ice. I was beginning to like this place.

"What's with the red dog?" I asked her.

"I had a poodle once," she said. "Reddish brown. A mean, miserable bitch. When I took this place over, I thought it would be like a trademark. Something different."

"Looks like it worked out just fine," I said, nodding toward the crowded dining rooms.

"I do all right," she acknowledged. "You should stop in some night, if you're looking for action."

"What kind of action?" I said cautiously.

She polished glasses for a few moments.

"Nothing heavy," she said. "Nothing rough. I run a clean joint. But at night, after the dinner crowd clears out, we get a real friendly drinking bunch. A lot of local girls from the farms and small towns around here. Not hookers; nothing like that. Just out for a good time. Have a few drinks, dance a little. Like that."

"And sometimes a trio on Saturday nights?" I asked.

She stopped polishing glasses long enough to look up at me.

"Who told you that?" she asked curiously.

"A loyal customer of yours," I said. "Millie Goodfellow. Know her?"

"Oh hell yes, I know her. Millie's a lot of woman. Life of the party."

"I figured," I said. "Can I buy you a drink?"

"Not till the sun goes down," she said.

"It's been down for the past five days," I said.

She considered that thoughtfully.

"You got something there," she said. "I'll have a short beer, and thank you."

"My pleasure."

She drew herself a small brew from the Michelob tap. She planted herself in front of me and lifted her glass.

"Health," she said, drained off the glass, and went back to her washing, drying, and polishing chores.

"How well do you know Millie?" she asked casually.

"Not very well. Just to talk to. I'm staying at the Coburn Inn."

She nodded.

"I know she's married to a cop," I added. "Ronnie Goodfellow."

Betty Hanrahan looked relieved.

"Good," she said. "As long as you know it."

"I'm not likely to forget it."

"Millie does," she said. "Frequently."

"It doesn't seem to bother him," I said.

"Uh-huh," she said. "Now I'll tell you a story. The same story I told Millie Goodfellow. Thirty years ago I was married—for the first and last time. His name was Patrick Hanrahan. My unmarried name is Dubcek, Betty Dubcek from Hamtramck, Michigan. Anyway, Pat turned out to be a lush, and I turned out to be Miss Roundheels of Detroit. I was a wild one in those days; I admit it. Pat knew about it, and didn't seem to mind. It went on like that for almost two years, with him trying to drink the breweries dry, and me making it with anyone who had a Tootsie Roll between his legs. I thought Pat just didn't care. Then one night he came home stone-cold sober and gave me this..."

She lifted a corner of that heavy wig. I saw a deep, angry scar that seemed to run across the top of her skull down to her left ear.

"He damned near killed me," she said. "After two years of taking it, and telling himself it didn't matter, and he couldn't care less, he blew up and damned near killed me. I should have known it would get to him eventually; he was a prideful man. They're like that. It may bubble along inside them for a long while, but sooner or later..."

"What happened to him?" I asked.

"Pat? He just took off. I didn't try to find him. Didn't even make a complaint to the cops; I had it coming. After ten years I got a legal divorce. But the reason I'm telling you this is because that Ronnie Goodfellow is the same kind of prideful man as Pat was. Millie thinks he doesn't care. Maybe he doesn't—now. Some day he will, mark my words, and then biff, bam, and pow."

"Thanks for the warning," I said. "Maybe I'll have some lunch now. What's good?"

"Try the broiled liver and bacon," she said. "Home fries on the side."

It was served to me right there on the bar, with slices of pumpernickel and sweet butter, and a small bowl of salad. It wasn't a great meal, but for a roadhouse like that, in the middle of nowhere, it was a pleasant surprise. I had a Ballantine ale, and that helped. And Betty Hanrahan mixed me some fresh Colman's mustard to smear on the liver. It was hot enough to bring the sweat popping out on my scalp. That's the way to eat broiled liver, all right.

I was on my second black coffee, wondering if I wanted a brandy or something else. Betty Hanrahan was down at the end of the bar near the door, checking her bottled beer supply. A guy came in wearing a fleece-collared trucker's jacket. He was still wearing his gloves, and didn't bother removing his badge-encrusted cap. He spoke to Betty for a few minutes, and I could see him gesturing toward the outside, toward the parking lot. Then the owner turned and stared at me. She came slowly down the bar.

"Mr. Todd," she said, "you don't, by any chance, drive a Grand Prix, do you?"

"Sure, I do," I said. "A dusty black job. Why?"

"You got trouble," she said. "Someone slashed your tires. All four tires."

"Son of a bitch!" I said bitterly.

Betty Hanrahan said she'd call the cops. I walked out to the parking lot with the trucker, and he told me what had happened. He had pulled his semitrailer onto the lot, and parked three spaces from my Pontiac. He and his mate got down from the cab, locked up, started for the roadhouse. They had to walk by the Grand Prix, and the mate was the first to see the tires had been slashed.

When we reached my car, the mate was hunkering down, examining one of the tires. He looked up at me.

"Your car?"

I nodded.

"Someone did a job on you," he said in a gravelly voice. "Looks to me like a hatchet, but it could have been a heavy hunting knife—something like that. One deep cut in every tire, except the left rear. That has two cuts, like the guy who did it started there, didn't cut deep enough on the first slash and had to swing again."

"How long do you figure it took?" I asked him.

The two truckers looked at each other.

"A couple of minutes, Bernie?" the mate asked.

"No more than that," the other said. "Just walked around the car hacking. The balls of the guy! In broad daylight yet. You got any enemies, mister?"

"Not that I know of."

"Haven't been sleeping in any strange beds, have you?" Bernie asked, and they both laughed.

I moved slowly around the Grand Prix. The car wasn't exactly on its rims, but it had settled wearily and was listing.

We heard the growl of a siren, and looked up. The Coburn constabulary cruiser, the same car I had seen thrice before, was pulling into the parking lot. One of the truckers waved his arms; the cruiser turned away from the roadhouse, came cutting across the lot toward us, pulled to a stop about ten feet away. The constable cut his flashing light and got out, tugging on his cap. He strutted toward us.

"What have we got here?" he demanded.

"Someone did a hatchet job on this man's tires," Bernie said. "All four of them."

The constable circled the Grand Prix. He was a short, hard bantam with a slit mouth and eyes like licked stones. He came back to join us and stood staring at the car, hands on his hips.

"Jesus," he said disgustedly, "ain't that a kick in the ass."

"I figure a hatchet," the mate said. "Hell, maybe it was an ax."

The constable stooped, fingered one of the cuts.

"Could be," he said. "Or a heavy knife. But I'd say you're right: a hatchet. No sign of sawing with a knife. Just one deep slash. Who discovered it?"

"We did," the mate said. "Pulled in, locked up, and started for the roadhouse. Then I seen it, and Bernie went on ahead to tell Betty, and I stayed here."

"How long ago was this?"

"Not more'n ten minutes. Right, Bernie?"

"About that. Fifteen tops."

The constable turned to me.

"Your car?"

"Yes, it's mine."

"How long you been parked here?"

I looked at my watch.

"Two hours," I said. "Give or take ten minutes."

"You were inside all that time? In the restaurant?"

He stared at me, waiting. The son of a bitch, he *had* seen Julie Thorndecker and me.

"Not all the time," I said. "I smoked a cigarette out here

first, then went in. I'd say I was in the bar about an hour and fifteen minutes. Something like that."

He kept staring at me, eyes squinted. But he didn't ask why it took me forty-five minutes to smoke a cigarette or why I hadn't gone into the roadhouse right after I parked.

"See anyone hanging around?" he asked me. "Anyone acting suspicious?"

"No," I said. "No one."

"I came through here a little after noon," he said, "just on routine patrol, you understand, and I didn't see anyone either." He paused thoughtfully. "Come to think of it, I don't recollect seeing your car."

"I was here," I said.

"Well," he said, "what the hell. A lot of cars here; I can't be expected to remember everyone I seen." He sighed deeply. "Crazy kids, I expect. Just doing something wild. We've had a lot of vandalism lately." He paused again, looking at me without expression. "Unless you got some idea of who'd do a thing like this to you?"

"No," I said. "No idea at all."

"Well, I'm sorry this had to happen, Mr. Todd," he said briskly. "It's a damned shame. I'll have to make out a report. Could I see your license and registration, please?"

"We'll be in the bar if you need us," Bernie said.

The constable waved a hand.

"Sure, boys, you go along. I'll drop by in a few minutes to get your names and addresses."

He used the hood of the Pontiac as a desk to copy information into a small notebook he took from a leather pouch strapped to his gunbelt.

"Some of these rotten kids," he said as he wrote, "you wouldn't believe the things they do. Smash windshields, rip off radio antennas, sometimes run a nail down a car they're walking by. Just to ruin the finish, you understand. No rhyme or reason to it. Damned trouble-makers."

He replaced the notebook in his gunbelt, handed the license and registration back to me. We started walking toward the roadhouse.

"New York City—huh?" he said. "I guess you're used

to shit like this. I hear the place is a jungle."

"Oh, I don't know," I said. "There are places just as bad. Maybe worse."

"Yeah," he said in a flat, toneless voice, "ain't it the truth? Well, you'll be needing a wrecker, I expect. Know any garages around here?"

"How about Mike's Service Station?" I asked. "Could they handle the job?"

"Oh hell, yes. They got a tow car. A job like this, I figure you won't get it today. Maybe tomorrow, if they put a rush on it. My name's Constable Fred Aikens. Mike knows me. Mention my name, and maybe he'll shave the price a little. But I doubt it," he added with a dry laugh.

We paused just inside the entrance of the roadhouse.

"We'll do what we can, Mr. Todd," Constable Aikens said, "but don't get your hopes up. A malicious mischief job like this, probably we'll never catch who done it unless they pull it again, and we get something to go on."

"I understand," I said.

"Besides," he said, "you got insurance—right?"

"I have insurance," I said, "but I'm not sure it covers malicious mischief. I'll have to call my agent."

"Well, I'm sorry it happened, Mr. Todd," he said again. "But at least no one got hurt—right? I mean, no bodily harm done. That's something to be thankful for, ain't it?" He smiled coldly. "Well, I got to find those truckers and get their names and addresses. You'll be hearing from us if we come up with anything."

He waved a hand, started toward the back of the bar where Bernie and his mate had joined the two truckers who had been there since I had first entered. All four of them were drinking boilermakers.

The black bartender was alone, and motioned me over.

"Miss Betty is upstairs in the office," he told me. "She'd like to see you up there, if you got a minute. Take that door over there, and it's at the head of the stairs."

"Thanks," I said. "I'll go up."

"She says maybe you better bring your hat and coat with you."

"Yeah," I said sourly, "maybe I better."

The door of the office was open. Betty Hanrahan was on the phone. She motioned me to come in, and pointed to a wooden armchair alongside her cluttered desk. I sat down, took out my cigarettes, offered the pack to Betty. She took one, and I lighted it for her as she was saying, "Yes, Dave ... Yes ... I understand, but I've never made a single claim before ..."

I lighted my own cigarette and looked around. It was about as big as a walk-in closet, with just enough room for a desk, two chairs, a scarred metal file cabinet, and a small, old-fashioned safe shoved into one corner: a waist-high job on big casters with a single dial and brass handles.

Betty Hanrahan leaned back in her oak swivel chair and parked her feet up on the desk. Good legs. Her rhinestone-trimmed shoes had heels at least four inches high, and I wondered how she could wait bar on those spikes. I also realized that in her stockinged feet, she'd be a small one. In length, not in width.

"Okay, David love," she was saying, "do what you can ... Fine ... Let me know as soon as you hear."

She leaned forward to hang up the phone. As she did, she looked at her skirt and tugged it down a bit over her knees.

"Nothing showing, is there?" she said.

"I didn't see a thing," I assured her.

"Well, what the hell, I'm wearing pants."

She opened a side drawer and pulled out a half-full bottle of Wild Turkey. She also set out a stack of paper cups.

"Build us a couple," she said.

I rose and began pouring the bourbon into two cups.

"I'll get you some water," she said, "if you want it."

"This'll do fine."

"I need a shot," she said. "I don't like rough stuff on my property. It scares me, and gives the joint a bad name. That was my insurance agent I was talking to. He thinks I'm covered against malicious mischief. But even if I'm not, I want you to know I'm picking up the tab."

"I appreciate that, Betty," I said. "But I may be covered myself. I'll wait till I get back to New York, and check it out."

"New York," she said, shaking her head. "That's funny. I had you pegged for Chicago. You don't talk like a New Yorker."

"Transplanted," I said. "Ohio originally. Could I use your phone? I want to call Mike's Service Station and see what they can do about my car."

"Let me call Mike," she said. "I know how to handle that old crook."

She took her feet off the desk, rummaged through a drawer, came up with a dog-eared business card. She had to put on a pair of glasses to read the number. The frames of the spectacles were sparkling with little rhinestones and seed pearls.

I listened to her explain to Mike what had happened. She told him she wanted the car picked up immediately, and new tires installed by 5:00 P.M. I heard an angry crackle on the phone. She screamed back, and finally agreed on the job being finished before noon on Saturday. Then they started talking cost, and another argument erupted. I didn't catch what the final figure was, but I do know she beat him down, and concluded by yelling, "And you make sure I get the bill, you goddamned pirate."

She slammed down the phone and grinned at me. She took off her glasses and put her feet back on the desk again. This time she didn't bother tugging down her skirt. She was right; she was wearing pants.

"They'll pick it up right away," she told me. "He claims he just can't get to it today. But they'll have it ready for you by noon tomorrow. They'll deliver it to the Coburn Inn. Okay?"

"Thanks, Betty," I said gratefully. "But you don't have to pay the bill. It wasn't your fault."

"It happened on my property, didn't it?" she said. "I'm responsible for the safety of my customers' cars."

"I'm not sure you are," I said. "Under the law."

"Fuck the law," she said roughly. "I feel responsible,

and that makes it so. Got any idea who did it?"

I had a lot of ideas.

"I have no idea," I said.

"Haven't been leaving your shoes under a strange bed, have you?"

"That's what one of the truckers suggested. But it just isn't so. As far as I know, I have no enemies in these parts. Maybe it was an accident. I mean that my car was hit. Maybe some joy-riding kids just picked on me because my heap was parked by itself, way down at the end of the lot."

"Maybe," she said doubtfully.

"That's what Constable Fred Aikens thinks. Claims you've had a lot of vandalism by wild kids lately."

"Constable Fred Aikens," she said with great disgust. "He couldn't find his ass with a boxing glove."

"Betty," I said, "tell me something... When you called the cops, when I went out to look at my car, did you tell them my name? Did you say the car was owned by Samuel Todd?"

She thought a moment, frowning.

"No," she said definitely. "I just told them a customer had gotten his tires slashed. I didn't mention your name."

"When Aikens showed up and was inspecting the car— this was before he checked my license and registration— he called me Mr. Todd. I just wondered how he knew who I was."

"Maybe he saw you around Coburn and asked who you were. Or maybe someone pointed you out to him."

"That's probably what it was," I said casually. "Someone pointed me out to him."

"Ready for another?" she asked, nodding toward the bottle.

"Sure."

"Use fresh cups. They begin to leak if you use them too long."

I poured us two more drinks in fresh cups. She drank hers with no gasps, coughs, or changes of expression. I hardly saw her throat move; she just tilted it down. No way was I going to try keeping up with this lady.

"You're in Coburn on business, Mr. Todd? If you don't mind my asking?"

"I don't mind," I said, and I told her, briefly, about the Bingham Foundation, the Thorndecker application, and how I had come to Crittenden to make a field investigation.

"I know that Crittenden bunch," she said. "The Thorndeckers have been over two or three times for dinner. That wife is a doll, isn't she?"

"Yes," I said. "A doll."

"And we get staff from the nursing home, and a lot of the young kids from the lab. Usually on Saturday and Sunday nights. A noisy bunch, but they mean no harm. Drink up a storm. Mostly beer or wine."

"Mary Thorndecker ever show up?"

"Never heard of her. Who is she?"

"Thorndecker's daughter. Stepdaughter actually. Twenty-seven. Spinsterish looking."

"I don't think I've ever seen her."

"How about Draper? Dr. Kenneth Draper?"

"Him I know. A loner. He comes in two or three nights a week. Late. Sits by himself. Drinks until he's got a load on. A couple of times he got a crying jag."

"Oh?" I said. "That's interesting. How about Stella Beecham? She's chief nurse at Crittenden Hall."

"Yeah," Betty Hanrahan said scornfully, "I know that one. I had to kick her ass out of here. She was hustling one of my young waitresses. Listen, I'm strictly live and let live. I don't care who screws who. Or how. But not on my premises. I got a license to think about. Also, this waitress's folks are friends of mine, and I promised to keep an eye on the kid. So I had to give that nurse the heave-ho. That's one tough bimbo."

"Yes," I agreed, "she is. Betty, I don't want you telling any tales out of school, but did Julie Thorndecker, the doll, ever come in with any man but her husband?"

"No," she said promptly. "At least not while I was working, and I usually am. You want me to ask around?"

"No, thanks. You've done plenty for me already, and I

appreciate it. Could I call a cab—if there is such a thing around here? I've got to get back to the Inn."

"I'll do better than that," she said. "You need wheels until Mike fixes up your car. I can take care of that. Not a car exactly. I drive a Mark Five; you can't have that, but we got a wreck, an old Ford pickup. We use it for shopping and put a plow on it to clear snow off the parking lot. It's not much to look at, but it goes. You're welcome to use it until you get your own car back."

I didn't want to do it, but she wouldn't take No for an answer. I kissed her thankfully. Much woman.

So there I was, twenty minutes later, rattling back to Coburn in the unheated cab of an ancient pickup truck that seemed to be held together with Dentyne and Dill's pipe cleaners. But it rolled, and I was so busy figuring out its temperamental gearbox, trying to coax it to do over thirty-five, and mastering its tendency to turn to the right, that I was back at the Coburn Inn before I remembered that I had forgotten to pay my lunch tab at Red Dog Betty's. When I returned to New York, I resolved, I would send Betty Hanrahan a handsome gift.

Something encrusted with rhinestones, seed pearls, and sequins. She'd like that.

Up in my room, I glared balefully at those two drinks lying quietly in the bottom of the quart vodka bottle, not doing anyone any harm. Not doing anyone any good either. I got my fresh bathroom glass and emptied the bottle. I flopped down and took a sip. So far that day I had swilled beer, Scotch, ale, bourbon and vodka. How had I managed to miss ouzo, sangria, and hard cider?

I drank morosely. I was not feeling gruntled. The slashing of my tires seemed such a childish thing to do. I knew it was intended as a warning—but how juvenile can you get?

I figured it had to be Constable Fred Aikens, acting on orders from Ronnie Goodfellow. I could even imagine how it went:

Aikens makes a routine patrol of the parking lot at Red Dog Betty's. Or maybe he's been tailing me since he saw me nosing around Crittenden Hall. Anyway, he spots me parked outside the roadhouse, thigh-to-thigh with Julie Thorndecker. If Aikens didn't actually see her face, he sure as hell recognized her blue MGB nuzzling my Grand Prix. So he hightails it to the nearest public phone. It must have gone something like this:

"Ronnie? Fred. Did I wake you up?"

"That's okay. What's going on?"

"I just spotted your girlfriend's car. Parked in the lot at Red Dog Betty's."

"So?"

"Right next to a black Grand Prix. She's sitting in the front seat of the Pontiac with this tall dude. Thought you might want to know."

Silence.

"Ronnie? You there?"

"I'm here. That son of a bitch!"

"You know him?"

"A snoop from the City. A guy named Todd. He's here to investigate Thorndecker about that grant."

"Oh. It's okay then? Them being together?"

Silence.

"I just thought you might want to know, Ronnie."

"Yeah. Thanks. Listen, Fred. Could you fix that smartass bastard?"

"Fix him?"

"Just his car. Don't touch him. But if you get the chance, you could do a job on the car."

"What for, Ronnie?"

"Just to give him something to think about."

"Oh, yeah, I get it. You know that hatchet you took away from Abe Tompkins when he was going to brain his missus?"

"I remember."

"The hatchet's still in the trunk. If I get the chance, maybe I can chop down that Grand Prix."

"Thanks, Fred. I won't forget it."

"You'd do the same for me—right?"

"Right."

I figured it went something like that. But solving the Mystery of the Slashed Tires gave me no satisfaction. Small mystery; small solution. It had nothing to do with the Thorndecker investigation.

I thought.

I sat there, trying to make the vodka last, glowering at nothing. In any inquiry there is an initial period during which the investigator asks, listens, observes, collects, accumulates, and generally lets things happen to him, with no control.

Then, when certain networks are established, relationships glimpsed, the investigator must start flexing his biceps and make things happen. This is the Opening Phase, when all those sealed cans get their lids peeled off, you lean close to peer in—and usually turn away when the stench flops your stomach.

It was time, I decided, to get started. One thing at a time. I chose the first puzzle of the Thorndecker inquiry. It turned out to be ridiculously easy.

But the simple ones sometimes take the most time to unravel. I remember working a pilferage case in a two-story Saigon warehouse. This place stored drugs for front-line medical units and base hospitals. An inventory turned up horrendous shortages.

The warehouse had three entrances. I had two of them sealed up; all military and civilian personnel had to enter and exit from one door. I doubled the guards, and everyone leaving the place had to undergo a complete body search. The thefts continued. I checked for secret interior caches, for tunnels. I even had a metal detector set up, the kind airports use, in case someone was swallowing the drugs in small metal containers, or getting them out in capsules up the rectum.

Nothing worked. We were still losing drugs in hefty amounts, and I was going nuts trying to figure how they were getting the stuff out of the place.

Know how I solved it? One day I was sitting at my desk in the security office. I took the last cigarette out of a pack. I crumpled the empty pack in my fist and tossed it negligently out an open window. I then leapt to my feet and shouted something a little stronger than "Eureka!"

That's how they were doing it, all right. A bad guy was dropping the stuff out a second-story window, right into the arms of a pal standing in an alley below. Simple? Sure it was. All the good scams are. Took me three weeks to break it.

But finding the author of the note, "Thorndecker kills," wasn't going to take me that long. I hoped.

I grabbed up my hat and trenchcoat, and went back down to the lobby, using the stairs. Twice as fast, I had learned, as waiting for Sam Livingston's rheumatic elevator.

I glanced toward the cigar counter, but Millie Goodfellow had a customer, one of the antediluvian permanent residents. He was leaning over the counter, practically falling, trying to read the sign on the front of her tight T-shirt.

"What?" I heard his querulous voice. "What does it say? I left my reading glasses upstairs."

I went to the desk, and the baldy on duty looked up, irritated at being interrupted in his contemplation of the *Playboy* centerfold.

"Yes?" he said testily.

"I need a new typewriter ribbon," I said. "You got any place in town that sells office supplies?"

"Of course we do," he said in an aggrieved tone, angry because he thought I doubted Coburn could provide such an amenity.

He told me how to find Coburn Office Supplies, a store located one block north of the post office.

"I'm sure they'll have everything you need," he said stiffly.

I thanked him, and started away. Then my eyes were caught by the right shoulder of his blue serge suit. He saw me staring, and twisted his head and looked down, trying to see what I was looking at. I reached out and brushed his shoulder twice with the edge of my hand.

"There," I said. "That looks much better."

"Thank you, Mr. Todd," he said, humble and abashed.

There was nothing on his shoulder, of course. God, I can be a nasty son of a bitch.

I found Coburn Office Supplies, a hole-in-the-wall with a dusty window and a sad display of pencils, erasers, faded stationery, and office gadgets already beginning to rust. The opening door hit a suspended bell that jangled in the quiet of the deserted store. I looked around. The place was a natural for a Going-Out-of-Business Sale.

And the little guy who came dragging out of the back room was perfectly suited to be custodian of this mausoleum. All I remember about him was that he wore shredded carpet slippers and had six long strands of hair (I counted them) brushed sideways across his pale, freckled skull.

"Yes, sir," he sighed. "Can I help?"

That last word came out "hep." In fact, he said, "Kin ah hep?" Southern, I thought, but I couldn't place it exactly. Hardscrabble land somewhere.

I had intended to waltz him around, but he was so beaten, so defeated, I had no desire to make a fool of him. Life had anticipated me. So I just said:

"I want to bribe you."

The pale, watery eyes blinked.

"Bribe me?"

I took out my wallet, extracted a ten-dollar bill. I dangled it, flipping it with my fingers.

"This is the only office supply store in town?"

"Wull . . . sure," he said, eyeing that sawbuck like it was a passport to Heaven, or at least out of Coburn.

"Good," I said. "The ten is yours for a simple answer to a simple question."

"I don' know . . ." he said, anxious and cautious at the same time.

"You can always deny you talked to me," I told him. "No one here but us chickens. Your word against mine."

"Yeah," he said slowly, brightening, "thass right, ain't it? Whut's the question?"

236

"Anyone in town buy ribbons for an Olympia Standard typewriter?"

"Olympia Standard?" he said, licking his dry lips. "Only one machine like that in town as I know of."

"Who?"

"Mary Thorndecker. She comes in ever' so often to buy—"

I handed him the ten.

"Thanks," I said.

"Mebbe ever' two months or so," he droned on, staring down at the bill in his hand. "She always asks—"

The bell over the door jangled as I went out.

I strutted back to the Coburn Inn, so pleased with myself it was sickening. As a reward for my triumph, I stopped off at Sandy's and bought another quart of Popov, a fine Russian-sounding vodka distilled in Hartford, Conn. But by the time I entered Room 3-F, my euphoria had evaporated; I didn't even open the bottle.

I lowered myself gingerly into one of those grasping armchairs and sat sprawled, staring at nothing. All the big problems were still there. Mary Thorndecker may have written the note, and Ronnie Goodfellow may have tried to recover it. An interesting combo. Tinker to Evers to Chance. But who was Chance?

How's this?

Mary Thorndecker types out a note, "Thorndecker kills," and leaves it for me. What's her motive? Well, maybe she's driven by something as innocent as outrage at the vivisection being practiced at the Crittenden Research Laboratory. If she's a deeply religious woman, a fundamentalist, as everyone claims, she could be goaded to write, "Thorndecker kills." Anyway, she writes the note, for whatever reason.

Now, who might Mary tell what she had done? She could tell Dr. Kenneth Draper. But I doubted that; he was deeply involved in the activities of the research lab. She might tell her half-brother, Edward Thorndecker. That made more sense to me. She wants to protect Edward from what she conceives to be an evil existing in Crittenden.

Let's say she does tell Edward, and hints to him that she intends to end what she sees as wickedness pervading the tiled corridors of Crittenden. But Edward, smitten by Julie's beauty and sexuality—I had observed this; it was more than a crush—tells his stepmother what Mary is up to. Especially the note left in my box at the Coburn Inn.

Julie, wanting to protect her husband, the "great man," before the letter can be used as evidence to deny Thorndecker's application for a grant, asks Constable Ronnie Goodfellow to recover the damned, and damning thing. For all Julie knows, it could be a long bill of particulars signed by Thorndecker's stepdaughter.

And because he is so pussy-whipped, Goodfellow gives it the old college try (using his wife's passkey), and strikes out. Only because I had already mailed the note to Donner & Stern for typewriter analysis.

All right, I admit it: the whole thing was smoke. A scenario based on what I knew of the people involved and how they might react if their self-interest was threatened. But it all made sense to me. As a matter of fact, it turned out to be about 80 percent accurate.

But it was that incorrect 20 percent that almost got me killed.

I had something to eat that evening. I think it was a tunafish salad and a glass of milk; the size of my gut was beginning to embarrass me. Anyway, I dined lightly and had only two vodka gimlets for dessert at the Coburn Inn bar before I climbed into Betty Hanrahan's pickup truck, drove happily out of Coburn, and rattled south on the river road. I was heading for Mary Thorndecker's church. It wasn't that I was looking for salvation, although I could have used a small dollop. I just wanted to touch all bases. I wanted to find out why a young, intelligent woman seemed intent on destroying a man she reportedly loved.

I've attended revival meetings in various parts of the country, including a snake-handling session in a tent pitched on the outskirts of Macon, Georgia. I've heard members of fundamentalist churches speak in tongues, and I've seen apparent cripples throw away their crutches or rise from wheelchairs to dance a jig. I'm familiar with the oratorical style of backwoods evangelists and the fervor of their congregations. This kind of down-home religion is not my cup of vodka, but I can't see where they're hurting anyone—except possibly themselves, and you won't find anything in the Constitution denying a citizen the right to make a fool of himself.

So I thought I knew what to expect: a mob of farmers, rednecks, and assorted blue-collar types shouting up a storm, clapping their hands, and stomping their feet as they confessed their piddling sins and came forward to be saved. All this orchestrated by a leather-lunged preacher man who knew all the buzzwords and phrases to lash his audience to a religious frenzy.

I was in for a surprise.

The First Fundamentalist Church of Lord Jesus was housed not in a tent or ramshackle barn, but in a neat, white clapboard building with well-kept grounds, a lighted parking area, and a general appearance of modest prosperity. The windows were washed, there were bright boxes of ivy, and the cross atop the small steeple was gilded and illuminated with a spotlight.

I had expected a junkyard collection of battered sedans, pickup trucks, rusted vans, and maybe a few motorcycles. But the cars I saw gave added evidence of the economic well-being of the congregation: plenty of Fords, Chevys, VW's, and Toyotas, but also a goodly sprinkling of imported sports cars, Cadillacs, Mercedes-Benzes, and one magnificent maroon Bentley. I parked Betty Hanrahan's heap amongst all that polished splendor, feeling like a poor relation.

They were singing "Jesus, Lover of My Soul" when I entered. I slid into an empty rear pew, opened a hymnal, and looked around. A simple interior painted an off-white, polished walnut pews, a handsome altar covered with a richly brocaded cloth, an enormous painting of the crucifixion on the wall behind the altar. It was no better and no worse than the usual church painting. Lots of blood. The seated congregation was singing along with music from an electronic organ up front against the left wall. There was a door set into the opposite wall. I assumed it led to the vestry.

There wasn't any one thing about the place that I could label as definitely fake or phony. But I began to get the damndest feeling that I had wandered into a movie or TV set, put together for a big climactic scene like a wedding or funeral, or maybe the church into which the bullet-riddled hero staggers to cough his last on the altar, reaching for the cross.

Trying to analyze this odd impression, I decided that maybe the *newness* of the place had something to do with it. Churches usually look used, worn, comfortably shabby. This one looked like it had been put up that morning; there wasn't a nick, stain, or scratch that I could see. It even smelled of paint and fresh plaster.

Maybe the congregation had something to do with my itchy feeling that the whole thing was a scam. There were a few blacks, but most of them were whites in their twenties and thirties. The men favored beards, the women either pigtails or hair combed loosely to their waist. Both sexes sported chain necklaces and medallions. Most of them, men and women, wore jeans. But they were French jeans, tailored jeans, or jeans with silver studs, appliques, or designs traced with bugle beads and seed pearls.

All I could do was guess, but I guessed there was a good assortment of academics, writers, artists, musicians, poets, and owners of antique shops. They looked to be the kind of people who had worked their way through Freudian analysis, high colonics, est, Yoga, TM, primal scream, communal tub bathing, and cocaine. Not because they particularly needed any of these things, but because they had been the *in* things to do. I'd make book that the First Fundamentalist Church of Lord Jesus was only the latest brief enthusiasm in their fad-filled lives, and as soon as they all got "born again," the whole crowd would decamp for the nearest disco, with shouts of loud laughter and a great blaring of horns.

The hymn came to an end. The congregation put their hymnals in the racks on the pew backs in front of them. A young man in the front pew stood up and faced us. "Faced" is an exaggeration; he had so much hair, beard, and mustache, all I could see were two blinking eyes.

"Welcome to the First Fundamentalist Church of Lord Jesus. My name is Irving Peacock, and I am first vestryperson of your church. Most of you I know, and most of you know each other. But I do see a few brothers and sisters who, I believe, are here for the first time. To these newcomers, may I say, 'Welcome! Welcome to our family!' It is our custom, at the beginning of the service, for each sister and brother to turn to the right and left and kiss their neighbors as a symbol of our devotion to the love and passion of Lord Jesus. Now, please, all kiss. On the lips now! On the lips!"

The congregation stood. I rose along with them, wondering what kind of a nuthouse I had strayed into. I watched, fascinated, as men and women turned right and left, embracing and kissing their neighbors. A great smacking of lips filled the room.

I was alone in the rear pew and figured I was safe. But no, a grizzly bear of a man in the pew in front of me kissed right and left, then turned suddenly and held out his arms to me.

"Brother!" he said.

What could I do—say, "Please, not on the first date?" So I kissed him, or let him kiss me. He had a walrus mustache. It tickled. Also, he had just eaten an Italian dinner. A cheap Italian dinner.

After this orgy of osculation, the congregation sat down, and Irving Peacock announced the offertory. Contributions would be accepted by vestrypersons John Millhouse and Mary Thorndecker, and we were urged to give generously to "support the splendid work of Father Michael Bellamy and to signify our faith in and love for our Lord Jesus."

The two vestrypersons started down the center aisle. Brass trays, velvet-lined to eliminate the vulgar sound of shekels clinking, were passed along each pew, hand-to-hand, then returned to the aisle. I saw that Mary Thorndecker was collecting on the other side. I slipped across the aisle, into the empty rear pew on her side. I watched her approach, features still and expressionless.

She was wearing an earth-colored tweed suit over a death-gray sweater. Opaque hose and flat-heeled brogues. Her hair was drawn back tightly, pinned back with a barrette. No jewelry. No makeup. I wondered if she was making herself as unattractive as possible in reaction to Julie's obvious charms.

She moved slowly down the aisle toward me, not looking up. Even when she took the brass tray from the pew in front of me, she still hadn't seen me. I had time to note the plate contained a nifty pile of coins and folding money. Father Michael Bellamy was doing all right.

Then she was at my pew. Her eyes rose as she proffered the tray.

"Why . . . Mr. Todd!" she said, not quite gasping, her face flushing.

I looked at her. I may have smiled pleasantly.

"Thorndecker kills?" I said.

Down went the brass tray. Coins clanged, bounced, rolled. Bills fluttered to the floor. For a moment I thought she was going to cave. Her face went putty-white, then greenish. A pale hand fluttered up to her hair, and just hung there, waving futilely.

Then she was gone, dashing out the double-door. I thought I heard a sound: a sob, a moan. I let her go. I helped others gather up the spilled coins, the scattered bills. I added a fin of my own. Atonement.

The collection plates were returned to the first vestryperson; everyone settled down. A few moments passed while the congregation gradually quieted. Nothing happened. But I felt the expectation, saw heads turning toward the vestry door. Still nothing. A very professionally calculated stage wait. Tension grew.

Then the effete lad at the Hammond organ played something that sounded suspiciously like a fanfare. The vestry door was flung open. Father Michael Bellamy, clad in flowing white robes, swept into the nave, arms outstretched to embrace his followers.

"Blessings on my children!" he intoned.

"Blessings on our father!" they shouted back.

He stood before the altar, arms wide, head thrown back, eyes turned heavenward.

"Let us pray together a moment in silence," he declaimed. "Let our souls' voices merge and rise to Lord Jesus, asking love, understanding, and redemption for our sins."

All heads bowed. Except mine. I was too busy studying Father Michael Bellamy.

A big man, maybe six-four. Broad shoulders and chest. I couldn't see much more because of those robes, but got an impression of a comfortable corporation. A marvelous head of wavy, snow-white hair. If it wasn't a carpet, it had enjoyed the attentions of an artful coiffeur. No one's hair could be that white or that billowy without aid.

The hair was long enough and full enough to cover what I guessed were big, meaty ears. I reckoned that from the rest of his face, also big and meaty. A nose like a sausage, a brow like a rare roast, chin and jowls like beef liver. The man was positively appetizing. Stuck in all this rosy suet were glistening eyes, round and hard as black marbles.

The voice was something; it made the electronic organ sound like a twopenny whistle. Orotund, booming, it not only filled the church but rattled the windows and, for all I knew, browned the ivy in the outside window boxes. That voice conquered me; it was an instrument, and if a good soprano can shatter a wine glass, this guy should have been able to bring down the Brooklyn Bridge.

"Children," he said, and his praying family looked up, "tonight we shall speak of sin and forgiveness. We shall speak of the unutterable lusts that corrupt the human heart and soul; and how we may all be washed clean in the blood of our Redemptor, Lord Jesus Christ of Nazareth."

Then he was off. I had heard the sermon before, but never so well delivered. The man was a natural, or practiced preacher. His magnificent voice roared, whispered, entreated, scorned, laughed, hissed, wailed. There was nothing he could not do with that voice. And the gesturings and posturings! Waves, flappings, pointings, clenched fists, pleading palms, stoopings, leaps, stridings from one side of the platform to the other. And tears. Oh yes. The eyes moist and brimming on demand.

Did they listen to his words? I wasn't sure. I found it difficult to listen, so overwhelming was his physical performance. He was a whirlwind, white robes streaming in the tempest, and what he said seemed of less importance than the presence of the man himself. Behind him, on the wall, Christ bled and died on the cross. And Father Michael Bellamy, the white-haired prophet incarnate, stamped the boards before this image and mesmerized his trendy flock with a performance worth four Oscars, three Emmys, two Grammys, one Ike, and a platinum record. The man was a master.

As I said, the sermon was familiar. He told us that the human heart was a fetid swamp, filled with nasty crawling things. We were all sinners, in thought or in deed. We betrayed the best impulses of our souls, and turned instead to lechery, lust, and lasciviousness. (The Father was big on alliteration.)

He gave a fifteen-minute catalogue of human sins of the flesh, listened to attentively by the congregation who, I figured, wanted to find out if they had missed any. This portion of the sermon was all stern denunciation, a jeremiad against the permissiveness of our society which condoned conduct that in happier times would have earned burning at the stake, or at least a holiday weekend in the stocks.

And where was such lewdness and licentiousness leading us? To eternal damnation, that's where. To a hell which, according to Father Bellamy's description, was something like a Finnish sauna without the snowbanks.

But all was not lost. There was a way to redeem our wasted lives. That was to pledge our remaining days to the service of Lord Jesus, following in His footsteps. It was being born again, finding the love and forgiveness of the Father of Us All, and dedicating our lives to walking the path of righteousness.

Up to this point, the sermon had followed the standard revivalist pattern: scare 'em, then save 'em. But then Bellamy got into an area that made me a little queasy.

He said there was only one way to prove sincere relinquishment of a wicked life. That was by full public confession, acknowledgment of past sins, and whole-hearted and soul-felt determination to make a complete break with the past, to seek the comforting embrace of Lord Jesus and be saved.

"O, my children!" cried Father Bellamy, throwing his gowned arms wide like a great white bat. "Is there not one among ye willing to stand now, this moment, and confess your most secret vices openly and honestly in the presence of Lord Jesus and these witnesses?"

As a matter of fact, there was more than one amongst us; several leaped to their feet and clamored for attention. What followed convinced me that this mob had come to church directly from a grass-uppers-LSD buffet, or was on leave from a local acorn academy.

A young woman, tears streaming down her cheeks, described, graphically, how she had been unfaithful to her husband on "myriad occasions," and how she was tortured by the memories. During this titillating recital, her hand was held by the young man seated beside her. He was, I presumed, the betrayed husband. Or he could have been one of the tortured memories.

A young man, twisting his fingers nervously, told how he had been seduced by his aunt when he was wearing his Boy Scout uniform, and how the relationship continued until he was wearing a U.S. Army uniform, at which time the aunt deserted him, leaving him with a seared psyche and a feeling of guilt that frequently resulted in nocturnal emissions.

Three witnesses, in rapid succession, testified to how much they hated their mother/father/brother/sister, and wished them dead.

A woman confessed to unnatural sex acts with a dalmatian owned by her local fire company.

A stuttering lad, desperately sincere, confessed to a secret passion for Madame Ernestine Schumann-Heink, who died in 1936. He had come across her photograph in an old magazine, and her image had haunted his waking hours and dreams ever since.

A wispy blond girl, eyes glazed and enormously swollen, said she had this "thing." She could never get rid of this "thing." She thought about it constantly and she wanted Lord Jesus, or at least Father Michael Bellamy, to exorcise this "thing."

It went on and on like that: a litany of personal confessions that had me squirming with shame and embarrassment. I am, by nature, a private man. I could match anyone of them sin for sin, depravity for depravity, in dream or in deed, but I'd be damned if I'd stand voluntarily before a jury of my peers and spill my guts. It was just none of their business. I don't think I could do it in a confessional booth either. I can't even watch TV talk shows. Listen, if we all told one another what we really did, thought, and dreamed, the world would dissolve into mad laughter, helpless with despair, and then who would have the strength and resolve to plan wars?

So I rose quietly from the rear pew and slipped out the church door, just as an older, bearded man was describing how he had been abusing himself ever since he picked up a weight-lifting magazine in a barber shop and, as a consequence, had become a chronic bed-wetter.

I climbed into the dank cab of the pickup. I turned up the collar of my trenchcoat and slouched down. I lighted a cigarette and waited. I wasn't bored; I had a lot of questions to ponder.

Like: were those idiots inside who were stripping themselves naked in front of friends and strangers really sincere about this confession and redemption jazz? Or was it just another kick like Zen or rolfing?

Like: had any bright young sociologist ever written a PhD thesis on the remarkable similarities between bucolic American revival meetings and sophisticated American group therapy sessions? Both had a father-leader (preacher/psychiatrist). Both demanded public confession. Both promised salvation.

Like: where did Mary Thorndecker run after I jolted her? I figured she'd have to call me, that night or Saturday morning. I put my money on a morning call, after she had a desperate night wondering how I had fingered her as the author of the anonymous note.

Three cigarettes later, the service ended. The congregation of the First Fundamentalist Church of Lord Jesus streamed forth into the cold night air, presumably cleansed and rejuvenated. I had been right: there were bursts of raucous laughter and a great tooting of horns as they roared away from the parking lot. Kids let out of school.

Still I sat there in Betty Hanrahan's broken wreck. The spotlight illuminating the steeple cross went out. The interior lights of the church went out. Only one car remained in the parking area: that impressive maroon Bentley. Of course, it would be his.

I got out of the truck slowly, being careful not to slam that tinny door. I made a slow circuit of the church building. Lights still burned in a side extension of the nave: the vestry. I went back to the main entrance. The double-door was still unlocked. I slid in, tiptoed up the aisle. Even in broad daylight a church is a ghostly place. At night, in almost total darkness, it can spook you. Don't ask me why.

The only illumination was a thin bar of light coming from the interior door of the vestry. I heard laughter, the clink of glasses. I pulled down my tweed hat to shadow my eyes, stuck my hands deep in the trenchcoat pockets. All I needed was a Lone Ranger mask.

I shoved the door open with my foot and stalked in. I was thinking of a joke a cop had told me: this nervous robber goes into a bank on his first job and pulls out a gun. "All right, you mother-stickers," he snarls. "This is a fuck-up."

There were two of them in there. Father Michael Bellamy had doffed his pristine robes. Now he was wearing a beautifully tailored suit of soft, gray doeskin with a Norfolk jacket, lavender shirt, knitted black silk tie. I had time to eyeball his jeweled cufflinks: twin Kohinoors. He was seated behind a desk, counting the night's collection. Piling the coins in neat columns, tapping the bills into square stacks.

The other gink was the limp young man I had seen playing the organ. He was a washed-out lad with strands of lank blond hair falling across his acned forehead. The acne was hard to spot under the pancake makeup. He was wearing a ranch suit: faded blue jeans and jacket. With high-heeled western boots yet. He looked as much like a Wyoming cowpoke as Joan Powell looks like Sophie Tucker.

There was a bottle of Remy Martin on the desk. Bellamy was taking his straight in a little balloon glass. The organist was diluting his cognac with a can of Pepsi, which is like blowing your nose in a Gobelin tapestry.

The effete youth was first to react to my entrance. He jerked to his feet and glared at me, not knowing whether to shit, go blind, or wind his watch.

Bellamy didn't pop a capillary.

"Easy, Dicky," he said soothingly. "Easy now." Then to me, brightly: "Yes, sir, and how may I be of service?"

I gave them the silent treatment, looking at them, one to the other, back and forth.

"Well?" Bellamy said. "If it's spiritual advice you're seeking, my son, I must tell you I conduct personal sessions only on Tuesdays and Thursdays, beginning at twelve noon."

I said nothing. He leaned forward a little to stare at my shadowed face.

"At the service tonight, weren't you?" he said in that rich, rolling voice. "In the rear pew, left side?"

"Keen eyes," I said. "What were you doing, counting the house?"

I had been keeping watch on nervous Dicky. But as I

spoke, he relaxed back in his chair, apparently reassured. But he never took his glittering eyes off me.

"If this is a robbery," Father Bellamy said steadily, "you're welcome to everything you see before you. Just don't hurt us."

"It isn't a robbery," I told him, "and why should I want to hurt you?"

That Bellamy was one cool cat. He sat back comfortably, took out a pigskin cigar case, and went through all the business of selecting, cutting off the tip, and lighting it with a wooden match. The whole ceremony took about two minutes. I waited patiently. He took an experimental puff to see if it was drawing satisfactorily. Then he blew a plume of blued smoke at me.

"All right," he said, "what's this all about?"

"It's a grift, isn't it?" I asked him.

"Grift?" he said perplexedly. "I don't believe I'm familiar with that term."

"Bullshit," I said. "You're in the game. It's all a con."

"A con?" he said. "Could you possibly be implying trickery? That I, as an ordained minister of the First Fundamentalist Church of Lord Jesus, am running a confidence game designed to deceive and defraud my parishioners?"

"Tell you what," I said, "you call the cops and tell them I'm threatening you. I'll wait right here until they come. No rough stuff, I promise you. Then, when they take me in, I'll ask them to run a trace. The Feds should have you in their files. Or someone, somewhere. They'll find out about the outstanding warrants, skips, and like that. Well? How about it?"

He looked at me with a beatific smile, rolling the cigar around in his plump lips.

"Mike, for Christ's sake!" Dicky cried. "Let's throw this turd out on his ass."

"Now, sonny," I said, "be nice. Have a little respect for a seeker of the truth. How about it, Mr. Bellamy?"

He sighed deeply, running a palm lightly over his billowy white hair.

"How did you tumble?" he asked me curiously.

"You're too good," I said. "Too good for the come-to-Jesus scam. With your looks and voice and delivery, I figure you for Palm Beach or Palm Springs, peddling cheesy oil stock. Or maybe in a Wall Street boardroom, trading conglomerates. You don't belong in the boondocks, Mr. Bellamy."

The Father smiled with great satisfaction. He raised his brandy snifter to me.

"Thank you for those kind words, sir," he said. "Did you hear that, Dicky? Haven't I told you the same thing?"

"Lots of times," Dicky grumbled.

"But I haven't asked your name, sir," Bellamy said to me.

"Jones," I said.

"To be sure," he said. "Very well, Mr. Jones. Assuming—just assuming, mind you—that your false and malicious allegations are correct, where do we go from here?"

"Mike, what are you doing?" the organist yelled. "Can't you see that this crud—"

Bellamy whirled on him.

"Shut your trap!" he said in a steely voice, the black eyes hard. "Just sit there and drink that loathsome mixture and don't say word one. Understand?"

"Yes, Mike," the youth said meekly.

"As I was saying," Bellamy went on blandly, turning back to me, "where do we go from here?"

I was still standing. There were two empty chairs in the room, but he didn't ask me to sit down. That was okay. Oneupsmanship. You keep a guy standing in front of your desk, he becomes the inferior, the supplicant.

"I don't want to blow the whistle on you," I assured him. "You got a nice thing going here, and as far as I'm concerned, you can milk it until you run out of sinners. I just want a little information. Whatever you can tell me about one of your vestrypersons."

He took a sip of cognac, a puff of his cigar. Then he dipped the mouth of the cigar in the brandy and took a pull on that. He looked at me narrowly through the smoke.

"Are you heat?"

"No. Just a concerned citizen."

"Aren't we all?" he said, smiling again. "Who do you want?"

"Mary Thorndecker."

"Mike, will you stop it?" the damp youth agonized. "You don't have to tell this creep anything, except to get lost."

"Sonny, sonny," I groaned, "can't you be civilized? The Father and I have reached a cordial understanding. Can't you see that? Now just let us get on with our business, and then I'll climb out of your hair, and you can go back to counting the take. Won't that be nice?"

"Listen to the gentleman, Dicky," Bellamy rumbled. "He is obviously a man of breeding and a rough but nimble wit. Mary Thorndecker, you said? Ah, yes. A plain jane. And yet I have the feeling that with the advice and assistance of a clever hairdresser, corsetiere, and dress designer, our dull, drab Mary might blossom into quite a swan indeed. Do you share that dream, Mr. Jones?"

"Could be," I said. "But what I really came to find out is anything you know about her private life, especially her family. Has she ever had one of those private consultations with you on Tuesdays and Thursdays, beginning at noon?"

"On occasion."

"And?"

"A very troubled young woman," he said promptly, staring over my head. "A difficult family situation. A stepmother who is younger and apparently much prettier than Mary. A man who wishes to marry her and who, for some reason she has not revealed to me, she both loves and loathes."

"And?" I said.

"And what?"

"That's it? That's all she talked about in those private sessions?"

251

"Well..." he said, waving a hand negligently, "she did confess to a few personal peccadilloes, a few minor misdeeds that could hardly be dignified as sins. Would you care to hear them?"

"No," I said. "And that's all there is?"

He smoked slowly, frowning in an effort to remember conversations in which, I was sure, he had no interest whatsoever. He leaned forward to pour himself another cognac. I licked my lips as obviously as I could. It won me an amused smile, but no invitation.

"Mike," Dicky said loudly, "you've told this jerk enough. Let's bounce him."

"Sonny," I said, "I'm trying very hard to ignore you, but it's a losing battle. If you'd like to—"

"Now, now," Bellamy interrupted smoothly, raising a palm. "There is no room for animosity and ill-feeling in God's house. Calm down, you two; I detest scenes." He took another sip of brandy, closing his eyes, smacking his wet lips. Then he opened his eyes again and looked at me thoughtfully. "She did say something else. Ask something else. In the nature of a hypothetical question. To wit: what is the proper course of conduct for a child of Lord Jesus who becomes aware that her loved ones are involved in something illegal? They are, in fact, not only sinning but engaged in a criminal activity."

"Did she tell you who the loved ones are?"

"No."

"Did she tell you the nature of the criminal activity?"

"No."

"What did you tell her to do?"

"I suggested she report the entire matter to the police," he said virtuously. "I happen to be a very law-abiding man."

"I'm sure you are," I said.

I decided not to push it any further; he was obviously tiring. After his physical performance at the church service that evening, considering his age it was a wonder he wasn't in intensive care.

"Nice doing business with you, Father," I said. "Keep

up the good work. By the way, I put a finif in the plate tonight. You and sonny have a drink on me."

"Don't call me sonny!" the infuriated youth screamed at me.

"Why not?" I said innocently. "If I had a son, I'd want him to be just like you." I paused at the door, turned back. "Father, just out of curiosity, is Mary Thorndecker a heavy mark?"

"She is generous in contributing to God's work on earth," he said sonorously, rolling his eyes to heaven.

"Could you give me a ballpark figure?" I asked him. He inspected the soaked stump of his cigar closely.

"It is a very large ballpark," he said.

I laughed and left the two of them together. They deserved each other.

I chugged back to Coburn, glad I couldn't coax any more speed out of that groaning heap, because I had some thinking to do. Up to that moment I had vaguely suspected Dr. Telford Gordon Thorndecker might be cutting corners in that combined nursing home-research-lab organization of his. I was thinking along the lines of unethical conduct: not an indictable offense but serious enough to put the kibosh on his application for a grant. Something like trying out new drugs without an informed consent agreement. Or maybe persuading doomed patients to include a plump bequest to the Crittenden Research Laboratory in their wills. Nasty stuff, but difficult, if not impossible, to prosecute.

But Mary Thorndecker hinted at something illegal. A criminal activity. I couldn't guess what it was. I did know it was heavy enough to get Ernie Scoggins chilled when he found out about it. And heavy enough to give Al Coburn the shakes when *he* found out about it.

I must have dreamed up a dozen ugly plots on my way back to Coburn. I had Thorndecker rifling the bank accounts of guests, hypnotizing them into signing over their estates, working on biological warfare for the U.S. Army, trying to determine safe radiation dosages with human subjects, even raping sedated female patients. I went wild, but nothing I imagined really made sense.

I pulled into the parking lot at the Coburn Inn. It was a paved area, lighted with two floods on short poles. They cast puddles of weak yellowish illumination, but most of the lot was either in gloom or lost in black shadow. Still, that was no excuse for what happened next. After the Great Slashed Tire Caper, I should have been more alert.

I parked, got out of the truck, turned to struggle with a balky door lock. The next thing I knew, I was face down on cold cement. That was the sequence: I went down first, and *then* I felt the punch that did it, a slam in the kidneys that spun me around and dumped me. Strange, but even as I realized what had happened, I remember thinking, "That wasn't so bad. It hurt like hell, but this guy is no pro." Probably the last thoughts of every man who's been killed by an amateur.

On the ground, I went into the approved drill: draw up the knees to protect the family jewels, bend neck, cover face and head with folded arms, make yourself into a tight, hard ball. All this to endure the boot you've got to figure is coming. It came, in the short ribs mostly. And though it banged me something fierce, there wasn't any crushing force, and I never came close to losing consciousness. I remember the other guy breathing in wheezing sobs, and thinking he was as much out of condition as I was.

So there I was, lying on my side on a hard bed, curled into a knot. After a few ineffectual kicks to my crossed arms, thighs, and spine, I began to get annoyed. At myself, not the guy who was trying so hard and doing such a lousy job of messing me up.

I recalled an army instructor I had who specialized in unarmed combat. His lecture went something like this:

"Forget about trying to fight with your fists. Forget about those roundhouse swings and uppercuts you see in the movies and on TV. All that'll get you is a fistful of broken knuckles. While you're trying the Fancy Dan stuff, an experienced attacker will be cutting you to ribbons, even if you're a Golden Gloves champ. Rule

Number One: hug him. If he's a karate or judo man, and you stand back, he'll kill you. So get in close where he can't swing his arms or legs. Rule Number Two: there are no rules. Forget about fair play and the Marquis of Queensberry. A guy is trying to murder you. Murder him first. Or at least break him. A knee in the nuts is very effective, but if he's fast enough, he'll turn to take it on his thigh. A punch to the balls is better. A hack at the Adam's apple gets good results. If you can get behind him, put two fingers up his nostrils and yank up. The nose rips. Very nice. Also the eyes. Put in a stiff thumb and roll outward. The eyeball pops out like a pit from a ripe peach. And don't forget your teeth. The human jaw can exert at least two hundred pounds of pressure—enough to take off an ear or nose. Shin kicks are fine, and if you can stomp down on the kneecap, you can get his legs to bend the wrong way. Pretty. Pulling hair comes in handy at times, and fingers bent backward make a nice snapping sound."

He went on and on like that, telling us what we could do to stay alive. So after taking a series of nondisabling kicks, I peeked out from under my folded arms, and the next time I saw a stylish black moccasin flashing for my ribs, I reached out, grabbed an ankle, and pulled hard. He landed on his coccyx, and his sharp yelp of pain was music to my ears.

Then I swarmed all over him. A hard knee into the testicles. A knuckled chop at his throat. I stiffened my thumb and started for the eyes when I suddenly saw that if I carried through, Edward Thorndecker would need a cane and tin cup.

"Oh for God's sake," I said disgustedly.

I dragged myself to my feet, tried to catch my breath. I dusted myself off. I left him lying there, weeping and puking. After my breathing returned to normal, and I had satisfied myself that I had no broken bones or cracked ribs, just bruises and wounded pride, I dug the toe of my boot into his ass.

"Get up," I told him.

"You keep away from her," he croaked, in rage and

frustration. "If you go near my stepmother again, I'll kill you. I swear to God I'll kill you!"

All in that half-lisp of his, sobbed out, coughed out, spluttered out. All in a cracked voice after that hack on his voice box.

I reached down, got a good grip on his collar, hauled him to his feet. I propped him back against the door of the pickup and patted him down. Just in case he was carrying a lethal weapon, like a Ping-Pong paddle or a lime Popsicle. Then I opened the door, shoved him inside, and climbed in after him. I rolled down the windows because he had upchucked all over himself. I lighted a cigarette to help defuse the stench.

I smoked patiently, waiting for his snuffling and whimpering to fade away. I wasn't as calm as it sounds. Every time I thought of how close I came to wasting that young idiot, I'd get the shakes and have to go to deep breathing to get rid of them. I handed over my handkerchief to help him clean himself. But he was one sad looking dude, hanging onto his balls and bending far over to cushion the hurt.

We must have sat there in the damp cold for at least fifteen minutes before he was able to straighten up. He didn't know which part of his anatomy to massage first. I was glad he was aching; his attack had scared me witless. I had thought it was Ronnie Goodfellow, of course. But if *he* had punched me in the kidneys, I'd have been peeing blood for three weeks. After I came to.

"All right," I said, "let's get to it. What makes you think I'm annoying your stepmother?"

"I don't want to talk about it," he said sullenly.

I turned sideways, and laid an open palm against his chops. His head snapped around, and he began crying again.

"Sure you want to talk about it," I said stonily. "Unless you want another knock on the cojones that'll have you singing soprano for the rest of your life."

"She said so," he mumbled.

"Julie told you I made a pass at her?"

"She didn't tell me. She told father. I heard her."

I didn't doubt him.

We sat there in silence. I gave him a cigarette and lighted another for myself. He began to feel a little better; his nerve came back.

"I'm going to tell my father that you beat me up," he said angrily.

"Do that," I told him. "Tell your father that we met by accident in the parking lot of the Coburn Inn, at an hour when you should be home studying, and I suddenly attacked you for no reason at all. Your father is sure to believe it."

"Julie will believe me," he said hotly.

"No one will believe you," I said cruelly. "Everyone knows you're a sack of shit. The only thing you've got going for you is that you're young enough to outgrow it. Possibly."

"Oh God," he said hollowly, "I want to die."

"Love her that much, do you?" I said.

"I saw her naked once," he said, in the same tone of wonderment someone might use to say, "I saw a flying saucer."

"Good on you," I said, "but she happens to be your father's wife."

"He doesn't appreciate her," he said.

What's the use? You can't talk to snotty kids. They know it all.

"All right, Edward," I said, sighing. "I could tell you that I never propositioned your stepmother, but I know you wouldn't believe me. Now you tell me something: what's going on in the research lab?"

"Going on?" he said, puzzled. "Well, you know, they do experiments. I don't understand that stuff. I'm not into science."

"Oh? What are you into?"

"I like poetry. I write poems. Julie says they're very good."

Full circle. Thorndecker's father was a poet. Thorndecker's son was a poet. I hoped the son wouldn't die as his grandfather had.

"And you've got no idea of anything strange going on out there?"

"I don't know what you're talking about."

I believed him.

He said he had "borrowed" Julie's sports car and parked it a block away. I told him that if he was smart, he'd drive directly home, soak in a hot tub, and keep his mouth shut about what had happened.

"I'm here to check on your father's qualifications for a grant," I said. "I don't think he or Julie would be happy to hear you tried to dent my head tonight."

I don't believe he had thought of that. It sobered him. He got out of the truck, then turned back to stick his head through the open window.

"Listen," he said, "my father's a great man."

"I know," I said. "Everyone tells me so."

"He wouldn't do anything wrong," he said, then walked away into the shadows. I watched him go. After awhile I got out, locked up, trotted to the Inn.

I'd had my fill of parking lots for one day.

Up in Room 3-F, I stripped down and inspected the damage. Not too bad. Some scrapings, bruises, minor contusions. I took a shower as hot as I could stand it, and that helped. Then I cracked that bottle of vodka I had purchased ten years ago and bought myself a princely snort.

I sat there in my skin, sipping warm Popov, and wondering why Julie Thorndecker had done it. Why she had told her husband that I had, ah, taken liberties. I couldn't blame it on the "woman scorned" motive; she was more complex than that.

This is what I came up with:

She was preparing ammunition in case I gave Thorndecker a negative report, as she feared I might. Then, having reported my churlish behavior to her husband, she might prevail upon him to write the

Bingham Foundation claiming that my reactions were hardly objective, but had been colored by my unsuccessful attempt to seduce his wife.

I could imagine the response of Stacy Besant and Mrs. Cynthia to such an allegation. They might not believe it entirely; they'd tell me they didn't believe it. But they might think it wise to send a second field investigator to check out the Thorndecker application. An older investigator. More mature. Less impetuous. And on the strength of *his* report, Thorndecker might squeak through.

I believed Julie was capable of such a Byzantine plot. Not entirely for her husband; self-interest was at work here. In Coburn, she had said, I'm a big frog in a little pond—and that was true. Most women are conservative by nature; she, in addition, was conservative by circumstance. The little she had let drop about the rackety life she led before she met Thorndecker convinced me that she enjoyed and cherished the status quo, didn't want it to change. She had found a home.

Having settled the motives of Julie Thorndecker, and resolving to meet with her husband as soon as possible to see how much damage she had done, I got back to my favorite topic: what was going on at the Crittenden Research Laboratory? I came up with another choice assortment of wild and improbable scenarios:

Thorndecker was developing a new nerve gas. Thorndecker was a Frankenstein, putting together a monster from parts of deceased patients. Thorndecker was engaged in recombinant genetic research, combining the DNA of a parrot with that of a dog, and trying to breed a schnauzer who talked. The more Popov I inhaled, the sappier my fantasies became.

What gave me nightmares for months afterward was that I had already come up with the solution and didn't know it.

The Sixth Day

THE PHONE WOKE me up the next morning. I have a thing about phones. I claim that when I'm calling someone who isn't at home, dialing a number that no one will answer, I can tell after the second ring. It has a hollow, empty sound. Also, I think I can judge the mood of anyone who calls me by *their* ring: angry, loving, good or bad news. Tell me, doctor, do you think I . . . ?

In this case, coming out a deep, dreamless sleep, the ring of the phone sounded desperate, even relayed through the hotel switchboard. I was right. It was Mary Thorndecker, and she had to see me as soon as possible. It couldn't be at the Coburn Inn. It couldn't be at Crittenden Hall. It couldn't be anywhere in public. I figured that left the Carlsbad Caverns, but she insisted on the road that led around the Crittenden grounds, in the rear, past the cemetery. She said eleven o'clock, and I agreed.

I got out of bed feeling remarkably chipper. Unhungover. You can usually trust vodka for that. After all, it's just grain alcohol and water. Very few congeners. Drink vodka all your life, and everything will be hunkydory—except you may end up with a liver that extends from clavicle to patella.

A shower, a shave, a fresh turtleneck—and I was ready for a fight or a frolic. When I went out into the hall, the brass indicator showed the elevator was coming down. I rang the bell, waited, watched Sam Livingston come slowly into view in his cage: feet, ankles, knees, hips, waist, shoulders, head. A revelation. The elevator shuddered to a stop. I stepped in.

"Sam," I said, "you suckered me."

He knew immediately what I meant.

"Nah," he said, with almost a smile, "I just told you he puts on a good show."

"The guy's a phonus-balonus," I said.

"So? He gives the folks what they want."

"Aren't you ashamed of yourself? You got Mary Thorndecker driving you out there. She thinks she's bringing in another convert, and all the time you're laughing up your sleeve."

"Well . . ." he said solemnly, "it's better'n TV. Hear you had a little trouble with your car."

"Good gracious me," I said, "word does get around. Mike's is delivering it with new tires, I hope, at noon today. If I'm not here, will you ask them to leave the keys at the desk? No, scratch that. Will you keep the keys for me?"

He explained that he expected to leave by 1:00 P.M., to take care of his cleaning chores at the Episcopal church. He'd keep my car keys until then. If I hadn't returned by one o'clock, he'd leave the keys on the dresser in my room. I said that would be fine.

We descended slowly past the second floor. In the old Greek plays, the gods must have come down out of heaven in their basket at about our speed.

"Sam," I said, "you know Fred Aikens? The constable?"

"Seen him around," he said cautiously.

"What's your take?"

He didn't answer.

"I wouldn't want to stroll down a dark alley with him," I offered.

"No," he said thoughtfully, "don't do that."

"Is he buddy-buddy with Ronnie Goodfellow?"

The old man turned to stare at me with his yellowish eyes.

"You ever know two cops who weren't?" he asked. "And they don't even have to *like* each other."

We inched our way down to the lobby. Millie was chatting it up with two customers at the cigar counter, and didn't notice me as I sneaked into the restaurant. It was practically empty, which surprised me until I remembered it was Saturday morning. I assumed the bank and a lot of offices and maybe some stores were closed. Anyway, I was able to get a table to myself and spread out.

After that tunafish salad for dinner the night before, I was ravenous. I shot the works with an Australian breakfast: steak and eggs, with a side order of American home-fries and a sliced tomato that tasted like a tomato. First one like that I had eaten in years.

I started my second cup of black coffee, and looked up to see Constable Ronnie Goodfellow standing opposite. From where I sat, he looked like he was on stilts. Did I tell you what a handsome guy he was? A young Clark Gable, before he grew a mustache. Goodfellow was as lean and beautiful, in a tight, chiseled way. I'm a het, and have every intention of staying that way. But even the straightest guy occasionally meets a man who makes him wonder. This is what I call the "What-if-we-were-marooned-on-a-desert-island Test." I don't think there's a man alive who could pass it.

"Morning," I said to him. "Join me for a cup?"

"I'd like to join you," he said, "but I'll skip the coffee,

thanks. Four cups this morning, so far."

He took off his trooper's hat, and sat down across from me. He removed his gloves, folded them neatly inside the hat on an empty chair. Then he put his elbows on the table, scrubbed his face with his palms. He may have sighed.

"Heavy night?" I asked him.

"Trouble sleeping," he said. "I don't want to start on pills."

"No," I said, "don't do that. Try a shot of brandy or a glass of port wine."

"I don't drink," he said.

"One before you go to sleep isn't going to hurt you."

"My father died a rummy," he said, with no expression whatsoever in his voice. "I don't want to get started. Listen, Mr. Todd, I'm sorry about your car."

I shrugged. "Probably some wild kids."

"Probably. Still, it doesn't look good when it happens to a visitor. I stopped by Mike's Service Station. You'll have your car by noon."

"Good."

Then we sat in silence. It seemed to me we had nothing to say to each other. I know I didn't; he'd never tell me what I wanted to know. So I waited, figuring he had a message to deliver. If he did, he was having a hard time getting it out. He was looking down at his tanned hands, inspecting every finger like he was seeing it for the first time, massaging each knuckle, clenching a fist, then stretching palms wide.

"Mr. Todd," he said in a low voice, not looking at me, "I really think you're prying into things that are none of your business, that have nothing to do with your investigation."

Then he raised those dark eyes to stare at me. It was like being jabbed with an icepick.

I took a sip of coffee that scalded my lips. I moved back from the table, fished for my cigarettes. I lighted one. I didn't offer the pack to him.

"Let me guess," I said. "That would be the Reverend

Father Michael Bellamy reporting in. Sure. How could a grifter like him operate around here without official connivance? Tell you about our little conversation, did he?"

"I don't know what you're talking about," he said, face impassive.

"Then what are *you* talking about?"

"As I understand it, you came up here to take a look around, inspect Dr. Thorndecker's setup, make sure it was what he claimed it was. Is that right?"

"That's about it."

"Well? You've looked over the place. It's what he said it was, isn't it?"

"Yes."

"So? Why are you poking into things that have nothing to do with your job? Private matters. You get some kind of a kick trying to turn up dirt? You really shouldn't do that, Mr. Todd. It could be dangerous."

What I said next I know I shouldn't have said. I knew it while I was saying it. But I was so frustrated, so maddened by hints, and eyebrow-liftings, and vague suggestions, and now so infuriated by this cop's implied threat, that I slapped cards on the table I should have been pressing to my chest.

I made a great show of sangfroid, old nonchalant me: sipped coffee, puffed cigarette, stared at him with what I hoped was amusement, insolence, secret knowing—the whole bit.

"I get kicks out of a lot of things," I told him. "Of seeing a guy named Chester K. Petersen being stuck in the Crittenden cemetery at two in the morning. Of being told by one person that he died of internal cancer, and by another person that he died of congestive heart failure. Of discovering that a remarkable number of patients at Crittenden Hall have died of congestive heart failure, with most of the death certificates signed by the same doctor. Let's see—what else? Oh yes—the mysterious disappearance of one Ernie Scoggins, a Crittenden employee. With blood stains on the rug in his trailer. Did you spot those during your investigation, *Constable* Goodfellow? Anything more? Not much—except rumors and hints and insinuations that something unethical, illegal, and probably criminal is going on out at Crittenden. I suppose I could add a few things, but they're mostly supposition. Like Dr. Thorndecker owns this village and every soul in it. I use the word 'soul' loosely. That Thorndecker has a finger in every pie in town. That this place is dying, and if he goes down, you all go down. That's about all I've got. Private matters? Nothing to do with my job? You don't really believe that, do you?"

I'll say this for him: he didn't break, or gulp, or give any indication that what I was saying was getting to him. He just got harder and harder, turned to stone, those black eyes glittering. Maybe he got a little paler. Maybe the hands spread out on the table trembled a little.

But he made no reply, no threat. Just stood, pulled on gloves and hat with precise movements, staring at me all the time.

"Goodby, Mr. Todd," he said tonelessly.

And that was enough to set my nerve ends flapping. "Goodby." Not So-long, or See you around, or *Ciao*, baby. Just "Goodby." Final.

I was glad I hadn't mentioned anything about Al Coburn. That was the only thing I was glad about. It didn't help. I had talked too much, and knew it. I tried to persuade myself that I had told Goodfellow all that stuff deliberately, to let everyone know what I knew, to stir them up, spook them into making some foolish move.

But I couldn't quite convince myself that I had just engineered an extremely clever ploy. All I had done was blab. I got up, signed my check, and strolled into the bar whistling. Like a frightened kid walking through a graveyard on his way home.

The restaurant may have been dying, but that bar was doing jim-dandy business for an early Saturday morning. Most of the stools were taken; three of the booths were occupied. The customers looked like farmers killing time while their wives shopped, had their hair done, or whatever wives did in Coburn on a Saturday morning. I finally caught Jimmy's eye, ordered a stein of beer, took it over to a small table away from the babble at the bar.

I had started the day in a hell-for-leather mood, but my little confabulation with Constable Goodfellow had brought that to a screeching halt. A new Samuel Todd record: one hour from manic to depressive. I sipped my beer and reflected that Coburn and the Coburnites had that effect: they doused the jollies, and nudged you mournfully into the Slough of Despond. I think I've already reported that I heard no laughter on the streets. Maybe, I thought, the Board of Selectmen had passed an anti-giggling ordinance. "Warning! Levity is punishable by a fine, imprisonment, or both."

I watched one of the customers climb down from his bar stool, waddle over to the door of the Men's Room, and try to get in. But the room was occupied; the door was locked. The guy rattled the knob angrily a few times, then went growling back to the bar. A very ordinary incident. Happens all the time. The only reason I mention it is that seeing the customer rattle the knob on the locked door inspired, by some loony chain of thought, a magnificent idea: I would break into Crittenden Hall and the Crittenden Research Laboratory late at night and look around.

My first reaction to that brainstorm was a firm conviction that I was over the edge, around the bend, and down the tube. First of all, if I got caught, it would mean my job, even if I was able to weasel out of a stay in the slammer. Second, how could I get over that high fence, avoid the armed guards, and gain entrance to the locked buildings? Finally, what could I possibly hope to find that I hadn't been shown on my tour of the premises?

Still, it was an enticing prospect, just the thing to keep me awake and functioning until it was time to drive out for my meet with Mary Thorndecker.

The more I chewed on it, the more reasonable the project seemed to me. I could get over the fence with the aid of a short ladder. There were only three guards I knew

LAWRENCE SANDERS

of: the rover with shotgun and attack dog, the guy on the gate, and the bentnose inside the nursing home. A sneaky type like me shouldn't find it too difficult to duck all three.

The stickler was how to get inside the locked buildings without smashing windows or breaking down doors. That business of opening a lock with a plastic credit card— beloved by every private eye on TV—works only when there's no dead bolt. And, I had noted on my visit, the doors at Crittenden had them. I'm no good at picking a lock, even if I owned a set of picks, which I don't. Also, I don't wear hairpins. That left only one impossible solution: keys.

But even assuming I got inside undetected, what did I expect to find? The answer to that was easy: if I knew what I'd find, a break-in wouldn't be necessary. This would be what the sawbones call an exploratory operation. It really was the only way, I acknowledged. Waiting for one of the cast of characters to reveal all was getting me nowhere.

I bought myself another beer, and went into the campaign a little deeper. Dr. Kenneth Draper had mentioned that his eager, young research assistants sometimes worked right through till dawn. But surely there wouldn't be many in the labs on Saturday or Sunday night. Even whiz-kids like to relax on weekends, or so Betty Hanrahan had said. As for the nursing home, it would probably be quiet at, say, two in the morning, with a skeleton night staff drinking coffee in offices and labs when they weren't making their rounds.

See how easy it is to talk yourself into a course of action you know in your heart of hearts is dangerous, sappy, and unlikely to succeed? Talk about Father Bellamy being a grifter! His talents were nothing compared to the skills we all have in conning ourselves. Self-delusion is still the biggest scam of all.

I know it now, I knew it on that Saturday morning in Coburn. I told myself to forget the whole cockamamie scheme.

But all I could think about was how I could get the keys

to those locked Crittenden doors.

"Hey, Todd," Al Coburn said in his cracked voice, kicking gently at my ankle. "You dreaming or something?"

"Or something," I said. "Pull up a chair, Mr. Coburn."

He was carrying his own beer, and when I pushed a chair toward him, he flopped down heavily. His hands were trembling. He wrapped them around his beer glass and held on for dear life.

"*Mister* Coburn," he said, musing. "You got manners on you for a young whipper."

"Sure," I said. "I'm also trustworthy, loyal, friendly, brave, clean, and reverent. Boy Scout oath."

"Yeah," he said, looking around absently. "Well, you remember what we were talking about before?"

"The letter from Ernie Scoggins?"

"What happened was this: I got in touch with the, uh, party concerned, and maybe it was all like a misunderstanding."

I looked at him, but he wouldn't meet my eyes. His vacant stare was over my head, around the walls, across the ceiling.

"You're a lousy liar," I said.

"No, no," he said seriously. "I just gabbed more than I should. That Ernie Scoggins—a crazy feller. I told you that. He blew it all up. Know what I mean? So I'm having a meeting late this afternoon, and we'll straighten the whole thing out. Everything's going to be fine. Yes. Fine."

I felt sick. I leaned across the table to him, tried to hold his gaze in mine. But he just wouldn't lock eyes.

"Your notes at the bank?" I said. "They got to you?"

I was doing it: using the word "they." Who? The CIA, the FBI, the KGB, the Gold Star Mothers, the Association for the Investigation of Paranormal Phenomena? Who?

"Oh no," he said, very solemn now. "No no no. This has nothing to do with my notes. Just a friendly discussion. To come to an agreement for our mutual benefit."

That wasn't Al Coburn talking. "An agreement for our mutual benefit." I knew he was quoting someone. It smelled of con.

"Mr. Coburn," I said slowly and carefully, "let's see if I've got this right. You're going to meet someone late this afternoon and talk about whatever is in that letter Ernie Scoggins left you? Is that it?"

"Well . . . yeah," he said, looking down into his beer. "It'll all get straightened out. You'll see."

"Want me to come along?" I asked him. "Maybe it would be better if you had—you know, like a witness. I won't say a word. I won't do anything. I'll just *be* there."

He bristled.

"Listen, sonny," he said, "I can take care of myself."

"Sure you can," I said hastily. "But what's wrong with having a third party present?"

"It's confidential," he said. "That was the agreement. Just him and me."

I grabbed that.

"Him?" I said. "So you're meeting just one man?"

"I didn't say that."

"No, you didn't. I guessed it. Am I wrong?"

"I'm tired," he said fretfully.

I looked at him, and I knew he was telling the truth: he *was* tired. The head was bowed, shoulders slumped, all of him collapsed. Tired or defeated.

"I don't want no trouble," he mumbled.

What was I to do—hassle a weary old man? The years had rubbed away at him. As they do at all of us. Will slackens. Resolve fuzzes. Worst of all, physical energy leaks out. We just don't have the verve to cope. A good bowel movement becomes life's highest pleasure, and we see a tanned teenager in a bikini and think bitterly, "Little do you know!"

I wanted to take his stringy craw in my fists and choke the truth from him. Who was the guy he was going to meet? What was in Scoggins's letter? What were they going to agree about? But what the hell could I do— stomp it out of him?

I'm pretty good at self-control. I mean I don't rant and

rave. The stomach may be bubbling, but the voice is low, level, contained.

"Look, Mr. Coburn," I said, "this meeting of yours—I hope it comes out just the way you want it. That everything is solved to your satisfaction. But just in case—in *case*, you understand—things don't turn out to be nice-nice, don't you think you should have an insurance policy? An ace in the hole?"

Then, finally, he looked at me. Those washed-out eyes focused on my stare, and I knew I had him hooked.

"Like what?" he said.

I shrugged. "A copy of Scoggins's letter. Left some place only you and I know about. Doesn't that make sense? Gives you a bargaining point, doesn't it? With the guy you're meeting? A copy of the letter, or the original, left in someone else's hands. In case..."

True to the Coburn tradition, I didn't finish that sentence. I didn't have to. He understood, and it shook him. I started from the table to buy him another beer, but he wagged his head and waved me back. All he wanted to do was think, ponder, figure, reckon. He may have been an old man, but he wasn't an old dummy.

"Yes," he said at last. "All right. I'll go along with that. It'll be in the glove compartment of my pickup. In case. But I won't need to use it; you'll see. I'll call you right after the meeting. You'll be here?"

"What time are you talking about?"

"Five, six this evening. Around there."

"Sure," I said, "I'll be here. If not, you can always leave a message. Just tell me everything's okay."

He nodded, nodded, like one of those Hong Kong dolls, the spineless head bobbing up and down.

"That's a good way," he said. "I'll call you to tell you everything's okay. Hey, maybe we can eat together tonight. Listen, Todd, I made a good stew last night. You come out and eat with me. I'll tell you about stew: you cook it, and then you let it cool, and you eat it the next day, after it's got twenty-four hours of soaking. Tastes better that way."

"Sounds good to me," I said. "I'll wait for your call.

271

Then I'll come out, and we'll have the stew. What's in it?"

"This and that," he said.

I began to have second thoughts. Not about the stew, but about the arrangements we had made. Too many things could go wrong. Murphy's Law.

"Well, look," I said, "I expect to be in and out all day, so maybe you'll call and I won't be here, and those nut-boys at the desk will forget to deliver your message. So why don't you give me your phone number now, and tell me how to locate your place?"

He wasn't exactly happy about that, but I finally got his phone number and directions on how to find his home. He said he lived in a farmhouse not too far from the foot of Crittenden Hill, and if I looked for a clumsy clapboard house set on cinder blocks, that was it. I'd know it by a steel flagpole set in cement in the front yard. He flew Old Glory day and night, no matter what the weather. When the flag got shagged to ribbons, he bought a new one.

"If I get six months out of a flag," Al Coburn said, "I figure I'm lucky. But I don't care. I'm patriotic, and I don't give a damn who knows it."

"Good for you," I said.

I watched him stumble out of there. He was trying to keep his shoulders back, chest inflated. I wanted to be like that when I was his age: cocky and hopeful. None of us can win the final decision. But, with luck, we can pick up a few rounds. I hoped old Al Coburn would pick up this round.

That blighted week... The sharpest memory I have is my Saturday morning phone call to Dr. Telford Thorndecker. I planned it: what I would say, what he might say, what I would reply.

I got through to Crittenden Hall with no trouble, but it took them almost five minutes to locate Thorndecker. Then I was told he was in his private office at the Crittenden Research Laboratory, and didn't wish to be disturbed except in case of emergency. I said it was an emergency. A string of clicks, and he finally came on the line. Angry.

"Who is this?" he demanded.

I told him.

"Oh yes," he said. "Mr. Todd. Did you get that report I promised you?"

"I did," I said, "and I want to—"

"Good," he said. "Then I presume the grant will be forthcoming shortly."

"Well, not exactly. What I really—"

"The skeptics," he said disgustedly. "The nay-sayers. Don't listen to them. We're on the right track now."

"Dr. Thorndecker," I said, "I was wondering if—"

"Of course there's a lot to be done. We've just scratched the surface. No one knows. No one can possibly guess."

"If you could—"

"I don't know when I've been so optimistic about a research project. I mean that sincerely. It just seems like everything is falling into place. The Thorndecker Theory. That's what they'll call it: the Thorndecker Theory."

All this in his booming baritone. But I missed the conviction the words should have conveyed. The man was remote: that's the only way I can describe it. I didn't know if he was trying to convince me or himself. But I had a sense of him being way up there in the wild blue yonder, repeating dreams.

"Dr. Thorndecker," I said, trying again, "I have some questions only you can answer, and I was hoping you might be able to spare me a few moments this afternoon."

"Julie," he said. "She'll be so proud of me. Of course. What is it you wanted?"

"If we could meet," I said. "For a short time. This afternoon."

"Delighted," he shouted. "Absolutely delighted, Now? This minute? Are you at the gate? I'm in my lab."

"Well...no, sir," I said. "I was thinking about this afternoon. Maybe three o'clock. Around there. Would that be all right?"

There was silence.

"Hello?" I said. "Dr. Thorndecker? Are you there?"

"What's this about?" he said suspiciously. "Who is this?"

Once more it occurred to me that he might be on

something. In never-never land. He wasn't slurring; his speech was distinct. But he wasn't tracking. He wasn't going from A to B to C; he was going from K to R to F.

I tried again.

"Dr. Thorndecker," I said formally, "this is Samuel Todd. I have a few more questions I'd like to ask you regarding your application to the Bingham Foundation for a grant. Could I see you at three this afternoon?"

"But of course!" he said heartily. Pause. "Perhaps two o'clock would be better. Would that inconvenience you?"

"Not at all," I said. "I'll be out there at two."

"Excellent!" he said. "I'll leave word at the gate. You come directly to the lab. I'll be here."

"Fine," I said. "See you then."

"And Mary and Edward," he said, and hung up.

It was Loony Tunes time. I figured I might as well be equipped. I found a hardware store that was open, and bought a three-cell flashlight with batteries, a short stepladder, 50 feet of cheap clothesline, and a lead sash weight. They didn't have any ski masks. I stowed my new possessions in Betty Hanrahan's pickup and headed out to Crittenden to meet Mary Thorndecker. If she had showed up in a Batman cape, I wouldn't have been a bit surprised. The whole world had gone lunatic. Including me.

She wasn't hard to find. Parked off the road in a black car long enough to be a hearse. I pulled up ahead of her, figuring I might want to get away in a hurry and wouldn't want to be boxed in. I got out of the pickup, ready to sit in her limousine. It had to be warmer in there. The Yukon would be warmer than Betty Hanrahan's pickup.

But Mary Thorndecker got out of her car, too. Slammed the door: a solid *chunk* muffled in the thicker air. Maybe she didn't want to be alone with me in a closed space. Maybe she didn't trust me. I don't know. Anyway, we were both out in the open, stalking toward each other warily. High Noon at Crittenden.

But we waded, actually. Because there was a morning ground fog still swirling. It covered our legs, and we pushed through it. It was white smoke, billowing. The earth was dry ice. And as we breathed, long plumes of vapor went out. I glanced around that chill, deserted landscape. Bleak trees and frosted stubble. A blurred etching: fog, vapor, my slick trenchcoat and her heavy, old-fashioned wrap of Persian lamb. I hadn't seen one of those in years.

She wore a knitted black cloche, pulled down to her eyes. Her face was white, pinched, frightened. Everything that had seemed to me mildly curious and faintly amusing about the Thorndecker affair suddenly sank to depression, dread, and inevitability. Her demonic look. Bleached lips. Her hands were thrust deep into her pockets, and I wondered if she had brought a gun and planned to shoot me dead. In that lost landscape it was possible. Any cold violence was possible.

"Miss Thorndecker," I said. "Mary. Would you—"

"How did you know?" she demanded. Her voice was dry and gaspy. "About the note? That I wrote the note?"

"What difference does it make?" I said. I stamped my feet. "Listen, can we walk? Just walk up and down? If we stand here without moving for fifteen minutes, we'll never dance the gavotte again."

She didn't say anything, but dug her chin down into her collar, hunched her shoulders, tramped beside me up the graveled road and back. Behind the fence was the Crittenden cemetery. On the other side were the winter-shredded trees. Not another car, a sound, a color. We could have been alone on earth, the last, the only. Smoke swirled about us, and I wanted a quart of brandy.

"Why did you write it?" I asked her. "I thought you loved your father. Stepfather."

She tried to laugh scornfully.

"*She* told you that," she said. "I hate the man. *Hate* him! He killed my mother."

"Can you prove that?"

"No," she said, "but I *know*."

I wondered if she was out to lunch, if her fury had corroded her so deeply that she was lost. To me, herself, everyone.

"Is that why you wrote: 'Thorndecker kills'? Because

you think he murdered your mother?"

"And his father," she said. "I know that, too. No, that's not why. Because he's killing, now, in that lab of his."

"Scoggins?" I suggested. "Thorndecker killed him?"

"Who?"

"Scoggins. Ernie Scoggins. He used to work at Crittenden. A maintenance man."

"Maybe," she said dully. "The man who disappeared? I don't know anything about him. But there were others."

"Petersen?" I asked. "Chester K. Petersen? They buried him a few days ago. Pelvic cancer."

"No," she said, "he was a heart patient. That's why he came to Crittenden Hall. I saw his file. Angina. No close relatives. A sweet old man. Just a sweet old man. Then, about three months ago, he began to develop tumors. Sarcomas, carcinomas, melanomas. All over his body. On his scalp, his face, hands, arms, legs. I saw him. I visited him. He rotted away. He smelled."

"Jesus," I said, looking away, remembering the dying chimp.

"But he was only the latest," she said. "There were others. Many, many others."

"How long?" I demanded. "How long has this been going on?"

She thought a moment.

"Eighteen months," she said. "But mostly in the past year. Patients with no medical record of cancer. Cardiacs, mentals, alcoholics, addicts. Then they developed horrible cancers. They decayed. He's doing it to them. Thorndecker is. I *know* it!"

"And Draper?" I said softly. "Dr. Kenneth Draper?"

A hand came swiftly out of her coat pocket. She gnawed on a chalky knuckle.

"I don't know," she said. "I ask him. I plead with him. But he won't *tell* me. He cries. He worships Thorndecker. He'll do anything Thorndecker says."

"Draper is in on it," I told her flatly. "He's the physician in attendance. He signs the death certificates. But *why* are they doing it? For the bequests? For the money the dead patients leave to the lab?"

The question troubled her.

"I don't know," she said. "That's what I thought at first, but that can't be right. Some of them didn't leave the lab anything. Most of them didn't. I don't know. Oh my God . . ."

She began weeping. I put an uncomfortable arm about her shoulders. We leaned together. Still stamping back and forth, wading through that twisting fog.

"All right," I said, "let's go over it . . . A patient checks in. A cardiac case, or a mental, drugs, alcoholic, whatever. Young or old?"

"Mostly old."

"Then after awhile they develop cancer and die of that?"

"Yes."

"The same way Petersen died? Or internal cancer, too? Lung cancer? Stomach? Spleen? Liver?"

"All ways," she said in a low voice.

"In how long a time? How long does it take them to die of the cancer?"

"At first, when I became aware of what was going on, it was very quick. A few weeks. Lately it's been longer. Petersen was the most recent. He lasted almost three months."

"And they're all buried here on the grounds?"

"Or shipped home in a sealed coffin."

"But all of them tumorous?"

"Yes. Decayed."

"And no complaints from relatives? No questions asked?"

"I don't know," she said. "Probably not. People are like that. People are secretly relieved when a sick relative dies. A problem relative. They wouldn't ask questions."

"You're probably right," I said sadly. "Especially if they're inheriting. And Draper hasn't told you a thing about what's going on?"

"He just claims Thorndecker is a genius on the verge of a great discovery. That's all he'll say."

277

"He loves you."

"He says," she said bitterly, "but he won't tell me anything."

We paced back and forth in silence. It was the pits, absolutely the pits.

"What will you do to find out?" I asked her finally.

"What? I don't understand."

"How far will you go to discover what's going on? How important is it to you to stop Thorndecker?"

Suddenly she came apart. Just splintered. She stopped, jerked away from my shielding arm, turned to face me.

"That cocksucker!" she howled. Her spittle stung. I took a step back, shocked, bewildered. "That murderer!" she screamed. "Turdy toad! Wife killer! You think I don't— And he—with that slimy wife of his rubbing up against everything in sight. He has no right. No right! He must suffer. Oh yes! Skin flayed away. Flesh from his bones. Rot in the deepest, hottest hell. Vengeance is mine, sayeth the Lord! Naked! The way she dresses! Licking up to every male she meets. Edward! Oh my God, poor, young, innocent Edward. Yes, even him. What does she *do* to them? And he, *he*, lets her go her way, his life destroyed by that wanton with her filthy ways. Ruining him. Her body there. For everyone! Oh yes, I know. Everyone knows. The whore! The smirking whore! Den of iniquity. That house of wickedness. Oh God, strike down the evil. Lord Jesus, I beg you! Smite this filth. Root out—"

She went on and on, using words I could hardly believe she knew. The schoolteacher gone beserk. The spinster wrung by an orgasm. Obscenity, jealousy, sexual frustration, religious frenzy: it was all in her inchoate shouts, words tumbling, white stuff gathering in the corners of her mouth, something leaking from her eyes.

And love there. Oh yes; love. Julie hadn't been so wrong. This woman had to love Thorndecker to damn him so viciously, to want him so utterly destroyed. Every woman deserves one shot at the man she loves, and this was Mary's, this wailed revilement, this hysterical abuse that frightened me with its intensity. The vapor of her screams came at me in spouts of steam smelling of acid and ash.

I wondered if I might shake her, slap her, or take her in my arms and say, "There, there," and commiserate over her wounded soul, lost hopes, wasted life. Finally, I did nothing but let her rant, rave, wind down, lose energy, become eventually silent, just standing there, mouth open, trembling. And not from cold, I knew, but from pain and shame. Pain of her hurts, shame for having revealed it to another.

I put a hand on her arm as gently as I could, and led her back to her car. She came willingly enough, and let me get her seated behind the wheel. I pulled up her collar, folded the coat carefully over her knees, did everything but tuck her in. I offered her a cigarette, but I don't think she saw it. I lighted up, with shaking fingers, smoked like a maniac. I finally had to open the window on my side just a crack.

When, after a few moments, I turned to look at her, I saw her eyes were closed, her lips were moving. She was praying, but to whom or for what, I did not know.

"Mary?" I said softly. "Mary, can you hear me? Are you listening to me?"

Lips stopped moving, eyes opened. Head turned, and she looked at me. The focus of her eyes gradually shortened until she saw me.

"I can help you, Mary," I whispered. "But you must help me do it."

"How?" she said, in a voice less than a whisper.

I laid it out for her:

I wanted to know the number of exterior and interior security guards on duty Sunday night. I wanted to know their schedules, when the shift changed, their routines, where they stayed when they weren't patrolling.

I wanted to know everything she could find out about alarms, electric and electronic, and where the on-off switch or fuse box was located. Also, the location of the main power switches for the nursing home and the research laboratory.

I wanted to know the number of medical staff on duty Sunday night in Crittenden Hall and who, if anyone, might be working in the laboratories.

Finally, most important, I wanted that big ring of keys that Nurse Stella Beecham carried. If she wasn't on duty late Sunday night—say from midnight till eight Monday morning—she probably left the keys in her office. I wanted them. If Beecham was on duty, or if she handed over her keys to a night supervisor, then I needed at least two keys: to the Hall and to the research lab. If those were impossible to obtain, then Mary Thorndecker would have to let me in from the inside of the nursing home, and I'd have to get into the lab by myself, somehow.

It took me a long time to detail all this, and I wondered if she was listening. She was. She said dully: "You're going to break in?"

"Yes. I'm going to find out about those cancer deaths."

"You're going to get the evidence?"

I felt like weeping. But I had no compunction, none whatsoever, about using this poor, disturbed woman.

"Yes," I said, "I'm going to get the evidence."

In my own ears, it sounded as gamy and cornball as if I had said, "I'm going to grab the boodle and take it on the lam."

"All right," she said firmly, "I'll help you."

We went over it again in more detail: what I wanted, what she could get, what we might have to improvise.

"How will you get over the fence?" she asked.

"Leave that to me."

"You won't hurt anyone, will you?"

"Of course not. I don't carry a gun or a knife or any other weapon. I'm not a violent man, Mary."

"All you want is information?"

"Exactly," I said, nodding virtuously. "Just information. Part of my investigation of Thorndecker's application for a grant."

That seemed to satisfy her. Made the whole scam sound more legal.

We left it like this: she was to collect as much of what I

wanted as she could, and on Sunday she was to call me at the Coburn Inn.

"Don't give your real name to the switchboard," I warned her. "Just in case they ask who's calling. Use a phony name."

"What name?"

"Joan Powell," I said instantly, without thinking. "Say your name is Joan Powell. If I'm at the Inn, don't mention any of this over the phone. Just laugh and joke and make a date to meet me somewhere. Anywhere. Right here would be fine; it's deserted enough. Then we'll meet, and you can tell me what you've found out. And give me the keys if you've been able to get them."

"What if I call the Coburn Inn, and you're not there?"

"Call every hour on the hour. Sooner or later I'll be there. Any time before midnight on Sunday. Okay?"

We went over the whole thing once more. I wasn't sure she was getting it. She was still white as paper, and every once in awhile her whole body would shudder in a hard fit of trembling. But I spoke as quietly and confidently as I could. And I kept touching her. Her hand, arm, shoulder. I think I made contact.

Just before I got out of the car, I leaned forward to kiss her smooth, chill cheek.

"Tell me everything's going to be all right," she said faintly.

"Everything's going to be all right," I said.

I knew it wasn't.

I drove back to Coburn as fast as Hanrahan's rattletrap would take me. I kept watching for a public phone booth. I had a call to make, and didn't want it to go through the hotel switchboard. My paranoia was growing like "The Blob."

I found a booth on Main Street, just before the business section started. I knew the offices of the Bingham Foundation were closed on Saturday, so I called Stacy Besant at his home, collect. He lived in a cavernous nine-room apartment on Central Park West with an unmarried sister older than he, three cats, a moth-eaten poodle, and a whacking great tank of tropical fish.

Edith Besant, the sister, answered the phone and agreed to accept the call.

"Samuel!" she caroled. "This *is* nice. Stacy and I were speaking of you just last night, and agreed you must come to us for dinner as soon as you return to New York. You and that lovely lady of yours."

"Well, ah, yes, Miss Edith," I said. "I certainly would enjoy that. Especially if you promise to make that carrot soup again."

"Carrot vichyssoise, Samuel," she said gently. "Not soup."

"Of course," I said. "Carrot vichyssoise. I remember it well."

I did, too. Loathsome. But what the hell, she was proud of it.

We chatted of this and that. It was impossible to hurry her, and I didn't try. So we discussed her health, mine, her brother's, the cats', the poodle's, the fishes'. Then we agreed the weather had been miserable.

"Well, my goodness, Samuel," she said gaily, "here we are gossiping away, and I imagine you really want a word with Stacy."

"Yes, ma'am, if I could. Is he there?"

"Of course he is. Just a minute."

He came on so quickly he must have been listening on the extension.

"Yes, Samuel?" he said. "Trouble?"

"Sir," I said, "there are some questions I need answers to. Medical questions. I'd like to call Scientific Research Records and speak to one of the men who worked on the Thorndecker investigation."

"Now?" he asked. "This minute? Can't it go over to Monday?"

"No, sir," I said. "I don't think it can. Things are moving rather rapidly here."

There was a moment of silence.

"I see," he said finally. "Very well. Wait just a few minutes; I have the number somewhere about."

I waited in the closed phone booth. It was an iced

coffin, and I should have been shivering. I wasn't. I was sweating.

He came back on the phone. He gave me the number of SRR, and the name of the man to talk to, Dr. Evan Blomberg. If SRR was closed on Saturday, as it probably was, I could call Dr. Blomberg at his home. The number there was—

"Mr. Besant," I interrupted, "I know this is an imposition, but I'm calling from a public phone booth for security reasons, and I just don't have phone credit cards, although I have suggested several times that it would make your field investigators' jobs a lot easier if you—"

"All right, Samuel," he said testily, "all right. You want me to locate Dr. Blomberg and ask him to call you at your phone booth. Is that it?"

"If you would, sir. Please."

"It's that important?"

"Yes," I said. "It is."

"Let me have the number."

I read it off the phone. He told me it would take five minutes. It took more than ten. I was still sweating. Finally the phone shrilled, and I grabbed it off the hook.

"Hello?" I said. "Dr. Evan Blomberg?"

"To whom am I speaking?" this deep, pontifical voice inquired. I loved that "To whom." Much more elegant than, "Who the hell is this?"

I identified myself to his satisfaction and apologized for calling him away from his Saturday relaxation.

"Quite all right," Dr. Blomberg said stiffly. "I understand you have some questions regarding our investigation of the application of Dr. Telford Gordon Thorndecker?"

"Well, ah, in a peripheral way, doctor," I said cautiously. "It's just a general question. A general medical question."

"Oh?" he said, obviously puzzled. "Well, what is it?"

I didn't want to say it. It was like asking an astronomer, "Is the moon *really* made of green cheese?" But finally I nerved myself and said:

"Is it possible to infect a human being with cancer?

That is, could you, uh, take cancerous cells from one human being who is suffering from some form of the disease and inject them into a healthy human being, and would the person injected then develop cancer?"

His silence sounded more shocked than any exclamation.

"Good God!" he said finally. "Who would want to do a thing like that? For what reason?"

"Sir," I said desperately, "I'm just trying to get an answer to a what-if question. Is it possible?"

Silence again. Then:

"To my knowledge," Dr. Evan Blomberg said in his orotund voice, "it has never been done. For obvious reasons. Unethical, illegal, criminal. And I can't see any possible value to any facet of cancer research. I suppose it might be theoretically possible."

Try to get a Yes or No out of a scientist. Hah! They're as bad as lawyers. Almost.

"Then you could infect someone with cancer cells, and that person would develop cancer?"

"I said theoretically," he said sharply. "As you are undoubtedly aware, experimental animals are frequently injected with cancer cells. Some host animals reject the cells completely. Others accept them, the cells flourish, the host animal dies. In other words, *some* animals have an immunity to *some* forms of cancer. By extension, I suppose you could speculate that *some* humans might have or develop an immunity to *some* forms of cancer. It is not a chance I'd care to take."

"I can understand that, Dr. Blomberg, but—"

"Different species of animals are used for different kinds of cancer research, depending on how similar they are to humans insofar as the way they react to specific types of cancer. Rats, for instance, are used in leukemia research."

"Yes, Dr. Blomberg," I said frantically, "I can appreciate all that. Let's just call this speculation. That's all it is: speculation. What I'm asking is if healthy humans are infected with cancer cells from a diseased human, will the healthy host develop cancer?"

"Speculation?" he asked carefully.

"Just speculation," I assured him.

"I'd say the possibility exists."

"Possibility?" I repeated. "Would you go so far as to say 'probability'?"

"All right," he said resignedly. "Since we're talking in theoretical terms, I'm willing to say it's probable the host human will develop cancer."

"One final question," I said. "We have been talking about injecting a healthy human host with cancerous cells from a live but diseased human donor. You've said it's probable the host would develop cancer. Does the same hold true of abnormal cells that have been cultivated *in vitro*?"

"Good God!" he burst out again. "What kind of a nightmare are you talking about?"

I wouldn't let him off the hook. "Would it be possible to infect a healthy human being with cancerous cells that have been grown *in vitro*?"

"Yes, goddammit," he said furiously, "it would be possible."

"In fact—probable?" I asked softly. "That you could infect a healthy human being with cancerous cells grown in a lab?"

"Yes," he said, in such a low voice that I could hardly hear him. "Probable."

"Thank you, Dr. Blomberg," I said, hung up gently and wondered if I had spoiled his weekend. The hell with him. Mine was already shot.

I drove the rest of the way into Coburn, reflecting that now I knew it could be done, what Mary Thorndecker feared. But why? *Why?* As Blomberg had said, who would want to do a thing like that? For what reason?

The Grand Prix was waiting for me in the parking lot of the Coburn Inn. Not only had it been equipped with new radials, but the car had been washed and waxed. I walked around it, kicking the tires with delight. But gently! Then I transferred my new purchases from the pickup to the trunk of the Pontiac.

In the lobby, a tall, skinny gink with "Mike's Service Station" stitched on the back of his coveralls was leaning over the cigar counter, inspecting Millie Goodfellow's cleavage with a glazed stare. He had a droopy nose and looked like a pointer on scent. Any minute I expected him to raise a paw and freeze.

I interrupted their tête-à-tête—and guessing the subject of their conversation, that's the only phrase for it. I asked the garageman about the bill for the tires and wax job. He said Betty Hanrahan had picked up the tab; I didn't owe a cent. I handed him a ten for his trouble, and he looked at it.

"Jesus, Mr. Todd," he said, "Betty told me I wasn't to take any money from you *a*-tall. She find out about this, she'll bite my ass."

He and Millie laughed uproariously. At last—Coburn humor. The hell with the quality; people were laughing, and after the way I had spent the last two hours, that was enough for me.

"I won't tell Betty if you don't," I said. "Can you get her pickup back to the Red Dog?"

"Sure," he said happily. "No problem. Hey, Millie, I'm a rich man now. Buy you a drink tonight?"

"I'll be there," she nodded. "For the ten, you can look but don't touch."

He said something equally as inane, and they gassed awhile. It was that kind of raunchy sexual chivying you hear between a man and woman who have been friends a long time and know they'll never go to bed together. I listened, smiling and nodding like an idiot.

Because I can't tell you how comforting it was. Their smutty jokes were so *normal*. There was nothing deep, devious, or depraved about it. It had nothing to do with cancerous cells and fluorescent tumors. No one dying in agony and pushed into frosted ground. That stupid conversation restored a kind of tranquillity in me; that's the only way I can describe it. I felt like an infantryman coming off the front line and being handed a fresh orange.

Fondling it, smelling it, tasting it. Life.

I waved goodby and went up to my room. I had an hour to kill before my meeting with Dr. Thorndecker. I didn't want to eat or drink. I just wanted to flop on my bed, dressed and booted, and think about the man and wonder why he was doing what he was.

I think that investigators work on the premise that most people act out of self-interest. The kicker is that a lot of us don't know, or can't see, our true self-interest. Case in point: my breaking up with Joan Powell. I thought I acted out of concern for my own well-being. All I got was a galloping attack of the guilts and a growing realization that I had tossed away a relationship that was holding me together.

What was Telford Gordon Thorndecker's self-interest—or what did he *think* it was? Not merely avarice, since Mary had said the lab didn't profit from the deaths of many of the victims. Then it had to be some kind of human experimentation that might result in professional glory. A different kind of greed.

I tried that on for motive. Mary had reported that Dr. Draper had said Thorndecker was a genius on the verge of a great discovery. Thorndecker himself had admitted to me that human immortality was his true goal. So far the glory theory made sense. Until I asked myself why he was injecting cancer-free patients with abnormal cells. Then the whole thing fell apart. The only fame you achieve by that is on the wall of a post office.

The man was such a fucking enigma to me. Inspired scientist. Paterfamilias. Skilled business administrator. Handsome. Charming. Energetic. And remote. Not only from me, I was convinced, but from wife, children, friends, staff, Coburn, the world. Either he had something everyone else was lacking, or he lacked something everyone else had. Or perhaps both.

Have you ever seen one of those intricately carved balls of ivory turned out by Oriental craftsmen? It only takes about ten years to make. The artist starts with a solid sphere of polished ivory. The outer shell is carved with fanciful open designs, and within a smaller sphere is cut free to revolve easily. That second ball is also carved with a complex open design, and a third smaller ball cut free to revolve. And so on. Until, at the center, is a ball no larger than a pea, also intricately incised. Spheres within spheres. Designs within designs. Worlds within worlds. The carving so marvelously complicated that it's almost impossible to make out the inscription on that pea in the center.

That was Dr. Telford Gordon Thorndecker.

Who had carved him?

But all that was purple thinking, ripe fancy. When I came back to earth, all I saw was a big man standing in the shadows, watching his young wife's bangled ankle flashing in the back of a cop's cruiser. And the man's face showing no defeat.

An hour later I was on my way out to Crittenden again. The only pleasure I had in going was being behind the wheel of the Grand Prix. After bruising my kidneys in Betty Hanrahan's junk heap, the Pontiac's ride felt like a wallow in a feather bed. I took it up to seventy for a minute or two, just to remind myself what was under the hood. The car even smelled good to me. More important, the heater worked.

I had no trouble at the gate. The guard came out of his hut when I gave the horn a little *beep*. Apparently he recognized the car; he didn't ask for identification. I watched his routine carefully. He had a single key attached by a chain to a length of wood. He opened the tumbler lock. The gates swung inward. After I drove through, I glanced in my rearview mirror. He swung the gates back into place, locked up, went back into his hut. He was a slow-moving older man wearing a pea jacket. No gun that I could see. But of course it could have been under the jacket or in the hut.

I didn't like the idea of those iron gates opening inward. I would have preferred they swung outward, in case I had to bust through in a hasty exit. But you can't have everything. Some days you can't have *anything*.

The gate guard must have called, because when I got to the front door of the Crittenden Research Laboratory, Dr. Kenneth Draper was waiting for me. He looked like a stunned survivor. He was staring at me, but I wasn't sure he saw me.

"Dr. Draper," I said, "you all right?"

He came out of his trance with a slight shake of his head, like someone trying to banish an ugly dream. Then he gave me a glassy smile and held out his hand.

He was wearing a white laboratory coat. There were dark brown stains down the front. I didn't even want to wonder about those. His hand, when I clasped it, was cold, damp, boneless. I think he tried to press my fingers, but there was no strength in him. His face was white as chalk, and as dusty. When he led me inside, his walk was stumbling and uncertain. I thought the man was close to collapse. I didn't think he'd suddenly fall over, but I had an awful vision of him going down slowly, melting, joints loose and limbs rubber. Then he'd end up sitting on the floor, knees drawn up, head down on his folded arms, and weeping softly.

But he made it up to the second floor, painfully, dragging himself hand over hand on the banister. I asked him if many staff were working on Saturday. I asked him if his research assistants worked through the weekend. I asked him if lab employees worked only daylight hours, or was there a night shift. I don't think he heard a word I said. I know he didn't answer.

So I looked around, peeked into the big laboratories. There were a few people at the workbenches, a few peering through microscopes. But not more than a half-dozen. The entire building had the tired silence of a Saturday afternoon, everything winding down and ready to end.

Draper led me to the frosted glass door of one of the small private labs. He knocked. No answer. He knocked again, louder this time, and called, "Dr. Thorndecker.

Mr. Todd is here." Still no reply.

"Maybe he fell asleep," I said, as cheerfully as I could. "Or stepped out."

"No, no," Dr. Draper said. "He's in there. But he's very, uh, busy, and sometimes he ... Dr. Thorndecker! Mr. Todd is here."

No one answered from inside the room. It was getting embarrassing, and just a little spooky. We could see lights burning through the frosted glass door, and I thought I heard the sounds of small movements.

Finally Draper hiked the skirt of his lab coat, fished in his pants pocket, and came out with a ring of keys which he promptly dropped on the floor. He stooped awkwardly, recovered them, and pawed them nervously, trying to find the one he wanted. He unlocked the door, pushed it open cautiously, peeked in. My view was blocked.

"Wait here," Draper said. "Please. Just for a moment."

He slipped in, closed the door behind him. I was left standing alone in the corridor. I didn't know what was going on. I couldn't even guess. I didn't think about it.

Draper came out in a minute. He gave me a ghastly smile.

"Dr. Thorndecker will see you now," he said.

He brushed closely past me. I caught an odor coming from him, and wondered if it was possible to smell of guilt.

The laboratory was small, with minimal equipment: a blackboard, workbench, a fine compound microscope, stacks of books and papers, a slide projector and screen, a TV monitor.

Dr. Telford Gordon Thorndecker was seated in a metal swivel chair behind a steel desk. He didn't rise when I entered, nor did he smile or offer to shake hands. He was wearing a laboratory coat like Draper's, but his was starched and spotless. In addition, he was wearing white cloth gloves with long, elasticized gauntlets that came to his elbows.

I did not think the man looked well. His face was pallid, but with circles of hectic flush high on his cheeks,

and lips almost a rosy red. I think what startled me most
was that his head was covered with a circular white cloth
cap, similar to the type worn by surgeons. But the cap did
not cover his temples, and it was apparent that
Thorndecker was losing his hair in patches; the sideburns
I remembered as full and glossy were almost totally gone.

But that resonant baritone voice still had its familiar
boom.

"What is of paramount importance," he said sternly,
"is the keeping of careful, accurate, and detailed records.
That is what I have been doing: bringing my journal up to
the present, to this very minute."

"Yes," I said. "May I sit down, Dr. Thorndecker?"

He gestured toward the book in which he had been
writing. It was a handsome volume bound in buckram.

"More than two hundred of these," he said. "Covering
every facet of my professional career from the day I
entered medical school."

I slid quietly into the tubular chair alongside his desk.
He was looking down at the journal, and I couldn't see his
eyes. But his voice was steady, and his hands weren't
trembling.

"Dr. Thorndecker," I said, "I have a few questions
concerning your work here at the research lab."

"Two hundred personal diaries," he mused. "A
lifetime. I remember a professor—who was he?—telling
us how important it was to keep precise notes. So that if
something should happen, an accident, the work could be
continued. Nothing would be lost."

Then he raised his eyes to look at me. I saw nothing
unusual in the pupils but it seemed to me the whites were
clouded, with a slight bluish cast, like spoiled milk.

"Mr. Todd," he said, "I appreciate your coming by. I
regret I have not been able to spend more time with you
during your visit, but I have been very involved with
projects here at the lab. Plus the day-to-day routine of
Crittenden Hall, of course."

"Dr. Thorndecker, when I spoke to you on the phone
this morning, you seemed excited about a potential

breakthrough in your work, a development of considerable importance."

He continued to stare at me. His face was totally without expression.

"A temporary setback," he said. "These things happen. Anyone in scientific research learns to live with disappointment. But we are moving in the right direction; I am convinced of that. So we will pick ourselves up and try a new approach, a different approach. I have several ideas. They are all here." He tapped the open pages of his journal. "Everything is here."

"Does this concern the X Factor, Dr. Thorndecker? Isolating whatever it is in mammalian cells that causes aging and determines longevity?"

"Aging..." he said.

He swung slowly in his swivel chair and stared at the blackboard across the room. My eyes followed his gaze. The board had been recently erased. I could see, dimly, the ghost of a long algebraic equation and what appeared to be a few words in German.

"Of course," he said, "we begin dying at birth. A difficult concept to grasp perhaps, but physiologically sound. I always wanted to be a doctor. Always, for as long as I can remember. Not necessarily to help people. Individually, that is. But to spend my life in medical research. I have never regretted it. Never."

This was beginning to sound like a valedictory, if not a eulogy. I knew I was not going to get answers to specific questions from this obviously troubled man, so I thought it best to let him ramble.

"Aging," he was saying again. "Perhaps rather than study the nature of senescence, we should study the nature of youth. My wife is a very young woman."

I wondered if he would now mention what his wife had told him about my alleged advances. But he made no reference to it. Perhaps he was inured to his wife's infidelities, real or fancied. Anyway, he kept staring at the erased blackboard.

"Are you a religious man, Mr. Todd?"

"No, sir. Not very."

"Nor I. But I do believe in the immortality of the human race."

"The *race*, Dr. Thorndecker? Not the individual?"

But he wasn't listening to me. Or if he was, he disregarded my question.

"Sacrifices must be made," he said quietly. "There can be no progress without pain."

He had me. I knew he was maundering, but the shields were coming down; he was revealing himself to me. I wanted to hear more of the aphorisms by which he lived.

"Did I do wrong to dream?" he asked the air. "You must dare all."

I waited patiently, staring at him. I had an odd impression that the man had shrunk, become physically smaller. He was effectively concealed by the lab coat and long gloves, of course, but the shoulders seemed narrower, the torso less massive. The back was bowed; arms and legs thinner. Perhaps his movements gave the effect of shriveled senescence. They had slowed, stiffened. The exuberant energy, so evident at our first meeting, had vanished. Thorndecker appeared drained. All his life force had leaked out, leaving only a scaly husk and dry memories.

He said nothing for several minutes. Finally I tried to provoke him...

"I hope, Dr. Thorndecker, you have no more surprises for me. Like admitting your application to the Bingham Foundation was not as complete as it should have been. I haven't yet decided what to do about that, but I wouldn't care to discover we have been misled in other things as well."

Still he sat in silence, brooding. He looked down at his closed journal, touched the cover with his gloved fingertips.

"I could never take direction," he said. "Never work under another man's command. They were so slow, so cautious. Plodders. They couldn't fly. That's the expression. None of them could fly. I had to be my own man, follow my instincts. What an age to live in. What an age!"

"The past, sir?" I asked. "The present?"

"The future!" he said, brightening for the first time since I had entered the room. "The next fifty years. Oh! Oh! It's all opening up. We're on the edge of so much. We are so close. You'll see it all within fifty years. Human cloning. Gene splicing and complete manipulation of DNA. New species. Synthesis of human blood and all the enzymes. Solution of the brain's mysteries, and mastery of immunology. And here, in my notebooks, the ultimate secret revealed, human life extended—"

But as suddenly as he had become fervent, he dimmed again, seemed to dwindle, retreat, lose his glowing vision of tomorrow.

"Youth," he said, and his voice no longer boomed. "The beauty of youth. She made me so happy and so wretched. On our wedding night we...The body. The youthful human body. The design. The way it moves. Its gloss and sweet perfume. A man could spend his life in...The taste. Did you know, Draper, that a—"

"Todd, sir," I said. "Samuel Todd."

"A proved diagnostic technique," he said. "Oh yes. Taste the skin. Acidity and—and—all that. So near. So close. Another year perhaps. Two, at most. And then..."

"You think it will be that soon, sir?"

"Please let me," he said. "Please."

I had a sudden feeling of shame listening to him. Watching the statue crumble. Nothing was worth witnessing that destruction. I stood abruptly. He looked up at me in surprise.

"Finished?" he said. "Well, I'm glad we've had this little chat, and I'm happy I've been able to answer your questions and clear up your doubts. Could you give me some idea of when the grant might be made?"

He was serious. I couldn't believe it.

"Difficult to say, sir. I turn in my report, and then the final decision is with my superiors."

"Of course, of course. I understand how these things

work. Channels, eh? Everything must go through channels. That's why I... Forgive me for not seeing you out, Mr. Todd, but—"

"That's perfectly all right."

"So much to do. Every minute of my time."

"I understand. Thank you for all your help."

Again he failed to rise or offer to shake hands. I left him sitting there, staring at an erased blackboard.

I had hoped I might have the chance to snoop around the labs unattended, but Linda Cunningham, Draper's chubby assistant, was waiting for me in the corridor.

"Hi, Mr. Todd," she said brightly. "I'm supposed to show you the way out."

So that was that. I was in the Pontiac, warming the engine, when suddenly Julie Thorndecker was standing alongside the window. I don't know where she came from; she was just there. She was wearing jodhpurs, tweed hacking jacket, a white shirt, ascot, a V-necked sweater. I turned off the ignition, lowered the window.

"Mrs. Thorndecker," I said.

Her face was tight, drawn. Gone were the pouts and moues, the sensuous licking of lips. I glimpsed the woman underneath: hard, wary, merciless.

"We're not getting the grant, are we?" she said.

"For God's sake," I said roughly, "get your husband to a doctor."

"For God's sake," she replied mockingly, "my husband *is* a doctor."

I was in such a somber mood, so confused and saddened, that I didn't trust myself to speak. I watched her put a thumb to her mouth and bite rapidly at the nail, spitting little pieces of matter onto the gravel. I had the feeling that if I could look into her brain, it would not be a cold, gray, convoluted structure; it would be a live lava bed, bubbling and boiling, with puffs of live steam.

"Well," she said finally, "it was nice while it lasted. But all good things must come to an end."

"Also," I said, "a stitch in time saves nine, and a rolling stone gathers no moss."

She looked at me with loathing.

"You're a smarmy bastard," she said, her face ugly. "When are you leaving?"

"Soon. Probably Monday."

"Not soon enough," she said, turning away.

I was less than a mile outside the gates when I passed a Coburn police cruiser heading toward Crittenden. Constable Ronnie Goodfellow was driving. He didn't look at me.

When I got back to Coburn I realized that on the big things, my mind wasn't working. It wouldn't turn over. But on the little things, it was ticking right along. It knew that the next day was Sunday, and liquor stores would be closed. So off I went to Sandy's to pick up a quart of vodka, a fifth of Italian brandy, and a fifth of sour mash bourbon. The vodka and brandy were for me. The sour mash was for Al Coburn. Somehow I figured him for a bourbon man, and I saw us having a few slugs together before digging into that stew he promised. And a few shots after. I also picked up two cold six-packs of Ballantine ale. I reckoned I might need them early Sunday morning.

I carted all these provisions back to the Coburn Inn. I stopped at the desk long enough to ask if there were any messages for me. There weren't, but then I didn't expect any; it was barely 3:30, too early to expect Al Coburn to call. So up I went to 3-F. I put the six-packs out on the windowsill. If they didn't slide off and brain a passing pedestrian, I could count on cold ale for Sunday breakfast. I opened the brandy, and had a small belt with water from the bathroom tap. It tasted so good that I had another to keep it company. Then I fell asleep.

It wasn't that I was tired; it was emotional exhaustion. If I've given you the impression that investigative work is a lark, I've misled you. The physical labor is minimal, the danger is infinitesimal. But what gets you—or rather, what gets *me*—is the agitation of dealing with people. I don't think this is a unique reaction. Doctors, lawyers, psychiatrists, waiters, cab drivers, and shoe clerks suffer from the same syndrome. Anyone who deals with the public.

People exert a pressure, deliberately or unconsciously. They force their wills. Their passion, wants, angers, lies, and fears come on like strong winds. Deal with people, and inevitably you feel you're being buffeted. No, that's no good. You feel like you're in a blender, being sliced, chopped, minced, ground, and pureed.

The problem for me was that I could appreciate the hopes and anxieties of everyone in Coburn I had interviewed. I could understand why they acted the way they did. I could *be* them. And everyone of them made sense to me, in a very human way. They weren't monsters. Cut anyone of them, and they'd bleed. They were sad, deluded shits, and I had such empathy that I just couldn't take any more pain. So I fell asleep. It's the organism's self-defense mechanism: when stress becomes overwhelming, go unconscious. It's the only way to cope.

I awoke, startled, a little after five. It took me a moment to get oriented. It was early December. I was in Coburn, N.Y. I was staying at the Coburn Inn, Room 3-F. My name was Samuel Todd. After that, everything came flooding back. I grabbed up the phone. The desk reported no messages. Al Coburn hadn't called.

I splashed cold water on my face, dried, looked at my image in the bathroom mirror. Forget it. The Monster Who Ate Cleveland. I went downstairs and told the baldy on duty that I'd be in the bar if I got a call. He promised to switch it.

The bar was almost empty. But Millie Goodfellow was sitting alone at one end.

"Join you?" I asked.

"Be my guest," she said, patting the stool alongside her.

She was wearing a white blouse with a ruffled neckline cut down to her two charlotte russe. She had obviously gussied up after getting off work; her hair looked like it had been worked on by a crew of carpenters, and the perfume was strong enough to fumigate a rice warehouse. She was trying.

She drank crazy things like Grasshoppers, Black Russians, and Rusty Nails. That night she was nibbling on something called a Nantucket Sleighride. I don't know exactly what it was, except that it had cranberry juice in it and enough *spiritus frumentum* to give the 2nd Airborne Division a monumental hangover.

I ordered her a new one, and a vodka gimlet for me.

"Millie," I said, gesturing toward her tall glass, "I hope you know what you're doing."

"I don't know," she said, "and I don't care."

"Oh-ho," I said. "It's like that, is it?"

"What are you doing tonight?" she asked.

I took out my cigarettes and offered her one. She shook her head. She waited until I lighted up, then took out her own pack of mentholated filtertips. She put one between her lacquered lips and bent close to me.

"Light my cold one with your hot one," she said.

It was so awful, so *awful*. But obediently, I lighted her cigarette from mine.

"How can you drink those things?" I asked, when Jimmy brought our drinks.

"One is an eye-opener," she said, swinging around to face me, putting a warm hand on my knee. "Two is a fly-opener. Three is a thigh-opener."

Oh God, it was getting worse. But I laughed dutifully.

"You didn't answer my question," she said. "What are you doing tonight?"

"Right now? Waiting for a phone call. Haven't seen Al Coburn around, have you?"

"Not since this morning. You're waiting for a phone call from *him*?"

"That's right. I'm supposed to have dinner with him."

"Instead of *me*?"

"It's business," I said. "I'd rather have dinner with you."

She wasn't mollified.

"*You* say," she sniffed. "What if he doesn't call?"

"Then I guess I better call him. Right now, in fact. Excuse me a minute."

I used the bar phone. It went through the hotel switchboard, but I couldn't see any danger. Anyway, Al Coburn didn't answer. No one answered.

I sat at the bar with Millie Goodfellow for another hour and two more drinks. I called Coburn, and I called him, and I called him. No answer. I was surprised that I wasn't alarmed, until I realized that I never did expect to hear from him.

"Millie," I said, "let's have dinner together. But I've got an errand to run first. Take me maybe an hour. If I can't get back, I'll call you here at the bar. You'll be here?"

"I may be," she said stiffly, "and I may not."

I nodded and turned away. She grabbed my arm.

"You won't stand me up, will you?"

"I wouldn't do that."

"And if you can't make it, you'll call?"

"I promise."

"You promise a lot of things," she said sadly.

That was true.

So there I was, back in the Grand Prix, heading out toward Crittenden for the third time that day. I felt like a commuter. My low beams were on, and I drove slowly and carefully, avoiding potholes and bumps. I had the bottle of bourbon on the seat beside me.

It was a sharp, black night, and when I thought of complaisant Millie Goodfellow waiting for me back in that warm bar, I wondered just what the hell I thought I was doing. I knew what I'd find at Al Coburn's place.

I've read as many detective-mystery-suspense paperbacks as you have—probably more—and there was only one ending to a situation like this:

I'd walk into Coburn's house and find him dead. Bloodily dead. Horribly mutilated maybe, or swinging on a rope from a rafter in a faked suicide. His home would be turned upside down because his killer would have tossed the place for that letter left by Ernie Scoggins.

I knew that was what I'd find. The only reason I was going out was the skinny hope that the old man had done what he promised: left the Scoggins letter or a copy in the glove compartment of his pickup. If he had the strength to withstand the vicious torture he had undergone.

Dramatic? You bet. Maybe I was disappointed, because it wasn't like that at all.

I could have driven past Al Coburn's farmhouse a dozen times without picking it out of the gloom if it hadn't been for that flagpole in the frontyard. Old Glory was hanging listlessly, barely stirring. I pulled into a gravel driveway and looked around. No lights anywhere. And no pickup truck.

I left my headlights beamed against the front door and got out of the car, taking the bourbon with me. I found my new flashlight, switched it on, started toward the house. I got within a few yards before I noticed the door was open. Not yawning wide, but open a few inches.

I pushed the door wider, went in, switched on the lights. It was a surprisingly neat home, everything clean and dusted. Not luxurious, but comfortable and tidy. And no one had turned it upside down in a futile search.

I didn't find the Scoggins letter. I didn't find evidence of murder most foul. I didn't find Al Coburn either. I found nothing. Just a warm, snug home with an unlocked door. I went through it slowly and carefully, room to room. I looked in every closet and cupboard. I poked behind drapes and got down on my knees to peer under beds and couches. I opened the trap to the unfinished attic and beamed my flashlight around in there. Ditto the half-basement.

Nothing.

No, not quite nothing. In the kitchen, on an electric range, a big cast-iron pot of stew was simmering. It smelled great. I turned off the light.

I went outside and made three circuits of the house, each one a little farther out. I found nothing. I saw nothing that might indicate what had happened to Al Coburn. He was just gone, vanished, disappeared. I came back into the house and lifted his phone. It was working normally. I called the Coburn Inn, identified myself, asked if anyone had called me. No one had.

I stood there, in the middle of the silent living room, looking around dazedly at the maple furniture with the cretonne-covered cushions. "Al Coburn!" I yelled. "Al Coburn!" I screamed. "Al Coburn!" I howled.

Nothing.

I think the quiet of that empty house spooked me more than a crumpled corpse. It was so like what had happened to Ernie Scoggins: now you see him, now you don't. Only in this case there wasn't even a blood-stained rug as a tip-off. There was nothing but a pot of stew simmering on a lighted range.

What could I do—call the cops and tell them a man hadn't phoned me as he promised? Ask for a search, an investigation? And then have Al Coburn waltz in with two quarts of beer he had gone to buy for our dinner?

But I knew, I *knew*, Al Coburn was never going to waltz in on me or anyone else, that night or any night. He was gone. He was just gone. How it had been managed I couldn't figure. It had to be some kind of a scam to get him out of the house. To get rid of him and his pickup truck. If the man he met had threatened, Al Coburn would have fought; I was convinced of that. And I would have found evidence of violence instead of just a pot of simmering stew. So he had been tricked. Maybe he had been conned to drive his truck himself to some other meeting place, some deserted place. And there...

I left the unopened bottle of bourbon in the kitchen. To propitiate the Gods? I turned off the lights inside the house. I closed the door carefully. I looked up at the flag still drooping from the staff. Patriotic Al Coburn. His folks had founded the town.

Then I drove slowly back into Coburn.

When I entered the lobby of the Inn, a gaggle of permanent residents was clustered about the desk, chattering excitedly. As I walked by, the clerk called out, "Hey, Mr. Todd, hear the news? They just found Al Coburn and his truck in the river. He's deader'n a doornail."

They had heard about it in the bar. "You won't be

having dinner with Al Coburn," Millie Goodfellow said. "No," I said. "He probably had one too many and just drove in," Jimmy said. "Yes," I said. "Another gimlet?" he asked. "Make it a double," I said. "Just vodka. On the rocks."

That's where I was—on the rocks. I won't pretend to remember all the details of that Walpurgisnacht. But that's how it began—on the rocks. Millie and I drank at the Coburn Inn for another hour or two. I wanted her husband to come in and catch us together. I don't know why. I think I had some childish desire to bend his nose.

"Why don't we go out to Red Dog Betty's for dinner?" Millie suggested.

"Splendid idea."

I drove, and not too badly. I mean I wasn't swarming all over the road, and I didn't exceed the limit by more than five or ten. Millie snuggled against me, singing, "You Light Up My Life." That was okay with me. I might even have joined in. Anything to keep from thinking.

Betty's joint was crowded, but she took one look at us, and hastily shoved us into a booth in a far dining area.

"Get your car all right?" she asked me.

"Did indeed," I said. "For which much thanks."

I leaned forward to kiss her.

"If you can ditch Miss Tits," she said, "I'll be around."

"Hey, wait a minute," Millie protested, "I saw him first."

Betty Hanrahan goosed her, and went back to the bar. Millie and I ordered something: skirt steaks I think they were. And we drank. And we danced. I saw people from Crittenden, including Linda Cunningham. I waved at her. She stuck her tongue out at me. I like to think it was more invitation than insult.

We kept chomping a few bites, finishing our drinks, then rushing back to the dance floor when someone played something we liked on the juke. Millie was a close-up dancer. I mean she was *close*.

"Carry a Coke bottle in your pocket?" she asked.

"Something like that."

"Come on," she yelled gaily in my ear. "Have fun!"

"Sure," I said.

So I had fun. I really did. I drank up a storm. Told hilariously funny stories. Asked Betty Hanrahan to marry me. Sang the opening verse of "Sitting One Night in Murphy's Bar." Bought drinks for Linda Cunningham's table. And threw up twice in the men's room. Quite a night.

Millie Goodfellow must have seen worse. Anyway, she stuck with me: conduct above and beyond the call of duty. She'd leave occasionally to dance with a trucker she knew, or with the tall, skinny gink from Mike's Service Station. But she always came back to me.

"You're so good to me," I told her, wiping my brimming eyes.

"You're not going to pass out on me, are you?" she asked anxiously.

Betty Hanrahan came back to persuade me to switch to beer. I agreed, but only, I told her, because she had bought me four "radical" tires. I may have kissed her again. I was in a kissing mood. I kissed Millie Goodfellow. I kissed Linda Cunningham. I wanted to kiss the black bartender, but he said he was busy.

Millie drove us back to Coburn.

"What a super car," she said.

"Super," I said.

"You need some black coffee," she said.

"Super," I said. "Millie, you drop me at the Inn, and then you go home."

"You really want me to go home?"

"No," I said.

"Super," she said.

It was then, I estimate, about 2:00 A.M. The lobby of the Coburn Inn was deserted, but the bar was still open. Millie sat me down in one of the spavined armchairs and disappeared. I sat there, content and giggling, until she returned with a cardboard container of black coffee. She helped me to my feet.

"Up we go," she said.

303

"Up we go," I said.

We took the stairs. It didn't take long, no more than a month or so, but eventually we arrived in Room 3-F. Millie locked the door behind us.

"Madam," I said haughtily, "do you intend to seduce me?"

"Yes," she said.

"Excuse me," I said suddenly, grabbed the black coffee, ran for the bathroom, and just did make it. I had let myself think about Al Coburn. So I threw up for the third time that night. Brushed my teeth. Showered. For some reason I'll never know, washed my hair and shaved. Finished the coffee. Put on a towel. Came out feeling mildly human. Millie Goodfellow was still there.

"You've very patient," I told her. "For a seductress."

"I found the brandy," she said cheerfully. "It's very good. Want one?"

"Do I ever!" I said.

She was using my sole glass, so I drank from the bottle. Not elegant, but effective.

"I'm sorry," I told her.

"What for? You weren't so bad."

"Bad enough. Did I pay the tab at Betty's?"

"Of course you did. And left too much tip."

"It couldn't have been too much," I groaned. "Betty and I are still friends?"

"She loves you."

"And I love her. Nice lady."

"Who was the little butterball you were slobbering over?"

"Linda Cunningham? She works at the Crittenden lab."

"You like her?"

"Sure. She's nice."

"You love her?"

"Come on, Millie. Tonight was the third time I've seen her. Just an acquaintance."

"I'm jealous."

I picked up her hand and kissed her fingertips.

"I like that," I said, grinning. "You jealous! You've got every guy in Coburn popping his suspenders."

"It's just a game," she said. "You play the game, and you get the name."

"And don't do the crime if you can't do the time."

"That's very true," she said seriously.

There I was in my towel. She was still fully clothed, sitting rather distantly in one of the sprung armchairs. I poured her another brandy.

"I talked to Al Coburn just this morning," I said. "Hearing he was dead hit me hard."

"I figured," she said. "You okay now?"

"Oh sure. I'm even sober. Sort of."

"I am, too," she said. "Sort of. I think Ronnie's going to leave me."

I tilted the brandy bottle again. I wasn't gulping. I was tonguing the opening. Little sips. It was helping.

"What makes you think that?" I asked her.

"I just know," she said. "A woman's instinct," she said virtuously.

"Well... if he does, how do you feel about it?"

"It's that chippy," she burst out. "It's because of her."

"Julie? Julie Thorndecker?"

"She'll be the end of him." Millie Goodfellow said. "He's pussy-whipped. If he wanted to leave me for some nice, sweet homebody who likes to cook, I could understand it, and wish him the best. But that hoor? She'll finish him."

I looked at her with awe. You never know people. Never. You think you've got them analyzed and tagged. You think you know their limits. Then they surprise you. They stagger you and stun you. They have depths, complexities you never even imagined. Here was this nutty broad mourning her husband's infidelity, not for her own injury, but because of the pain he would suffer. I admired her.

"Well, Millie," I said, "I don't think there's a thing you can do about it. He's got to make his own mistakes."

"I suppose so," she said, staring into her glass of

brandy. "If I come to New York, could you do anything for me? I don't mean money—nothing like that. I mean introduce me to people. Tell me how to go about getting a job. Would you do that?"

"Of course," I said bravely.

"Oh hell," she said, shaking her head. "Who am I kidding? I'll never leave Coburn. You know why?"

"Why?"

"Because I'm scared. I watch television. I see all these young, pretty, bright girls. I'm not like that. I sell cigarettes at the Coburn Inn. They could put in a coin machine, but I bring guys around to eat in the restaurant and drink at the bar. Think I don't know it? But I'm safe here. I'll never leave. I might dream about it, but I know I'll never leave. I'll die in Coburn."

I groaned. I went down on my knees, put my head in her lap. I took up her hand again, kissed her palm.

"You'll be nice to me, won't you?" she asked anxiously. It was a pleading, little girl's voice. "Please be nice."

I nodded.

From the way she dressed and the way she came on, I expected her to be sex with four-wheel drive, a heaving, panting combination of Cleopatra, Catherine the Great, and the Dragon Lady. But she undressed with maidenly modesty, switching off all the bedroom lamps first, leaving only the bathroom light burning with the door open just wide enough to cast long shadows across the softly illuminated bed.

She turned her back to me when she took off her clothes. I think she was humming faintly. I watched her in amazement. She didn't come diving eagerly between the sheets like a chilled swimmer entering a heated pool. She slid in next to me demurely, her back still turned. All cool indifference.

I pulled her over to face me.

"Be nice," she kept murmuring. "Please be nice."

That Picasso clown makeup ended at her neck. On almost a straight line. Above was the painted, weathered, used face of a woman who's been through the mill twice:

306

seams and wrinkles, crow's feet and puckers, worried eyes and a swollen, hungry mouth. She looked like she had been picked up by the heels and dipped in age.

But below the pancake makeup line, from neck to toes, her body was fruit, as fresh and as juicy. It was a revelation. She was made of peach skin and plum pulp: a goddamned virgin.

"Millie," I said. "Oh Millie . . ."

"Please be nice," she said.

Nice? I was in bed with a white marble Aphrodite, a faintly veined Venus. Having sex with her was like slashing a Rubens or taking a sledge to a Michelangelo. Screwing that woman was sheer vandalism.

I made love to her like an archeologist, being ever so careful. I didn't want to break or mar anything. After awhile she lay on her back, closed her eyes, and stopped saying, "Be nice," for which I was thankful. But she gave me no hint, no clue as to what I might do that would bring her pleasure. She made small sounds and small movements. If she felt anything, it was deep, deep, and there were few outer indications that she might not be falling asleep.

It became evident that I could do anything to her or with her, and she would slackly submit. Not from desire or unendurable passion, but simply because this was what one did on Saturday night in Coburn, N.Y., after a drunken dinner at Red Dog Betty's. It was ritual.

But something happened to me. I think it was caused by the texture of her skin: fine-pored, tight and soft, firm and yielding. Joan Powell had skin like that, and holding a naked Millie Goodfellow in my arms, putting lips and tongue to her warm breast, I thought of Powell.

"Aren't you going to *do* anything?" she breathed finally.

So I knew that if I did not *do* something, Europe would be the less. She expected tribute; denial would have demolished what little ego survived. Almost experimentally, and certainly deliberately, I began a long, whispered hymn of love.

"Oh Millie," I declaimed into her ear, "I've never seen a woman like you. Your body is so beautiful, so beautiful. Your breasts are lovely, and here, and here. I want to eat your sweetness, take all of you into me. This waist! Legs! And here behind your knees. So soft, so tender. This calf. These toes..."

On and on. And as I reassured her, she came alive. Her magnificent body warmed, began to twist and writhe. Her sounds became stronger, her pulse beat more powerfully, and she pressed to me.

"How lovely," I carried on, "how wonderful. You have a perfect body. Perfect! Never have I seen nipples so long. And this slender waist! Look, I can almost put my hands around it. And down here. So warm, so warm and loving."

It wasn't my caresses, I knew. It was the con, the scam. Is it so awful to be wanted? She awoke as if my words were feathers between her thighs. Her eyes opened just a bit, wetly, and I thought she might be weeping from happiness.

"Don't stop," she told me. "Please don't stop."

So I continued my sexual gibberish as she became fevered and bursting beneath me. In all things I was gentle, and hoped it was what she meant by, "Be nice." And all the time, delivering my cocksman's spiel, I was remembering Joan Powell, tasting *her* skin, kissing *her* skin, biting *her* skin. I loved Millie Goodfellow, and loving her, loved Joan Powell more.

I'll never understand what it's all about.

The Seventh Day

I GUESS IT was the clanking of the radiator that woke me up Sunday morning. Of course it might have been the clanking in my head, but I didn't think so; I wasn't hissing and spitting.

It was nice in that cocoon of warmed sheets and wool blankets. For the second time since I arrived in Coburn, I debated the wisdom of staying there for the rest of my life. I could pay Sam Livingston to bring me bologna sandwiches and take away the bedpan. What I had to do that day offered no hope of jollity. Maybe it's a sign of age (maturity?) when the future holds less than the past.

I turned to look at the other pillow, still bearing the dent of Millie Goodfellow's architectural hairdo. I leaned across to sniff. It still smelled of her scent but, faded, it didn't seem as awful as it had the night before. Now it seemed warm, fragrant, and very, very intimate. I kissed the pillow like a demented poet.

We had dressed shortly before what laughingly passes for dawn in Coburn, N.Y., and I had escorted Millie down to her car in the parking lot. An affecting parting. We clung to each other and said sappy things. It wasn't the world's greatest love affair—just a vigorous one-night stand—but we liked each other and had a few laughs.

Then I had returned to my nest for five good hours of dreamless sleep. When I awoke, other than that crown of thorns (pointed inward) I was wearing, the carcass seemed in reasonably efficient condition: heart pumping, lungs billowing, all joints bending in the proper direction. Bladder working A-OK; I tested it. Then I rescued a cold ale from the windowsill. See how rewarding careful planning can be?

Sat sprawled naked, sipping my breakfast calories, and tried to remember what goofy things I had done the night before. But then I gave up on the self-recriminations. I've played the fool before, and will again. You'd be surprised at how comforting that acknowledgment can be.

Finished the ale, went in to shave and discovered I had shaved the night before. In fact, at about two in the morning. Beautiful. So I showered and dressed, happy to feel the headache fading to a light throb. Went to the window again, not expecting to see the sun, and didn't. Had another chilled ale while planning the day's program. I didn't want to stray too far from the hotel in case Mary Thorndecker called. But there was one thing I decided I had to do: try to convince the local cops to let me take a look at Al Coburn's pickup truck, especially the glove compartment. It wasn't a job I was looking forward to, but I figured I had to make the try.

Went down to the lobby to discover the restaurant and bar didn't open until 1:00 P.M. I decided that a day-long fast wouldn't hurt me. After my behavior the night before, maybe a week-long penance would be more appropriate.

Sam Livingston came to my rescue. He found me in the lobby, trying to get a newspaper out of a coin machine. Sam showed me where to kick it. Not only did you get your newspaper, but your money came back. Then I accepted his invitation to join him in his basement apartment for coffee and a hunk of Danish.

It was snug in that warm burrow, and the coffee was strong and hot. We sat at the little table with the ice cream parlor chairs, drank our coffee, chewed Danish, and grunted at each other. It wasn't till the second cup and second cigarette that we started talking. That may have been because this wise old man was putting a dollop of the 12-year-old Scotch in the drip brew. Coffee royal. Nothing like it to unglue the tongue on a frosty Sunday morning.

"I keep hearing things," he told me.

"Voices?" I asked idly.

"Nah. Well... them too. I was talking about gossip."

"Thought you didn't believe in gossip?"

"Don't," he said stoutly. "But this was about something you asked me, so I listened."

"What did you hear?"

He poured us each a little more coffee, a little more whiskey. It was warming, definitely warming. The headache was gone. I began to expand.

"I should have been a detective," he said. "Like you."

"I'm not a detective; I'm an investigator."

"There's a difference?"

"Sometimes. Sometimes they're the same. But why should you have been a detective?"

"Well, you've got to know that in a place small like this, we ain't got too much to talk about. Small town; small talk. Like Mrs. Cimenti had her hair dyed red. Aldo Bates bought a new snow shovel. Fred Aikens bounced a bad check at Red Dog Betty's. Little things like that."

"So? What did you hear?"

"On Friday, one of the regulars here told me he stood behind Constable Ronnie Goodfellow at the bank, and Goodfellow closed out his account. More'n three hundred dollars. Then that fellow from Mike's Service Station, he told Millie Goodfellow that her husband had brought in their car for a tune-up. Then one of the clerks from Bill's Five-and-Dime happened to mention that Ronnie

Goodfellow stopped in and bought the biggest cardboard suitcase they got. Now you put all those things together, and what do you get?"

I grinned at him.

A trip," I said. "Constable Goodfellow is cutting loose."

"Yeah," he said with satisfaction, taking a sip of the coffee royal, "that's what I figured."

"Thanks for telling me," I said. "Any idea where he's going?"

"Nope."

"Any idea who he's going *with*?"

"Nope, except I know it ain't his wife."

"Sam," I said, "why would Goodfellow go about planning this trip so openly? He must know how people talk in this town. Is it that he just doesn't give a damn?"

That seamed basalt face turned to me. He showed the big, yellowed teeth in what I supposed was intended as a smile. The old eyes stared, then lost their focus, looking inward.

"You know what I figure?" he said. "I figure it's part what you say: he don't give a damn. But why don't he? I tell you, I think since he took up with that woman—or she took up with him—he ain't been thinking straight. I figure that woman scrambled his brains. Just stirred him up to such a hot-pants state, he don't know if he's coming or going. I hear tell of them two..."

"All right," I said, "that fits in with what I've heard. Sam, you think he'd kill for her? You think he'd do murder for a woman he loves?"

He reflected a moment.

"I reckon he would," he said finally. Then he added softly, "I did."

I froze, not certain I had heard him aright.

"You killed for a woman?"

He nodded.

I glanced briefly at his bookcase of romantic novels. I wondered if what he was telling me was fact or fiction. But when I looked at him again, I recognized something I had

312

never before put a name to. That unreadable, inward look. Speaking with a minimum of lip movement. The ability to turn a question. The coldly suspicious, standoffish manner. Friendly enough, genial enough. To a point. Then the steel shutter came rattling down.

"You've done time," I told him.

"Oh yes," he said. "Eleven years."

"Couldn't have been manslaughter. Murder two?"

He sighed. "My woman's husband. He was a no-good. She wanted him gone. After awhile, I wanted him gone, too. I'd have done anything to keep her. Anything. Murder? Sheesh, that wasn't nothing. I'd have cut my own throat to make her happy. Some women can do that to you."

"I guess," I said. "Did she wait for you?"

"Not exactly," he said. "She took up with others. Got killed when a dancehall burned down in Chicago. This happened a long time ago, whilst I was inside."

He just said it, without rancor. It was something that had happened a long time back, and he had learned to live with it. Memories blur. Pain becomes a twinge. Can you remember the troubles you had five years ago?

"So you think Goodfellow would do it?"

"Oh, he'd do it; no doubt about that. If she said, 'Jump,' he'd just say, 'How high?' You think he did?"

I started to say yes, started to say I thought Ronnie Goodfellow had murdered both Ernie Scoggins and Al Coburn. But I shut my mouth. I had nothing to take to a D.A. Nothing but the sad knowledge of how a tall, proud Indian cop might become so impassioned by sleek, soft Julie Thorndecker that the only question he'd ask would be, "How high?"

We finished our coffee. I thanked Sam Livingston and left. He didn't rise to see me out. Just waved a hand slowly. When I closed the door, he was still seated at the table with empty cups and a full ashtray. He was an old, old man trying vainly to recall a dim time of passion and resolve.

When I got up to the lobby, the desk clerk motioned

me over and said I had a call at ten o'clock. A Miss Joan Powell had called.

I was discombobulated. Then insanely happy. Joan Powell? How had she learned where I was? What could she—? Then I remembered: it was the name Mary Thorndecker was to use.

"Did she say she'd call again?"

"Yes, sir, Mr. Todd. At eleven." He glanced at the wood-cased regulator clock on the wall behind him. "That'll be about twenty minutes or so."

I told him I'd be in my room, and asked him to switch the call. Upstairs, I sat patiently, flipping the pages of my Sunday newspaper, not really reading it or even seeing it. Just turning pages and wondering if I'd ever meet a woman I'd kill for. I didn't think so. But I don't suppose Sam Livingston or Ronnie Goodfellow ever anticipated doing what they had done.

I remember meeting a grunt in Vietnam, a very shy, religious guy who told me that during training he had given the matter a great deal of painful thought, and had decided that if he got in a firefight, he'd shoot over the heads of the enemy. He just believed it was morally wrong to kill another human being.

Then, less than a week after he arrived in Nam, his platoon got caught in an ambush.

"How long did it take you to change your mind?" I asked him. "Five minutes?"

"About five seconds," he said sadly.

I grabbed up the phone after the first ring. I might have had my fingers crossed.

"Samuel Todd," I said.

"This is Joan Powell," Mary Thorndecker said faintly. "How are you, Mr. Todd?"

"Very well, thanks. And you, Miss Powell?"

"What? Oh yes. Fine. I'm going to church this morning. The Episcopal church. The noon service, and I was wondering if you were planning to attend?"

"As a matter of fact, I am. The noon service at the Episcopal church. Yes, I'll be there."

"Then maybe I'll see you."

"I certainly hope so. Thank you, Miss Powell."

I hung up slowly, and thought about it. I decided she was a brainy woman. A crowded church service would offer a good opportunity to talk. There's always privacy in mobs. I glanced at my watch and figured I had about forty-five minutes to kill.

I wandered out to the vacant streets of Coburn. A drizzle was beginning to slant down from a choked sky. I turned up my collar, turned down the hat brim. It seemed to me that my boots had been damp for a week, and soggy pant and sleeve cuffs rubbed rawly. I passed a few other Sunday morning pedestrians, hunched beneath black umbrellas. I didn't see any cars moving. The deserted village.

I walked over to River Street, stood at the spot where Ronnie Goodfellow and I had paused a week ago to watch the garbage-clogged water slide greasily by. Then I turned away and went prowling through the empty streets. There were some good storefronts beneath the grime. A few bore the date of construction: 1886, 1912, 1924.

A paint job and clean-up drive would have done wonders for Coburn. Like putting cosmetics on a corpse. I had told Goodfellow that if history teaches anything, it teaches change. That people, cities, nations, civilizations are born, flourish, die. How fatuous can you get? That may be the way things are, but knowing it doesn't make it any easier to accept. Especially when you're a witness to the senescence of what had once been a vital, thriving organism.

Coburn was dying. Unless I had misread the signs, Dr. Telford Gordon Thorndecker was dying. If he went, the village would surely go, for so much of the town's hopes seemed built on his money, his energy, his dreams. They would vanish together, Thorndecker and his Troy.

I shouldn't have felt anything. This place meant nothing to me. It was just a mouldering crossroad on the way to Albany. But once, I suppose, it had been a busy, humming community with brawls and parades, good times, laughter, a sense of growth, and a belief it would last forever. We all think that. And here was Coburn now, the damp and the rot crumbling away brave storefronts and streaking dusty glass.

If this necropolis and the sordid Thorndecker affair meant anything, they persuaded me to feel deeply, cherish more, smell the blooms, see the colors, love, laugh at pinpricks and shrug off the blows. What do the Hungarians say? "Before you have time to look around, the picnic is over." The picnic was ending for Coburn. For Thorndecker. Nothing but litter left to the ants.

· I plodded back to the Coburn Inn. I had a sudden vision of this place in twenty years, or fifty. A lost town. No movement. No lights. No voices. Dried leaves and yellowed newspapers blowing down cracked pavements. Signs fading, names growing dim. Everyone moved away or dead. Nothing but the rain, wind, and maybe, by then, a blank and searing sun.

You're as old as you feel? Bullshit. You're as old as you look. And you can't fake youth, not really. The pain is in seeing it go, grabbing, trying to hold it back. No way. Therefore, do not send to ask for whom the ass sinks; it sinks for thee. Forgive me, Joan Powell. I cast you aside not from want of affection, but from fear. I thought by rejecting an older mate I might stay young forever: the Peter Pan of the Western World. Why do we think of the aged as lepers when we are all registered for that drear colony?

So much for Sunday morning thoughts in Coburn, N.Y. Gloomsville-on-the-Hudson. But I met this emotional wrench with my usual courage and steadfastness. I rushed up to Room 3-F and had a stiff belt of vodka before setting out for the noon service at the Episcopal church.

My nutty fantasy of the morning had been the right one: I should have stood in bed.

I was a few minutes late getting to the church. But I wasn't the only one; others were hurrying up the steps, collapsing their umbrellas, taking seats in the rear pews. I stood a moment at the back of the nave, trying to spot Mary Thorndecker. A robed choir was singing "My Faith Is a Mountain," and not badly.

I finally saw her, sitting about halfway down on the aisle. Next to her were Dr. Kenneth Draper, Edward Thorndecker, and Julie. *Julie?!* I couldn't figure out what she was doing there, unless she was screwing the choir.

I noticed Mary was turning her head occasionally, glancing toward the rear of the church, searching for me. I moved over to one side, and the next time she looked in my direction, I raised a hand and jerked a thumb over my shoulder. I thought she nodded slightly. I went back outside. I wasn't about to sit through the service. If Mary could get out while it was going on, so much the better. If not, I'd wait outside until it was over.

I stood on the pillared porch, protected from the rain. I lighted a cigarette. The Reverend Peter Koukla had practically said it was a sin to smoke on church grounds. But it wasn't a 100 mm. cigarette, so it was really a *small* sin.

I was leaning against a pillar watching the rain come down—almost as exciting as watching paint dry—when an old guy came around the corner of the church. Another of Coburn's gnarled gaffers. He had to be 70, going on 80. Coburn, I decided, had to be the geriatric capital of the U.S.

This ancient was wearing a black leather cap, rubberized poncho, and black rubber boots. He was carrying a rake and dragging a bushel basket at the end of a piece of soggy rope. He was raking up broken twigs, sodden leaves, refuse, and dumping all the slop in his basket.

When he came close to me, I said pleasantly, "Working on Sunday?"

"What the hell does it look like I'm doing?" he snarled.

It was a stupid question I had asked, so I was willing to endure his ill-humor. I pulled out my pack of cigarettes and held it out to him. He shook his head, but he dropped rake and rope, and climbed the steps to join me on the

porch. He fished under his poncho and brought out a
blunt little pipe. The shank was wound with dirty
adhesive tape. The pipe was already loaded. He lighted it
with a wooden kitchen match and blew out an explosion
of blue smoke. It smelled like he had filled it with a piece
of the wet rope tied to his bushel basket.

"No church service for you?" I said.

"Naw," he said. "I been. See one, you seen 'em all."

"You're not a religious man?" I asked.

"The hell I'm not," he said. He cackled suddenly.
"What the hell, it don't cost nothing."

I looked at him with interest. All young people look
different; all old people look alike. You see the bony nose,
wrinkled lips, burst capillaries. The geezer sucked on his
pipe with great enjoyment, looking out at the wet world.

"How come you ain't inside?" he asked.

"Like you," I said, "I been."

"I got no cause to go," he said. "I'm too old to sin. You
been sinning lately?"

"Not as much as I want to."

He grunted, and I hoped it was with amusement. At
that moment, a religious nut I didn't need.

"You the sexton?" I asked.

"How?"

"Sexton. Church handyman."

"Yeah," he said, "I guess you could say that. Ben
Faber."

"Samuel Todd," I said.

His hands were under his poncho. He didn't offer to
shake, so I lighted another cigarette and dug my chilled
hands back into my trenchcoat pockets.

"You don't live hereabouts?" he said.

"No."

"Just passing through?"

"I hope so."

He grunted again, and then I was certain it was his way
of expressing amusement.

"Yeah," he said, "it's a pisser, ain't it? Going down the
drain, this town is. Well, I won't be here to see it."

"You're moving?"

"Hell, no," he said, astonished. "But I figure I'll be six feet under before it goes. I'm eighty-four."

"You look younger," I said dutifully.

"Yeah," he said, puffing away. "Eighty-two."

I was amazed at how this chance conversation was going, how it seemed a continuation of my melancholy musings of the morning.

"It doesn't scare you?" I asked him. "The idea of dying?"

He took the pipe out of his mouth long enough to spit off the porch into a border of shrubs tied up in burlap sacks.

"I'll tell you, sonny," he said, "when I was your age, it scared me plenty. But don't worry it; as you get along in years, the idea of croaking gets easier to live with. You see so many people go. Family. Friends. It gets familiar-like. And then, so many of them are shitheads, you figure if they can do it, you can do it. Then too, you just get tired. Nothing new ever happens. You've seen it all before. Wars and accidents. Floods and fires. Marriages. Murders. People dying by the billions, and billions of babies getting born. Nothing new. So just slipping away seems like the most natural thing in the world. Naw, it don't scare me. Pain, maybe. I don't like that. Bad pain, I mean. But as for dying, it's got to be done, don't it?"

"Yes," I said faintly, "it surely does."

He knocked the dottle from his pipe against the heel of his rubber boot. It made a nice mess on the porch, but that didn't seem to bother him. He took out an oilskin pouch, unrolled it, began to load the pipe again, poking the black, rough-cut tobacco into the bowl with a grimy forefinger.

"Want some advice, sonny?" he said.

"Well...yeah, sure."

"Do what you want to do," he said between puffs, as he lighted his pipe. "That's my advice to you."

I thought that over a moment, then shook my head, flummoxed.

"I don't get it," I told him. "I always do what I want to do."

The grunts came again. But this time he showed me a mouthful of browned, stumpy teeth.

"The hell you do," he said. "Don't tell me there ain't been things you wanted to do, but then you got to thinking about it. What would this one say? What would that one say? What if this happened? What if that happened? So what you wanted to do in the first place never got done. Ain't that right?"

"Well . . . I guess so. There have been things I wanted to do, and never did for one reason or another."

"I'm telling you," he said patiently. "I'm giving you the secret, and not charging for it neither. What it took me eighty-four years to learn. I ain't got a single regret for what I done in this life. But I'll go to my grave with a whole lot of regrets for things I wanted to do and never did. For one reason or another. Now you remember that, sonny."

"I surely will," I said. "Tell me, Mr. Faber, how long do you figure this service will last?"

"What time you got?"

I glanced at my watch. "About ten to one."

"Should be breaking up any minute now. The Ladies' Auxiliary, they're serving coffee and doughnuts in the basement. Think I'll get me some right now. You coming?"

"No, thanks. I'll stay here."

"Waiting for someone?"

"Yes."

"A woman?"

I nodded.

He cackled again, then clumped down the steps to pick up his rake and rope tow to the wet bushel basket.

"A woman," he repeated. "I don't have to fret about *that* no more. But you remember what I said: you want to do something, you just *do* it."

"I'll remember," I said. "Thanks again."

He grunted, and trudged away in the rain. I watched him go. I wasn't sure what the hell he had been talking about, but somehow I felt better. He had found a kind of peace, and if that's what age brought, it might be a little easier to endure varicose veins, dentures, and a truss.

I moved back toward the doors and heard the swelling sonority of the church organ. A few people came out, buttoning up coats and opening umbrellas. I stood to one side and waited. In a few minutes Mary Thorndecker came flying out, face flushed. The long Persian lamb coat was flapping around her ankles. She was gripping a black umbrella. She grabbed my arm.

"The others are having coffee," she said breathlessly. "I don't think they saw you. I only have a minute."

"All right," I said, taking the umbrella from her and opening it. "Let's go to my car."

"Oh no," she cried. "They may come out and see us."

"This was your idea," I said. "What do you want to do?"

"Let's walk across the street," she said nervously. "Away from the church. Just a block or two. It won't take long."

I took her arm. I held the big umbrella over both of us. We crossed the street and walked away from the church on the opposite sidewalk.

"There are three guards," she said rapidly. "The gate guard, one on duty in the nursing home, and a man with a dog who patrols outside. They come on at midnight. A day shift takes over at eight in the morning."

"No guard in the lab?"

"No. Each building has its own power switches and alarm switches. In the basements of both buildings. The switch boxes are kept locked."

"Shit," I said. "I beg your pardon."

"I can't get Nurse Beecham's keys," she went on. "She hands them over to the night supervisor, a male nurse. He carries them around with him."

"Listen," I said, "I've narrowed it down. There's only

321

one place I want to go, one thing I want to see. Your stepfather's private office. On the second floor of the research laboratory."

"I can't get the keys."

"Sure you can," I said gently. "Dr. Draper has keys to the main lab building and to your stepfather's private lab. Get the keys from Draper."

"But how?" she burst out desperately. "I can't just ask him for them."

"Lie," I told her. "Where does Draper live?"

"In Crittenden Hall. He has a little apartment. Bedroom, sitting room, bathroom."

"Good," I said. "Wake him up about two o'clock tomorrow morning. Tell him Thorndecker is working late in Crittenden Hall and wants his journal from the lab. Tell him anything. You're a clever woman. Make up some excuse, but get the keys."

"He'll want to get the journal himself."

"Not if you handle it right. Just get the keys. By fifteen minutes after two, I'll be inside the fence. I'll be waiting at the back entrance to the research lab. The door at the end of that covered walk that comes down the hill from the nursing home."

She didn't say anything, but I felt her shiver under my hand. I thought I might have thrown it at her too fast, so I slowed down and went over it once again. Get the keys from Draper at 2:00 A.M. Let me into the lab at 2:15.

"I'm not going to steal anything," I told her. "You'll be with me; you'll see. I just want to look in Thorndecker's journal."

"What for?"

"To see what he's been doing, and why. He said he keeps very precise, complete notes. It should all be there."

She was silent awhile, then ...

"Do I have to be with you?" she asked. "Can't I just give you the keys?"

I stopped and turned her toward me. There we stood under that big, black umbrella, the rain sliding off it in a circular curtain. She wouldn't meet my eyes.

"You don't really want to know, do you?" I asked softly.

She shook her head dumbly, teeth biting down into her lower lip.

"Mary, I *need* you there. I need a witness. And maybe you can help me with the scientific stuff. You must know more of that than I do. Anyone would!"

She smiled wanly.

"And also," I said, "I need you with me for a very selfish reason. If we're caught, it'll be impossible to charge me with breaking-and-entering if I'm with a member of the family."

She nodded, lifted her chin.

"All right," she said. "I'll get the keys. Somehow. I'll let you in. I'll go with you. We'll read the journal together. I don't care how awful it is. I do want to know."

I pressed her arm. We started walking back toward the church. Her stride seemed more confident now. She was leading the way. I had to hurry to keep up with her. We stopped across the street from the church. We faced each other again.

"I know how to get the keys from Kenneth," she said, looking into my eyes.

"Good," I said. "How?"

"I'll go to bed with him," she said, plucked the umbrella from my hand, dashed across the street.

I just stood there, hearing the faint hiss of rain, watching her run up the church steps and disappear. And I had thought her prissy.

It was a few minutes before I could move. I felt the drops pelt my sodden tweed hat. I saw the rain run down my trenchcoat in wavery rivulets. I knew my boots were leaking and my feet were wet.

Simple solution: "I'll go to bed with him." Just like that. Maybe old Ben Faber was right. You want to do something, then *do* it.

I got back in my car, still in a state of bemused wonderment. I drove around awhile, trying to make sense of what was going on, of what people were doing, of what

I was doing. What amazed me most was how Telford Gordon Thorndecker, unknowingly, was impinging on the lives of so many. Mary. Dr. Draper. Julie. Edward. Ronnie and Millie Goodfellow. The "best people" of Coburn. And me. Thorndecker was changing us. Nudging our lives, for better or for worse. None of us would ever be the same.

The man was a force. It went out in waves, affecting people he didn't even know. Joan Powell, for example. Thorndecker was the reason I had come to Coburn. Coburn was changing the way I felt about Joan Powell. Her life might be turned around, or at least altered, by the influence of a man she had never met.

I wondered if all life was like this: a series of interlocking concentric circles, everything connected to everything else in some mad scheme that the greatest computer in the world would digest and then type out on its TV monitor: "Insufficient data."

It was a humbling thought, that we are all pushed and pulled by influences that we are not even aware of. Life is not a bowl of cherries. Life is a bowl of linguine with clam sauce, everything intertangled and slithery. No end to it.

Maybe that was the job of the investigators. We're the guys with the fork and the soup spoon, lifting high a tangle of the strands, twirling fork tines in the bowl of the spoon, and producing a neat, palatable ball.

It made me hungry just to think of it.

The Coburn Civic Building looked like it had shrunk in the rain. I didn't expect bustling activity on a Sunday afternoon, but I thought *someone* would be on duty in the city hall, minding the store. I finally found a few real, live human beings by peering through the dirty glass window in the wide door of the firehouse. Inside, four guys in coveralls sat around a wooden table playing cards. I would have bet my last kopeck it was pinochle. I also got a view of their equipment: an antique pumper and a hose truck that looked like a converted Eskimo Pie van. Neither vehicle looked especially clean.

I walked around the building to the police station in

the rear. It was open, desolate, deserted. It smelled like every police station in the world: an awful amalgam of eye-stinging disinfectant, vintage urine, mold, dust, vomit, and several other odors of interest only to a pathologist.

There was a waist-high railing enclosing three desks. A frosted glass door led away to inner offices. This splintered room was tastefully decorated with *Wanted* posters and a calendar displaying a lady in a gaping black lace negligee. I thought her proportions highly improbable. She may have been one of those life-size inflatable rubber dolls Japanese sailors take along on lengthy cruises.

From somewhere beneath my feet, a guy was singing— sort of. He was bellowing, "Oh Dolly, oh Dolly, how you can love." That's all. Over and over. "Oh Dolly, oh Dolly, how you can love." From this, I deduced that the drunk tank was in the basement.

"Hello?" I called. "Anyone home?"

No answer. One of these days, some smart, big-city gonnif was going to drop by and steal the Coburn police station.

"Hello?" I yelled again, louder. Same result: none.

I pushed open the railing gate, went over to the frosted glass door, opened that, stepped into a narrow corridor with four doors. Three were unmarked; one bore the legend: Chief. One of the unmarked doors was open. I peeked in.

My old friend, Constable Fred Aikens. He was sprawled in a wood swivel chair, feet parked up on the desk. His hands were clasped across his hard, little pot belly. His head was thrown back, mouth sagging, and he was fast asleep. I could hear him. It wasn't exactly a snore. More like a regular, "Aaagh. Aaagh. Aaagh." There was a sheaf of pornographic photos spread out on his desk blotter.

I stared at Coburn's first line of defense against criminal wrongdoing. I had forgotten what a nasty little toad he was, with his squinchy features and a hairline that seemed anxious to tangle with his eyebrows. I had an insane impulse. I'd very carefully, very quietly tiptoe into the office and very slowly, very easily slide his service revolver from his holster. Then I'd tiptoe from the room, from the building, and drive back to the Coburn Inn where I'd finish the vodka while laughing my head off as I thought of Fred Aikens explaining to the Chief Constable how he happened to lose his gun.

I didn't do it, of course. Instead, I went back to the main room. I slammed the gate of the railing a few times, and I really screamed, "Hello? Hello? Anyone here?"

That did the trick. In a few minutes Aiken came strolling out, uniform cap squared away, tunic smoothed down, every inch the alert police officer.

"Todd," he said. "No need to bellow. How you doing?"

"Okay," I said. "How *you* doing?"

"Quiet," he said. "Just the way I like it. If you came to ask about those slashed tires of yours, we haven't been able to come up with—"

"No, no," I said. "This is about something else. Could I please talk to you for a couple of minutes?"

I said it very humbly. Some cops you can handle just like anyone else. Some you can manipulate better if you start out crawling. Fred Aikens was one of those.

"Why, sure," he said genially. "Come on into my private office where we can sit."

I followed him through the frosted glass door into his room. He jerked open the top desk drawer and swept the pornographic photos out of sight.

"Evidence," he said.

"Yes," I said. "Terrible what's going down these days."

"Sure is," he said. "You park there and tell me what's on your mind."

I sat in a scarred armchair alongside his desk, and gave him my best wide-eyed, sincere look.

"I heard about Al Coburn," I said. "That's a hell of a thing."

"Ain't it though?" he said. "You knew him?"

Those mean, little eyes never blinked.

"Well...sure," I said. "Met him two or three times. Had a few drinks with him at the Coburn Inn."

"Yeah," he said, "old Al liked the sauce. That's what killed him. The nutty coot must have had a snootful. Just drove right off the bluff into the river."

"The bluff?"

"A place we call Lovers' Leap. Out of town a ways."

"How did you spot the truck? Someone call it in?"

"Hell, no," he said. "Goodfellow saw him go over. Had been tailing him, see. Coburn was driving like a maniac, all over the road, and Ronnie was trying to catch up, figuring to pull him over. Had the siren and lights going: everything. But before he could stop him, Al Coburn drives right off the edge. There's been talk of putting a guard rail up there, but no one's got around to it."

I shook my head sadly. "Hell of a thing. Where is he now? The body, I mean."

"Oh, he's on ice at Markham's funeral parlor. We're trying to locate next of kin."

"You do an autopsy in cases like that?" I asked him casually.

"Well, hell yes," he said indignantly. "What do you think? Bobby Markham is our local coroner. He's a good old boy."

"Coburn drowned?"

"Oh sure. Lungs full of water."

"Was he banged up?"

"Plenty. Listen, that's more'n a fifty-foot drop from Lovers' Leap. He was a mess. Head all mashed in. Well, you'd expect that. Probably hit it on the wheel or windshield when he smacked the water."

I didn't say anything. He looked at me curiously. Something wary came into those hard eyes. I knew: he was wondering if he had said too much.

"What's your interest in this, Todd?"

"Well, like I said, I knew the guy. So when I heard he was dead, it really shook me."

"Uh-huh," he said.

"Also," I said, "something silly. I'm embarrassed to mention it."

He leaned back in his swivel chair, clasped his hands across his belly. He regarded me gravely.

"Why, you go right ahead," he said. "No need to be embarrassed. I hear a lot of things right here in this office, and it never gets past these walls."

I bet.

"Well," I said hesitantly, "I had a drink with Al Coburn yesterday morning. A beer or two. Then afterward, he wanted me to see where he lived. The flagpole and all."

"Oh yeah," he laughed. "Old Al's flagpole. That's a joke."

"Yes," I said. "Anyway, I own a gold cigarette lighter. Not very valuable. Cost maybe twenty, thirty bucks. But it's got a sentimental value—you know?"

"Woman give it to you?" he said, winking.

I tried a short laugh.

"Well...yeah. You know how it is. Anyhow, I remember using it while I was in Al Coburn's pickup. And then, a few hours later, after I got back to the Inn, it was missing. So I figure I dropped it in Coburn's truck. Maybe on the floor or back between the cushions. I was wondering where Coburn's pickup is now?"

"The truck?" he said, surprised. "Right now? Why, it's out back in our garage. We're holding it until everything gets straightened out on his estate and will and all. You think your gold cigarette lighter is in the truck?"

"I figured it might be."

"I doubt it," he said, staring at me. "When we went down to get Coburn out, we had to pry open the doors, and the river just swept through. Then we winched the truck out of the water. Nothing in it by then. Hell, even the back seat cushion was gone."

"Well," I said haltingly, "I was hoping you'd let me take a quick look...."

"Why not?" he said cheerily, jerking to his feet. "Never

can tell, can you? Maybe your gold cigarette lighter got caught in a corner somewhere. Let's go see."

"Oh, don't bother yourself," I said hastily. "Just tell me where it is, I'll take a quick look and be on my way. I imagine you have to stick close to the phones and all."

"No bother," he said, his mouth smiling but not his eyes. "Nothing happens in Coburn on a Sunday. Let's go."

I had pushed it as far as I thought I could. So I had to follow him out of the station house, around to a corrugated steel garage. He unlocked the padlock, and we went in.

Al Coburn's pickup truck was a sad-looking mess. Front end crumpled, windshield starred with cracks, doors sprung, seat cushion soaked, steering column bent.

And the glove compartment open and empty.

"Stinks, don't it?" Aikens said.

"Sure does," I said.

I made a show of searching for a cigarette lighter. The constable leaned against the wall of the garage and watched me with iron eyes.

I crawled out of the sodden wreck, rubbing my palms.

"Ahh, the hell with it," I said. "It's not here."

"I told you," he said. "Nothing's there. The river got it all."

"I suppose," I said dolefully. "Well, thanks very much for your trouble."

"No trouble," he said. "I'm just sorry you didn't find what you were looking for."

"Yes," I said, "too bad. Well, I guess I'll be on my way."

"Leaving Coburn soon?"

That's what Julie Thorndecker had asked me. And in the same hopeful tone.

"Probably tomorrow morning," I said.

"Stop by and see us again. Happy to have you."

"Thanks. I might do just that."

We grinned at each other. A brace of liars.

Nothing's ever neat. The investigator who's supposed

to twirl a tight ball of linguine with fork and spoon usually ends up with a ragged clump with loose ends. That's what I had: loose ends.

I didn't know how it was managed, but I knew Al Coburn never drove off that cliff deliberately. His truck was nudged over, or driven over with a live driver leaping out at the last second, leaving an unconscious or dead Al Coburn in the cab. An experienced medical examiner could have proved those head injuries were inflicted before drowning, but not Good Old Boy Bobby Markham.

Maybe the glove compartment had been searched before the truck was pushed over. Maybe after it was hauled out. Or maybe the river really did sweep it clean. It didn't make any difference. I knew I'd never see the letter Ernie Scoggins had left with Al Coburn.

I could guess what was in the letter. I could guess at a lot of things. Loose ends. But in any kind of investigative work, you've got to live with that. If you're the tidy type, take up bookkeeping. Business ledgers have to balance. Nothing balances in a criminal investigation. You never learn it all. There's always something missing.

I got out to Red Dog Betty's about 3:30 in the afternoon. That crawl through Al Coburn's death truck had affected me more than I anticipated. When I held out a hand, the fingertips vibrated like tuning forks. So I went to Betty's, for a drink, something to eat, just to sit quietly awhile and cure the shakes.

This time I parked as close to the entrance to the roadhouse as I could get, hoping it would discourage the Mad Tire Slasher from striking again. I hung up hat and coat, sat at the bar, ordered a vodka gimlet. I asked for Betty, but the black bartender said she wouldn't be in until the evening.

The barroom and dining areas had that peaceful, dimmed, hushed atmosphere of most watering places on a Sunday afternoon. No one was playing the juke. No voices were raised. The laughter was low-pitched and rueful. Everyone ruminating on their excesses of the night before. I knew that Sunday afternoon mood; you move carefully and slowly, abjure loud sounds and unseemly mirth. The ambience is almost churchlike.

I must have been wearing my head hanging low, because I saw them for the first time when I straightened up and looked in the big, misty mirror behind the bar. Sitting in an upholstered banquette on the other side of the room were Nurse Stella Beecham, editor Agatha Binder, and the cheerleader type from the *Sentinel* office, Sue Ann. Miss Dimples was seated between the two big women. They looked like massive walnut bookends pressing one slim volume of fairy tales.

If they had noticed me come in, they gave no sign. They might have been ignoring me, but it seemed more likely they were too busy with their own affairs to pay any attention to anyone else. Beecham was wearing her nurse's uniform, without cap. Binder had a clean pair of painters' overalls over a black turtleneck. The lollipop between them had on a pink angora sweater with a long rope of pearls. She kept nibbling on the pearls as the two gorgons kept up a running conversation across her. The older women were drinking beer from bottles, scorning their glasses. The young girl had an orange-colored concoction, with a lot of fruit and two long straws.

I stole a glance now and then, wondering what the relationship of that trio was, and who did what to whom. About 3:45, Nurse Beecham lurched to her feet and moved out from behind the table. She smoothed down her skirt. That was one hefty bimbo. Get an injection in the rump from her, and the needle was likely to go in the right buttock and come out the left.

She said something to the other women, bent to kiss them both. She took a plastic raincoat and hat from the rack, waved once, and was gone. I figured she was heading for Crittenden Hall, for the four-to-midnight shift.

The moment the nurse disappeared, Agatha Binder turned slightly sideways and slid one meaty arm across Sue Ann's shoulders. She leaned forward and whispered something in the girl's ear. They both laughed. Chums.

I saw Miss Dimples' drink was getting low, and the editor was tilting her beer bottle high to drain the last few drops. I got off my barstool and went smiling toward them.

"Hi!" I said brightly. "How are you ladies?"

They looked up in surprise. The nubile one with some interest, Agatha Binder with something less than delight.

"Well, well," the editor said, "if it isn't supersnoop. What are you doing here, Todd?"

"Recovering," I said. "May I buy you two a drink?"

"I guess so," she said slowly. "Why not?"

"Won't you join us?" Sue Ann piped up, and I could have kissed her.

I moved onto the seat vacated by Stella Beecham, ignoring Binder's frown. I signaled the waitress for another round, and offered cigarettes. We all lighted up, and chatted animatedly about the weather until the drinks arrived.

"When are you planning on leaving Coburn?" Agatha asked. Same question. Same hopeful tone. It's so nice to be well-liked.

"Probably tomorrow morning."

"Find out all you need to know about Thorndecker?"

"More," I said.

We sampled our drinks. Sue Ann said, "Oh, wow," and blushed. She was so fresh, so limpid and juicy, that I think if you embraced her tightly, she'd squirt mead.

"Well, he's quite a man, Thorndecker," the editor said. "Very convincing."

"Oh yes," I said. "Very. I'll bet he could get away with murder."

She looked at me sharply. "What's that supposed to mean?"

"Figure of speech," I said.

She continued to stare at me. Something came into her eyes, something knowing.

"This is yummy," Miss Dimples said, sucking happily at her straws. Lucky straws.

"He's not going to get the grant, is he?" Binder demanded.

"When is your next edition coming out?" I asked her.

"We just closed. Next edition is next week."

"Then I can tell you," I said. "No, he's not going to get the grant. Not if I have anything to do with it, he isn't."

"Well . . . what the hell," she said. "I figured you'd find out."

"You mean you knew?"

"Oh Christ, Todd, everyone in Coburn knows."

I took a deep breath, sat back, stared into the air.

"You're incredible," I said. "You and everyone else in Coburn. Something like this going on under your noses, and you just shrug it off. I don't understand you people."

"Sometimes I have a Tom Collins," the creampuff giggled, "but I really like this better."

"You know, Todd, you're an obnoxious bastard," the editor said. "You come up here with your snobbish, big-city, sharper-than-thou attitude. You stick your beezer in matters that don't concern you. And then you condemn Thorndecker because of the way his wife acts. Now I ask you: is that fair?"

My stomach flopped over. Then I just spun away. My hand stopped halfway to my glass. I tried to slow my whirling thoughts. I had a sense of total disorientation. It took awhile. A minute or two. Then things began to harden, come into focus again. I understood: Agatha Binder and I had been talking about two different things.

"I tried beer a few times," Miss Dimples volunteered, "but I really didn't like it. Too bitter."

I drained my glass, motioned toward their glasses.

"Ready for another?" I asked hoarsely.

"Hell, yes," the editor said roughly.

Sue Ann said, "Whee!"

By the time my fresh gimlet arrived, I had it organized: how I would handle it.

"You think Thorndecker knows about it?" I asked cautiously.

"Oh hell," she said, "he has to know. Those trips to

Albany and Boston and New York. Once to Washington. To talk to potential sponsors. Big-money guys who might dip into their wallets for the Crittenden Research Laboratory. Then Thorndecker would come back alone. Julie would return a day or two or a week later. And a day or two after *that*, the contribution would come in. It wasn't hard to figure out what was going on."

I nodded as if I was aware of this all along.

"I knew you'd catch on," Agatha Binder said morosely. "Listen, is what they do so bad? It's in a good cause. You talk like it's a federal case or something."

"No," I said thoughtfully, "it's not so bad. Maybe a little shabby, but I suppose it's done in other businesses every day in the week."

"You better believe it," she said, nodding violently.

"I'm hungry," Sue Ann said.

I mulled over this new information. An angle I hadn't even considered. Was this the "conspiracy" that all the Coburnites shared? Pretty sleazy stuff.

"A very complex woman, our Julie," I said wonderingly. "I'm just beginning to appreciate her. My first take was of a bitch with a libido bigger than all outdoors. But now it seems there's more to her than that. Why does she do it, Agatha? Is it the sex? Or just the money to keep her lifestyle intact?"

Binder punched gently at the tip of her nose with one knuckle. Then she took a deep swig from her beer bottle.

"When are we going to eat?" Sue Ann asked plaintively.

"A little of both," the big woman said. "But mostly because she loves Thorndecker. *Loves* him! And believes in him, in his work. She worships him, thinks he's a saint. She's really a very loving, sacrificing woman."

I literally threw up my hands.

"It's a masquerade," I said hopelessly. "Everyone wearing masks. Do you all take them off at midnight?"

"You come up here from the big city and think you're dealing with simple country bumpkins. It's obvious in your attitude, in your sneers and jokes. Then you act like

334

we've been misleading you when it turns out that we're not cardboard cutouts, that we're as screwed-up as everyone else."

I thought about that for a few moments.

"You may be right," I admitted. "To some extent. I've underestimated most of the people here I've met; that's true. But not Thorndecker. I never sold him short."

"Oh, he's one of a kind," Agatha Binder said. "You can't judge him by ordinary standards."

"I don't," I said. "I just wonder what kind of a man would endure what his wife is doing. Encourage her to do it. Or at least accept it without objection."

"His work comes first," the editor told me. "That's his only test. Is it good or bad for his work?"

"A monomaniac?" I suggested.

"Or a genius," she said.

"Obsessed?" I said.

"Or committed," she said.

"Insensitive?" I said.

"Or totally dedicated," she said.

Then we were both silent, neither of us certain.

"Maybe a hamburger," Sue Ann said dreamily. "A cheeseburger. With relish."

I sighed and stood up.

"Feed the child," I told Agatha Binder, "before she collapses. Thanks for the talk."

"Thanks for the drinks."

Unexpectedly, she thrust out a hand, hard and horny. I shook it. I won't say we parted friends, but I think there was some respect.

I went back to the bar. I had intended to have something to eat there, but I decided to return to the Coburn Inn. I didn't want to look into a misty bar mirror and see Agatha Binder sticking her tongue in Sue Ann's ear. Then I knew I was getting old. It upset me to see things in public that people used to do only in bedrooms after the lights were out and the kids were asleep.

On the drive back to the Coburn Inn, I tried not to think of what the editor had told me about Julie

335

Thorndecker. But it bothered me that what she had revealed came as such an unexpected shock. The whole Thorndecker business had been like that: unfolding slowly and painfully. I wondered if I stayed in Coburn another week, a month, a year, if it would all be disclosed to me, right down to the final surprise.

Agatha Binder's accusation rankled because it was true. Partly true. I *had* assumed that these one-horse-town denizens were a different species, made of simpler, evident stuff, their motives easily perceived, their passions casually analyzed. There was hardly one of them who hadn't proved my snobbery just by being human, displaying all the mysterious, inexplicable quirks of which humans are capable. I should have known better.

The dining room at the Coburn Inn was moderately crowded; I ate in the bar. Had two musty ales with broiled porkchops, apple sauce, a baked potato, green beans with a bacon sauce, and rum cake for dessert. Well, listen, the fast I vowed that morning had lasted almost nine hours. After all, I *am* a growing boy.

Went up to my room and began packing. I wasn't planning to leave until the following morning, but I was nagged by the feeling that after my criminal enterprise scheduled for 2:00 A.M., I might want to make a quick getaway. So I packed, leaving the two suitcases and briefcase open.

Then, using hotel stationery, I wrote out a precis of the Thorndecker affair. I tried to keep it brief and succinct, but included everything I had discovered, and what I hadn't discovered: Thorndecker's motive for infecting his nursing home patients with cancer.

It ran to five pages, front and back, before I had finished. I read it over, made a few minor corrections, then sealed it in an envelope addressed to myself at the address of the Bingham Foundation in New York. I remembered what Thorndecker had said about keeping precise, complete notes "in case of an accident." Then someone else could carry on the work.

If there was no "accident" (like driving off Lovers'

Leap), I could destroy the manuscript when I got back to the office on Tuesday. If, for some reason, I didn't return, someone at the office would open the letter. And know.

Put on coat and hat again, went down to the lobby, bought stamps at the machine on the cigar counter.

"Mail that for you, Mr. Todd?" the baldy behind the desk sang out.

"No, thanks," I said. "I'll take a walk and drop it in the slot at the post office."

"Wet walking," he said.

"The farmers need it," I said.

I liked saying that. A Coburn tradition. A hurricane could hit, decimating Coburn and half of New York State, and someone was sure to crawl painfully from the wreckage, look up at the slashing, ripping sky, and croak, "Well, the farmers need it."

When I got back to Room 3-F, I shucked off wet coat, wet hat, wet boots, and fell into bed. I had heard that if you fall asleep concentrating on the hour you want to awake, you'll get up on the dot. So I tried it, thinking, "Get up at midnight, get up at midnight, get up at midnight." Then I conked off.

I awoke at 1:15, which isn't bad, considering it was my first try. But I did have to rush, making sure I was dressed completely in black, sneaking down the stairs, waiting until the lobby was deserted and the desk clerk was in the back office. Then I strode swiftly out to the parking lot. Still raining. I figured that was a plus. That roaming shotgun-armed guard with the attack dog would probably be inside someplace dry and warm, reading *Penthouse* or *The Wall Street Journal*. Something like that.

I drove out to Crittenden at a moderate speed. I didn't want to be late for my rendezvous with Mary Thorndecker—I doubted if her nerves could endure the wait—but I didn't want to be too early either, chancing discovery by one of the guards.

I cruised slowly by the gate. There were outside lights burning on the portico of Crittenden Hall, and I could see

Julie Thorndecker's blue MGB parked on the gravel driveway. It seemed odd that the car wasn't garaged on a night like that.

There were a few lights burning on the main floor of the nursing home, none on the second and third floors. No lights in the laboratory. There was a dim bluish glow (TV?) coming from the gatekeeper's hut.

I passed the gate, followed the fence until it began to curve around toward the cemetery. Then I pulled well off the road, doused my lights, waited until my eyes became accustomed to the dark. I opened the car door cautiously, stepped out, closed the door but left it unlatched.

Gathered my equipment: stepladder, clothesline, sash weight, flashlight. I stuck the flash and weight in my hip pockets. My pants almost fell down.

Carried ladder and rope across the road to the fence. Still raining. Not hard, but steadily. Straight down. A rain that soaked and chilled.

Tied one end of the rope to the top of the aluminum stepladder. Threw the loose coils over the fence. Then I set up the ladder carefully, making sure the braces were locked. I climbed up.

You've seen movies where James Bond or one of his imitators goes over a high fence by leaping, grabbing the top, pulling himself up and over. Try that little trick some time. Instant hernia. It's a lot easier to carry your own stepladder.

I stood on the top rung, swung one leg over the fence, straddled, swung the other leg over and jumped, remembering to land with flexed knees. Then I pulled my rope, and the ladder came up the outside of the fence. It took me a few minutes to jiggle it over, but eventually it dropped down inside. I caught it, and set it up against the inside of the fence, ready for a quick escape.

Now I was inside the grounds. I had selected a spot where the bulk of Crittenden Hall came between me and the gate guard. I hoped I was right about the roving sentry keeping out of the rain. But just in case, I crouched a few moments in the absolute dark and strained to hear. A silence like thunder. No, not quite. I heard the rain hitting my hat, coat, the ground. But other than that—nothing.

Moved warily toward the nursing home and its outbuildings. Didn't use my flash, so twice I blundered into trees. Didn't even curse. Did when I tripped over a fallen branch and fell to my hands and knees.

Figure it took me at least fifteen minutes to work my way slowly around Crittenden Hall. A light came on briefly on the second floor, then went out. I hoped that was Mary Thorndecker with the keys, leaving the apartment of Dr. Kenneth Draper, starting down to meet me.

Sudden angry barking of a dog. I froze. The barking continued for a minute or two, then ended as abruptly as it began. I moved again. Slowly, slowly. Trying to peer through the black, through the rain. Nightglow was practically nonexistent. I was in a tunnel. Down a well. Buried.

Came up to Crittenden Hall. Eased around it as noiselessly as I could, fingertips lightly brushing the brick. Reflected that I was no outdoorsman. Not trained for this open-country stuff. I could navigate a Ninth Avenue tenement better than I could a copse, stubbled field, meadowland, or hills.

Found the covered steps leading down from the nursing home to the back door of the Crittenden Research Laboratory. Kept off the paved walk, but moved in a crouch alongside it. Tried to avoid crashing through shrubbery or kicking the slate border.

Finally, at the door. No Mary. I hunkered down. Put flashlight under the skirt of my trenchcoat. Risked quick look at my wristwatch. About 2:20. Sudden fear that I had missed her at 2:15, and she, spooked, had gone back to Draper's bed.

Waited. Hoping.

Heard something. Creak of door opening. Pause. Soft thud as it closed. Wiped my eyes continually, peering up the hill. Saw something lighter than the night floating down. Tensed. Watched it draw closer.

Mary Thorndecker. In white nightgown partly covered by old-fashioned flannel bathrobe cinched with a cord. Heavy brogues on bare feet. She was carrying the big umbrella, open. Beautiful. But I didn't feel like laughing.

She almost fell over me. I straightened up. She jerked back. I grabbed her, palm over her mouth. Then she steadied. I released her. Shoved my face close to hers under the umbrella.

"The keys?" I whispered.

Felt rather than saw her nod. Rings of keys pressed into my hand. I put my lips close to her ear.

"I'm going to give you the flashlight. Before you switch it on, put your fingers across the lens. We just want a dim light. A glimmer. Just enough to show the lock. Understand?"

She did just fine. We stood huddled at the door, blocking what we were doing with our bodies. She held the light, her fingers reducing the beam to a reddish glow. I tried three keys before the fourth slid in. I was about to turn it, then stopped. Still.

"What is it?" she said.

There had to be an alarm.

I left the keys in the lock. Took her hands in mine, turned the flashlight slowly upward along the jamb of the door. There, at the top, another lock taking a barrel key.

"Alarm," I breathed in her ear. "Got to be turned off first before we open the door. There's a barrel key on the ring. Let's hope it—"

At that moment. Precisely. Two sounds. Muffled. Indoors. From the nursing home. They were not snaps. More like dulled booms.

"What—?" Mary said.

I put a hand on her arm. We waited. In a few seconds, four more hard sounds in rapid succession. These were louder, more like cracks. They sounded closer.

"Handgun," I said in my normal voice, knowing it had all come apart. "Heavy caliber. You stay here."

"No," she said, "I'm coming with you."

I grabbed the flashlight from her. Took her hand. We

went stumbling up the walk, the open umbrella ballooning behind us, a puddle of light jerking along at our feet.

Reached the back door of Crittenden Hall. Both of us panting.

The door was locked.

"The keys," I said.

"You left them in the door of the lab."

"What a swell burglar I am," I said bitterly.

I took out the sash weight, smashed the pane of glass closest to the lock. Hammered the shards away from the frame so I wouldn't slit my wrists. Then reached in, opened the door.

We ran into a brightly lighted corridor. Chaos. Alarms and excursions. Shouts and screams. People in white running, running. All toward the main entrance hall.

And a shriek that shivered me. A wailing shriek, on and on. Man or woman? I couldn't tell.

"That's Edward," Mary Thorndecker gasped. "Edward!"

We dashed like the others. Debouched into the lobby. Joined the jostling mob. All circling. Looking down.

The shriek was all wail now. A weeping siren. It rose and fell in hysterical ululation.

"Shut him up!" someone yelled. "Slap him!"

I pushed roughly through, Mary following. No one saw us. Everyone was looking at what lay on the marble floor, at the foot of the wide staircase.

They must have been shot while coming down the stairs. Then they fell the rest of the way. Ronnie Goodfellow, clad in mufti, hit first. He was prone, face turned to one side. His right leg snapped under him when he hit. A jagged splinter of bone stuck out through the cloth.

Julie Thorndecker had landed near him, on her back. One side of her head was gone. Her arms were thrown wide. Her coat was flung open, skirt hiked up. One naked, pale, smooth, beautiful leg was lying across Goodfellow's neck.

Two pigskin suitcases had fallen with them. One had snapped open on impact, the contents cascading across the floor. Blue panties, brassieres, a small jewel case, negligees, the silver evening pajamas and sandals she had been wearing the night I met her.

I don't think the first two shots killed them. But then he followed them down and emptied his gun. The blood was pooling, beginning to merge, his and hers, and trickle across the marble tiles.

Like the others, I stared at the still, smashed dolls. Dr. Draper knelt alongside, wearing a raincoat, bare shins sticking out. He fumbled for a pulse at their throats, but it was hopeless. Everyone knew it. He knew it. But his trembling fingers still searched.

When I first glimpsed them, Edward Thorndecker was sitting cross-legged on the floor, his stepmother's torn head in his lap. His head was back, face wrung, and that shrieking wail came out of his open mouth continuously, as if he needed no breath but only grief to produce that terrifying scream. Finally, hands reached down, pulled him away, took him off somewhere. They half-carried him, his toes dragging on the marble. The shriek faded, faded, then stopped suddenly.

Surprisingly, Mary Thorndecker took charge.

"Don't touch anything," she commanded in a loud, sharp voice. "Kenneth, you call the police. At once. Did anyone see where he went?"

Where *he* went. There was no doubt in her mind, nor in anyone else's, who had done this slaughter.

The gorilla-butler, with a shoulder holster and gun strapped across a soiled T-shirt, pushed forward.

"Out the back door, Miss Thorndecker," he said. "I heard the shots and come running. I seen him. Out the back door and onto the grounds."

Mary Thorndecker nodded. "Alma, you and Fred see to the patients. Some of them may have heard the commotion. Calm them down. Sedation, if needed. The rest of you get your hats and coats. Bring flashlights and lanterns. We must find him. He is not a well man."

I pondered that: "He is not a well man." And Hitler was "disturbed."

It took us maybe ten minutes to get organized. Mary Thorndecker ordered us around like a master sergeant. I couldn't fault her. She got us spread out on a ragged line, at about fifteen-foot intervals. Most of the beaters had flashlights or lanterns. One guy had a kerosene lamp. And all the interior lights of Crittenden Hall were switched on, cutting the gloom in the immediate vicinity.

At a command from Mary, we started moving forward, trying to keep the line intact. Once we were out of the Hall's glow, the dark night closed in. Then all I could see was a bobbing, wavering necklace of weak lights, shimmering in the rain.

"Thorndecker!" someone called in a quavery voice, and the others took up the cry.

"Thorndecker!"

"Thorndecker!"

"Thorndecker!"

Then it became a long, wailing moan: "Thooorndecker!" And we all, scarcely sane, went stumbling across the slick, frosted fields, lights jerking up and down, calling his name again and again, echoing his name, while the cold rain pelted a black and ruined world.

Oh yes, we found him. We had passed through the cemetery and were slowly, fearfully working the stand of bare trees on the far side. There was a shout, the wild swinging of a lantern in wide circles. We all ran, breathless and blundering, to the spot. We clustered.

He lay on his back, spreadeagled, face turned to the falling sky. He wore only pajama pants. He was almost completely bald; only a few wet tufts of hair were left. Bare feet were bruised and bleeding. His eyes were open. He was dead.

Arms, shoulders, torso, neck, face, scalp—all of him exposed to view was studded with suppurating tumors. Great blooms of red and yellow and purple. Rotting excrescences that seemed to have a vigorous life of their own, immortal, sprouting from his cooling flesh. They had soft, dough-like centers, and browned, crusted petals.

There was hardly an inch of him not choked by cancerous growths. Eyes bulging with necrosis, mouth twisted, nose lumped, the limbs swollen with decay, trunk gnarled with great chunks of putrescent matter. The smell was of deep earth, swamp, and the grave.

The trembling circles of light exposed the horror he had become. I heard a sobbing, was conscious of people turning away to retch. Someone began to murmur a prayer. But I was stone, transfixed, looking down at what was left of Dr. Telford Gordon Thorndecker, wanting desperately to find meaning, and finding nothing.

The butler-thug volunteered to remain with the body. The rest of us wandered back to Crittenden Hall. We moved, I noted, in a tight group, seeking the close presence of others to help hold back the darkness, to prove that live warmth still existed in the world. No one spoke. Silently we filed through the cemetery, gravestones glistening in our lights, and straggled across the stubbled fields to the brightness of Crittenden Hall, a beacon in the black.

A half-hour later I was seated with Dr. Kenneth Draper in Thorndecker's private office in the Crittenden Research Laboratory. I had left Mary Thorndecker to deal with the police. I had latched onto Draper—literally. I took him by the arm and would not let him go, not for an instant, I am not certain if any of us were acting rationally that night.

I marched Draper upstairs to his apartment and let him dress. Then I pulled him into that marvelous Thorndecker sitting room where I swiped a bottle of brandy, and thought nothing of it. I made Draper gulp a mouthful, because his face was melting white wax, and he was moving like an invalid. I took him and the brandy back to the research lab. Found the keys, turned off the alarm, opened the door, turned on the lights.

In Thorndecker's private lab, I pushed Draper into the chair behind the desk. I peeled off my soaked hat and coat. I found paper cups, and poured us each a deep shot of brandy. Some color came back into his face, but he was racked with sudden shivers, and once his teeth chattered.

Thorndecker's journal, the one he had been working on the last time I saw him alive, still lay open on the desk. I shoved it toward Draper.

"When did it start?" I asked him.

"What will they do to me?" he said in a dulled voice. "Will I go to jail?"

I could have told him that if he kept his mouth shut, probably nothing would happen to him. How could they prove all those Crittenden Hall patients had died other than natural deaths? I figured the Coburn cops would be satisfied that Thorndecker had killed his wife and her lover, then died himself from terminal cancer. It was neat, and it closed out a file. They wouldn't go digging any deeper.

But I wanted to keep Draper guilty and quivering.

"It depends," I told him stolidly, "on how willing you are to cooperate. If you spell it out for me, I'll put in a good word for you."

I didn't tell him that I had about as much clout with the Coburn cops as I do with the Joint Chiefs of Staff.

"All right," I said, in the hardest voice I could manage, "when did it start?"

He raised a tear-streaked face. I poured him another brandy, and he choked it down. He stared at the ledger, then began turning the pages listlessly.

"You mean the—the experiments?"

"Yes," I said, trying not to yell at him, "the experiments."

"A long time ago," he said, in a voice so low I had to crane forward to hear him. "Before we came to Crittenden. We started with normal mammalian cells. Then concentrated only on normal human cells. We were looking for the cellular clock that causes aging and death. Dr. Thorndecker believed that—"

"I know what Thorndecker believed," I interrupted him. "Did you believe in the cellular clock theory?"

He looked at me in astonishment.

"Of course," he said. "If Dr. Thorndecker believed in it, I *had* to believe. He was a great man. He was—"

"I know," I said, "a genius. But you didn't find it? The cellular clock?"

"No. Hundreds of experiments. Thousands of man-hours. It's extremely difficult, working with normal human cells *in vitro*. Limited doublings. The cells become less differentiated, useless for our research. We confirmed conclusively that the cell determines longevity, but we couldn't isolate the factor. It was—well, frustrating. During that period, Dr. Thorndecker became very demanding, very insistent. Hard to deal with. He could not endure failure."

"This was before you came to Crittenden?"

"Yes. Dr. Thorndecker's first wife was still alive. Most of our research was being done on small grants. But we had no exciting results to publish. The grant money ran out. But then Dr. Thorndecker's first wife was killed in an accident, and he was able to buy Crittenden and establish this laboratory."

"Yes," I said, "I know. And then?"

"We had been here only a short time, when one night he woke me up. Very excited. Laughing and happy. He said he had solved our basic problem. He said he knew now what our approach should be. It was an inspiration. Only a genius could have thought of it. A quantum leap of pure reason."

"And what was that?" I asked.

"We couldn't keep normal cells viable *in vitro*. Not for long. But cancer cells flourished, reproduced endlessly. Apparently they were immortal. Dr. Thorndecker's idea was to forget about finding the factor in normal cells that caused senescence and death, and concentrate on finding the factor in abnormal cells that caused such wild proliferation."

"The factor that made cancer cells immortal *in vitro*?"

"Yes."

I took a deep breath. There it was.

I knew what was coming. I could have stopped right

there. But I wanted him to spell it out. Maybe I wanted to rub his nose in it.

"And you found the factor?"

He nodded. "But the problem was how to separate the longevity effect from the fatal effect. You understand? The cancer cells themselves simply grew and grew—forever, if you allowed them to. But they killed the host organism. So all our research turned to filtering out the immortality factor, purifying it in effect, so that the host's normal cells could absorb it and continue to grow indefinitely without harm. Very complex chemistry."

"It didn't work?" I said.

"It did, it did!" he cried, with the first flash of spirit he had exhibited. "I can show you mice and guinea pigs in the basement that have lived three times as long as they would normally. And they're absolutely cancer-free. And we have one dog that, in human terms, is almost two hundred years old."

"But no success with chimps?"

"No. None."

"So this essence of yours, this injection, wasn't always successful?"

"No, it wasn't. But animals are notoriously difficult to work with. Sometimes they reject the most virulent cancer cells. Sometimes a strain of rats supposed to be leukemia-prone will prove to be immune. Animals do not always give conclusive results, insofar as their reactions can be applied to humans. And animal experimentation is expensive, and takes time."

I leaned back and lighted a cigarette. Like most specialists, he tended to lecture when riding his own hobbyhorse. I probably knew as much about nuclear physics as he did, but bio-medicine was his world; he was confident there.

"Animal experimentation is expensive," I said, repeating his last words, "and it takes time. And Thorndecker never had enough money for what he wanted to do. But more than that, he didn't have the time. He was a man in a hurry, wasn't he? Impatient? Anxious for the fame the published discovery would bring?"

"He was convinced we were on the right track," Dr. Draper said. "I was, too. We were so close, so close. We had those animals in the basement to prove it—the ones who had doubled and tripled their normal life spans."

I rose and began to pace back and forth in front of the desk. Somehow I found myself with a lighted cigarette in each hand, and stubbed one out.

"All right," I said, "now we come to the worm in the apple. Whose idea was it to try the stuff on humans?"

He lowered his head and wouldn't answer.

"You don't have to tell me," I said. "I know it was Thorndecker's idea; you don't have the balls for it. I'll bet I even know how he convinced you. 'Look, Draper,' he said, 'there can be no progress without pain. Sacrifices must be made. We must dare all. Those patients in Crittenden Hall are terminal cases. How long do they have—weeks, months, a year? If we are unsuccessful, we'll only be shortening slightly their life span. And think of what they will be contributing! We can give their remaining days meaning. Think of that, Draper. We can make their deaths meaningful!' Isn't that what Thorndecker told you? Something like that?"

He nodded slowly. "Yes. Something like that."

"So you selected the ones you thought were terminal?"

"They were, they were!"

"You *thought* they were. You weren't sure. Doctors can never be sure; you know that. There are unexpected remissions. The patient recovers for no explainable reason. One day he wakes up cured. It happens. You know it happens."

He poured himself another cup of brandy, raised it to his pale lips with a shaking hand. Some of the brandy spilled down his chin, dripped onto his shirtfront.

"How many?" I demanded. "How many did you kill?"

"I don't know," he muttered. "We didn't keep—"

"Don't give me that shit!" I screamed at him. "Thorndecker kept very complete, precise records, and

you know it. You want me to grab up this journal and all
the others for the past three years, and take them to the
cops? You think you can stop me? Try it! Just try it! How
many?"

"Eleven," he said in a choked voice.

"And none survived?"

"No," he said. Then, brightly: "But the survival time
was lengthening. We were certain we were on the right
track. Dr. Thorndecker was convinced of it. I was, too.
We had purified the extract. A week ago we were
absolutely certain we had made the breakthrough."

"Why didn't you try it on another patient?"

Draper groaned.

"Don't you understand? If it had succeeded, how could
Thorndecker publish the results? Admit experiments on
humans? Fatal experiments? With no informed consent
agreements? They'd have crucified him. The only way was
to inject himself. He was so sure, so sure. He laughed
about it. 'The elixir of life, Draper,' he told me. 'I'll live
forever!' That's what he told me."

I marveled at the man, at Thorndecker. To have such
confidence, such absolute faith in your own destiny, such
pride in your own skill. To dare death to prove it.

"What went wrong?" I asked Draper.

"I don't know," he said, shaking his head. "Initially,
everything was fine. Then, in a short time, the first
symptoms appeared. Hair falling out, skin blotches that
signaled the beginning of tumors, sudden loss of weight,
loss of appetite, other things..."

"Thorndecker knew?"

"Oh yes. He knew."

"How did he react?"

"We've spent the last few days working around the
clock, trying to discover what went wrong, why the final
essence not only didn't extend life but produced such
rapid tumor germination."

"Did you find out what it was?"

"No, not definitely. It may have been in the purifying

process. It may have been something else. It could have been Dr. Thorndecker's personal immunochemistry. I just don't know."

"Julie Thorndecker was aware of this?"

"She was aware that her husband was fatally ill, yes."

"Was she aware of the experiments you two ghouls were carrying out?"

"No. Yes. I don't know."

I sat down again. I slumped, so exhausted that I could have slept just by closing my eyes.

Dazed, not thinking straight, I wondered what I could do about this guy. I could have him racked up on charges, but I knew a smart lawyer could easily get him off. Do what? Exhume the corpses and find they had died of cancer? He'd never spend a day in jail. There might be a professional inquiry, and his career would be ruined. But so what? I wanted this prick to *suffer*.

"What about Ernie Scoggins?" I asked him dully. "Was Scoggins blackmailing Thorndecker?"

"I don't know anything about that," he mumbled.

"You goddamned shitwit!" I yelled at him. "You were Thorndecker's righthand man. You know about it all right."

"He got a letter from Scoggins," Draper said hastily, frightened. "Not mailed. A note shoved under his door. Scoggins was working here at the time. He helped out with the animals occasionally. And when we had burials in the cemetery. He guessed something was wrong. All those tumorous corpses..."

"Did he have any hard evidence of what was going down?"

"He stole one of Dr. Thorndecker's journals. It was—ah—incriminating."

"Then what happened?"

"I don't know. Dr. Thorndecker said he'd take care of it, not to worry."

"And he got the journal back?"

"Yes."

"And Ernie Scoggins disappeared."

"Dr. Thorndecker had nothing to do with that," he said hotly.

"Maybe not personally," I said. "But he had his wife persuade Constable Ronnie Goodfellow to take care of it. She persuaded him all right. It wasn't too difficult. She could be a very persuasive lady. And I suppose the same thing happened when it turned out that old Al Coburn had a letter from Scoggins recounting what was in Thorndecker's journal. So Al Coburn had to be eliminated, and the letter recovered. Constable Goodfellow went to work again, and did his usual efficient job."

"I don't know anything about Al Coburn," Draper insisted, in such an aggrieved tone that he might have been telling the truth.

I couldn't think of anything else to ask. Not only was my body weary, but my brain felt flogged. Too many strong sensations for one night. Too many electric images. The circuits were overloaded.

I stood up, pulled on my sodden coat and hat, preparing to leave. I had a sudden love for that bed in Room 3-F.

"What's going to happen to me?" Dr. Kenneth Draper asked.

"Keep your mouth shut," I advised him resignedly. "Tell no one what you've told me. Except Mary Thorndecker."

"I can't tell her," he groaned.

"If you don't," I said, "I will. Besides, she's already guessed most of it."

"She'll hate me," he said.

"Oh, I think she'll find it in her heart to forgive you," I told him. "Just like Lord Jesus. Also, she'll probably inherit, and she'll need someone to help her run Crittenden Hall and the lab."

He brightened a little at that.

"Maybe she will forgive me," he said, almost to himself. "After all, I just did what Dr. Thorndecker told me to."

"I know," I said. "You just obeyed orders. Now where

have I heard that before? Goodnight, Dr. Draper. I hope you and Mary Thorndecker get married and live happily ever after."

There were two Coburn police cruisers, a car from the sheriff's office, and an ambulance in the driveway when I went outside. The gates were wide open. I just walked out, and no one made any effort to stop me.

Thirty minutes later I was snuggling deep in bed, purring with content. The last thing I thought of before I dropped off to sleep was that I had forgotten to pick up my aluminum stepladder before I left Crittenden. I was more convinced than ever that I just wasn't cut out for a life of crime.

The Eighth Day

I AWOKE ABOUT eleven Monday morning. I got out of bed
immediately. Showered, shaved, dressed. Finished
packing and snapped the cases shut. Took a final look
around Room 3-F to make certain I wasn't forgetting
anything. Then I rang for Sam Livingston, and asked him
to take the luggage down to my car. I told him he could
have what was left of the ale and vodka. I took the
remainder of the brandy with me.

The desk clerk wanted to talk about the terrible
tragedy out at Crittenden. That was his label: "Terrible
tragedy." I cut him short and asked for my bill. While he
was totaling it, I glanced over toward the locked cigar
stand. There was a sign propped on the counter. I went
over to read it.

"Closed because of death in the family."

I think that sad, stupid sign hit me harder than

anything I had seen the night before.

I paid my bill with a credit card, and said goodby to the clerk. Went into the bar to shake Jimmy's hand, pass him a five and say goodby. Went out to the parking lot and helped Sam Livingston stow the suitcases and briefcase in the trunk. Put my hat, coat, and brandy bottle in the back seat.

I gave Sam a twenty. He took it with thanks.

"Take care," I said, as lightly as I could.

That ancient black face showed nothing—no distress, sadness, sorrow. Why should it? He had seen everything twice. Like Ben Faber, the old sexton, had said: nothing new ever happens.

I got in the Grand Prix, slammed the door. I stuck my hand out through the open window. The mummy shook it briefly.

"Sam," he said, "you ain't going to change this world."

"I never thought I could," I told him.

"Um . . ." he said. "Well, if you ever get up this way . . ."

I drove away. It seemed only right that the last words I heard in Coburn were an unfinished sentence.

It was a long, brooding drive back to New York. I wish I could tell you that once Coburn was behind me, the sky cleared, the sun came out, the world was born again. It would have been a nice literary touch. But nothing like that happened. The weather was almost as miserable as it had been a week ago, when I drove north. A wild west wind scattered snow flurries across the road. Dark clouds whipped in a grim sky.

I stopped for breakfast at the first fast-food joint I came to. Tomato juice, pancakes, bacon, three cups of black coffee. Nothing tasted of anything. Sawdust maybe. Wet wallboard. Paste. The fault may have been mine. Back in the car, I cleansed my palate with a belt of brandy.

I hit the road again, driving faster than I should have. It was all automatic: steering, shifting, braking. Because I was busy trying to understand.

I started with Julie Thorndecker. Maybe, as Agatha Binder said, she was a loving, sacrificing wife. But deserting a fatally ill husband to run away with a young lover is not the act of a loving, sacrificing wife. I thought that in all Julie's actions there was a strain of sexual excitement. I do not mean to imply she was a nymphomaniac—whatever that is. I just believe she was addicted to illicit sex, especially when it included an element of risk. Some people, men and women, are like that. They cannot feel pleasure without guilt. And they cannot feel guilt unless there is a possibility of punishment.

I think Julie Thorndecker had the instincts of a survivor. If Thorndecker hadn't saved her at that Cambridge party, someone else would have. She was too young, too beautiful to perish. Her reactions were elemental. When she saw her husband dying, she thought simply: the game is up. And so she planned to move on. She may have loved him and respected him—I think she did—but she just didn't know how to grieve. Life was too strong in her. So she made ready to take off with a hot, willing stud. I'm sure she loved him, too. Goodfellow, that is. She would love any man who worshipped her, since he was just giving her back a mirror image of her own infatuation with herself, her body, her beauty. A man's love confirmed her good taste.

Telford Gordon Thorndecker offered a more puzzling enigma. I could not doubt his expertise in his profession. I'd agree with everyone else and say he was a genius—if I was certain what a genius was. But I think he was driven by more than scientific curiosity and a desire for fame. I think his choice of his particular field of research—senescence, death; youth, immortality—was a vital clue to his character.

Few of us act from the motive we profess. The worm is always there, deep and squirming. A man might say he wishes to work with and counsel young boys, to give them the benefit of his knowledge and experience, to keep them from delinquency, to help them through the agonies of adolescence. That may all be true. It may also be true that he simply loves young boys.

In Thorndecker's case, I think he was motivated by an incredible seductive, sexually active young wife as much as he was by the desire to pioneer in the biology of aging. I think, perhaps unconsciously, the disparity in their ages was constantly on his mind. He saw her almost every day: youthful, live, energetic, vibrant, physically beautiful and sexually eager. He recognized how he himself, more than twice her age, had slowed, bent, become sluggish, his blood cooling, all the portents of old age becoming evident.

The search for immortality was as much, or more, for himself as it was for the benefit of mankind. He was in a hurry to stop the clock. Because in another ten years, even another five, his last chance would be gone. There could be no reversal; he knew that. He dreamt that, with hard work and good fortune, he might never grow older while she aged to his level and beyond.

You see, he loved her.

Although he could understand the rational need for her infidelity with Goodfellow—his work must not be delayed!—jealousy and hatred cankered his ego. In the end, he could not endure the thought of those two young bodies continuing to exist, rubbing in lubricious heat, swollen with life, while he was cold mould.

So he took them with him.

Wild supposition, I know. All of it was. So I came to the dismal conclusion: how could I hope to understand others when I was a mystery to myself. I wanted desperately to tell the saga of Dr. Telford Gordon Thorndecker to Joan Powell. That brainy lady had the ability to thread her way through the tangles of the human heart and make very human sense.

It was raining in New York, too. I found a parking space only a half-block away from my apartment, and wrestled my luggage into the lobby in a single, shin-bumping trip. I collected my mail, and banged my way up the narrow staircase. Inside, door locked and chained, I made myself a dark Scotch highball and took it into the bathroom with me while I soaked in a hot tub. My feet had been wet and cold for a week; I was delighted to see the toes bend and the arches flex.

Came back into the living room, dressed casually, and went through the accumulated mail. Bills. Junk. Nothing from Joan Powell. I unpacked, put dirty laundry in the hamper, restored my toilet articles to the medicine cabinet.

Put something low and mournful on the hi-fi, and sat down to prepare an official report on the Thorndecker affair. The Bingham Foundation supplied its field investigators with a five-page printed form for such reports. It had spaces for Personal Habits, Financial Status, Religious Affiliation, Neighbors' comments, etc., etc. I stared at the form a few minutes, then printed APPLICANT DECEASED in big block letters across the top page, and let it go at that.

There was a can of sardines in the refrigerator, and I finished that with soda crackers. I also ate a few olives, a slice of dill pickle, a small wedge of stale cheddar, and a spoonful of orange marmalade. But that was all right; I wasn't hungry.

I watched the news on TV. All bad. I tried reading three different paperbacks, and tossed them all aside. I piled my outstanding bills neatly for payment. I sharpened two pencils. I smoked almost half a pack of cigarettes. I found a tin of rolled anchovies in the kitchen cupboard, opened it, and wolfed them down. And got thirsty, naturally.

About 9:30 P.M., on my third highball, I gave up, and sat down near the phone, trying to plan how to handle it. I brought over several sheets of paper and the sharpened pencils. I started making notes.

"Hello?" she would say.

"Powell," I'd say, "please don't hang up. This is Samuel Todd. I want to apologize to you for the way I acted. There is nothing you can call me as bad as what I've called myself. I'm phoning now to ask if there is any way we can get together again. To beg you. I will accept any conditions, endure any restraints, suffer any ignominy, do

357

anything you demand, if you'll only let me see you again."

It went on and on like that. Abject surrender. I made copious notes. I imagined objections she might have, and I jotted down what my answer should be. I covered three pages with humility, crawling, total submission. I thought sure that, if she didn't hang up immediately, I could weasel my way back into her favor, or at least persuade her to give me a chance to prove how much I loved her and needed her.

And if she brought up the difference in our ages again, I prepared a special speech on that:

"Powell, the past week has taught me what a lot of bullshit the whole business of age can be. What's important is enjoying each other's company, having interests in common, loving, and keeping sympathy and understanding on the front burner, warm and ready when needed."

I read over everything I had written. I thought I had a real lawyer's brief, ready for any eventuality. I couldn't think of a single way she might react, from hot curses to cold silence, that I wasn't prepared to answer.

I mixed a fresh drink, drained half of it, picked up the phone. I arranged my speeches in front of me. I took a deep breath. I dialed her number.

She picked it up on the third ring.

"Hello?" she said.

"Powell," I said, "please don't hang—"

"Todd?" she said. "Get your ass over here."

I ran.

Bestsellers you've been hearing about—and want to read

Bestselling Books for Today's Reader